Praise fo

"Johnston's page-turner is replete with romantic angst, sizzling sex, and the promise of an enduring love."
—*Publishers Weekly* (starred review)

"Joan Johnston continually gives us everything we want . . . fabulous details and atmosphere, memorable characters, a story that you wish would never end, and lots of tension and sensuality."
—*Romantic Times*

"A master storyteller . . . Joan Johnston knows how to spin a story that will get to the readers every time."
—*Night Owl Reviews*

"Johnston has a keen eye for quirky circumstances that put her characters, and the reader, through a wringer. Laughing one moment and crying the next, you'll always have such a great time getting to the happy-ever-after."
—*Romance Junkies Reviews*

"Johnston is a writer who can combine romance side by side with tragedy, proving that there is magic in relationships and that love is worth the risk."
—*Bookreporter*

By Joan Johnston

Bitter Creek Novels

The Cowboy	*The Next Mrs. Blackthorne*
The Texan	*A Stranger's Game*
The Loner	*Shattered*
The Price	*Invincible*
The Rivals	

Sisters of the Lone Star Series

Frontier Woman	*Texas Woman*
Comanche Woman	

Captive Hearts Series

Captive	*The Bodyguard*
After the Kiss	*The Bridegroom*

Mail-Order Brides Series

Texas Bride	*Montana Bride*
Wyoming Bride	*Blackthorne's Bride*

King's Brats Series

Sinful	*Surrender*
Shameless	

Connected Books

The Barefoot Bride	*The Inheritance*
Outlaw's Bride	*Maverick Heart*
Sweetwater Seduction	

Dell books are available at special discounts for bulk purchases for sales promotions or corporate use. Special editions, including personalized covers, excerpts of existing books, or books with corporate logos, can be created in large quantities for special needs. For more information, contact Premium Sales at (212) 572-2232 or email specialmarkets@penguinrandomhouse.com.

Surrender

A Bitter Creek Novel

JOAN JOHNSTON

DELL BOOKS • NEW YORK

Sale of this book without a front cover may be unauthorized. If this book is coverless, it may have been reported to the publisher as "unsold or destroyed" and neither the author nor the publisher may have received payment for it.

Surrender is a work of fiction. Names, characters, places, and incidents are the products of the author's imagination or are used fictitiously. Any resemblance to actual events, locales, or persons, living or dead, is entirely coincidental.

A Dell Mass Market Original

Copyright © 2018 by Joan Mertens Johnston, Inc.
Excerpt from *Sullivan's Promise* by Joan Johnston copyright © 2018 by Joan Mertens Johnston, Inc.

All rights reserved.

Published in the United States by Dell, an imprint of Random House, a division of Penguin Random House LLC, New York.

DELL and the HOUSE colophon are registered trademarks of Penguin Random House LLC.

This book contains an excerpt from the forthcoming book *Sullivan's Promise* by Joan Johnston. This excerpt has been set for this edition only and may not reflect the final content of the forthcoming edition.

ISBN 978-0-399-17776-7
Ebook ISBN 978-0-399-17777-4

Cover design: Lynn Andreozzi
Cover photograph: Rob Lang

Printed in the United States of America

randomhousebooks.com

9 8 7 6 5 4 3 2 1

Dell mass market original: March 2018

This book is dedicated
to the wildland firefighters
who have lost their lives
in the line of duty

Surrender

Chapter 1

DOES YOUR LIFE *really flash before your eyes when you know you're going to die?* Taylor Grayhawk was a great pilot, but there was nothing she could do with both engines flamed out. Her hands were shaking and a knot of fear had formed in her throat. Without the rumble of engines, the Twin Otter that had just dropped seven smoke jumpers on a raging inferno in Yellowstone National Park was eerily quiet.

She took a firmer grip on the control column as a way to keep herself—her emotions and her mind and her body—calm. The terrifying threat of plummeting into the fire, along with undeniable whiffs of choking black smoke in the cockpit, made it plain she didn't have much time left to figure out a way to save herself and the single passenger left on the plane.

Taylor had just dropped the last jumper to fight the blaze that had been burning for the past two weeks, when a whirlwind of fire had engulfed the Otter. Without power, she'd been slowly, but steadily, losing altitude. She turned, with eyes she hoped didn't reveal how frightened she was, to stare over her shoulder at the single smoke jumper remaining on the plane.

"You can still jump," she said loud enough to be heard over the unnerving whisper of wind in the open doorway at the rear of the Otter.

"Not without you," the jumper replied, pulling off his headset.

"I don't have a parachute."

"We can share mine."

Taylor calculated the odds of getting to the ground hanging on to Brian Flynn by her fingernails—and whatever other body parts she could wrap around him. She wasn't a gambler by nature, and she didn't like what she saw. Brian was wearing a yellow, padded jump jacket and Kevlar-reinforced pants, which acted like a cowboy's chaps, to protect the firefighter's trousers from being ripped by brush and tree limbs. She imagined herself falling—sliding down his body—into the scorching flames below, and shivered.

"I'll take my chances on getting the plane to the ground in one piece," she said, turning back to the control panel to see how much lift she could manage without the engines. Not much. She searched in vain for a meadow—any flat place, for that matter—where she might crash-land the plane. The only barren terrain she saw, in one of the most remote areas in the Lower 48, were steep mountain slopes leading straight down into the ferocious fire.

The spotter, who was required to be on all flights to gauge the wind, fire activity, and terrain, hadn't shown up for this 9 P.M. flight, which took advantage of the long August daylight. So Brian, already dressed in smoke-jumping gear, had doffed his Ram Air parachute and cage helmet in the corner of the plane, donned the spotter's harness and helmet, and served as spotter instead. After the last smoke jumper had gone out the door, Brian had suggested that Taylor drop down to survey the fire perimeter, in order to send the latest information back to base.

It was a judgment call whether the risk was worth the reward. But this fire had been frighteningly unpredictable, and she understood Brian's concern for the safety of his fellow smoke jumpers. It hadn't been easy to see anything through the cloud of black smoke, so she'd slipped even lower—and been engulfed in a sudden tornado of flame, rising hundreds of feet from the 250-foot conifers below.

They'd been drifting downward ever since.

Brian met her gaze with worried eyes. "This plane's headed straight into the fire," he said from the open doorway. "We need to jump now, while there's still time to hit a safe clearing. Get over here, Tag. Move your butt!"

The use of her nickname, which came from her initials—Taylor Ann Grayhawk—conjured powerful, painful memories. Brian had dubbed her with it when he was a junior and she was a freshman at Jackson High.

Taylor felt her stomach shift when the plane jolted, as the right wingtip was abruptly shoved upward by a scorching gust of air. Time was running out. Her eyes were tearing from the smoke, and her chin was trembling, despite her clenched teeth. In a voice that was hoarse, but surprisingly composed, considering the desperation she felt inside, Taylor reported their position on the radio, along with the information she'd gleaned from their survey of the fire and the fact that she'd been unable to restart the engines.

"I'm putting us down in the first clearing I find," she told the dispatcher.

"Roger," the dispatcher replied. "Good luck."

As Taylor surveyed the violent landscape, she figured it was going to take more than luck to survive. It was going to take a miracle. She didn't see an area large enough to allow her to land without going in nose first. If the crash didn't kill them, they would burn to death in the converging fire.

She knew her thoughts should be focused on wind currents and lift and drag. What consumed her instead was her greatest regret: *What would my life be like now, if I hadn't broken up with Brian Flynn in high school?*

Taylor had memories of the few autumn months she'd secretly dated Brian that were hard to forget. Laughter. Loving. Sharing and bonding. He'd seemed almost as perceptive of her feelings as her fraternal twin, which was saying something, because her life and Vick's had been wrapped, one around the other, like clinging vines.

It was easy to blame the tensions between their feuding families for driving them apart. Vick had been appalled when she discovered Taylor was dating one of "those awful Flynn boys" and demanded she stop seeing Brian. But ultimately, the decision had been hers. She was the one who'd given up on the possibility of loving and being loved. She was the one who'd walked away.

After college, Brian had become a firefighter and married someone else. She'd become a corporate jet pilot who flew CEOs to meetings around the country and found time during the summer to drop smoke jumpers from a twin-engine Otter. She'd been engaged three times, but she'd never married.

Since Brian's divorce a year ago, they were both single. During that year she'd done nothing to engage his interest, nothing to reignite the secret romance-of-a-lifetime that had been snuffed out thirteen years ago, like a campfire you were done with.

She'd often thought about approaching Brian once she learned he was free. But she'd waited too long. Very likely, they were going to die in the next few minutes.

But if we live through this . . .

"Tag?"

She focused her gaze on the tall, broad-shouldered man who'd been forbidden fruit when she was a teenager.

"I'm not leaving without you," Brian said from the doorway. "Get your beautiful ass over here!"

When their eyes met, she felt the past flooding back. All the things she should have done . . . and hadn't. All the things she shouldn't have done . . . and had.

The hope of a future with Brian almost had her rising. But there was too much water under the bridge. Or water over the dam. She'd been disappointed too many times by too many men. Some people were lovable, and some were not. She was just one of those people who wasn't destined to find a man who could love her. She no longer believed in the myth of "happily ever after." Her life was liable to end in an altogether more gruesome way.

"You should jump," she said turning back to search through the thick black smoke for the grassy clearing she knew had to be there somewhere.

A moment later she felt a strong hand grip her arm, yanking her out of her seat.

"I am not, by God, going to take the blame for leaving you behind, you stubborn brat!"

The plane shimmied again, and the wings tipped sideways.

"Let me go!" She reached back in an attempt to right the plane, but he pulled her inexorably toward the door, which was starting to tilt upward at an angle that might keep them both from escaping.

Taylor jerked free, her heart thundering in her chest, and grabbed the control column, bringing the plane back to level flight. Panting, breathless, her eyes locked with Brian's. "Just go! Someone has to keep the plane steady so you can get out the door."

"I'm not going without you, Tag. Get that into your head. So you can either join me in getting out of this plane, or we can both go down with it in flames."

Chapter 2

TAYLOR FOUGHT PANIC as the paint on the nose of the plane began to blister. The heat in the cockpit was insufferable. Any second the gas tank might blow. Brian was right. If she wanted to live, she had to abandon the Otter. *Now!*

She seized the bungee cord she'd used to hold a bunch of charts together and tied off the control column, then stumbled her way along the empty belly of the plane, grabbing at one of the storage racks along the side to keep from falling when the wings abruptly tipped and, just as suddenly, righted themselves. She was gasping with fear when she finally reached Brian. He was still wearing the spotter's helmet, but he'd replaced the spotter's harness with his smoke-jumping parachute.

"How do you want me to hang on, once we go out the door?"

"Come here," he said curtly.

Brian put a cage helmet, which normally protected a smoke jumper's face from being impaled by branches on the way down, onto her head and settled a spotter's harness around her chest. He secured the clip at the back, which had kept him attached to the plane while he was hanging out the door as the spotter, to a carabiner on his smoke jumper's rigging belt. When he was done, she stood in front of him at the door to the plane, her back arched slightly by the PG—personal gear—bag he had strapped to his stomach.

He pointed out the door. "See that spot? That's where we're headed."

Taylor looked where he'd gestured and saw a tiny circle, with patches of green and brown, surrounded by towering flames. Colored streamers he'd dropped to show the direction of the wind drifted downward through the black smoke. While she stood frozen, trying to fathom that this was really happening, that they really were going to jump into the inferno below, he kicked a tall, narrow cargo box used by smoke jumpers out the door. The box contained a sleeping bag and Brian's Pulaski tool, along with other supplies, including three days' worth of food and water.

She was still watching the descent of the cargo box parachute, which was headed in the same direction as the streamers, when Brian yanked her close.

"Trust the harness to hold you. Keep your arms crossed over your chest and your knees bent," he ordered tersely. "Lean your head back against my shoulder and lift your feet off the ground."

She barely had time to do as he'd asked, before he put his long, powerful arms around her and dropped out of the plane.

Taylor would have screamed as they fell, except she

was so frightened, she couldn't draw breath to make a sound. She whimpered when a flying cinder slipped through the metal cage protecting her face and landed on her cheek, but she was afraid to move her hands from the position she'd been told to take, so she shook her head frantically to get rid of it.

"Settle down," Brian said in an infuriatingly calm voice, tightening his hold until she thought her ribs might crack. "I have you."

It surprised her how much relief she felt at Brian's deep-voiced reassurance, but that small comfort didn't last, because she could see that they were headed straight into the hottest part of the fire. Any second, she expected to be impaled on a burning limb. She felt like she might throw up. How did smoke jumpers do this time after time after time?

Taylor followed the direction of the streamers far below, which seemed to be headed into the fiery blaze. Her search was interrupted by a jerk and a sudden reversal of direction upward, as Brian pulled the rip cord and the chute opened.

"I'm going to let go of you now. I need to adjust the risers."

Taylor felt herself slide downward and screamed, "Brian!"

"You're not going to fall. Just do as I say."

Then his arms were gone.

Taylor would have given anything to be facing the other way, holding on to Brian like a baby animal clutched to its mother's belly. It was torture watching the ground coming up at her faster and faster. She closed her eyes and felt their bodies sliding sideways as Brian adjusted the steering toggles. But the fearsome noise rising upward, as the fire hissed and growled like a multitude of predatory cats and carnivorous dogs, was too ominous to ignore.

Taylor forced herself to open her eyes, but her heart skipped a beat at the sight that greeted her.

An inferno. Nothing but death in every direction.

"There," Brian muttered, gesturing with his chin, which nudged the back of her head.

Taylor spied their supposed destination, a tiny, unburned meadow at the base of the mountain. It was about the size of a baseball field and was bounded everywhere she looked by giant burning spruces and pines. The patch of grass Brian had spotted was too small a target. They would never make it. "You can't—"

Taylor bit off the rest of her speech. The meadow he'd found was ridiculously tiny, but it was the only place she could see anywhere around them that wasn't licked by flames. She watched the cargo box land in rugged brush ringed by trees that crackled viciously as they burned. Black smoke rose ominously, so thick and hot it was difficult to breathe. Maybe they weren't going to be scorched to death after all. Maybe they were going to suffocate.

She heard Brian say, "Keep your knees bent, so they're off the ground when we land." Then he swore savagely, as a gust of wind caught the Ram Air chute and forced it twenty feet farther up into the air and sideways toward the inferno.

Taylor watched in horror as embers landed in the

rectangular canopy and felt sure the fragile nylon was going to dissolve in flames. Any second, she expected them to plummet to their deaths. Her stomach turned topsy-turvy, and she felt her tongue latch to the roof of her mouth.

"Not on my watch, you sonofabitch!" Brian muttered.

They suddenly swirled in a circle, and Taylor heard Brian's grunts as he wrestled the chute away from the devilish fire. But whichever way he turned them, they were surrounded by flames. There was no escape. Taylor blinked her tearing eyes and coughed as she breathed in the hot smoke that obscured everything. She had the awful feeling that the end was near, but because it was so dark, she was going to miss it.

Apparently Brian could see just fine, because he swore again.

Taylor tried to imagine the feat of superhuman strength it was taking to direct the parachute away from the flaming trees. Amazingly, a moment later, they were headed back toward the center of the meadow.

Taylor clutched her arms tighter across her chest when, once again, they shot higher into the air. This time, they dropped just as suddenly. The descent was horrifying because they ended up below the tops of the towering conifers, within the ring of excoriating fire. Sparks spit and flew. Taylor gasped and shook her head to put out another flaming ash that landed on her forehead.

She was suddenly aware of how fast they were falling. *Too fast. We're falling too fast!* Which was when it dawned on her that there was too much weight on the chute, that two of them hanging from the billowing nylon intended for just one was likely contributing to the difficulty Brian was having maneuvering them into the small open space.

"Keep your knees bent, so they're off the ground when we land," Brian repeated.

He knew she needed the reminder, because he knew this was her very first jump. She'd always thought it was stupid to purposely exit a perfectly functioning plane, even with a perfectly functioning parachute. She didn't respond because her breathing had gone wonky again.

Taylor was fully aware that, assuming the parachute opened, most jumping accidents occurred on landing. In fact, that was how most smoke jumpers got injured—impaled on a tree branch, falling as they tried to free themselves from a perch high in some towering pine, or running into some object on landing, like a boulder, that crushed bones. Not to mention ending up smack-dab in the middle of a raging fire.

It had been a running joke between the two of them, whenever she'd flown Brian on smoke-jumping missions over the past summer, that he was going to get her into a parachute and out of a plane someday. She fought the urge to laugh at the absurdity of the position in which she found herself and realized that she was on the verge of hysteria. This was the sort of dire emergency that happened only in novels or movies.

Except, this was real.

"Knees up!" Brian ordered.

She kept her knees raised as Brian landed, running to

keep up with the speed of the chute. But a gust of wind tore at the nylon and knocked him sideways onto the grass. She felt a stone jab her hip as he rolled them over, so she was on top of him.

We're down. And we're not on fire!

There was no time for exultation. The chute was still full of air, and it was dragging them along the ground, faster and faster.

"We're being pulled into the fire!" Taylor dug in her heels, but it didn't help.

Brian reached between them to release the carabiner. He tossed her aside and was on his feet an instant later, deflating the Ram Air and gathering it into a ball.

Taylor tried to shove her way upright, but her body didn't want to move. The air seared her lungs; the smoke was suffocating. She crouched close to the ground, where it was easier to breathe. She turned her head in a slow circle and felt her heart falter. She saw no break in the fire, no narrow passage between the burning trees through which they might escape. She had no idea why this meadow hadn't burned yet, but it was only a matter of time before the wind blew burning embers onto the dry grass and brush, or charred trees began crashing down on top of them.

They were safely on the ground, but all they'd done was postpone the inevitable . . . and ensure their deaths would be excruciating.

Chapter 3

BRIAN OFTEN HAD nightmares in which the fire he was fighting took him down, sweat-drenched dreams where, no matter how hard he battled, the fire won. When he'd stepped from the Twin Otter with Tag in his arms, his body charged with adrenaline, he hadn't allowed himself to consider what he would do if there was no path of escape once they reached the ground. His single goal was to survive.

But he'd never been in a situation quite this menacing. He'd never had the responsibility for the life of someone he loved—*had loved*—completely on his shoulders. He felt his pulse racing as he suppressed the knowledge of what might happen to them if they ended up in the burning trees.

He'd smelled scorched human flesh. He'd seen the remains of a charred human corpse, the face in agonized rictus. He forced that awful smell, that horrific image, from his mind, as he did every morning when he went to work. A firefighter couldn't afford to think of the worst-case scenario. Otherwise, he'd be no good at his job.

Fear—being scared shitless—led to indecision. And indecision led to disaster.

His heart galloped out of control as he searched for some tiny break in the cage of fire surrounding the meadow below—and found nothing. This fire was a gobbler, gorging on everything in sight. He estimated the flames rose sixty to eighty feet above the trees. Maybe Tag had been right. Maybe they should have stuck with the plane. He was the one who'd insisted they get out.

But he was a smoke jumper, and he worked best on the ground. He'd been sure that, if they could just get to solid footing safely, he could figure out a way to save them both. He could tell Tag was terrified, but she hadn't panicked, which would have made the situation worse.

Ordinarily, he would have been falling through the air at ninety miles an hour, but Tag's added weight made it much faster. He'd figured they would need the sixty-five pounds of stuff he'd packed into the pockets in his trousers and the supplies in his PG bag, so he hadn't discarded anything before they jumped.

To compensate for the increased speed caused by the extra weight, he'd simply ratcheted up the normal count before he opened the chute—*jump one thousand, look one thousand, reach one thousand, wait one thousand, pull one thousand*—each element an instruction for what he should be doing in the moments before he pulled the rip cord across his chest.

The multicolored streamers had revealed four hundred yards of drift and shown him the wind was stronger down low. The terrain was mountainous, but the valley into which they'd jumped was all forest. Black smoke made the ground nearly invisible, and he was worried that he wouldn't be able to hit the scrap of unburnt land he'd seen from the plane. He checked the surrounding forest and saw only fast-burning black and white spruce. His nose pinched at the acrid smell of pine tar and burning pitch.

There wasn't much wind, but he held his breath in an agony of suspense, hoping it wouldn't rise and send flying embers out into the grass and rugged brush, setting fire to the meadow before they landed. He couldn't figure out why it wasn't already in flames. Then he saw it—a natural barrier of rock, a ring of boulders and stones that kept the fire from spreading from the trees into the grass. All it would take was one good gust of wind to send sparks into the scrubland. After that, it wouldn't take long for the brush to burn—along with the two of them.

He aimed the chute toward the far end of the meadow, away from the direction of the wind. Like cattle drives, fires had different areas where the firefighters—the fire's drovers—positioned themselves: the head, the right and left flanks, and the tail. He hoped that landing near the tail of the fire, rather than closer to its head, might give them a few more seconds, seconds they would need to escape, if the meadow started to burn.

Once they were on the ground, he didn't stop to ask Tag how she was. He simply released the carabiner and hurried to collect the chute. They might need it to keep them warm overnight, assuming they didn't get rescued right away.

He found himself grinning like an idiot. He was worried about keeping *warm* overnight? They'd be lucky if they lived another half hour! He was glad Tag couldn't see him. She'd think he'd gone around the bend. His grin became a grimace when he realized there was no break visible in the fire that encircled them.

But he'd been in plenty of tight places before and managed to come through. He wasn't the kind of man to give up or give in. Otherwise, he never would have survived this long.

Brian's nose was already running, and his eyes were burning and tearing from the smoke. As soon as he had the parachute bunched, he headed for the cargo box, which held four plastic quart bottles of water. From his own experience, he knew Tag would appreciate a wet cloth to wipe her eyes and to tie around her nose, so she could breathe more easily.

Brian had just reached the three-foot-tall, one-foot-wide box when he saw a fast-moving shadow on his right. He figured it was some small animal fleeing its burrow, a sight common during forest fires.

"Brian! Look out!"

At Tag's shriek, he spun, then threw himself side-ways, as a set of monstrous claws that would have ripped his guts out, slashed through his trouser leg instead. He was too startled to do more than spread his arms wide to make himself look bigger and shout at the top of his lungs. The young grizzly darted away, and Brian realized he had only seconds to find something with which to defend himself. When the ferocious bear realized there was nowhere to go, he'd be back.

Brian slammed open the cargo box and grabbed his

Pulaski—a firefighter's tool with an ax head on one side of the long wooden handle and a hoe for digging on the other—to defend himself when the bear attacked again. He didn't stand much of a chance against a five-hundred-pound grizzly's teeth and claws, but at least the ax gave him a chance. He shot a glance in Tag's direction and, when it looked like she might move toward him, shook his head violently to warn her away. He turned to face the grizzly, putting himself between the dangerous beast and the woman he was determined to protect.

As he stared, his heart in his throat, Pulaski in hand, the grizzly shoved through a burning bush and kept on running, roaring in tragic defiance as it disappeared into the fiery hell that surrounded them.

Brian was astonished, disbelieving. What had just happened? The animal had to know it didn't stand a chance in the fire. But he'd watched people do equally desperate things when faced with a burning inferno and no obvious means of escape—like jump out of a twenty-story window knowing they would die when their bodies hit the ground. He saw the lumbering beast catch fire and heard it scream in agony before he turned away.

"Are you hurt?" Taylor called as she ran to him, coughing and choking from the smoke. She'd gotten rid of the helmet and spotter's harness and had her chambray shirttail up over her face, baring a naked midriff. "I saw it take a swipe at you and thought . . ." Her eyes were two wide white saucers surrounded by skin turned black by smoke.

He glanced at his trousers and shivered when he saw

the tattered cloth surrounding his right calf, which stung a bit, relieved that he'd survived the encounter with so little damage. He dumped the spotter's helmet on the ground and said, "I'm fine," as he turned to see where the grizzly had come from.

He made an instant decision and acted on it. If the cave opening was large enough for the young grizzly to exit, it was probably large enough for the two of them to get inside, where they could wait for the fire to burn itself out. A can of pork and beans fell from the ragged pocket in his trouser leg as he grabbed the cargo box with one hand, keeping the Pulaski in the other, and dragged it toward the hole, nearly hidden by brush, from which the animal had emerged.

"What's this?" Taylor asked as she picked up the can and trotted after him.

"Supper." The wind ruffled his hair, and he glanced at the trees and saw embers being blown about. The wind was coming up. Time was running out.

"Stand back," he said, when they reached the grizzly's hideaway. He let go of the cargo box and took the Pulaski in both hands, wary of what might be coming out next.

It was impossible to see very far inside the hole, but it was clearly too narrow for him to enter wearing his smoke-jumping gear. He slipped off his jacket and PG bag and let them drop. He had the fleeting thought that he should try to report on his Bendix King that they'd reached the ground alive. But without a repeater, the radio had a range of only three miles—and that was on flat land. They were surrounded by mountains. No sense confirming to Tag that they had no way of contacting the outside world. Better to wait until they were safe. They weren't out of danger yet. Not by a long shot.

He retrieved his headlamp from his PG bag and put it on, then emptied the rope from his shredded trouser pocket and left it coiled on the ground. He removed the frying pan from his other pants pocket, but left the steak, foil-wrapped potato, and another can of pork and beans where they were. He could collect the stuff he'd removed when he came back out.

Assuming I come back out, he thought grimly.

"Surely you're not going in there," Tag said.

"Do you see anywhere else to wait out this fire?" He didn't pause for an answer, simply dropped to his hands and knees. He'd planned to shove the cargo box through the hole ahead of him, thinking it would keep a grizzly's jaws and claws off him until he was inside the cave and could wield the Pulaski, which he still held. The box was too tall.

He seized the parachute instead, then settled onto his stomach, angled his broad shoulders, and began slithering into the tunnel, pushing the bulky fabric through ahead of him.

"Be careful!" Taylor called after him. "There might be another bear inside."

He heard the panic in Taylor's shrill voice and stopped long enough to yell back, "I'll be fine."

"You can't know that!"

Brian didn't bother arguing. He was willing to fight a grizzly for the refuge if necessary, because their only other choice was burning to death. The rock walls on either side of his body narrowed, squeezing the air from his lungs, as he struggled to get through the tapering entryway. Gravity suddenly caused the chute to slide away from him, and he heard it *swoosh* when it landed. He had a moment's terror when he realized he would be pretty much helpless if something tried to escape, now that the chute was gone, while his arms were confined by the rock walls.

"How the hell did that bear get through here?" he muttered.

"What?" Taylor called down to him.

He slid out of the tunnel into the cave like a baby leaving its mother's womb, but without the blazing light a newborn was likely to find waiting for him. He was grateful for the parachute, which allowed him a relatively soft landing.

He turned his head to illuminate the cave with his headlamp. The dark space looked about as tall and wide as his bedroom at home. He searched for anything else that might have decided to wait out the fire down here but saw nothing. He cautiously moved far enough away from the opening to determine that the cave narrowed again at the other end. He couldn't see light or feel any sort of breeze that would suggest another exit.

The surprisingly cool cave was empty.

Brian coughed as he inhaled a breath of smoke from the entrance. He realized that once they were both inside, he would need to block the opening, in order to keep out the smoke until the fire died down. He could do that with the chute.

He crawled back out again, Pulaski in hand, aware

that there might be other caves in the rocky area, with other feral animals intent on escaping. He needed to collect his coat and the rest of his gear, report their position, if that was possible, and retrieve his PG bag and the supplies from the cargo box.

"What's down there?" Taylor asked.

"A lot of bear scat and bat guano," he replied. "Otherwise, we'll have the place to ourselves." He surveyed the flames with a firefighter's eyes, noting the direction of the wind and seeing how the dry brush along the edge of the clearing was beginning to burn. Now that the wind had picked up, it might be only a matter of seconds before the fire was at their feet.

He quickly retrieved his PG bag and took out his Bendix King. He stuffed two of the quart water bottles from the cargo box into it, then added the skillet and the can of beans Tag was holding. He handed the heavy bag to her, along with his sleeping bag, and said, "Push this down ahead of you when you crawl in."

Tag eyed the hole skeptically, her blue eyes wide, her chin wobbling. "Where are you going to be?"

Then he remembered that she hated being alone in the dark. When they were teenagers, he'd thought she just wanted to see what the two of them were doing, when she'd insisted she didn't want to make love without a light on. He'd smirked and said, "Are you sure you're ready to see this big boy?"

She'd socked him in the arm and explained, "One of the maids my father hired to take care of us while he was gone locked me in a closet. I suppose I deserved some sort of punishment."

"What did you do?" he'd asked.

"I don't remember. The point is, she forgot about me, and I spent the rest of the day in the dark. None of my sisters were at home, and the maid must have gone shopping, because she didn't hear me screaming, either. Or she ignored me. I've never felt so helpless in my life."

"So you're not really scared of the dark?"

She'd shivered. "I was so alone. I never want to feel like that again."

Remembering the look on her face, Brian set down his Pulaski, then took off his headlamp and arranged it on her forehead. "Take this and go on inside. I need to report that we're on the ground and where we're holed up, so they can find us later, and collect the rest of the supplies from the cargo box. I'll be right behind you."

"All right. Please hurry, Brian."

He had to hand it to her. She might look and sound scared, but Tag was a trooper. She dropped to her knees and shoved everything through the hole ahead of her, before she flattened onto her stomach and slithered into the narrow opening.

He'd just started up the rock face above the tunnel, in hopes of getting better radio reception, when he heard an earsplitting *crraaaaccck*.

Brian saw a gigantic, 200-foot spruce begin to fall, its trunk massive enough to seal the cave opening. He didn't think, he just reacted. He tripped and dropped the radio as he scrambled back down the rock, but there was no time to retrieve it. He ran full tilt for the tunnel and dove inside, just as the mighty tree, limbs on fire, crashed to the ground in a horrendous cacophony of breaking branches and crackling flames. The colossal spruce shut out what little sunlight had made it through the smoke, leaving them trapped in the pitch-black cave . . . with no way out.

Chapter 4

"BRIAN?" TAYLOR'S HEART racketed in her chest as the cave suddenly became the dark, suffocating closet she'd been locked in as a child. She focused the bright stream of light from her headlamp where she thought the tunnel entrance should be and watched Brian drop onto the parachute that lay where it had fallen when he'd first entered the cave.

She hurried over to help him to his feet. "What happened?"

"A tree came down and sealed up the entrance."

Taylor stared in horror at the smoldering, fire-blackened branches intruding through the narrow opening. "We're trapped?"

Brian grimaced, his expression providing all response necessary.

"Are you hurt?" she asked.

"No." He turned to look at the blocked opening, shaking his head and swearing under his breath.

"Are you sure you're all right?"

"I'm just pissed off. I had to leave a bunch of stuff out

there when that tree came down, including my ax, which I could have used to hack a way back out of here." He hesitated, then added with disgust, "I lost the radio."

"But you called them—"

"I didn't have time."

Taylor's lungs couldn't seem to suck air. She gasped and said, "They don't know where we are?"

"They have the last location you gave them."

"But we're miles from there!"

"They'll take that into account when they start their search."

"How are they going to find us down here?" she cried, turning in a circle within the cave, hoping against hope for some sliver of light, some breath of fresh air. "They won't even know there is a cave unless that tree burns up!" She crossed to Brian, focused the light on his sooty face and asked, "Is there any chance it will? Burn enough to reveal the opening, I mean?"

Brian shook his head. "Probably not. Now that it's on the ground, once the grass around it burns away, the trunk will likely stop burning, too."

Taylor put a hand to her heart, which was battering against her ribs. "So we're really, truly trapped in here?"

"You're shivering."

"I'm cold. So cold."

"You're in shock."

"I'm scared!" she retorted. "We're trapped and it's dark and—"

His arms closed around her, pulling her snug against powerful muscle and sinew. "We're alive, Tag. We survived."

"You're trembling, too, Brian."

"Yeah. Well. Shit. I made a jury-rigged tandem jump with you into a pea-sized meadow surrounded by fire and didn't get either one of us killed. A grizzly attacked me, and I walked away unscathed. A tree nearly crushed me flat, but here I am. I think I'm entitled."

She felt him quiver as he pressed his face against her neck.

"It's just adrenaline," he muttered, his whole body shaking uncontrollably. "Too much adrenaline."

Her arms slid around his neck offering comfort, and she pressed her body close, seeking support in return. "I can't believe we didn't end up burning to cinders."

"Yeah. Me, too. That's kind of a nightmare of mine."

She shuddered. They could have died. They still might. She suddenly sobbed and whispered, "Brian."

He lifted his head to look into her eyes.

She had time to notice his pupils were dilated so wide his blue eyes were nearly black, before he shoved the light off her head. She heard it clatter to the stone beneath them and saw a splash of light hit the dirt wall as his mouth found hers. She wasn't sure who was more desperate for the life-affirming contact, but their mouths clung as his tongue came searching for solace.

Her hands shoved at the suspenders holding up his Kevlar pants, forcing them off his shoulders, then reached for his T-shirt, yanking it up and out of the way, wanting to feel the warmth of his living flesh, proof they were both still alive.

He tore at the buttons on her shirt and thrust it off her

shoulders, then released her bra clasp and removed the last thing keeping their naked bodies apart.

They stood cleaved to each other, panting.

It wasn't close enough. Not for her. And not for him, either, because he unsnapped her jeans and shoved down the zipper, even as she tugged at his Kevlar pants, pushing them down to reach the metal buttons on his jeans. Their boots stayed on, and their trousers tangled at their ankles.

He backed her in short steps to the pile of nylon on the ground and tumbled them onto it. She felt his desperation as he stripped down her panties, even as she tore at his briefs.

A moment later he was inside her and they were joined. It was a simple confirmation that he was man, she was woman, and they were alive. The sex was carnal. Animalistic. Savage and satisfying.

She cried out, her body clenching around his as he threw his head back with a guttural sound of triumph, a vocal celebration of the simple joy of having survived.

He sank onto her, his weight surprisingly comforting, solid and strong. She wrapped her arms around his waist and held him close, not wanting to let go, not wanting the moment of mindless release to end.

A moment later, he rolled onto his back and slung an arm across his face. He heaved a sigh. Started to speak. Stopped, then said, "I didn't mean for that to happen."

"I needed you. And you needed me. We needed each other, Brian."

She suddenly felt very much alone. She wanted to reach out to him but lacked the confidence to act. The adrenaline—and fear—that had forced them together seemed to have dissipated.

She shivered, and he must have noticed, because he said, "We'd better get dressed."

He suited word to deed. He kicked off his Kevlar pants, then pulled up his shorts and jeans, lifting his hips to get them over his butt. He stood and said, "Did you see where I threw my T-shirt?"

Taylor covered her breasts with her hands, suddenly aware of her nakedness, like Eve in the Garden of Eden, when she realized she'd sinned.

What had just happened? How had it happened? She'd just made love—had sex—with Brian Flynn!

She was staring into the darkness when she felt something drop into her lap.

"Your bra," he said. "I'll see if I can find your shirt."

Well, if he wasn't going to make a big deal about what had just happened, neither was she.

Taylor glanced at Brian to make sure his back was turned, then slipped on her bra. By the time he returned with her shirt hanging over his arm, she'd pulled up her panties and jeans and was on her feet.

"Thanks." When she tried to take the shirt from him, he settled the lamp back on her head and held on, forcing her to look at him.

"Tag, I . . . I've heard about things like what just happened to us occurring in a crisis. I should have recognized what it was and—"

"What was it, Brian? Because it felt like pretty good sex to me."

She saw his disappointment at her attempt to downplay their need for human contact—for each other—in such a desperate moment.

He rested his palm on her cheek. "It was comfort, Tag. Proof that we're both still here and kicking. Nothing more." He hesitated before adding, "And nothing less."

She heaved a sigh. "What happened was just so . . . unexpected."

"I know. For what it's worth, I'm sorry."

She managed a crooked smile and said, "For what it's worth, I'm not."

Chapter 5

"WHY DON'T WE cook that steak I brought along," Brian suggested. "I'm hungry. How about you?"

It took a moment for Taylor to realize she was famished. She'd been so busy dropping smoke jumpers all day she'd missed both lunch and dinner. "I could eat a bite or two."

She wrapped her arms tightly around her chest to steady nerves that were still on edge, as Brian dug a fire pit with his Swiss army knife in a spot that was mostly dirt. He used paper from a small notebook he'd brought along and shavings from limbs that weren't burned through for kindling, and added a few thicker branches on top from the charred tree that blocked the entrance. He lit the fire with a match from the tin he'd carried in his PG bag.

"You made that look easy," Taylor said.

He waggled his eyebrows. "I'm as good at starting fires as I am at putting them out."

Taylor couldn't believe he was joking at a time like this. Her composure was rattled, and she was barely holding herself together. But if Brian could conquer his fear, so could she. "What can I do to help?"

"Check my bag. See if you can find that potato wrapped in foil. When the fire's hot enough, we'll throw it on the coals."

"Steak and a baked potato? On a fire line? Who knew?"

"You forgot about the pork and beans."

She wrinkled her nose. "Not my favorite."

"Sorry the menu is so limited, but food is food. Unfortunately, we don't have a lot of it. So, no beans tonight. At some point, we're going to have to take inventory and figure out how much—or little—we can eat every day. While you're scrounging, see if you can find the skillet I dropped in there when I was cleaning out the pockets of my Kevlar trousers."

She held it up and shook her head in disbelief. "For heaven's sake, Brian. You brought along a *frying pan*?"

He lifted a dark brow. "You expected me to impale my steak on a stick and hold it over the fire like some Neanderthal? We smoke jumpers are civilized human beings."

She laughed as she handed him the pan and lobbed the foil-wrapped potato at him. "This is ridiculous. All of this." She turned in a circle, her hands widespread. "I can't believe this is happening. We're going to have a steak dinner in a cave where we're trapped with no way out."

"I haven't investigated the rest of our humble abode yet," Brian said. "I noticed it narrows at the other end, but I was only looking for more wildlife. There may, in fact, be another way out."

Taylor turned to study the opposite end of the cave. It was murky and musky-smelling. She felt Brian's hand on her shoulder, before he turned her and gently urged her into his embrace.

"There's no sense worrying now, Tag," he murmured. "We can't go anywhere until the fire outside dies down. Meanwhile, we're both safe."

Taylor laid her cheek against his chest. She could hear his heart thumping hard and fast beneath his T-shirt, so he wasn't as calm as he wanted her to think. She hoped he couldn't tell how distraught she was. She'd flown a lot of smoke jumpers in life-threatening conditions, and staying cool in an emergency was one of her best qualities.

Besides, it wasn't the idea of being trapped that was freaking her out. It was the idea of being trapped *in the dark*. "Am I wearing the only headlamp?"

He ducked down under the light and looked her in the eye. "Afraid so."

"How long do these batteries last?"

She was surprised when Brian answered with a precise number. "Twenty-two hours on high beam—"

She turned to face him directly, and he squinted as the light hit him in the eyes. "That's less than a day!"

"And a hundred and sixty hours on low," he finished.

Taylor backed out of his arms. She tried to do the math in her head but was too anxious to think clearly. "How many days is that?"

"Six for sure. Maybe seven, if the batteries last as long

as they're supposed to last. Those have been in there for a while."

"These batteries aren't new?"

"No."

Taylor realized the numbers had been on the tip of Brian's tongue because he'd need to know that information when he and his team were left in the wilderness for days at a time fighting a fire. She had a sudden thought and asked, "Do we have more batteries?"

"I've got four more in my PG bag."

Taylor didn't speak the unspeakable. If they weren't found before the extra set of batteries wore out, she would be alone with Brian in the dark until they were. Her stomach did a quick somersault but didn't land on its feet. She felt queasy. Surely they would be able to figure out some way to get out of here. Or they'd be found.

It occurred to her that they would be turning the lamp off when they were asleep, so maybe six days could be stretched to twelve. Or maybe fourteen. And they had time left on these batteries.

She had another thought that put an ironic, idiotic grin on her face, a sure sign of how out of it she was. *We're probably going to starve to death, or die of thirst, long before the batteries wear out.*

Taylor hadn't said she needed reassurance, but Brian's strong arms folded around her again. She released an anxious breath as she pressed her cheek against his and slid her arms around his waist. He didn't say anything. Neither did she. They simply stood there and held each other.

She was reminded of why she'd liked Brian so much in

high school. He was the one boy who'd always held her after sex. Taylor wondered what had made him do something so wonderful, something that, in her experience, wasn't typical teenage-boy behavior. Especially since there had never been anything like love involved in their brief relationship. Well, Brian might have said the word "love" once upon a time, but she hadn't believed him.

It was a wonder they'd stayed together as long as they had. Three months was an eternity to a fifteen-year-old girl, especially since Taylor had never been good at keeping a boyfriend. Her twin had accused her of dropping the boys she dated, like half-eaten apples, before the thought of dropping her could form in their minds.

"I'm just cutting my losses," she told Vick in her defense. "It wouldn't have lasted anyway." As far as Taylor was concerned, it was better to be the one leaving than the one being left.

With his black hair and blue eyes, his broad shoulders and athletic build, she'd thought Brian Flynn was *hot*. When she'd mentioned that fact in the kitchen one night, her eldest sister, Leah, had told her in no uncertain terms, "Stay away from him. Don't speak to him. Don't even look at him. He's trouble you don't need."

Leah had good reason for the warning. Their father, King Grayhawk, and Brian's father, Angus Flynn, had been mortal enemies for more years than anyone could count. Their battle had been taken up by the four youngest Grayhawk girls, better known around Jackson Hole as King's Brats, and Angus's four boys.

What had begun as pranks played on one another— shaving a patch of hair from a competition 4-H cow or putting salt in a competition 4-H cherry pie—had graduated, as they became teenagers, to letting the air out of all four tires or encasing an entire truck in Saran wrap in below-zero temperatures. Until finally, it had morphed into something more hazardous—like sliced saddle cinches during a junior rodeo competition that had resulted in a broken arm for Taylor's youngest sister, Eve, and a broken leg for Brian's eldest brother, Aiden.

Needless to say, there was no love lost between Grayhawks and Flynns when Taylor had turned her eyes toward Brian. But Leah telling her to stay away from him was like telling her not to touch a hot stove. She had to test it, to see if it really was going to burn her.

She watched Brian roughhouse with his jock friends on the way to class. Watched him attack his sack lunch in the cafeteria. Sat in the stands during football practice and watched him run wind sprints. He must have noticed all that attention, because he started saying, "Hi," whenever they passed each other in the hall. She put her nose in the air and pretended she wasn't interested.

One day, he didn't let her get away with walking past him. He stepped in front of her, stopping her in her tracks. "Hi."

Nothing more. Nothing to make it any easier for her. Heart slamming against her rib cage, she glanced up at him from beneath lowered lashes, her most successful flirting technique.

He didn't let her get away with that, either. He slid a forefinger under her chin and lifted her face so she was forced to meet his gaze. "I said, 'Hi.'"

She felt a blush rising and had no idea how to stop it.

"Hi." It came out sounding like some movie starlet, whispery and breathless.

His lips tilted in a lopsided smile. "Now that I have your attention, how about going out with me on Friday night?"

She jerked free. "Are you crazy?"

"Not that I've noticed. How about it?"

"You're a—"

"Flynn," he finished for her. "So what? I've always thought this whole feud thing was ridiculous. I don't see why we have to be a part of it."

Taylor was thrown for a loop. Now that she'd caught the tiger by the tail, she had no idea what to do with him. She had visions of Vick catching them together and tattling to Leah. Vick saw things in black and white. Rules were rules. Besides, Taylor was a lot more concerned about getting caught disobeying Leah than she was about disappointing one of "those awful Flynn boys." After their mother had run off with one of their father's cowhands, ten-year-old Leah had taken her place and raised her three much younger half sisters.

Taylor let her eyes flash with disdain. "I wouldn't date you if you were—"

He laughed, a soft, teasing sound. "You've been wagging that tail of yours at me like some lost puppy for the past three weeks." Then his eyes did something funny. Softened. And lightened. His callused thumb moved across her cheek in a tender caress. "I've always had a soft spot for strays."

She felt horrified at his characterization of her as someone who wandered through life without any particular purpose or destination, mostly because it was so close to the mark. But it was too late to escape. She'd already fallen headlong into those two deep, dangerous blue pools that remained focused intently on her.

So Taylor went out with him.

She convinced herself she wasn't betraying her family. She endured without comment the censuring looks Leah gave her at the supper table when, inevitably, her older sister found out. She told Vick that she was merely on a mission to get Brian to fall for her so she could dump him. It would simply be one more trick played by one of King's Brats on one of "those awful Flynn boys." She almost believed it herself.

Things hadn't gone at all as she'd planned.

Taylor wondered how Brian had known she needed closeness and comfort all those years ago. And how he'd known she needed it now. She was heartened by the thought that, although she was probably going to die in this cold, creepy place, at least she wasn't going to die all alone.

"Brian?"

"What?"

She lifted her head from his chest and pointed toward the spot where her light had been aimed. "There's water streaming down that stone wall."

Brian took several steps, following the beam of light, and pressed his hand against the wall. "I'll be damned."

Taylor followed him to the wall and drifted her fingers through the cool stream of water trickling down the stone. It collected in a six-inch-round pool at the bottom, then ran in a groove along the wall toward the back of the cave. "Do you suppose we can drink it?"

"If the choice is between dying of thirst and drinking it, yeah, I think we can drink it." A grin flashed, and he gave her a quick, hard hug before letting her go again. "I suddenly feel a lot better about being stuck in here. Maybe, while that potato cooks, we'd better take inventory and see just how bad off we are."

The good news was that the PG bag contained the two quart plastic bottles of water he'd retrieved from the cargo box. Once they were emptied, Taylor was sure Brian could figure out a way to refill them from the water streaming down the wall. The bad news was that most of the food—a three-day supply of dried and canned food and two more bottles of fresh water that had been in the cargo box—had never made it inside.

At least they had a sleeping bag—big enough for one. That should make things interesting.

Brian's personal gear bag was a treasure trove of odds and ends. The items that seemed most useful to her included a flashlight with extra batteries, a T-shirt, baby wipes, ibuprofen, a brand-new bar of Irish Spring soap, a toothbrush and paste, and a first-aid kit.

The pickings were slim where food was concerned: two Snickers bars and a McIntosh apple.

When they searched Brian's Kevlar pants pockets, they found another can of pork and beans and twelve packets of instant coffee.

"Why so much coffee?" she asked.

"When I'm running out of energy I dump a couple of

packets in my mouth and swallow them down with water."

"Dry, *unbrewed* coffee? That sounds disgusting."

"Not when it's three A.M. and the fire is winning and you need the caffeine to stay awake and fight it."

Taylor marveled, not for the first time, at the tremendous dedication of wildland firefighters. She knew for a fact they often worked forty-eight to seventy-two hour shifts without a break.

"Here's something we can use," Brian said, holding up an unmarked plastic bottle filled with brown liquid.

"What is it?"

"My old friend Jack Daniel's."

She arched a disbelieving brow. "I thought you smoke jumpers drank coffee on the line, not whiskey."

"It's purely medicinal," he said with a grin and a wink.

She focused her attention back on his pants pocket. "Look what I found! A sweatshirt."

"I haven't had a chance to wash that. It might stink."

She put it to her nose and inhaled. It did smell. Like wood smoke and sweat . . . and Brian. "I think I can tolerate it."

She immediately slipped it over her head and stuck her arms in the sleeves, pushing them up so they wouldn't drape over her fingers.

"Are you still cold?"

"I'm always cold. Too skinny, I guess."

"Having just held your breasts and your butt in my hands, Tag, I'd say you're pretty damn perfect."

Taylor was surprised, and surprisingly pleased, by the

compliment. "Thanks, Brian." As her face began to flush, she turned away for one last check through his trouser pockets, which were now empty. She felt the same way about Brian, except he was more than perfect, but she felt awkward about returning the compliment. That would suggest she'd kept an eye on him all these years. Which was true, of course, but she didn't want him to know it.

She'd seen the announcement of his wedding in the local paper, and another article when he'd divorced five years later. He'd been single for an entire year, but Taylor had resisted getting in touch with him outside of the work they did together fighting fires—her flying, him jumping. She'd heard high school romances stuck with you for a long time. All she knew was that she'd never felt with another man what she'd felt in those few months she'd spent with Brian Flynn in high school.

Taylor had thought about it a lot and couldn't quite put a finger on what it was she'd found in Brian's arms. *Peace. Joy.* Which were strange words to use for a high school fling. She'd never really sat down to figure it out. She just knew how she'd felt when she was with Brian. *Valued. Cherished.*

Her feelings for Brian had been as powerful as they were confusing. *Respect. Adoration.* And *something else.* Something she'd never named. She'd made a point not to say "I love you," since she was supposedly only dating him with the intention of breaking up with him.

Fear had kept her from getting in touch with him over the past year. Fear that he would laugh at the very idea. Fear that he would reject her. Fear that she'd imagined all those feelings she'd felt in high school, feelings she'd been unable to re-create with any man since.

Taylor felt Brian's hand on her shoulder and bit back a surprised gasp.

"I didn't mean to startle you. You were quiet so long, I wanted to be sure you're okay."

She stood up, causing his hand to fall free, aware of his body heat. She noticed how, even though she was tall, her chin came only to his shoulder. Taylor caught a whiff of whatever piney aftershave he'd used that day. She realized she ought to make some explanation for her lengthy silence, but she couldn't come up with anything.

Instead she said, "I don't have much to contribute to our store of food and supplies." She reached into her back jeans pocket. "My phone." She turned it on and said, "No service," and threw it onto the pile. She fished into her front jeans pocket. "A granola bar. Squashed, but edible." She patted her shirt pocket and came out with a package of Kleenex. She held it up so he could see. "That's it."

He grimaced. "Pretty slim pickings. At least we have the parachute."

She watched a smile flash briefly before he added, "We already know it makes a pretty comfortable bed."

She felt her insides tighten and her nipples bud at the memory of how they'd used the nylon bedding, especially knowing that, with their lovemaking, some threshold had been crossed. The long silence between them had ended. It was up to her what she did with this opportunity. If she'd learned anything from this experience, it was that there were no guarantees in this life. Not even, it seemed, a guarantee of life itself.

Taylor studied the sparse amount of food, then met Brian's gaze. "How long can we survive on what we have here?"

"Rule of three," he said with surprising cheerfulness.

"What's that?"

"Three minutes without air, three days without water, three weeks without food. We'll be hungry, but it'll take us a while to starve."

Taylor eyed the two cans of pork and beans, the steak and potato, the apple, the two Snickers, the granola bar, and the packaged coffee. That was it. All the sustenance they had.

Smoke jumpers usually lost weight fighting a fire, since they needed five to six thousand calories of energy each day and didn't have time to stop and eat enough to sustain themselves. She probably didn't eat more than twelve hundred.

"What's the minimum number of calories we can eat and survive long enough to be found?" she asked.

Brian shrugged. For once, he didn't seem to have the answer. "Whatever it is, we'll need a lot less if we keep our activities to a minimum."

Despite Brian's optimism, their odds of survival seemed slim. Taylor didn't want to wander through life anymore. She was tired of being the meandering stray Brian had named her so many years ago. She decided to take the risk of asking for something that had seemed impossible as recently as yesterday. "If we're going to die anyway," she said, "I don't see why we can't enjoy the time we have left."

"What did you have in mind?"

"That we use that sleeping bag for more than sleeping."

Chapter 6

BRIAN WAS CAUGHT off-guard by Tag's suggestion, and his body surged to life so quickly he felt like a randy, sex-starved teenager again. He wanted her. Badly. He fought back the impulse to do what his body was demanding. It was easy to see from the bleak look in Tag's eyes, not to mention her offer of sex, that she didn't believe they were going to get out of here. He wasn't willing to admit defeat. Not yet.

Which meant he had to say no.

"Let's not jump the gun."

She lifted her chin and said, "The offer is open. Whenever you're in the mood." She began untying the sleeping bag to make a bed for them. He knelt beside her to help, aware of her in a way he hadn't been a mere twenty-four hours ago.

He still couldn't quite believe they'd made love. *Had sex,* he corrected. He reminded himself that, even though he'd been inside her, even though he'd heard those almost-forgotten gasps and moans as he came, their coupling had been more an act of desperation than anything else.

And yet, he'd been forcefully reminded of the softness and fullness of her breasts, the tight, sucking wetness that surrounded him as he thrust inside her, the taste of her that he'd never forgotten, but couldn't quite remember, either.

Brian wished Tag hadn't made her offer, because now all he could think about was what it might be like to make love when they were both naked and taking their time. He imagined capturing her mouth with his, tasting her, tangling her naked body with his own, while he stuck his nose in her long blond hair and smelled her flowery shampoo.

Brian hadn't let himself even *think* about sex in the year since his divorce, but the possibility of putting himself inside Tag again turned his body hard as stone. And made him chuckle. *I sure ended my year of celibacy with a bang.* Which turned his chuckle into a chortle. Followed by a snort and a snicker.

Tag shot him a nervous look, but luckily, didn't ask him what was so funny.

He grabbed the flashlight and said, "I'm going to check out the back of the cave."

He beat a hasty retreat before he did something he would regret. He didn't want Tag thinking all hope was lost. He was pretty sure she would draw that conclusion if he didn't keep his wits about him and resist temptation.

He hadn't been in a big hurry to examine the rest of the cave because he was pretty sure what he was going to find: no way out. The knot of fear in his stomach tightened. He didn't see how they were going to survive this disaster, but he had to be strong for Tag. The longer he could keep her from realizing the truth, the better.

The truth was they were probably going to die in here.

Brian figured if he had to spend the last few days of his life with someone, Tag wasn't a bad choice. At seventeen, he'd fallen hard for her. In those days, she'd had a smile that lit up his day, stunning blue eyes that sparkled with mischief, and a body that begged to be touched.

He hadn't seen much of her over the past few years, except when she was flying a plane from which he was smoke jumping. He'd noticed the smile wasn't present anymore, and the mischief in her eyes had been replaced by caution, but her body still implored a man to touch. Brian didn't understand why one of the dozens of guys she'd dated hadn't grabbed her up. Or maybe she was the one who'd rejected them.

As she'd rejected him.

They'd dated long enough in high school for Brian to discover that Tag had a lot of hang-ups about a lot of stuff, not the least of which was the fact that she had no mother and a mostly absent father. Her father had stayed away in Cheyenne for eight years, serving two terms as Wyoming governor, and sent Tag to boarding school in Switzerland for middle school.

Brian wasn't sure why he'd taken the chance of hooking up with a Grayhawk, even someone as enticing as Tag, when their fathers were constantly looking for ways to cut each other's throats. But he'd been at an age when he rebelled against just about everything, and dating Tag had been one more way to defy his father and irk his three brothers.

He'd quickly discovered that he and "that Grayhawk girl" had a lot in common. He had no mother, either. She'd died birthing his youngest brother, Devon. And his father was also absent, even though he never left home, if that made sense. Angus Flynn ruled the roost from his study, where he manipulated everyone and everything around him from sunrise till late into the night.

Maybe the feud between their fathers was so bitter because, a long time ago, Angus Flynn and King Grayhawk had been best friends. In fact, Angus's sister, Jane, had been King's first wife. Unfortunately, after King divorced Aunt Jane, she'd retreated to the Flynn family ranch, gotten hooked on barbiturates, and died of an overdose. Brian would never forget the anguished cry that had echoed through the house when Angus discovered his sister's dead body. His father blamed King for Aunt Jane's death and had been exacting revenge, in large ways and small, ever since.

Brian wondered how his relationship with Tag might have turned out if Aiden hadn't caught them naked together after the junior prom. Although Aiden's appearance had interrupted their lovemaking, horribly embarrassing the two of them, his older brother hadn't confronted Brian immediately. He'd merely walked away, not saying a word until Brian came home that night.

Then he'd let him have it.

"One of King's Brats?" he'd ranted. "Are you crazy, Brian? Or just plain stupid?"

"I like her."

"She's just using you."

Brian had never considered the possibility. The sex between them was something he'd never imagined. It was good. No, great. Holding Tag afterward, while they talked and laughed together, was the best part of all. He wasn't about to give that up. He shot back, "If she is using me, it's my problem, not yours."

"End it. Now. Or I'll tell Dad."

Brian had opened his mouth to say he wasn't afraid of his father and shut it again. Angus would have ten fits if he found out what Brian was doing. What Brian didn't understand was Aiden's interest in his love life. "Why are you threatening me, Aiden? Why should it matter to you what I do?"

"I don't want you hurt."

Brian frowned. "Hurt?" It was an odd thing to say. "What the hell are you talking about?"

Aiden's eyes suddenly became shuttered. "Just drop her, Brian. Or you'll be sorry."

Brian had decided to keep on dating Tag, despite Aiden's warning. It was Tag who'd opted out of the relationship. He'd been shocked and unbearably hurt, the kind of hurt where your heart actually *aches* inside your chest, when she'd sent him a brief note to tell him she was breaking up with him. She hadn't even had the decency to tell him to his face. She hadn't given a reason why she was walking away, and he'd been too wounded to ask. After what Aiden had said, he'd nursed his broken heart—and his bruised pride—in private.

Maybe, over the next few days—or sometime before they succumbed to starvation—he'd finally get an answer for what had happened all those years ago. It was too bad they had plenty of water. Starving to death would take a lot longer—two or three weeks, maybe—than dying of thirst. He honestly wasn't sure how long it would take, with the supplies they had on hand, to starve.

"Brian?"

Brian wondered how long he'd been standing, staring at a back wall that ended abruptly, silently contemplating their curtailed futures. He turned so his voice would carry and said, "What?"

"Should I come back there?"

"No. I'll come to you."

When he returned from the back of the cave, he flashed the light on her face. He watched her try to smile. And fail.

"Shouldn't we be doing something?" she asked.

"What did you have in mind?"

Her eyes looked scared, but her chin stuck out like she was ready to take on the world. He'd always admired her backbone. Never more than now.

"Is there another way out at the other end of the cave?" she asked, turning her head—and the light—in that direction.

"Not that I saw."

"I want to look for myself."

He realized he'd spent more time thinking and worrying than searching and said, "Sure. Let's go."

He was grateful that, even at six foot four, the cave ceiling was high enough for him to stand upright. Tag, who'd sprouted like a weed in high school, was a mere six inches shorter, which reminded him how well their bodies fit together in all the right places. He forced his mind away from physical pleasure and focused on survival. Once they were out of here, he could pursue a relationship with her, if she was still willing.

Except the chances of them getting together—for anything—if they were ever rescued, were nil to nothing. Grayhawks and Flynns were like oranges and jelly. They just didn't mix.

Or rather, that had been the case in the past. Things had changed—were changing—faster than he could have imagined a year ago when he was still a happily married man.

His younger brother Connor had recently married Tag's youngest sister, Eve. He'd thought Connor was out of his mind, even if it had been a marriage of convenience on both their parts. Connor, who was a widower, had needed someone to take care of his two-year-old son and four-year-old daughter. Eve had needed a ranch where she could keep her rescued herd of wild mustangs.

He sneered inwardly. A true marriage made in heaven. He supposed he'd gotten soured on the institution by his own experience with lifelong commitment. As far as he was concerned, enduring, lifelong love didn't exist. Connor should have hired a babysitter. And Eve should have taken her horses somewhere out of expensive Teton County, where she could afford to support them.

"Watch your head," Tag said as she made a left-hand turn at the far end of the cave where the ceiling was lower.

As he bent to avoid hitting his head, Brian searched

the sides of the cave, this time focusing his attention on where it should have been all along, looking for any crack that might be a way in or out. He saw nothing encouraging, just a few roots growing out of the wall about shoulder height, before the ceiling tapered, over another dozen feet, all the way to the ground. He followed Tag as she dropped to her knees and kept crawling forward, until she came to the end of the cave.

She sat on her butt and turned to face him. "It ends here. There's no way out."

Chapter 7

IN HER HEART of hearts, Taylor had been sure there was another way out of the cave. It was crushing to realize she'd been wrong. She clenched her hands into frustrated fists.

We're stuck in here with no way out.

She dropped her chin to her chest. When she did, the light fell on the torn leg of Brian's jeans and the ragged flesh beneath it.

"You're bleeding!"

"It's nothing."

"It won't be nothing when it gets infected," Taylor retorted. Getting angry was good. Anger pushed back her debilitating fear. "I noticed a first-aid kit in your PG bag. Is there any Neosporin?" She'd used the antibacterial ointment on minor abrasions with good results.

"Should be."

"Then let's go."

She followed Brian as he began crawling back in the other direction. When they reached the other end of the cave, she said, "Take off your pants."

He shot her a sideways look, and she felt her heart flutter.

"I need to treat your leg," she said in a voice made breathless by the suggestive gleam in his blue eyes.

"If you say so."

"I do." She put both hands on top of his shoulders and said, "You might as well sit down and take off your boots."

He shrugged and sat.

As she watched him unlace and remove his steel-toed logger's boots, Taylor realized how much broader Brian's shoulders were than they'd been in high school. His biceps and forearms were visions of corded muscle and sinew. The back-breaking work of fighting forest fires required that sort of physical fitness, but to Taylor, Brian looked invincible. She felt her stomach sink. If someone didn't find them, this beautiful, powerful man was going to starve to death right along with her.

Brian unbuttoned his jeans, lifted his hips, and began sliding them down. The denim got stuck at the site of the wound on his calf. He flinched and made a guttural sound. "What the hell?"

He awkwardly rearranged his rear end on the bundled-up sleeping bag and extended both legs, which were caught in his jeans, in her direction. He grunted when a piece of tattered material that must have been stuck in his wound came loose.

Taylor noticed—not that she cared—that he'd switched from the sexy, formfitting underwear that outlined his masculinity, which he'd worn in high school, to boxers.

She barely restrained a gasp when she finally aimed the headlamp at Brian's injury.

Taylor saw four distinct, surprisingly deep lines where the grizzly's claws had raked his flesh along the side of his calf. Blood had streamed from the wounds and been soaked up by his wool sock.

She turned the lamp toward Brian, searching for the pain that should be reflected on his face. There was a hint of something amiss in his eyes, but she saw no twitch in the muscles of his jaw that suggested his teeth were clenched. "This must be hurting you. Why didn't you say something, so this could be treated sooner?"

"When it happened, it just stung a little. I didn't think it was that bad. I guess adrenaline kept me from feeling anything."

"And now?"

"My leg is pounding like an Oglala drum."

"These wounds are deep, Brian. Deep enough to need stitches."

"Lucky me, there's no needle in that pack," he quipped. "My hands got callused enough to stop getting blisters, so I stopped carrying a needle to pop them."

"You need more than a little Neosporin." Besides the antibacterial salve, the first-aid kit contained alcohol swabs, along with gauze and tape, and a few Band-Aids. She didn't have enough supplies to change the bandage more than once or twice. Keeping the injury clean was going to be a problem.

Taylor stared at the ugly wound. Her stomach curled in on itself at the thought of the pain she would have to cause to clean up those claw marks. "I'm not sure where to start."

"Try rinsing it out with some bottled water. I guess it's a good thing we don't have to ration it."

Taylor retrieved one of the plastic bottles and used a piece of gauze as a sterile rag, rinsing the wound as thoroughly as she could, pointedly ignoring Brian's hisses and gasps.

"Ow!" he said, as she eased the sides of the deepest cut apart to make sure she was getting out all the dirt and debris. "That hurts!"

"I'm sorry. I need to be able to see what's there." To her dismay, the deepest of the four claw marks was still seeping blood. "I'm going to need to tape the skin together to get this to stop bleeding."

"Do what you have to do," Brian said, his hands knotted on his thighs.

Taylor cleaned her forefinger with one of the alcohol swabs, then squeezed out a line of Neosporin on her finger. She fought back nausea as she forced the edges of the deepest wound apart and daubed the Neosporin into the crevice. Then she pulled the skin together and put tape across it to hold it closed.

The other three slashes were already scabbed, but she added a layer of Neosporin on top of them as well.

"Where did you learn to play doctor?" Brian asked.

"In high school, of course."

"I wasn't talking about *that* kind of playing doctor."

She shook her head in disbelief. How could he still be joking at a time like this? She gave him a pointed look and said, "I took a basic first-aid class."

"And you remember it all these years later?"

"I remember everything from high school."

Too late, Taylor realized what she'd said. She refocused her gaze on the wounds she was treating and waited for Brian to make another smart remark.

When he spoke, his voice sounded gruff and surprisingly tender. "I remember everything, too."

She lifted her head to look at him, but he squinted and turned away when the bright light hit his eyes. She lowered her gaze again and said, "I'm not sure this is the right time to dig up the past."

"Why not? What else do we have to do?"

"High school was a long time ago. We've barely exchanged two words in a row in all the years since."

"To my regret."

She stared at him in shocked surprise, causing him to put up a hand to keep the light out of his eyes. She lowered her head again, alarmed by his confession. Her only defense against the sudden rush of regret she felt herself was denial. "Moments we shared in the past have nothing to do with our lives now."

"Our lives now." He hesitated, then said, "Our time together in this cave may very well be all the life we have left. Have you considered that?"

"I'd rather not."

She raised her eyes to Brian's face without lifting her head, so the light would stay focused on his leg. "What are we going to do, Brian? There must be some way to get a message out of here. Maybe we can dig ourselves out through the walls or the ceiling, where all those roots are hanging down. Or chop our way past that tree blocking the exit."

"You do realize how far-fetched those options are."

"Then what are we supposed to do? Sit here and wait to die?" Taylor heard the panic in her voice and bit her lip to keep from whimpering with despair.

Brian reached out and took her hand, threading their fingers together.

She felt the rough calluses and the comforting warmth as he gave her hand a reassuring squeeze.

He waited until she looked at him and said, "I'm betting our families will find us."

"*Our* families? You think they'll be working together?"

He shrugged. "Why not? None of them, not your sisters or my brothers, will give up until they find us. They'll pool their efforts because that'll be the most efficient way to search. Not to mention the fact that, knowing our fathers, they'll have all the resources money can buy. Don't give up hope, Tag. I expect everyone to keep looking until they find us."

Or our bodies, Taylor thought with a cynical twist of her mouth. "That's all very well. But isn't there something we can do to help ourselves?"

"We can conserve our energy, make our food last as long as we can, and be sparing with the headlamp and flashlight batteries. I have my Swiss army knife. Once I get rid of all those intruding limbs, I can chip away at the top of that charred stump and make an opening wide enough to let a little light in here."

"Big enough so that searchers can hear us yelling for help?"

"That, too."

Taylor pulled her hand free and reached for a piece of gauze. She laid it along the side of Brian's leg to cover the entire wound, then taped it in place. "That's the best I can do."

"Feels better already."

"You're lying."

He grimaced. "Yeah, I'm lying. I'm pretty sure I have ibuprofen in that bag of mine. Can you get me a couple?"

Taylor brought him the pills and handed him a bottle of water, then watched his Adam's apple bob as he swallowed the pills. His face was shadowed with dark beard, and she realized she hadn't seen a razor in his pack. She supposed there wasn't time—or the need—to shave when he was fighting fires.

She settled beside him and noticed he was folding his jeans rather than putting them back on. "You're not going to dress?"

"I'd just have to take everything off again when we hit the sack. And I'm a little worried how that denim is going to feel against my leg."

"What now?"

"Supper."

The potato had been in the fire for a while, and he set the pan on the coals and added the steak, which looked like it had already been liberally sprinkled with salt and pepper.

"How do you like your steak?" he asked.

"Medium rare."

"Works for me. I've only got one set of utensils, so we'll have to share."

"Works for me." Taylor was surprised, when Brian forked the potato out of the fire and removed the foil, to discover that it had been pre-coated with salt and butter. He dumped it in the skillet with the steak and cut it into smaller chunks they could eat with a fork.

When the steak was done, Brian said, "I'm going to let it sit for a few minutes, so the juices will stay in the meat when I cut it."

Taylor smiled. She supposed with all the men in the Flynn house they spent a lot of time grilling meat—and letting the juices settle. She found it charming—and heartening—to receive cooking tips from Brian. It presumed they were going to have a life outside this cave where she might need to use them in the future.

While they were waiting, Brian said, "Scoot over here. There's something I've been wanting to do for you."

She shot him a quizzical look but inched over so they were side by side.

He picked up the bottle of water she'd used to clean his wound and poured some of it onto the extra T-shirt he'd carried in his bag, then took her chin in his hand and used the cloth to dab at her face. "You look like a raccoon," he said, smiling to temper the unflattering description. "It can't hurt to get some of this soot off your skin."

She hissed when he cleaned the burn on her cheek, and again, when he touched a raw spot on her forehead.

"Hand me that Neosporin," he said.

She handed it over and sat still as he carefully dabbed some on each injury.

"There. That should do it." He recapped the Neosporin and gave it back to her, then surveyed his work. "Oops. Missed a little soot on your chin."

Her headlamp lit his face, so she saw the softness in his blue eyes that matched his gentle touch as he finished washing her face. She'd enjoyed too little of this sort of male attention. It felt good.

When he was done, she took the T-shirt from him and said, "Might as well clean you up, too." She found an unsoiled spot on the shirt, poured more water, and wiped away the soot on his forehead, nose, cheeks, and chin. When she was done, she said, "Your face is full of bristles."

He put his hands up to his cheeks. "Guess I'll forgo the shave, since I don't have anyone to impress."

"And no razor to shave with," she added wryly.

He laughed. "Ready for some steak?"

"I'm ravenous."

"Remind me to keep my body parts away from your mouth until you're fed."

It took Taylor a moment to realize he was teasing her, and that his words were filled with sexual innuendo. One of the things they'd both enjoyed as teenagers was pleasuring each other with their mouths and tongues. She fought a blush and lost. Her only comfort was the realization that he probably couldn't see her reaction in the dark. She arched a brow and said, "You can't say you weren't warned."

He laughed and held out a bite of steak on the fork. "Eat, woman."

Taylor ate.

When half the steak and half the potato were left Brian said, "I think we better save this for tomorrow."

Taylor was still hungry, but she realized the wisdom of having something to fill her empty belly on another day.

Brian took the foil that had been on the potato and used it to cover the skillet, which contained the leftovers. He set the pan aside, then rose and said, "I'll dig a latrine at the back of the cave."

"Oh." Taylor realized Brian was used to managing without facilities and was grateful that he'd made the suggestion. "I'll go when you get back."

When Taylor returned from her trip to the back of the cave, she saw Brian had unzipped his sleeping bag and opened it to make a double-wide bed. He'd wadded up his T-shirt and laid it on one side for a pillow, and used the PG bag as a pillow for the other side.

"You going to wear your clothes to bed?" he asked.

"I suppose not." She leaned down to untie her hiking boots, then toed them off, setting them carefully beside the sleeping bag where she could find them in the dark, if necessary.

Then she unsnapped and unzipped her jeans. She pushed her Levi's down and off, leaving her perfectly decent, since her chambray shirt had tails long enough to cover her bikini underwear. She didn't want to sleep in her bra, so she began unbuttoning her shirt.

"Give me a break, Tag," Brian said in a harsh voice. "Do that where I can't see you."

She glanced up and saw his gaze focused on the narrow strip of skin she'd bared, which was lit by the headlamp she was wearing. "I'm sorry. I wasn't thinking." She buttoned the shirt back up, but unbuttoned the sleeves. Then she reached up under the back of the shirt to release the clasp on her bra and pulled the straps down through her sleeves one at a time. A moment later, the bra fell into her hand.

"How did you do that?"

"Magic," she said with a grin. She folded the bra inside her jeans and set them beside her boots.

Brian had gathered up the parachute and said, "Lie down and I'll cover you."

Taylor eased herself onto the ground, lying flat so the headlamp faced the ceiling. She noticed the roots again and wondered if the fact that she could see them meant that the layer of dirt over their heads wasn't very deep. Maybe they could claw their way out.

What if you start digging, and the whole cave collapses on top of you?

Taylor shuddered. Maybe excavating the dirt in the ceiling wasn't such a good idea. She turned on her side and arranged Brian's T-shirt, which was nearly dry, under her head. It smelled like soap from the laundry— and the smoky soot from their faces.

Brian hissed in a breath as he settled beside her, and she realized he must have jostled his injured leg. "You okay?"

"Yeah. Are you going to sleep in that headlamp?"

"Oh." She'd forgotten she had it on. And she wasn't ready to turn it off. When she did, it would be dark. *Completely* dark.

"Here. Let me help." Brian sat up so he could ease it off her head. He laid it on top of her jeans and turned it off. "You saw where I left it. Right there beside your pillow. That way you can find it when you need it."

Taylor's whole body tensed when the light went out. It was terrifyingly dark, and she babbled to keep the fear she felt at bay. "I can't remember the last time I went to bed this hungry. What's on the menu for tomorrow?"

"If we eat half of what's left of that steak and potato for breakfast, we can save the other half for dinner."

Taylor realized he hadn't mentioned lunch. Which meant they were going to skip it.

"I guess I'm finally going to lose that extra five pounds I've put on since March."

"March, huh? That five pounds have anything to do with your half brother Matt showing up out of the blue and taking over your dad's ranch?"

"Everything to do with it," Taylor muttered.

"I heard about the raw deal you Grayhawk girls got. It's hard to believe King gave the ranch to a Black Sheep who hid himself away in Australia for twenty years and left you four girls out in the cold."

"Kingdom Come won't belong to Matt until he's lived there for three-hundred-sixty-five consecutive days. If we four girls have anything to say about it, he won't last that long."

"Devon told me you let King's Tennessee walker stallion into the pasture with Matt's quarter horse broodmares. That was *inspired* deviltry. He must have been furious."

"We were paying him back for forcing Eve to move her wild mustangs off that pasture so he could put his mares there instead."

"Reminds me of all the tricks you Grayhawk girls pulled on us Flynn boys over the years."

"We aren't called 'King's Brats' for nothing." Taylor heard the tremor in her voice. Merely talking wasn't getting the job done. She was scared witless. "Brian?"

"Hmm?"

"Would you please hold me?"

Chapter 8

BRIAN HAD BEEN anticipating Tag's request. He'd known, when she'd nearly refused to part with the headlamp, that she dreaded the impending darkness. He was perfectly willing to provide the support she needed to allay her fear. He just wasn't sure he could stick with offering comfort, when what he really wanted to do was make love to her.

He fought the desire to kiss her and caress her and bring them both indescribable pleasure, because making love—taking the chance of getting emotionally involved—would create its own set of problems. If there was any chance they were going to die, and the odds of living weren't currently in their favor, the last thing he wanted to do was fall back in love with Tag. It would be easy enough to do. But that would be asking for a bitch of a heartache when he had to watch her die, or died himself, knowing he was leaving her all alone.

Tag's erratic breathing was loud in the silence, and Brian wasn't nearly as detached as he wished he could be.

"Come here," he said at last.

She threw herself at him, their chins bumping, her arms clinging to his neck, her body aligned with his from chest to hips as his arms slid around her to hold her tight.

"Thank you," she whispered against his throat. "I'm sorry to be such a baby about this."

He tried to lighten the situation by saying, "The pleasure is all mine," which must have been clear to her, from the heat and hardness of his arousal pressing against her belly.

She reached between them and traced the ridge beneath his thin cotton boxers with her fingertips.

He caught her hand and said in a harsh voice, "Don't."

"Why not?"

"This won't help anything, Tag."

"It can't hurt anything, either. I want you, Brian. Don't you want me?"

Their previous bout of sex had done no more than blow the foam off the beer, so to speak, and his body was clamoring for what Tag was offering. Even so, he might have refused her, except he'd heard, in her wistful voice, the girl who hadn't believed him in high school when he'd told her he loved her. The girl who'd scoffed and said, "No one's ever loved me. What you love is what I do with you . . . and to you."

He'd known she meant all the times she'd put her mouth on him and brought him to climax. To his shame, he hadn't contradicted her. He'd been too shocked and embarrassed by what she'd said. And too young to realize the pain concealed by her mocking words.

In the darkness, he took her head between his hands

and brought his mouth to hers, feeling the softness, the willingness in her supple lips. He kissed each closed eye, then each cheek, and finally, each side of her mouth, before easing her head to his shoulder.

His body was urging him to throw caution to the winds. His head was telling him that making love to Taylor Ann Grayhawk—when it wasn't the direct result of surviving several harrowing, life-threatening events—was a really bad idea. He couldn't believe what he was about to say.

"I want to make love to you, but I don't think we should."

"Why not?"

He tucked a strand of hair that was tickling his nose behind her ear. It gave him a few moments to think of the best way to explain how he felt. "Considering our situation, it would be easy to do what we want and say to hell with the consequences. But there's still a chance we're going to get out of here eventually, and then what?" He blew one of her stray curls away from his cheek. "We haven't been a couple for a long time. How the hell many years has it been, anyway, since we were together?"

"I was fifteen. I'm twenty-eight. You do the math."

"Good lord. That's a lot of years. I guess that makes what I'm about to say even more amazing. The time we spent together is stuck in my mind as tight as that row of Flynn cowboy boots you Brats glued to the mudroom floor."

"Really? I feel the same way."

He heard the amazement in her voice and realized she must have felt more for him than she'd admitted at the time. "The point is I have enough good memories from the months we spent together to be glad you're the one who ended up in here with me. Like it or not, I suspect we're going to get to know each other a lot better before we get out of here. If we ever do."

She made a hitching sound that might have been a repressed sob. He hadn't meant to scare her with that last statement, but it was better if they both faced the facts.

He continued, "Whatever happens—or doesn't happen—between us, I want you to know up front that I'm never making a commitment to another woman."

"What does that have to do with our making love now?" She gripped his waist more tightly and said, "Maybe you'd better tell me why you're planning to spend the rest of your life as a lone wolf."

"That's none of your business."

"It is my business, if it's keeping you from making love to me now."

Brian was sorry he'd said anything. He should have kept his mouth shut, ordered his body to behave itself, and held Tag until she fell asleep. No one knew the truth about why his marriage had broken up, not even his brothers. He was too ashamed to tell them.

Tricia had been another stray he'd rescued, lost on campus and looking helpless. He'd offered to show her the way to the student union, and the rest was history. Looking back, he realized he might not have been as much in love with her as she'd seemed to be with him. In light of recent events, it appeared she'd needed a savior more than a spouse. Obviously, it had taken her a long time to grow up. When she finally did, several years into their marriage, she hadn't needed him anymore.

"Well?" Tag prodded. "I'm waiting. What happened to make you swear off relationships with women?"

Brian could feel Tag's breasts snug against his chest and her soft belly pressed invitingly close, and he wanted desperately to make love to her. The problem was he knew he shouldn't. So he told her what he'd never told anyone else—to remind him why he'd sworn off women.

"Tricia left me because she fell in love and cheated on me . . . with another woman."

"Oh. I'm so sorry, Brian. That must have been terrible for you, to lose her to someone else."

"Not just someone else. *Another woman.*"

"Is that worse than her leaving you for another man?"

"Hell, yes!"

"Why?"

"Because it means my whole marriage was a sham. Tricia couldn't have loved me, if she was sexually attracted to women from the start."

"Maybe she loved you for all the qualities that make you a good person. Maybe she didn't know how she felt about women when she married you."

Brian barked a laugh. "Don't you see? If Tricia could fool me so completely, how can I ever trust myself not to make the same mistake again?"

"So you're giving up on relationships?"

He heard the incredulity in her voice. What he'd given up on was any physical involvement with a woman that might lead to a deeper relationship. In a word, *sex*. At least, for the past year, while he'd been licking his wounds.

"But you *know* I prefer men," Tag protested.

"Do I?"

She laughed low in her throat, a sound that made his shaft pulse with need.

"Trust me," she said in a husky voice. "You do. And since getting out of here is something that seems unlikely at the moment, I vote we make love to each other as often as the mood strikes. Like now."

She sucked lightly on his throat, raising gooseflesh all over his body.

There was no reason not to surrender. It seemed they both wanted the same thing. To live in the present. To take pleasure where it was offered and give it in return.

Brian unerringly found Tag's mouth in the darkness. She opened to him and their tongues dueled, even as their bodies wrestled for dominance. He grunted when he jarred his wounded leg as he tore at her panties.

She laughed and said, "Don't rip them! They're all I have." The playful sound echoed back to him from the length of the cave. Then she arched her hips off the ground, so he could easily slide the fragile silk down her long legs.

He moved his hand upward along the length of her leg to cup the heart of her, loving the feel of her smooth, warm flesh. He hadn't realized how starved he was for this. He relished the feast all the more because Tag was sharing it with him.

She shoved his boxers down so she could hold him in

her hand, causing him to groan as she smoothed her thumb over the tiny drop of liquid at the tip.

He kicked the cloth out of his way, as she urged him with whispered words to put himself inside her, forgoing tenderness in favor of passion.

But he was a boy no longer, and he owed her more pleasure than she was likely to get if he took what he wanted without giving her at least as much joy.

So he held her hips down when she would have bucked beneath him, inflaming him further, and reached under the chambray shirt to cup her naked breast and tease the nipple.

"Oh."

She said it with a release of breath that showed how surprised she was that they weren't headed from kissing to climax in two quick steps.

"Easy now," he whispered in her ear. "We have all the time in the world to get where we're going. And nothing and no one to interfere or stop us from getting there."

Chapter 9

TAYLOR WAS CONFUSED by Brian's behavior. In high school, she'd always, always focused on giving pleasure, rather than receiving it. Brian had never failed to hold her close afterward, which she'd craved far more than the sex they shared. His behavior tonight was different. *He* was focused on giving pleasure to *her*. And she wasn't quite sure how to respond.

Since she couldn't see his expression, she stopped what she was doing and asked, "What's going on, Brian?"

He lowered his head to kiss her throat beneath her ear. "I'm making love to you. Slowly. So we can enjoy ourselves."

"I was enjoying myself," she said with a pout that was wasted in the dark.

A moment later he reached her mouth, his tongue dipping inside to taste and to tease, and the pout disappeared. She threaded her fingers into his hair and gave herself up to the novel experience of having Brian search out the best ways to arouse her. She writhed in his arms, her moans and gasps and wrenching groans filling the deep silence of the cave, as she waited for the moment when their roles would revert to those they'd played in the past.

But the kisses didn't stop. And Brian never headed for third base, let alone home plate. It was as though the two of them were teenagers making out, with no intention of doing anything more. She quivered when Brian touched her breast with the reverence of a boy tracing its shape for the first time. He outlined her ear with his tongue, causing her insides to clench.

He'd never left a hickey on her neck in high school, because she'd shuddered at the thought of explaining one to Leah or Vick. But the gentle suction of his mouth on her throat became more insistent, and she felt her body responding to the intense pleasure-pain.

Brian tore his mouth from her throat and threaded his fingers into her hair, shoving it away from her face so he could plant surprising, petal-soft kisses on her eyes and cheeks, before he finally found his way back to her mouth.

His tongue dipped inside and withdrew, teasing, taunting. She moaned and opened her mouth wider, inviting him inside. She thrust her tongue into Brian's mouth, while her hips writhed against his engorged shaft, trying to incite him to finish what he'd started. She'd never been so ready for a man, never desired a man so much.

It didn't occur to her to simply ask Brian for what she wanted, because she'd never done it in the past—with him, or any other man. Wanting something from another person meant making herself vulnerable to the pain of rejection. In her experience, it was better not to get her hopes up in the first place.

She loved what Brian was doing and wondered if she would ever again be satisfied with moving from "at bat" to "home plate" without so much as a pause in between.

If I didn't know better, I'd say Brian cares about me.

Taylor found that thought terrifying. She wanted to get this interlude over with so she wouldn't have to deal with all the unwelcome baggage that had been churned up along with it. Like knowing she was not the sort of woman to whom men got attached. Like feeling unlovable. Like knowing she was unloved.

Taylor wondered if the rush of frightening emotions she was fighting, as Brian devoted himself to the simple acts of kissing and touching, was being magnified by the dark. Otherwise, she had no explanation for why her throat ached and her eyes had filled with unshed tears.

"Brian," she whispered.

"What?"

"I wish I could see your face."

"Why?"

"So I'd know if you're enjoying all this kissing as much as I am."

He chuckled, and pressed his hard, hot length more tightly against her. "What does that tell you?"

"I'm not sure."

"Take a guess."

"That you'd rather be inside me?"

He lifted himself up on his arms, and she could feel his consternation in the sudden tenseness of his muscles. "We have all the time in the world. Why hurry?"

Because I don't want this to mean something when it doesn't. Because I'm feeling too much. Because it hurts to want what I don't believe I'll ever have.

She swallowed past the rawness in her throat and said, "I just want to be sure you're satisfied."

"This isn't about *you* pleasing *me*," he replied. "It's about *us* pleasing *each other*."

"Oh." It was a sign of how little she'd asked for from the men she'd dated that Taylor found the concept of shared joy unnerving. Fortunately, because it was pitch-black, Brian couldn't see how uncomfortable she was with the idea of giving up even a little of the control of their lovemaking to him.

Unless Brian had changed a great deal, she knew the places on his body where he was most sensitive, and she did what she knew would arouse him, smoothing her fingertips over his sweat-slick shoulder, then letting her hand roam to a small spot under his armpit that she knew was almost ticklish.

She felt him grunt and wriggle away, before lying still and inviting her touch. She slid her hand down his side to his hip, to the crevice between his groin and leg. Before she could do more than touch, she felt his hand cupping the heart of her, and his finger finding its way inside.

"You're wet," he said.

She was glad for the darkness that hid her sudden blush. No one had ever said such a thing to her out loud. It was the sort of frankness between partners that would have required knowing each other well, and Taylor had never stayed long enough with a man, or sought such intimacy, even with the three men to whom she'd been engaged. Very briefly engaged.

Taylor wanted to be in a loving relationship. She wanted to be married and have children. But she was short on trust. She'd never been sure any of her fiancés would really hang around through thick and thin. She couldn't shake the thought that the men who'd sworn to love her would run away at the first sign of trouble, the way her mother had. Or abandon her without a backward look to follow their personal dreams, as her father had.

Her parents' behavior had left Taylor feeling like a person without a lot of worth to anybody. Was it any wonder she expected a man to take off when the going got tough? Consequently, she always made sure she found a reason to leave first. She couldn't face the thought of being abandoned—yet again—by someone she loved.

Because Taylor was always ready and willing to walk away, she'd been careful never to let her feelings get too engaged. What Brian was doing to her now brought back memories of the time they'd spent together and reminded her that she'd given more of herself to him than she had to anyone else before or since. All those teenage feelings of wanting to be loved and seeking to belong were surging over her like a tidal wave, threatening to drown her with needs she'd shoved aside for far too many years.

She had to do something to end this. Now. Before things got completely out of control.

Taylor reached for Brian's hardened shaft, but her fingertips merely grazed the heat of his throbbing flesh, before he laughed and angled his body away, forcing her to let go.

"Back off, lady. I'm enjoying myself too much to want this to be over anytime soon." He continued kissing her mouth, letting his hands work their magic on her body.

In the end, she didn't let him have things entirely his way. Her hands roamed his back and shoulders, caressing and gently scratching, reveling in the play of muscle over bone. She could feel and smell—and indulged herself enough to taste—the faint layer of slick, salty sweat that coated his shoulders. Her fingertips dipped into the tiny dimples at the top of his sinewy buttocks and then slid down to lovingly cup them. She caught him off-guard when she captured the delicate, soft sacs below, caressing until his breathing was ragged.

Trapped as they were in the darkness, time ceased to have meaning. Every time Taylor thought she couldn't endure another moment of pleasure, Brian would find another place to kiss, another place to tease, another place to touch with greedy hands that demanded her attention.

When Brian finally entered her, she rose to meet him. Their bodies came together joyfully, with the sucking sounds of thrust and parry. She wrapped her legs around his hips and arched upward to urge him deeper inside. Their tongues mimicked the dance of their bodies below, as each sought the pleasure to be found in the other.

She had never felt so full. Never felt such yearning to be closer to another human being. Never felt such a need to give—and to take. Never experienced such wonder and joy and sheer carnal desire. Taylor didn't think she could survive it. Her glass was full and spilling over in torrents of exhilarating, almost excruciating, pleasure.

Their bodies continued to plunge and escape until, at last, their guttural grunts and agonized groans of satisfaction filled the dark void.

Afterward, Brian lay atop her, slick with sweat, his lungs heaving. She slid her arms around him to hold him tight, loving the feel of his solid weight on her body.

Too soon he said, "I'm too heavy for you," and slid to her side.

She felt bereft. But only for a moment, because he reached out and slid his arm around her, pulling her close, as he murmured, "Come here."

She snuggled against him, her nose at his throat, smelling his piney aftershave, the faded scent of which must have been released by their exertions, and the pungent scent of sex. Once they were lying still, Taylor quickly became chilled.

When she shivered, Brian said, "You must be cold." He snatched up the parachute, and dragged it over them.

"You ready to sleep now?" he asked.

"It's too dark to sleep."

He chuckled. "Don't you usually sleep with the lights out?"

"Actually, no."

"Why not? Oh, right. The whole 'scared of the dark' thing."

"Sort of."

"Sort of? Now I'm curious. Spill."

"Aren't you sleepy?" she asked, unwilling to keep him

awake, if he was tired, to hear something she wasn't sure she should share in the first place.

"A little. Go ahead and tell your story. You can give me an elbow in the ribs if I nod off."

"I wouldn't do that!"

"My brothers have done a lot worse. I'm listening."

She pursed her lips, trying to decide whether to reveal another piece of herself to him. But she was too keyed up to sleep, so she might as well talk.

"I was already scared of the dark by the time I got to that boarding school in Switzerland where King sent me."

"Let me interrupt."

She laughed. "Already?"

"Why do you call your dad 'King' instead of 'Dad'?"

She shrugged, realized he couldn't see the gesture and explained, "Since King was gone so much of the time, Leah was the only parent my sisters and I had growing up. She called my father King because she was five years old when he married our mother and became her stepfather. We followed her lead and called him King, too." Taylor thought of times when she'd referred to her father as "Daddy" or "Dad" and amended, "Well, most of the time, anyway."

"Do you ever hear from your mother?"

"No. I have no idea what happened to her." She was tempted to add, "And I don't care!" But that would have been a lie. Not knowing was awful. Wondering was even worse. With the Internet, she probably could have tracked her mother down, but when all she felt was animosity toward the woman, it hadn't seemed like a good idea.

"Sorry I brought it up," Brian said. "Go on with your story."

"As I said, I was already afraid of the dark when I arrived at that Swiss boarding school."

"Did you like it there?"

"Vick loved it. I did everything I could to get myself kicked out."

"What was wrong with it?"

"Nothing, I guess. Except it was thousands of miles from home. I begged King not to make me go. Leah said she'd take care of me, but he wouldn't budge. Being at that school was proof that I was merely another problem my father had to solve. Most of the shit I pulled was just a way to get him to pay attention to me.

"It didn't work. He never came to visit. Not once. He just kept paying for the damage I caused, along with a bit more for the inconvenience I'd become, and I was stuck there for three long years."

"How did you finally get him to let you come home?"

"I set a fire that nearly burned down the dormitory."

She'd forgotten he was a firefighter, but his appalled voice reminded her of that fact when he asked, "You're an arsonist?"

"I didn't do it on purpose! It was an accident."

He made an accusatory sound in his throat.

"Honestly, it wasn't my fault."

"Sounds to me like a lot of folks, including you, could have been killed."

"I would rather have been dead than stuck where I was," she muttered, resentful of his judgmental tone.

"It couldn't have been that bad."

"You weren't there," she retorted. "The other girls were tired of all the trouble I was causing and decided to teach me a lesson. Vick had told a friend I was scared of the dark, to explain why we always had a small light on in our room at night. The story must have been passed around, because they fixed the light switch in the cellar so it wouldn't turn on and locked me in there all alone in the dark.

"It was my worst nightmare come to life."

He reached out to brush her shoulder with his hand but didn't speak. Why couldn't her father have done that, just that, when he'd learned about her terrifying experience in the cellar? King hadn't been sympathetic when he'd heard what she'd been through. He'd been livid.

"What happened next?" Brian asked.

"It was bitterly cold, and I didn't have a coat. And, of course, it was dark enough to be the setting for some monster movie. They imprisoned me down there shortly after Vick left to spend the weekend with a friend. The other girls told the headmistress that I'd gone with Vick to Paris."

"Those little bitches," Brian muttered.

"I yelled and banged on the cellar door, but it was thick, and besides, there was no one around to hear me. I was down there, alone in the dark, when I accidentally started the fire."

"How could you start an 'accidental' fire in the dark?"

"I found a candle on Friday. I didn't find the matches until Sunday afternoon. Those were the darkest, longest, loneliest three days of my life."

"I'm so sorry, Tag. That must have been awful."

"It was." Her throat clogged in response to Brian's sympathy. She swallowed over the painful lump and continued, "I must have put the candle too close to the straw used to pack the wine stored down there, because I woke up choking from the smoke. It never occurred to me that such an ancient cellar would have sprinklers, but I suppose they put them in when they started using the building overhead as a dormitory for wealthy young ladies.

"At any rate, the sprinklers went off, the fire engines showed up, and I got myself thrown out and sent home. Vick was pissed off because she got kicked out right along with me."

"And you showed up at Jackson High in the fall, where I took one look and fell hard for you."

"You didn't do that."

"Didn't I?"

She heard Brian's jaw crack when he yawned.

"Sorry to be keeping you up," she said.

"I haven't had much sleep over the past two weeks while we've been fighting that fire."

"Believe it or not," she murmured, "I forgot about the fire." Making love with Brian, and then lying in his arms, had made their circumstances fade away. At least, for a little while. "Go to sleep, Brian."

"If you can't sleep, count some sheep." His voice was slurred, as though he were already half asleep.

Taylor lay there for a long time, staring into nothingness. She shouldn't have let Brian talk her into that last "low and slow" survey of the fire. Then none of this would have happened. But she was the pilot. She could have refused. She was more to blame for the hopeless situation in which they found themselves than he was.

Her stomach growled. Taylor hardly ever thought of food. She ate to nourish her body, plain and simple. Now, all she could think about was how great an enormous bison cheeseburger and a plate of Big O rings at Liberty's would taste, followed by a huge, homemade huckleberry ice-cream cone from Moos.

Taylor's mouth filled with saliva. For heaven's sake, she was drooling! She stuck her head under Brian's chin and squeezed her eyes, just to make sure they were closed, then sighed in disgust. She might as well try counting sheep. Tomorrow was liable to be a very long day.

One sheep. Two sheep. Red . . . sheep . . . Blue . . . sheep . . .

Chapter 10

AIDEN FLYNN LOOKED from one dog-tired, soot-blackened face to the next along the fire line. His heart hurt when he saw the look of despair in his two younger brothers' eyes. They were all suffering as a result of Brian's disappearance. His heart sank to his feet when he considered how the loss of her sister was going to affect the woman he loved.

In a miracle of cooperation, Grayhawk and Flynn had been working side by side for the past sixteen hours fighting the Yellowstone fire. Connor and Devon stood nearby with Pulaski tools slung over their shoulders, their eyes bleak, their hips canted in exhaustion. Matthew Grayhawk's nose and eyes dripped clear fluids in a useless effort to rid themselves of smoke, and the blond ponytail that ran halfway down Leah Grayhawk's back beneath her hard hat was peppered with ash.

The grueling, backbreaking, mind-numbing effort to curb the fire, beating back flames with tree limbs, digging furrows in the earth with a Pulaski tool—with its hoe on one side of the metal head and ax on the other—

and cutting down trees with a chain saw to make a fire-break, gave them a way to fight back against the fear and worry they all felt at the disappearance—without a trace—of Brian Flynn and Taylor Grayhawk.

Within the past hour, word had reached them that the fire-breathing dragon had been curbed. The flames weren't completely squelched, but the Yellowstone fire was no longer burning out of control. Now a more thorough search for the missing plane, and possible survivors, could begin.

As Aiden approached Leah, his heart began thumping erratically. He tried to look casual. He felt anything but. His voice was raspy from smoke. He coughed to clear his throat and said, "You look beat."

Instead of admitting to fatigue, she focused her red-rimmed eyes on him and said, "I'm just thirsty."

He handed her the canteen from his PG bag.

She opened it and drank before handing it back to him. She sighed, then removed her hard hat and used the back of her wrist to shove the bangs off her forehead. She pursed her lips and shook her head as she eyed the blackened cuff of her khaki shirt. "I need to go to the command post. I promised to find something for us to eat."

Aiden took a step to block her way. "You haven't said two words to me since we got here. You didn't say much more than that on the drive here from Jackson."

"Not now, Aiden."

"When, Leah? When are you going to believe I love you?"

She glanced around to make sure no one was close

enough to hear and rounded on him, her eyes fierce, her voice a harsh whisper. "Leave me alone. Stop harassing me."

"Give me a chance to explain. If you're still determined to be rid of me, I'll walk away."

"I know everything I need to know. You bet Brian you could get me to fall in love with you. You won. End of story."

"You're my wife."

Her nostrils flared with anger. "Not for long. The minute I find the time to fly back to Vegas, this marriage is over."

"Catholics don't believe in divorce."

"Brian got a divorce."

He saw the flash of regret in her eyes that she'd mentioned his missing brother. He swallowed the knot of raw pain in his throat and said, "I'm not Brian."

It was Brian who'd talked him into the bet. When he'd told his brother to stop moping over his broken marriage and move on with his life, Brian had countered that Aiden hadn't even managed to get a woman to fall in love with him, let alone marry him. He was in no position to lecture Brian on his love life.

Aiden remembered bragging, "I can get any woman I want."

"*Any* woman?" Brian had countered. "How about Leah Grayhawk?"

"Who'd want her? That female's nothing but piss and vinegar." In fact, Leah could be downright vicious when it came to defending her sisters against Flynn pranks. Aiden had the scars to prove it.

In retaliation for Connor cutting Eve's cinch before the barrel race competition at a junior rodeo, causing Leah's youngest sister to break her arm when the saddle came free, Leah had cut the cinch on Aiden's saddle before the calf-roping competition at the same event. He'd ended up breaking his leg. It still ached on cold days.

"You said *any* woman," Brian jibed.

Aiden eyed his brother sideways. What was Brian's game? He rubbed his thigh and said, "Not Leah."

Brian made clucking sounds. "You're afraid to try because you know you'll fail. Leah isn't likely to fall for your tricks. She knows too much about your exploits with women."

Leah was the same age as he was. They'd been in most of the same classes in high school. They hadn't had much to do with each other since, but Jackson Hole was a small place, and he was sure she'd heard whatever gossip there was about him. "I could have her swooning at my feet"—he snapped his fingers—"like that." Even as he said it, Aiden realized how silly the whole conversation had become. At thirty-three, he didn't need to prove his prowess with women. He'd had plenty of willing partners over the years. Getting involved with one of King's Brats was a dumb move.

"I have no doubt you could charm Leah into a date or two," Brian said. "But could you get her to fall in love with you?"

"That's ridiculous."

Brian bent his elbows and flapped his arms. "Like I said, *cluck, cluck, cluck*. You think it's easy to get a woman to trust you enough to give you her love? Put your money where your mouth is. I'll bet you my Harley that you can't get Leah Grayhawk to fall in love with you."

Aiden had been coveting Brian's Harley-Davidson ever since his brother had bought it. He could have bought a motorcycle of his own, but that would have felt too much like he was copying Brian. As the firstborn, he always had been, and always would be, the leader in the family.

"I have to admit I'm tempted," he told Brian. "That's a fine ride."

"If you lose," Brian said, "you never say another word about me getting on with my life." Brian then extended his hand. "Do we have a bet?"

It had seemed harmless enough at the time. All Aiden had to do was put his best foot forward with Leah. He'd never seen her date, even in high school. He supposed she'd stayed home to keep an eye on her sisters. She wasn't as pretty as the twins or Eve, but she wasn't bad-looking, either. She had really beautiful golden brown eyes that reflected what she was feeling. At least he would have that much of a head start figuring out what was going on inside her. He liked a challenge, and he was sure Leah would give him a run for his money.

He put his hand in Brian's and said, "You're on."

Even making contact with Leah hadn't been easy. Both of them worked on their fathers' ranches. The Flynn ranch, the Lucky 7, and the Grayhawk ranch, Kingdom Come, had a few common borders, but both ranch houses sat in the middle of thousands of acres of land. Unless he and Leah happened to be in Jackson

Hole at the same time shopping for supplies, or showed up at the same cattle auction or rodeo, there was no reason for their paths to cross.

When he finally tracked her down at the hardware store in town, Leah had been so suspicious of his motives—rightfully, as it turned out—that it took all his persuasion—and a small lie—to get her to go out with him.

"I was wondering if you'd help me out with a problem I'm having."

Her eyes had narrowed suspiciously. "What sort of problem?"

There was no problem. So he made one up. "Uh. It's about this girl I was dating. She broke up with me, and I can't figure out why."

Her lip curled cynically. "She must be blind. Or stupid."

He'd been shocked by her response, which suggested she liked his looks and maybe even him as a person. He shot her a coaxing smile and said, "Obviously, she's not as perceptive as you."

Leah snorted derisively. It was the sound a cowhand might make to another cowhand. There was nothing feminine about it. It dismissed the possibility that she thought he was anyone worth knowing.

He appreciated the fact that she hadn't gone all girly on him and said, "I hoped you'd be willing to hear me out, about the relationship, I mean, and let me know what you think I should have done differently."

Her gaze lowered to her feet and remained there for a few moments. He was almost rocked backward when her eyes finally locked with his. Those fierce, sun-lit orbs, which reminded him of a lioness on the hunt, challenged him to tell the truth. He suddenly felt guilty for the hoax he was perpetrating on her. He almost ended the bet right there.

Except, there was something else in her eyes. It was a feeling he had that she could see inside him to what he was thinking, what he was feeling. The experience was strange enough to keep him silent.

"Why don't you ask your brothers for advice?"

"They're no help with something like this. I need a female perspective."

"I haven't dated much, but I have three sisters with a lot of experience. Maybe you should speak to one of them."

He was surprised to hear her admit she hadn't dated, even though he knew it to be true. He was even more surprised that she'd offered to set him up with one of her sisters. "I have a suggestion. I don't know if you'll go for it, but here it is. Go out on a date with me. You can judge for yourself where you think I might have gone wrong."

"Why me?"

"I can count on you to tell me the brutal truth."

Her lips pursed and then flattened. "All right. I'll go on a 'pretend' date with you."

Leah had been a babe in the woods, falling for a line like he'd handed her. To this day, Aiden was ashamed of his underhanded tactics in getting her out on that first date. But he wasn't sorry he'd done it. Otherwise, he would have deprived himself of everything good that had followed.

Leah had greeted him with wary eyes at the Stage-coach Bar in Wilson, where they'd arranged to meet for their "pretend" date, and watched him with mistrust the rest of the night. The bar just outside Jackson, which had been around since the 1940s, catered to local work-ers, so they were less likely to run into someone they knew. The music was so loud, talking was difficult.

By the end of the evening, Aiden was ready to forget the whole thing, but he knew Brian would never let him hear the end of it. He walked Leah through the parking lot to her pickup, then put a hand on her elbow to turn her to face him.

"Well, what do you think? If this were a real date, would you go out with me again?"

"No."

Even though Aiden had no intention of going on an-other date with Leah, her rejection stung. "Why not?"

"You couldn't have had a good time tonight. We only danced the two-step twice. You passed on every waltz, when you could have used the opportunity to hold me in your arms. You drank one beer. I don't know if you just don't like beer, or whether you were afraid I'd take ad-vantage of you if you got drunk."

He laughed at the absurdity of her suggestion.

She held up a hand to keep him from explaining or making excuses and continued, "You didn't ask me any-thing about myself. Nor did you offer any information about yourself that would lead me to believe you're in-terested in the two of us getting to know each other any better."

He found her scathing honesty refreshing enough to

meet it with equal frankness. "Everything you've said is true enough. But I think there's something about this"—he gestured between the two of them—"that's worth exploring." It dawned on him that he meant it. There was *something* about her that he found intriguing, but he knew little more about her now than he had before the evening had begun. "So. Do you want to give it another try?"

She took a long time considering his suggestion. Instead of speaking, she rose on tiptoe and slid one arm around his neck, teasing her fingertips through the too-long hair on his nape, raising gooseflesh. Then she pressed her lips softly against his, her tongue dipping inside his mouth for a thrilling instant, spinning his insides as though he were on a Tilt-A-Whirl.

When she was done, Leah looked into his eyes and whispered, "Yes. This is worth exploring."

He felt as though he'd been poleaxed. He was dizzy, and his heart was pounding like it wanted out of his chest. Nothing even remotely like it had ever happened to him. Aiden fought the confusing feelings, because they frightened him. For a moment, he considered changing his mind. Then he realized that, if he did, he would have to give Brian a reason for giving up.

Flynns never quit. Which meant he had to see Leah again. He would just be more careful next time. He would make sure that he was the one in charge of any kissing they did. And he would find out everything about her. Once she was no longer a mystery to him, he would be able to walk away without a qualm.

He should have known it wouldn't be that simple.

Nothing was ever easy between Grayhawks and Flynns. Considering the way their relationship had started out, it was doomed from the start. Aiden never should have expected—or hoped—for anything else.

They met in secret for every date, because Leah was worried about what King—or Angus, for that matter—would do if he ever found out. Aiden couldn't disagree with her, because their fathers' hatred for each other was as virulent as ever. But the more fences she put in his way to keep them apart, the more determined he was to move over them, around them, or just knock them down.

Aiden wasn't sure when or how he'd fallen in love with her. It just happened. One day she was this fascinating creature who figuratively held a palm against his chest to keep him at arm's distance. The next she was this amazing woman he couldn't hold close enough to his heart.

Leah had put off having sex, arguing they needed more time to know each other first. It had dawned on him that, despite everything, she still didn't trust him. He debated admitting that he'd started dating her because of a bet with Brian. He would explain how his feelings had changed and grown into something genuine and true. But he was afraid she would use the bet as an excuse to walk away and never see him again.

That would break him apart.

Four months ago, when her sisters were all out of town, Aiden had surprised Leah with a trip to Vegas. He'd never seen her so carefree, so . . . happy. Until that weekend, he'd never seen her drink anything stronger than beer, and when he'd offered her champagne to celebrate, she'd liked it so much, she drank it like fruit punch. He'd done his share of celebrating as well.

As the evening wore on, her smile seemed broader to him and her laughter more jubilant. Getting married at the Golden Bells Wedding Chapel in the middle of the night seemed like a wonderful idea. As the gloriously happy bride and groom, they finally consummated their relationship.

Leah had been surprisingly remorseful the next morning.

"If it's because your sisters weren't at the wedding—"

"It's not that."

"Or because I didn't have a ring—"

"Or that, either."

"Then what? Was the sex not what you expected?"

She blushed a fiery red. "It was . . . You know what it was."

She'd been a virgin. He'd been half drunk and in a hurry. It hadn't been good.

Aiden had silently vowed to do better—to think more about her than himself—the next time. But Leah was already up and dressed and ready to leave by the time he woke up. He hadn't tried to coax her back into bed, which he didn't realize until much later was a terrible mistake. He simply got up and got dressed, all the while listening to the reasons why they shouldn't have done what they'd done.

"Where will we live, Aiden?"

"At the Lucky 7, of course."

She shook her head. "I don't know what I was thinking. Getting married was a bad idea."

"Then what have we been doing for the past five months? Do you love me, Leah?"

She refused to answer him. Refused to say what he'd already said to her more than once—without a like response. He thought he saw love in her eyes, but what she said was, "I can't live with you, Aiden. I need to be home for my sisters."

His face grew hot with anger. "Your sisters are grown women. They can take care of themselves."

"I'm the only mother they have," she argued. "Until they have homes of their own, I'm responsible for them. Besides, I could never live under the same roof as your father."

"I have a whole wing of the house to myself."

"But there's one kitchen, right? And one dining room?"

"Fine. We'll build a house of our own."

"Where?"

"My father has plenty of land where—"

"So does mine. In fact, Kingdom Come will be mine one day."

"I need to live at the main house, so I can take care of ranch business."

"So do I."

Frustrated, he said, "I want to stop sneaking around, Leah. I want to wake up with you in the morning. Think about coming to live with me. Please."

"We should have left things the way they were. We never should have gotten married."

"Don't say that. I love you. I want to spend my life with you."

She looked at him with the saddest eyes he'd ever seen. But she didn't say the words he longed to hear. Or even promise to think about coming to live with him. It was a problem without an easy solution, but one he was determined to solve.

They left Vegas that same day, with everything still unsettled, and returned home—where he'd made a fatal mistake. He'd sought out Brian, who was having lunch on the patio of the Sweetwater Restaurant, across the street from the Jackson Hole fire station where he was on duty, wanting to share the happy—if stunning—news that he and Leah had gotten married.

He'd been surprised at the sneer on Brian's face. "You won your bet, fair and square," his brother said. "I'll give you the keys to the Harley when my shift ends."

"I thought you'd be glad for me."

"What bet?" Leah interjected.

Aiden turned to find Leah standing right behind him. Apparently, she'd been sitting at a table by herself on the opposite side of the patio and had come over to speak to him.

"He didn't tell you?" Brian said.

"Tell me what?" Leah said.

Aiden felt a chill run down his spine when he met Leah's gaze. She looked like a whipped cur that expects nothing better than unkindness, or even cruelty, at the hands of others.

"What's going on?" she asked.

He never took his eyes off her as he said, "Keep your mouth shut, Brian."

"Aiden bet me he could get any girl he wanted to fall

in love with him," Brian said. "Even someone as full of piss and vinegar as you."

The blood leached from Leah's face so completely Aiden thought she might faint.

She stared at him with eyes so wounded he felt like throwing up. She opened her mouth to speak, then clamped it tight to still the wobble in her chin. In a voice like a rusty gate she asked, "Is that true?"

"Yes, but—"

He would never forget the look in her eyes as long as he lived. He had never seen such wrenching pain, or felt such pain himself. She tore her gaze from his as she whirled and ran.

Aiden snatched Brian out of his chair by his shirt front and smashed him in the jaw, sending him stumbling backward over the bench onto the ground. Aiden shook his throbbing hand as he railed, "What the hell were you thinking? Why would you hurt her like that?"

"You're a fool if you think love is forever, Aiden," he yelled back. "I did you a favor. See how fast she took off? Better she does it now than later."

Aiden shook his head in disgust and dismay. He didn't recognize the man sprawled in front of him. This wasn't the brother he knew. Brian's divorce had changed him— for the worse. "I don't know what your wife did to make you such a bitter sonofabitch, but figure it out and get over it. You better hope Leah forgives me, because if she doesn't . . ." He left the sentence unfinished. He didn't like the feelings roiling inside him. Anger and frustration. Fear and hate. He leaped the short fence that separated the patio from the sidewalk and raced after Leah.

She hadn't forgiven him, despite all his pleas since that awful day. But she hadn't gotten an annulment during the past four months. Or a divorce. At least, not yet.

He wasn't particularly encouraged by her delay in cutting the cord that bound them, because within a week of Brian's revelation, her life had been turned upside down.

Without any warning, the "Black Sheep" of the family, Matthew Grayhawk, who'd disappeared without a word twenty years ago, arrived at Kingdom Come with his nineteen-year-old daughter, Pippa, and six-year-old son, Nathan.

King had lured Matt back to Wyoming from Australia by promising him that, if he stayed at Kingdom Come for a full year, the ranch would be his. Matt's arrival had thrown the lives of the Brats into terrible turmoil, because Matt had made it clear that, when the year was up, he expected all of them—including Leah—to be long gone.

Aiden remembered how Leah had told him Kingdom Come would be hers one day. He tried to imagine how she must be feeling, now that her father had disinherited her, and her stepbrother was threatening to throw her out on her ass. But she wasn't speaking to him, so he could only guess how fuming mad she must be.

On the other hand, he saw in her situation an opportunity for the two of them. If Kingdom Come was lost to Leah, maybe she would agree to come live with him.

That is, if she ever forgave him.

Aiden was familiar with the trails Leah rode on horseback every morning, because it was one of the ways they'd managed their meetings when they'd been secretly dating. Recently, he'd intercepted her at a place where she couldn't see him soon enough to avoid him, and couldn't easily escape once she did lay eyes on him.

He'd angled his mount across the trail and asked, "What are you going to do about Matt's ultimatum?"

"Fight. Matt's not getting this ranch. Not if I have anything to say about it."

"You don't have anything to say about it," he pointed out. "The way I heard it, King has given Matt the authority to treat the ranch as though he already owns it."

"A lot can happen in a year. By the time I'm through with him, Matt will head back to Australia with his tail between his legs."

"You don't know Matt."

"And you do?"

"He lived with us for a while when he was a teenager, when he had that falling out with King that eventually sent him running off to Australia. Matt's not going anywhere. That man is grit personified."

"We'll see."

He leaned over to kiss her, but she turned her head away. "Is this the way it's going to be? I'm not even allowed to touch you?"

"I don't trust you," she shot back. "I don't know if I'll ever be able to trust you again."

She'd spurred her horse so its shoulder knocked into his mount, forcing it backward, and ridden away.

The first time she'd spoken willingly to him since that day was to ask for a ride to Yellowstone. Based on what, and how little, she'd said during the trip, it seemed her heart hadn't softened toward him.

Aiden loved his brother. But he hadn't confided in him or shared much of anything personal with him since their fight. Because Brian's wife had gotten his house in the divorce and Brian hadn't yet bought another place, they both still lived under the same roof. But for all intents and purposes, he'd cut his brother out of his life.

Brian couldn't die, because Aiden hadn't yet forgiven him for destroying his relationship with Leah. The mere possibility of never seeing his brother again made his stomach churn. Aiden knew Brian had suffered from his continued cold shoulder, but he'd nursed his grievance and let things hang.

Now it might be too late.

"I've got to get us some sandwiches, Aiden," Leah said. "Everyone's hungry."

He stepped aside. She couldn't avoid him forever. And she couldn't get out of this marriage without him signing papers of some kind. Which he had no intention of doing. Ever.

Chapter 11

LEAH FOUGHT TEARS as she walked away. She *would not* cry. Between Matt's return from Australia claiming the ranch that she'd expected to be her home for the rest of her life, Angus's most recent efforts to financially ruin her father, and her disastrous marriage to Aiden, her life was in chaos. Taylor's disappearance threatened to make the load of troubles she was carrying unbearable.

Leah pulled her cellphone from her pocket, but there was no service. She wondered how Vick was faring back at the ranch. She'd fallen apart when she learned Taylor was missing. The twins had bickered and brawled all their lives, but Vick would be lost without the sunshine to her shadow. Leah tried to stay optimistic that Taylor and Brian would be found alive and well, but it was ominous that nothing had been heard from either of them, considering the state-of-the-art communication equipment Brian had carried.

She heard the limbs of felled trees cracking underfoot behind her and gritted her teeth, certain it was Aiden. She whirled to confront him and found Matt dogging her heels. Matt was only four years older, thirty-seven to her thirty-three, but he'd done a world more of living. He'd been married and divorced twice, and had a grown daughter and a young son.

The crow's-feet at the edges of his blue eyes had been hard-won in the harsh Australian sun, where he'd managed a cattle station for the past twenty years—and where he'd learned to be every bit as ruthless as King. Matt was a worthy adversary, but Leah was determined that when all was said and done, she would be the one in possession of the ranch they both wanted.

"What's up?" she asked.

"I thought I'd come and help you cart everything back." He put a hand to the small of his back and twisted sideways. "Besides, I needed a break."

"Don't tell me you're tired."

"I think we all passed 'tired' twelve hours ago. I'm completely worn out."

"Then go home. Why are you here, anyway? Taylor's been awful to you, and you hardly know Brian."

She started walking again, and he fell into step beside her.

"Believe it or not," he said, "I don't wish any of you Brats ill."

"Really? Could've fooled me."

"All I've done is give you and your sisters a little nudge to move on with your lives."

"My life is—and always will be—at Kingdom Come."

"To be honest," Matt said, "I'm not sure either of us is going to end up with the ranch. What on earth was

King thinking when he bought a quarter of a million acres of ranchland in Argentina?"

"It wasn't a bad investment. He'd have been fine if Angus hadn't stuck his nose in where it didn't belong."

"I guess you know the banker isn't going to give King an extension on the loan, which is secured by the ranch and damn near everything else that's not tied down. You and I both know King doesn't have the assets to pay it off."

"He'll figure something out."

"He's running out of time. I think Angus may finally get the revenge he's been after all these years. I can't say I'm sorry to see it."

She eyed him sideways. "You're okay with King—your own father—losing everything?"

"Once upon a time, King caused me to lose everything I loved most in the world."

Leah frowned. "Is that why you disappeared without a word to anyone?"

Matt nodded curtly.

She hesitated, then asked, "What did King do?"

"When I was sixteen, he conspired with the parents of Jennie Fairchild, the girl I loved—who was pregnant with my child—to keep us apart."

"That doesn't sound so terrible. Lots of parents manipulate their children's lives for their own good."

"By the time Jennie's due date came around, I was frantic for information, and King finally provided it."

He was silent so long, she asked, "What did he say?"

"He told me Jennie had died during childbirth, along with our baby."

She came to an abrupt halt. "Oh, Matt! I'm so sorry."

"The sonofabitch lied. Jennie is alive and well to this day. And so is our child."

Leah gasped. "They didn't die?"

Matt shook his head. "Jennie's parents lied to her, too. They told her our baby died at birth, then placed our child with foster parents." Obviously agitated, Matt started walking again.

Leah quickly followed. She'd always known King was ruthless. But she hadn't known about this. "That sounds awful, Matt."

"It was. With Angus's help, I got custody of our daughter when she was a year old and took her as far away as I could from my father and Jennie's parents, where there was no chance they could find me and take her away again."

Leah had a sudden realization. That baby was Matt's nineteen-year-old daughter. "You're talking about Pippa!"

Matt nodded again.

"Did you ever get in touch with Jennie and tell her where you were and what you'd done?"

"I was too scared to try at first. Besides, Jennie was only fifteen. When she would have been old enough to join me, I couldn't find her. And later, when I knew where she was, I just . . . didn't."

Leah hissed in a breath. "Ever?"

"Not until six weeks ago. I found her living at her grandmother's ranch in Texas."

"And?"

"Jennie can't forgive me for what I did. For taking

Pippa and running away. But mostly, for never telling her our daughter was alive. I don't blame her, really."

"But you still blame King for losing your chance at a life together with her. And you're bitter enough about how things turned out that you'd be happy if King ends up ruined."

"Don't miss a thing, do you? Maybe now you can understand why I don't have a lot of sympathy for our father."

"Unfortunately, King's loss will be your loss," she pointed out. *And mine.* Except, Leah was betting on King. If the loan got renewed, the ranch would stay in King's possession. And if that happened, she needed a way to oust Matt from control of the ranch before he could meet the required three hundred sixty-five uninterrupted days of residence at Kingdom Come.

He might just have given her the information she needed to be rid of him.

What if she encouraged Matt to reunite with his lost love, who lived in faraway Texas? What if he needed to leave the ranch—and violate his agreement with King—to work things out with Jennie?

Leah glanced at Matt and asked, "Is there any hope you and Jennie might get back together?"

"The last time I spoke to her, she was pretty definite about never wanting to see me again."

"You're going to leave it at that?"

Matt shot her a crooked smile. "I suppose you wouldn't."

"I don't believe in giving up." Although that was exactly what she'd done with Aiden. Easy to give such advice. Difficult to take it.

Matt seemed to be considering what she'd said, so Leah fell silent. Her thoughts strayed inevitably, unerringly to Aiden. Even thinking about his betrayal made her throat tighten and her heart hurt. It had taken a great deal of courage to give her trust to any man. But she was a quick learner. Once burned, twice chary.

Maybe he does love you.

And maybe, someday, buffalo will fly.

When she was ten years old, Leah had learned her lesson about the fickleness of men from her mother. She'd never forgotten it: You can't trust a man to keep on loving you forever.

"A man only wants a wife who's beautiful, Leah," her mother had said. *"Nothing else is more important to him. When your looks are gone, he throws you away like an old tissue. I've borne King three babies, and lost my figure as a result. Nowadays, he seems more interested in politics and business than in me. I'm taking matters into my own hands. I've found someone who loves me as I am, and I've decided to run away with him."*

Her mother had paused. Perhaps what she said next was why the conversation had stuck so firmly in Leah's mind.

"My new man doesn't want any baggage along. So I have to leave you and my babies behind."

Leah tried to remember what she'd been feeling at that moment.

Panic. Disbelief. And horrible grief.

"I need you to take care of your sisters for me."

"But I've never taken care of anybody before. I won't know what to do."

"You'll figure it all out. Be a good girl and help with the little ones, and everything will be fine."

Leah hadn't forgotten that advice either. She'd been terrified that King would get rid of her, since she was no blood relation, when he realized that her mother had run away. Leah had been the most helpful, invisible, well-behaved ten-year-old a father could ask for, taking on responsibility far beyond her years.

She'd gone to bed every night for months afraid that the next morning would be the day King decided she wasn't earning her keep and sent her away. She'd devoted herself to caring for her siblings, because it was the only way she could see to earn herself a place in a home where she didn't belong.

Leah had never dated in high school, because she'd known she wasn't beautiful. She had her biological father's unremarkable hazel eyes and his straight-as-an-arrow, dishwater blond hair, not the vivid blue eyes and striking golden curls her mother had passed on to her three younger sisters. What boy would be interested in an ordinary-looking girl like her? And even if he did date her, how long would he hang around?

As a grown-up, she'd gone out with enough men—five, to be exact—to know it was an exercise in futility. Smart, attractive men had approached her, and she enjoyed spending time with the opposite sex. But whenever a man got serious, she bolted for the door.

Leah knew why she was so scared of commitment.

She should be over her childhood trauma by now. She wasn't her mother. And besides, her mother was wrong about men wanting only beautiful women. Even knowing that, she couldn't seem to stop herself from running for the hills whenever a man started talking about forever after.

Leah had been shocked by Aiden's invitation to go out on a date. And suspicious. What interest could he possibly have in her? But she'd been lonely, and she'd figured an evening together would be time enough to figure out what sort of Flynn monkey business he had planned for her.

Because she hadn't been forthcoming, Aiden had done most of the talking. She'd given him her attention because he'd talked about ranching. Neither shared any personal information. She'd been perplexed when Aiden asked for another date. She'd been intending to tell him good night and goodbye, one date with a Flynn was enough. Then she'd decided that, since she wouldn't be seeing him again, and she might not get another opportunity anytime soon, she might as well kiss him.

That kiss had changed everything, including her decision to walk away. Who would have thought pressing female lips to male lips could evoke such strong feelings. It had never happened to her before. Or that simply running her fingers through the hair at Aiden's nape could raise gooseflesh on her arms. Or that her belly would curl with desire when her tongue touched his.

After their kiss in the moonlight, she'd seen the confusion and curiosity in his eyes and realized he didn't understand what had happened between them any better than she did. Despite the warning bells going off in her head, Leah had agreed to see him again.

So many of her beliefs had been challenged over the next five months, as they spent time together. In the end, her mother had been right. You couldn't trust a man to keep on loving you. Or, in her case, to have ever loved you at all.

As she and Matt approached the command post, a man called out to them, "Hey! I'm looking for Aiden Flynn."

"We were just with him," Leah said. "Do you have a message? Have they been found?"

Chapter 12

"THE PLANE'S BEEN found," Leah announced as she approached the three Flynn brothers, her arms filled with sandwiches.

"Hallelujah!" Connor said, rising from his seat on a tree stump.

"Are they all right?" Devon asked, jumping up from a stone where he'd been perched.

Leah saw the look of hope as Aiden turned to her and watched the light in his eyes die when he saw her somber expression.

"What did you find out?" he asked.

Before answering either man, Leah handed out the ham and cheese sandwiches, knowing the three men had missed several meals. It was a sign of just how hungry they were that all three had already taken bites when she said, "The Twin Otter's a burned-out shell."

Aiden stopped chewing and stared.

She continued, "The good news is that no bodies were visible near the wreckage." That didn't mean they weren't burned beyond recognition. But Leah didn't want to put that thought in anyone's mind.

"Is there any sign of them?" Aiden asked. "Surely they would have stayed by the plane."

Leah focused her gaze on his anxious blue eyes. "The whole forest had been turned to ashes for a mile around the crash site. There's no way of knowing whether they escaped before the fire came through."

Leah wondered if her eyes looked as desolate as Aiden's. She gritted her teeth to still her quivering chin, then clenched her hands into fists to keep from reaching out to comfort the man she'd once loved . . . and now despised with a passion equal to the betrayal she felt.

"Unfortunately," she continued, "the plane is miles from the closest Forest Service road. We can only drive so far. We'll have to hike in the rest of the way to search for them."

"You keep saying 'we,'" Aiden said. "Does that mean you're coming with us?"

"I want to be there. Taylor might need me."

"How do we know they're not both dead inside the plane?" Connor said.

Leah watched Aiden visibly wince at Connor's statement.

"If that's the case, we'll know soon enough," he said.

"I need to go check on things at the ranch," Connor said. He was the only Flynn brother with children at home, and his ranch was set up as a haven where returning veterans could escape for a little R & R—rest and recuperation—before either going back to war or heading home to their families. "Keep me in the loop while I'm gone."

"Will do," Aiden replied.

"By the way, did Matt catch up to you?" Connor asked Leah.

"He's on his way home. His daughter just showed up at Kingdom Come, after spending six weeks visiting her mother in Texas. He said he'll be back on the hunt as soon as he checks on her."

Devon blurted, "Pippa's back?"

Leah nodded. Matt's teenage daughter had been so unhappy at Kingdom Come that she'd run away and ended up living with Devon, who'd offered her a room in his cabin in the mountains.

Leah continued, "It seems there's a brand-new fire burning in the Bridger-Teton forest, which puts it on the outskirts of your ranch, Devon. It's still small, and they're hoping to keep it under control. Whether they can is anybody's guess."

Devon turned to Aiden and said, "I'd better head home, in case I have to round up my cattle and trailer my horses someplace safe."

"And maybe see Pippa while you're at it?" Aiden said.

"She doesn't want anything to do with me," Devon replied. "She made that clear when she left for Texas."

"But she's back," Connor pointed out.

Leah saw the look of longing on Devon's face. But all he said was, "I'll rejoin the search the instant I can."

Aiden focused his gaze on each of his brothers in turn and said, "I'll let both of you know if we find out anything." And then, to Devon, "Let us know if you need help relocating your livestock."

"Will do."

Leah watched as Aiden and his brothers exchanged hugs—a bump of shoulders and a pat on the back that, nevertheless, conveyed how much they cared for one another—before Connor and Devon headed toward the road where they'd left their pickups. As they passed her, the two men each touched a respectful fingertip to the brim of his hard hat.

"Good luck," Connor said.

"Take care of yourselves," Devon said.

Once they were gone, Aiden murmured, "I wonder what we'll find when we get to the site of the crash."

"I'm guessing at least one of them is hurt," Leah said. "It has to be Brian."

"Why do you say that?"

"If Taylor were injured, Brian could carry her out."

"And if Brian's injured?"

Leah shrugged. "Taylor's strong. Maybe she managed to drag him to safety." A shiver of foreboding ran down her spine, and she spoke to counter it. "I'm betting they're lost in the forest and will be back with a story to tell."

Aiden took off his hard hat, shoved his sleeve across his sweaty forehead, then put his hat back on. "I hope you're right. We'd better get busy organizing a ground search. How big of an area are we talking about?"

Leah pulled a Forest Service Teton Wilderness map out of her back pocket. It had been marked to show the remote area where the fire still burned. "One of the su-

pervisors gave me this." She laid it out on the stone
where Devon had been sitting.

She pointed to an X on the map and said, "This is
where the Otter went down."

"Oh, my God," Aiden muttered. "That's the middle
of nowhere. How much terrain did you say is burned out
around the wreckage?"

Leah met his gaze, her eyes bleak. "I was told the
plane is surrounded by charred trees and vegetation for a
mile in every direction."

"Then how did they escape?"

Leah shrugged. "The fire must have come through
after the crash."

"And no one saw any bodies on the ground?"

Leah shook her head. "But bodies might be hard to
see from the air in that scorched landscape, especially if
Taylor and Brian aren't together, or if one or both of
them is inside the wreckage."

"Brian's good in an emergency. The only question is
whether he was physically able, after they crashed, to do
what needed to be done, especially if they had to escape
a fast-moving fire. That appears to be the case. Otherwise, they would have stayed near the plane."

"If they're up and on the move," Leah said, "why
weren't they spotted by the helicopter that discovered
the Otter? Or one of the planes out there searching?"

When Aiden reached out as though to take her in his
arms and comfort her, Leah gasped and took a step
backward. She ended up stumbling and would have
fallen if he hadn't caught her by the shoulders to hold
her upright.

"Let me go!"

"Leah, I—"

"Let me go, or I'll scream." Leah writhed and squirmed, repelling Aiden's touch precisely because she yearned to be held in his strong arms, yearned to feel his bristled cheek against her own, yearned to have his hands moving over her body. She'd needed all her willpower to resist the urge to listen to his excuses and forgive him. She didn't know how much time she could spend with him without breaking down entirely.

Aiden let go of her and held his hands up, palms out. In a harsh voice he said, "You're free. Settle down."

"Don't you dare tell me to settle down!"

"Then don't act like a five-year-old. Would you rather I let you fall on your ass?"

"That's exactly what you did, Aiden. Dumped me upside down and tossed me sideways. I hope you're happy, because I'm not! I trusted you. I lo—" She cut herself off, crossed her arms, and stared at him with her lips pressed flat.

"Please, Leah. Let me explain."

Leah glared at Aiden through narrowed eyes. "No. Not now. Not ever. Not ever again will I trust a Flynn. Especially not with my heart. If you bring up this subject again, you'll be searching for your brother by yourself."

Aiden dropped his hands to his sides and his chin to his chest. His shoulders slumped. When he met her gaze again, the pain in his eyes made her stomach knot. She hardened her heart and said, "Where do you want to start?"

"If there was any way on this earth to escape the furnace that burned that forest to ash, Brian will have found it. I suggest we start on the perimeter of the burned area, where there's still green forest."

"I have another idea I'd like to suggest."

"I'm listening," Aiden said.

"What if they didn't go down with the plane?"

"What do you mean? What other possibility—"

"Didn't you tell me earlier that Brian was supposed to jump the fire but ended up being the spotter instead?"

Aiden nodded. "I see where you're going. He probably boarded the plane with his parachute. Are we presuming the spotter's parachute never made it onto the plane, because the spotter never showed up?"

"What I'm suggesting is that Brian could have parachuted out of the plane before it crashed."

Aiden frowned. "Without Taylor? Not a chance."

"What if they jumped together with one parachute?"

"A tandem jump?" Aiden said. "Without the right gear that would be pretty risky. A Ram Air is intended for one person."

"Put yourself in their shoes," Leah argued. "The plane is going down. Taylor can't find a safe place to land because they're surrounded by mountains and sharply angled gullies. Brian could probably rig something to get the two of them down with one chute, don't you think?"

"I can check with the jumpers and see if Brian boarded the plane wearing his chute. That'll tell us if jumping was even an option."

"I wonder why they haven't contacted us on Brian's radio," Leah mused.

"Maybe it was damaged," Aiden said. "Even if it wasn't, his Bendix King doesn't have much range without a repeater in the area, and it's useless in mountainous terrain. Where was the last contact with the plane?"

Leah pointed to a red dot. "This is where Taylor gave their last position."

Aiden drew a line with his finger between the red spot where Taylor had last radioed her position to the X where the Twin Otter had crashed. "If they jumped somewhere along that line, we'll to need to search a lot of territory to find them. How far is it from one point to the other?"

The firefighter who'd handed Leah the map had already made the calculation, which she shared with Aiden. "Exactly 17.4 miles."

"That makes the search area—" Leah began.

"Too damn big," Aiden interrupted.

"We can search more efficiently if we start with the plane's location and move out from there," Leah said.

"Unless they jumped."

"The fire's still burning at the last location Taylor gave us on the radio," Leah said. "The fire is out where the plane crashed."

"I guess that settles that," Aiden said. "How many experienced searchers can we get?"

"You want to do a grid search?"

"I don't see a better way, do you?"

A grid search involved a long line of people, about twenty feet apart from one another, moving forward slowly and deliberately through an area. Leah knew about grid searches because she'd become a trained volunteer and participated in previous searches for missing backcountry skiers and hikers.

She also knew the math: twenty-five people to the mile with twenty feet between them meant 924 man hours. A trained team could cover *one square mile* in 3.5 hours. That meant they had to figure out a way to reduce the search area to make a realistic search possible.

"Why don't we take a look ourselves before we organize a larger search?" Leah suggested. "Especially since the area is so remote."

"All right," Aiden agreed. "Meanwhile, I'll get Dad to expand the air search."

"I'll speak to King as well. Will the Forest Service even allow us in there with the fire still burning?"

"I don't intend to ask," Aiden said. "That way they can't say no."

Leah smiled grimly. That sounded like the Flynn way of doing things. It was similar to the Grayhawk way of getting from point A to point B without a hitch. "Finish your sandwich," she said. "It may be a while before we have time to eat again."

"Leah—"

"I'm going to say this one more time. I don't want to hear explanations or apologies, Aiden. I don't want you to say a word to me that doesn't have to do with finding Taylor and Brian. Is that understood?"

She watched a muscle bunch in his jaw, watched his lips turn down, watched his eyes fill with frustration.

All he said was "Understood."

Chapter 13

"WHY AREN'T YOU married?"

Taylor laughed at the odd question and snuggled closer to Brian. They were sprawled on the sleeping bag, with the parachute draped over them. They'd spent the past six days sitting or lying together in the dark, because the more they moved around, the more calories they used, and they didn't have any to spare.

At least it wasn't pitch-black inside. Once Brian had trimmed away the spruce branches on the inside of the cave, they could see the trunk hadn't completely sealed the opening. A quarter-inch stream of light seeped through at the top.

It occurred to Taylor that they might have suffocated without that opening. Besides allowing air inside, the narrow slit permitted them to tell night from day, and to observe that the forest fire had burned out as far as they could see. The smoke was gone. The sky was blue. But the landscape had been reduced to charred ashes and skeleton trees. Devastation and desolation. No birds. No chipmunks or squirrels. No elk or moose or bears. Nothing living remained.

"We could barely tell there was a cave here before that tree came down," Taylor said. "How is anyone going to find us with that enormous tree blocking the opening?"

"Once I chip away enough of that spruce, we can shove part of the parachute out. It'll be a white flag on black soot. For anyone hunting from the air, it'll make something big to spot."

Taylor's stomach growled, and she looked to see if Brian had noticed. She hadn't yet turned out the headlamp after her early morning trip to the back of the cave, despite the knowledge that the batteries couldn't last. It was one more reason to be anxious.

Brian was stretched out with his head on his PG bag and his arm up across his eyes. If he'd noticed her stomach protesting, he wasn't saying anything. What was there to say? They were running out of food.

For the first time in her life, Taylor was truly starving. The sun had risen on their seventh day of captivity. Her stomach growled again.

Brian chuckled and said, "Insistent little bugger. Wants to be fed, I suppose."

"If I'm hungry, you must be starved."

"Don't change the subject."

"What's the subject?"

"Why aren't you married?"

"I'd rather talk about food. Or the lack of it. We're running out, Brian. What are we going to do?"

"Since there's nothing we can do, I prefer to talk

about other things. Like why you didn't marry one of those three guys you had on the hook."

"Do you realize that all we've eaten—between us—in six days, not counting that steak and potato, are two cans of beans, a granola bar, and an apple? That all we have left is two Snickers bars, and we're going to eat one of those for breakfast?"

"We still have six packets of coffee."

They'd used the frying pan to heat water to make hot coffee, and had shared a cup each day before they'd eaten their single meal, so their stomachs wouldn't realize how empty they were.

We really are going to starve. We should have eaten less. We shouldn't have been so greedy the past six days. We should have spread out our food to make it last longer.

Taylor was silent so long Brian prompted, "Well? Why aren't you somebody's wife?"

Instead of answering his question, Taylor reached up and turned off the headlamp and set it aside. They'd kept the headlamp off except to make meals or trips to the latrine, to treat Brian's wounds, and to allow him to mark the passing of each day by writing in the small notebook from his PG bag. Today, he hadn't even done that.

Taylor laid her ear against Brian's heart—she found its steady beat calming—and said, "Why do you care why I'm not married?"

"I just wondered."

"I could say 'nobody's asked' but you'd know I was lying." All three of her engagements had been announced not only in *The New York Times* but in the daily *Jackson Hole News & Guide*. "I suppose the truth is 'the right person hasn't asked.'"

"What was wrong with the three guys who gave you a ring?"

Taylor shrugged. She knew Brian could feel the gesture because they were lying so close. She'd spent all her waking hours talking about stupid stuff that didn't matter, until her throat was raw and sore, because talking about anything more significant suggested that she'd accepted the inevitability of their deaths. She didn't want to talk about important things, like why she'd stayed single instead of marrying one of the three men who'd professed to love her. She didn't want to accept the fact that her life might be ending when she had this awful, aching hole inside her that had never been filled.

So she said, "I'm dying for a Pinky G's pizza with sausage and pepperoni."

"Personally, I could go for a Liberty's bacon cheeseburger and sweet potato fries."

"I keep thinking of all the hungry children in Africa, and how Leah used them as a reason for us to clean our plates. I never really understood what it meant to be hungry."

"Now you do?" Brian asked.

"I'm starting to. I can't imagine living an entire life—start to finish—like this."

She fell silent, with the question Brian had asked hanging between them. She gritted her teeth and pressed her lips flat. She wasn't going to speak. She was going to keep her mouth shut and her problems private. This was

Brian Flynn. What if they did get out of here? Imagine the ammunition he would have to make her life miserable.

The silence stretched between them in the darkness.

At last Brian asked, "What's wrong, Tag?"

"You mean aside from the obvious?"

"You've been talking nonstop since we got stuck in here. I worry when you're quiet."

While she'd been blabbering away about clothes and makeup and vacations she'd taken and holidays with her sisters—innocuous facts about her life that didn't matter—Brian had been content to listen. Suddenly, he was probing for very private, very personal information about her three engagements.

What's changed?

She didn't like the answer that came to mind.

Brian doesn't think we're going to be found. He believes we're going to die of starvation. He just doesn't want to frighten me by admitting it aloud.

If all hope was gone, there was no longer any reason to keep anything from him. She took a deep breath, a breath of inevitability, and let it out.

"Shall I discuss the prime specimens of manhood who proposed marriage to me?" she said, breaking the silence.

"By all means."

"I should get a pass for getting engaged to Joe Bob Trent."

"Why is that?"

"I was only eighteen, too young and stupid to know better. I think I should get credit for calling that one off."

"Fair enough. What about Craig Rudolph Hempstead, III? You were twenty-four when I saw that announcement. Educated guy. Yale, according to the paper. Wealthy, due to inherit his father's copper mines in South America. Athletic, a sailor in the America's Cup. Philanthropic, supported Greenpeace. What was wrong with him?"

"He hit me."

She felt Brian's body go rigid.

"Just once," she hurried to add. "That was enough. I hightailed it as fast as I could."

"Good for you. And the third guy? The most recent one?"

Taylor sighed. "Dr. Harold Norwood? Nothing was wrong with him."

"Then why did you cut old Harry loose?"

"I don't know. I just . . . got cold feet." When Brian made no comment, she added, "You must admit, I don't have the greatest role models for the institution of marriage. King's been married and divorced four times. Most of those relationships caused havoc for everyone involved when they ended. My mom was married twice—that I know of—and quit both times. What's the point of getting married if it's going to end badly?"

"Who says it has to end badly?"

"Statistics," she said flatly.

"Then why get engaged in the first place?"

She made a face. "For the obvious reason, of course."

"What is that?"

Taylor reminded herself that what she said here was never going any further. It was all right to tell Brian her deepest desires, because they were the last thoughts she'd be revealing to anyone. "I want to share my life with someone who loves me as much as I love him."

"And none of those guys loved you?" He sounded incredulous.

When she didn't speak he said, "Oh. I see. *You* didn't love any of *them*. If that was the case, why get engaged?"

In a small voice she said, "I think there's something wrong with me."

"What are you talking about?"

"I want to be in love. I just . . . don't trust a man to keep on loving me. I figure he's going to get tired of me eventually, so I run before he can."

"Get tired of you? Are you crazy?"

"Admit it, Brian. If I hadn't walked away from you in high school, you would have left me eventually."

"I liked you, Tag. A lot."

She noticed his use of *liked,* even though he'd qualified it with *a lot*. That was a far cry from the *love* he'd supposedly felt and verbally expressed.

"I was willing to defy Aiden to keep dating you in high school. He thought you were going to hurt me if I stuck around. Turned out he was right."

"You were hurt when we broke up?" She felt him nod.

"I hadn't nearly had my fill of you."

"Be honest. How much longer would we have lasted as a couple?"

"I guess we'll never know."

"You sound mad."

"You didn't just walk away, Tag. You ran like a scared rabbit. You never gave us a chance. Now I see why. With you it's 'Don't get too close. Don't love too much. Or I'm out of here.' I guess I was lucky you left me when you did."

"I'm sorry if I hurt you, Brian. I did care for you. Too much, maybe."

"Why didn't you say something at the time?"

She put a palm to his bristly cheek. "I guess I was afraid."

"Of what?"

"That if I stayed, the pain of losing you would be devastating." She put a hand to his lips to keep him from interrupting. "When I thought the plane was going to crash and I might die, the thing I regretted most in my life was walking—all right, running—away from you in high school. I thought about what I might say to you if I got a second chance."

He eased her hand away from his lips and took it in his own. "What would that be?"

"That I wish we could try again. That there was a spark of . . . something . . . between us I think can be rekindled."

She felt his body stiffen. "You have feelings for me? Now? Still?"

"Leftover feelings. Unfinished feelings. 'Wonder if we could ever recapture what we had' feelings."

He eased her head off his shoulder onto the T-shirt she was using as a pillow and sat up. "I don't want to hear this. Not now. Not when it's too late."

His words confirmed their fate, the impending doom that had loosened her tongue. Their lives would end in this cave. She understood Brian's frustration. Why consider what might have happened between them, when there was no happily ever after to be had?

Brian held up his wrist so he could see the face of his watch, which glowed in the dark. "We missed breakfast. And lunch. You want to eat something now, or wait until later?"

She sat up, aware that, once again, she'd done most of the talking. Did Brian still have feelings for her? If he did, he wasn't admitting to them. Not even when he wouldn't have to act on them. She hadn't believed she could be hurt. But she was. She wasn't sure what she'd wanted him to say. Whatever it was, he hadn't said it. He hadn't said anything.

"Maybe we shouldn't eat anything today," she suggested.

"We keep eating until there's no food. I'll get a Snickers for us to split."

He hissed in a breath when he angled his leg to get up and she said, "We should check your wound first."

"Yeah. Okay."

She retrieved the headlamp and turned it on. "How does your leg feel?"

"It hurts."

His jeans had been shredded by the grizzly at the spot of the wound, but the second time she'd treated him, he'd ripped the opening wider, so he wouldn't continually have to strip. She aimed her headlamp at the wound and asked, "Does it feel better or worse than yesterday?"

Taylor had been worried that Brian's wounds would get infected, and she'd been insistent about cleaning the four claw marks with Jack Daniel's—for its antiseptic effect—and applying Neosporin at least twice each day. Unfortunately, they'd run out of Neosporin two days ago, and there was only a swallow or two of Jack Daniel's left in the plastic bottle.

"My skin feels tight," Brian said.

That likely meant the wounds were swollen. Swelling was one of the signs of infection. She pressed a fingertip against a red spot near the deepest gash.

"Ouch! Take it easy."

"I don't like the looks of that fourth gash."

"I don't much like it, either," he said. "But there's no pus, so I don't think it's infected."

Taylor wasn't so sure. She reached over to press her hand against his forehead to check for fever, but he swatted it away.

"I'm fine, Tag. Don't fuss."

His body always felt warm to her, but she made a note to feel his skin the next time they were lying close together to see if she could detect more warmth than usual. "I should put—"

"The whole thing's scabbed over," he said irritably. "I don't think we should waste the last of the whiskey. I'd rather drink it than pour it over my leg."

Taylor couldn't disagree. A scab had formed over each of the four stripes, but she didn't like the tenderness around the deepest wound. "All right," she said at last. "But if the swelling gets worse, let me know."

"Roger that. Your turn to yell your lungs out? Or mine?"

"Yours. But let's eat first."

They'd been taking turns, once every half hour during the daylight, crawling up to the cave opening and shouting for help for three minutes, in hopes that someone doing a grid search would hear and rescue them. So far, neither of them had detected any sound at all on the other side of the tree trunk—not even a birdcall or the skitter of a small animal.

Whoever was doing the yelling also used that three minutes to pry away slivers along the top of the trunk with Brian's Swiss army knife, expanding the opening a little bit more each time.

Brian unwrapped the Snickers bar and cut it in half. "I have to admit, when you're hungry, something full of sugar hits the spot."

"Think of all the protein we're getting from the peanuts," Taylor said with a wry grin.

She nibbled at the chocolate and nougat and peanuts, relishing the sweetness on her tongue. "You realize all this sugar is just going to make us hungrier in about a half hour."

"I don't think I could be any hungrier," Brian said. "I can't believe how little energy I have after a week on short rations."

She decided to broach the elephant in the room. "I wonder if we're just fooling ourselves. We're almost out of food, and there's no sign that anyone out there even knows we're still alive."

"I'm making progress on that stump."

Taylor didn't point out that the entire tree trunk would need to be gone for either one of them to get out. She licked her fingers to get the last bits of chocolate off them. She turned her headlamp toward Brian and saw a speck of chocolate on the side of his mouth.

"Hold still." She used her fingertip to catch the chocolate and then pressed it against his lips. "You missed a bit."

His tongue came out and licked it away.

"I would have kissed it off," she said, "but then I'd be getting all that sustenance instead of you."

"I would have been just as happy to retrieve it from your mouth as from your finger."

Taylor laughed. "Promises, promises. You haven't kissed me even once since the last time we made love."

Taylor flushed. She hadn't brought up the subject of their lovemaking, or rather, the absence of it since their first day in the cave. She wasn't sure why they hadn't indulged again. She'd been willing, and she thought Brian had been as well, but neither of them had done anything about it.

"I guess I owe it to myself to see if there's any more of that chocolate I might vicariously enjoy." Brian's hand cupped her nape to draw her close, and his mouth captured hers in a gentle kiss.

She felt a rush of pleasure as he teased her lips apart with his tongue and they tasted each other. Her hands slid into the hair at his nape, and she groaned as his hand cupped her breast.

Abruptly, he let her go. His breathing was uneven, and his eyes glittered with desire.

"Why did you stop?" she asked.

He took another step back and said in a voice harsh with unrequited desire, "I can't give up hope that we're getting out of here. I can't! I refuse to believe otherwise. If we do this, we're liable to end up with complications neither of us wants."

Taylor felt a flare of anger, followed by a painful ache in her chest. Obviously, Brian had been listening when she'd admitted to having "feelings" for him. She was appalled to see the result of her openness: he was concerned that she might make demands on him if they were ever free. At the same time, he'd made it more than clear—by his silence—that he had no intention of making any kind of commitment to her.

"Don't worry, Brian," she said, her voice filled with scorn. "I won't expect a proposal. Or a ring I'd eventually have to give back."

He grabbed her by her arms and shook her. "Damn it, Taylor! You aren't thinking straight. I didn't see a package of pills come out of your pocket. What if you get pregnant?"

She didn't have the heart to tell him that she hadn't been taking pills since she'd broken up with good old Harry.

"The chances—" she began.

"It might not happen," he interrupted. "It probably won't happen. But what if it did? I don't want either of us to be forced into a marriage we don't want. Or end up fighting over custody of a child."

She opened her mouth to speak, but before she could, he added, "And I wouldn't want you to end the pregnancy."

He let go of her and said, "I love having you close, but it's been hell keeping my hands off you. I'm not pushing you away because I don't want you. I want you all the time." He shoved a hand through his hair, leaving it askew. "I'm trying to be reasonable here."

She was shocked. And pleased. And confused.

He wanted her? He couldn't keep his hands off her? Was his desire merely physical? Or were there emotions attached? And who said they had to be reasonable? Especially at a time like this?

"All right," she conceded. "No sex. But I don't see why we can't enjoy a little kissing and cuddling."

Brian scoffed. "You don't?"

She shook her head.

"Aw, hell. Come here."

She pulled off the headlamp and stepped into Brian's open arms. They closed firmly around her, providing comfort and security. That was good enough for now.

He murmured, "If I could survive wanting you in high school without having you, I suppose I can survive wanting you without having you here. Turn that face up to me, so I can kiss you silly."

Taylor laughed. "I think I reached silly a day or so ago."

But she made sure he found her lips in the darkness.

Chapter 14

BRIAN WAS WORRIED about his leg. The way he saw it, he wasn't going to spend thirty days starving to death. He was going to die of sepsis in ten. He hated the thought of leaving Tag behind him to die alone, but there wasn't much he could do about it. Not if his leg was as badly infected as he feared it was.

As a firefighter, he knew a lot about treating minor wounds and the symptoms that heralded an infection, like the fatigue that had dogged him over the past forty-eight hours. Sure, he needed a lot more calories to sustain his muscular body than he was getting, but his reduced activity level should have compensated. It hadn't.

This morning, their seventh day in the cave, he'd woken up with more pain in his lower leg than he'd felt yesterday. That was a very bad sign. Obviously, the Neosporin had been doing more good than he'd thought, since he'd been healing fine for the first four days. Just as obviously, the lack of it was making a difference. He wondered how much time he had before he developed a fever. And how much time beyond that before it laid him low.

It was clear Tag suspected something was up. She'd noticed the additional redness on his leg and then reached out to see if his forehead was feverish. He'd have to make excuses to keep her from realizing the truth. Too soon for his peace of mind, it was going to be impossible to hide his condition.

Brian was scraping hard enough on the trunk with the knife to put a film of perspiration on his face. He took a break to swipe it away with his sleeve, then put his mouth close to the opening and yelled, "Anybody out there? Heeeeelp! We're stuck down here. Helloooooo! Can anybody hear me?"

He listened, hoping against hope for some response. He heard an airplane somewhere overhead. He was afraid the air search would already have swept this area by the time he made a hole big enough to slip something through that could be seen. He doubted the planes would come back to the same area again, but there was always the ground search. That was far more thorough, and more likely to result in someone discovering them.

Brian began chipping away at the log again, harder, deeper, trying to get the opening big enough to push through a piece of the parachute. Since everything was burned to ashes all around them aboveground, the parachute would show up like a spill of bleach on a black shirt. The only problem was how to keep the thin cloth from blowing away in the never-ending Wyoming wind. He figured he could tie a knot in the fabric on the inside, to keep it from slipping away. Hopefully the wind would make the parachute billow and the wafting nylon would be an attraction to anyone hunting for them.

"Hey!" Tag shouted. "Time's up."

"I want to work a little longer on this log."

"You're the one who set the rules, Brian. You need to abide by them."

She was right, but he'd set the rules before he'd known he was living on borrowed time. "Another five minutes. Then I'll quit."

"I'm going to hold you to that."

Both the Swiss army knife blade and its tiny saw were losing their edges, which made the work harder. Oh, what he would have given to have his Pulaski in here! He'd have made short work of this tree trunk.

"Brian! Come quick!"

Tag's piercing shriek made his blood run cold. He scurried backward as fast as he could down the tunnel, wondering what had happened. "Are you okay? What's wrong?"

By then he was dropping out of the hole, his system charged with adrenaline. He whirled to face her and was blinded by the headlamp. "Get that damned thing out of my eyes!"

She made a distressed sound in her throat and yanked it off. It was still aimed upward, so he could see her parchment white face in the stream of light.

"What happened? Why did you scream?"

She was staring at him with wide, frightened eyes. "I saw a fox. A red fox, with a white chest and pointy ears and a big bushy tail, like you see in kids' books for the letter F. You know, F is for fox?"

"What the hell are you talking about?"

She grabbed his arm, and he winced when her finger-nails pierced his skin. "I tell you I saw a fox! I was at the back of the cave with my pants down and I heard something scrabbling in the dark and I turned and . . . it suddenly appeared right in front of me."

Her jeans were still unsnapped and unzipped, so something had spooked her. But a fox?

"Are you sure it wasn't your imagination?"

"Brian, I'm not sick. I'm not crazy. I saw it!"

He might have believed her, if she'd said she'd seen a coyote or a wolf. Yellowstone had plenty of both. But a fox? They weren't unknown in the park, but they weren't common, either.

"Do you know what that means, Brian?"

He understood what she was saying. But he was pretty much convinced she'd dreamed up the fox, because she wished so badly for what the appearance of an animal in this cave suggested. "You think there's another way out of here."

"Yes! That fox had to come from somewhere. We must have missed something the first time we searched for another way to escape."

"And the second and tenth and twenty-fourth times," Brian muttered. Every time he'd gone to the back of the cave he'd looked again, but he'd never found anything, not even so much as a hint of light or a whiff of air to suggest a way out.

"I saw what I saw," she insisted.

"Assuming you weren't hallucinating."

"I had my headlamp on," she said, her voice rising. "I

heard a sound, and when I turned, the fox's eyes reflected the light. It looked as shocked to see me as I was to see it."

"I presume it took off. Did you watch where it went?"

"It ran away."

"You didn't follow it?"

Her face looked stricken. "I was . . . I guess I was too excited . . . and my pants were down around my ankles."

"Finish zipping yourself up, and let's go see what we can find. With any luck, your fox left a trail we can follow out of here."

Brian grabbed the flashlight he'd dropped near the tunnel and followed Tag to the back of the cave. He didn't think the animal was still around, but he kept the Swiss army knife open in his other hand, just in case they ran into something more dangerous. He slipped past Tag and used the flashlight to see if he could find the fox's tracks. But there was no paw print on the stone floor where Tag said the fox had appeared.

He sprayed the light from wall to wall looking for an animal sign, but he didn't find any. Which made sense. If any animal had been coming into the cave at this end, he would have seen the tracks on one of his previous forays.

"I don't see any sign of it. Are you sure—"

"I saw a fox!" she insisted. "It wasn't my imagination. It wasn't!"

Tag sounded almost hysterical, and Brian turned and swept her into his arms, hugging her tight. Her nose was pressed against his throat, and he could feel her quivering.

"It's all right, Tag. I believe you." That wasn't entirely

true. But he was willing to give her the benefit of the doubt, because he could see she desperately needed to believe in the hope of escape that her sighting of the fox had provided.

"Look again," she insisted, shoving him away. "That animal can't have come and gone without a trace."

Brian turned and searched again, scanning the floor of the cave, which was made up of stone and hard-packed dirt, with his flashlight. Then he saw it, near the wall of the cave, where the dirt was softer. Half a paw print.

"Tag," he said. "Look."

She pressed her hands to her mouth, and her eyes filled with tears. "Oh, my God. I didn't imagine it. The fox was here."

Tag joyously threw herself into his arms, and he held her tight, rocking her from side to side. She was half laughing, half sobbing, and he felt his own throat swell with emotion. They weren't going to die. At least, not in here. Although, that wasn't a sure thing, either. A hole big enough for a fox might not be big enough for a human. Especially one with big, broad, muscular shoulders.

But Tag might be able to fit where he couldn't. He gave her a quick hard kiss and freed himself. "Let's see where that print leads."

Brian had done plenty of tracking when he was hunting with his brothers. He looked to see whether the paw print was for a right or left foot, and whether it was a front or back paw. It was a right rear paw print. He looked for where the right front foot should be if the fox had left in a hurry and, sure enough, found the barest imprint right next to the wall. No sign of the left front or rear paws showed on the cave's stone floor.

Brian kept his light aimed along the edge of the wall and found another rear paw print in the dirt. And then another front paw print.

And then the prints simply disappeared.

Chapter 15

TAYLOR HAD BEEN choking back tears ever since she'd spotted the fox. She was afraid to hope, yet hope was making her heart beat hard and her breath come in frantic pants. She heard Brian swearing under his breath, and her throat closed so tight she ended up croaking, "What's wrong?"

He turned to her, his lips a flat, angry line and his brow furrowed in confusion. "I don't see any more tracks. Where the hell did it go?"

"What do you mean? It couldn't disappear into thin air."

"Well, it's not here, and I don't see any more tracks, or any opening where it could have escaped."

"Show me the last footprint you found."

He turned the flashlight toward a faint paw print. "There it is."

She took a step closer and leaned down on one knee to examine it. "Why is it so messy around the edges?"

His eyes narrowed. "Because it . . ."

"It what?"

"It pushed off. It leaped . . ." He turned the flashlight toward the opposite wall from the one along which he'd been following tracks. Starting at the bottom of the wall, he moved the flashlight slowly upward until he was nearly to the ceiling. He focused on an anomaly near the top of the opposite wall. "It leaped up there."

"Where up there?" Taylor asked. "I don't see anything."

There was no hole where there should have been one, only a bunch of roots sticking out from the dirt wall, the way they did in places all over the cave. She'd watched Brian tug on a few of those roots when they'd searched in the first few days after they'd been trapped, but they hadn't felt any air moving or seen any light, so they'd dismissed it as a possible exit. The bunched roots the fox had apparently penetrated were exactly like other patches of roots sticking out and hanging down all over the cave.

Brian shoved a hand through his hair, leaving it tousled. "I should have looked closer," he said. "I should have investigated every damned inch of these walls."

"Look at those bunched roots, Brian. Even now it seems impossible anything could have gotten through there."

Brian heaved a frustrated sigh. "I don't see how else he could have escaped."

She eyed the tangled mass high above her head. "So, there's a hole up there?"

"Has to be."

She walked over and stood right in front of the opening. "How could it have jumped so high?"

"It's not more than seven feet." Brian pointed to what he now recognized as claw marks, a foot or so below the opening. "It dug its rear claws in the last foot or so going up. I never took a second look when I saw those vertical lines in the wall." She heard the disgust in his voice as he added, "I figured they were caused by erosion."

"I wonder what it was doing in here."

"My guess is it came here for a drink of water."

Taylor eyed the mess of roots. "How wide do you think the opening might be?"

"Not wide enough for either one of us right now," he said. "But we can fix that." He eyed the distance up to the hole and said, "If I roll up the parachute in the PG bag, and stand on top of it, I should be able to reach that spot. While I chop roots, you start collecting water in our bottles. We're going to need it when we hike out of here."

Taylor felt a surge of joy so strong she threw her arms into the air and shouted, "We're saved, Brian! We're getting out! We're going home!"

"Hold off on the celebration," he snapped. "We've got a lot of work to do to get out of here, and a long way to go before we're home safe. Save your energy and get to work."

He stalked past her, she presumed to pack the parachute in his PG bag.

"You don't have to be so mean," Taylor retorted. "I don't know about you, but I'm *happy*. And I intend to stay happy. So there!"

He was already on his way back to her, hauling the

parachute and the bag. "I'll be happy when I see those water bottles filled."

"You sound like Leah. Work, work, work."

"Move your beautiful ass, Tag."

She turned, swaying her hips suggestively as she sauntered away. "Look your fill, because you've touched this ass for the last time, Mr. Flynn. We're getting out of here, which means all bets are off."

"Yeah, yeah, yeah. I've heard it all before."

"This time I mean it. I don't care if we end up trekking through the forest for another twenty days. My body is off-limits to you. When we finally get rescued—"

"You're presuming we get rescued," he said in a harsh voice. "It's not a sure thing, Tag."

She turned back to him, her hands on her hips, her chin upthrust. "Why do you always have to spoil everything? Why can't you let me believe everything is going to turn out all right? Why are you such a pessimist?"

She watched a muscle jerk in his jaw, but he didn't reply. His face was set in forbidding lines as he turned his attention to the roots that needed cutting.

She turned on her heel and stalked away. "Damned mule-headed Flynn," she muttered. "Giving orders and expecting me to follow them. We'll see how long that lasts, once we're out of this prison. I've spent as much time trekking in the wilderness as he has. There's nothing that says we have to find our way out of here together."

Nothing except common sense.

It was entirely possible they would encounter other dangers, once they were out of the cave. A myriad of wild animals—grizzlies, black bears, cougars, moose, and wolves—could cause them grief. Lots of pitfalls—rugged terrain, geysers, and acid springs, for instance—could make their journey a nightmare. Finally, there was no telling how long their bottled water would have to last before they found water they could boil and safely drink.

On the good side, they might be able to catch fish or set a trap for something they could eat, and there might be a few berries left on bushes they could scavenge. Even if they were lost for a long time in the woods, they probably wouldn't starve.

So why was Brian in such a foul mood?

Then it dawned on her. His leg. Once they started walking, he was liable to be in a lot of pain. His wounds might get even worse.

No wonder Brian wasn't looking forward to the journey ahead of them. She quelled the impulse to return and tell him she understood why he was worried. There would be time enough for that later. Right now she needed to do as he'd asked. If they were lucky, they might be able to leave this cave by tomorrow morning.

After she'd filled the water bottles, Taylor decided she ought to spell Brian. She observed him for a few minutes, seeing how he made short work of some roots and needed to chop harder at others. His face was covered with a film of perspiration, and his T-shirt was soaked with sweat down his back and under his arms. She watched the muscles and sinews in his forearms stretch and bow. He must be tired, but he was hacking at the roots even harder now than he had been when she'd started watching.

"I can take over for a while," she said.

"No need. I'm pretty much done. As a matter of fact, I'd like to give you a shove and see how far up this hole you can get before you're stopped."

"You want *me* to go in there? What about spiders?"

"You can wear my gloves and squash them."

"And snakes?"

"The fox scared them away."

"What about a grizzly waiting for me at the other end?"

"I think we've already seen the only grizzly in these parts. Come on, Tag. You can do this."

She crossed her arms protectively over her chest. In the past, she'd been adventurous to the point of recklessness. But no one would ever have called her brave. They were two entirely different things. "Why don't you do it?"

"You're smaller. I need to know whether there's any chance of me getting out this way, or whether you're going to have to leave me behind and head out on your own."

"I'm not leaving you behind."

"Don't argue with me! Just get over here and check out the dimensions of this tunnel."

She was shocked by the harshness of his voice and the demand for obedience. She flashed her headlamp on his face and saw the desperation in his eyes.

He doesn't think he's going to be able to get through

that small opening. He thinks I'm going to have to leave him here and find help all by myself.

Her stomach knotted as she turned the light back toward the foxhole. Even though all the roots had been cleared, no light or air was coming through. What if the tunnel was too tight for her to squeeze through? She shivered. Just how long—and narrow—was it?

"Let me get your gloves," she said, "and I'll be right back."

The gloves he used while fighting fires were too big for her, and they were filthy with soot and sweat. But they would protect her hands from spiders or the bite of a small animal, like another fox coming in while she was headed out.

"Let me give you a hand up." Brian cupped his hands as though he was going to help her mount a horse.

Taylor put her foot in his hands and when he lifted, she dove headfirst into the hole he'd made. She winced and grunted when several roots gouged her sides but kept wriggling forward.

"This is pretty narrow," she called back.

"Uh-huh. What can you see ahead of you?"

Exhilarated, she shouted back, "It gets wider!" She scooched a little farther, and her spirits sank as quickly as they'd risen. "Uh-oh."

"What?"

"It just stops."

"That's impossible."

"Oh. It turns! It's almost a right angle turn. That's why we couldn't see any light and why no air was coming in."

"I can barely hear you," he shouted. "Talk louder."

Taylor was too excited to talk. The tunnel took one more turn in the opposite direction, and she could suddenly smell the charred landscape. She could feel fresh air on her face. She could, quite literally, see the light at the end of the tunnel.

She paused at the opening to look around for any danger that might be lurking, before she shoved herself all the way out. She tumbled into powdery black soot, and brushed herself off as she stood and looked around. She was in the forest, on the far side of the large boulder that had initially concealed the entrance to the cave.

Or rather, what was left of the forest after the fire had turned everything to ash. Black skeletons that had once been trees stood sentinel over carcasses of animals both small and large. Her nose pinched at the smell of burned and rotting flesh. Few trees remained standing. Most had fallen across one another like Pick-Up Sticks, as though an atom bomb had leveled the timberland.

She turned in a circle, looking for something—anything—green in the distance. There was nothing to see but scorched devastation in every direction.

"Oh, my God," she whispered. "There's nothing left." She had the urge to hurry back through the tunnel to tell Brian about the calamity she'd discovered and give him the news that the tunnel was large enough for him to escape along with her. But she thought of something else that couldn't wait.

She needed to see if Brian's communication equipment had survived the fire. After all, he'd dropped his smoke-jumping coat as well. Maybe it had protected the equipment.

It quickly became apparent that getting back to the front of the cave was no simple matter. Enormous downed trees and blackened vegetation blocked her way. She hadn't gone very far before she realized she'd been gone a long time, and Brian must be worried. It might be better if she turned around, and they looked for the missing equipment together.

She picked her way back to the tunnel and crawled into the opening through which she'd emerged. It wasn't until she'd passed the second turn that she heard Brian's frantic shouts.

"I'm here!" she called back. "I'm fine. We can both get out this way."

When she reached the cave again, she fell forward into his waiting arms. He pulled her close and slid down the wall until he was sitting with her in his lap.

"Don't ever do that again!" he snarled.

"Do what?"

"Leave me to go crazy wondering what happened to you. Why did you stop talking?"

"I didn't realize I had," she admitted. "The tunnel's plenty wide for your shoulders. It makes two dogleg turns. That's why there's no light or air on this end."

"What did you see?"

"Everything's gone. Burned up, I mean. There's nothing green in any direction."

"That doesn't surprise me. We'd better get ourselves packed up and out of here."

"Now? Why not spend the night inside, where it's safe, and leave in the morning?"

"It doesn't get dark until nearly ten. That gives us four or five hours to find our way to forest that hasn't been burned."

"Why don't we just stay here? I mean, now that we can come and go from the cave, we could open up the parachute and wait to get spotted from the air."

"What if they've already searched here?"

"There's still the ground search. We would have heard them, or they would have heard us, if they'd been anywhere near here."

"They can't possibly search the whole forest, Tag. There's too much territory to cover. They could miss us by a mile. And from what you've described, there's no food to be had around here. We'd just starve to death aboveground, instead of below it."

She hadn't let herself think about the fact that there were no berries on bushes, no small animals to trap. Brian was right. Although the cave was a safe refuge, it could end up becoming a death trap.

"Do we really have to leave right now?" she said. "I mean, one more day—"

"One more day could mean the difference between living and dying," he said in a harsh voice.

She eyed Brian sideways. Then she leaned her cheek against his, as though conceding her willingness to do as he asked. In reality, she was checking to see why his face was still flushed, long after he'd stopped working. She draped her arms around his shoulders and held him close.

He was burning up with fever.

Now she knew why Brian was in such a hurry to leave. They had a matter of days to get back to civilization, back to a hospital where his wounds could be treated with antibiotics. They were in a deadly race to save Brian's leg—and maybe his life.

Chapter 16

BRIAN WAS BATTLING against time. He felt feverish, which was the beginning of the end, where sepsis was concerned. The first thing he did, once he was outside the cave, was check to see if their communication equipment had survived the fire. He found his Bendix King, but the radio had melted. *We won't be calling for help on this.* He left it where it was.

His Pulaski tool and the cargo box, which had contained additional food, were buried under the giant spruce that had come down over the cave opening. He fought off a wave of despair. *I should have gotten this stuff inside. I should have found that foxhole and gotten us out of that cave. I should have done better . . . at everything.*

"Now what?" Tag asked.

He took a deep breath and let it out. *No sense worrying over spilled milk.* He had to focus on getting the two of them back to civilization in one piece.

Tag's face bore streaks of soot where she'd shoved her windswept blond hair behind her ears with blackened hands. In the waning light, the ravages of the seven days they'd spent in the cave were evident. Deep hollows furrowed her cheeks, and her beautiful blue eyes looked bleak. He resisted the urge to offer comfort. He didn't want to suggest their situation was hopeless.

But it's pretty damn bad.

There was no telling how much timberland the fire had consumed. Until they reached green forest they had no hope of finding berries or something they could trap and eat. Nor did they have wood for a fire to keep away wild animals that might be foraging for food in the devastation, like wolves and coyotes—and the vultures that soared overhead.

Brian had slung his PG bag over one shoulder and settled the rolled-up parachute across the other. "Are you okay with that sleeping bag?" Tag had offered to carry something, and it had a strap she could throw over her shoulder.

"I've got it. We should get moving, Brian. The sun's heading down."

It had taken far longer than he'd expected to work his way around the rock to search for the items they'd left behind, which had turned out to be an exercise in futility. He retrieved his compass from his PG bag. It had been useless while they were trapped in the cave but was absolutely necessary now. "We were headed west when we left the Otter. I think our best bet is to head back to the open area where we dropped the smoke jumpers. There's a slight chance they haven't been evacuated yet, and even if they're gone, they may have left some supplies behind."

When their job was done, smoke jumpers packed up their gear, leaving the forest as pristine as they'd found it, and hiked, sometimes several hours, to a spot where they could be picked up by a vehicle. If the site was too remote, as this one was, they'd be airlifted out by helicopter, once the fire was under control. Brian knew from experience that the odd bit of food—a heavy can or damaged item too inconvenient to haul away—might be left behind.

He tripped when his bad leg didn't make it over a downed limb and swore as he recovered his balance.

"Are you okay?" Tag asked.

"Don't be asking me every five minutes how I am," he answered curtly. "Save your breath for walking."

She shot him a look that said he was being a prick. "God forbid a Grayhawk should ask about the well-being of a Flynn. I don't know what I was thinking."

Doesn't she understand I'm trying to protect her from the truth? Doesn't she understand I want to get her somewhere she can survive on her own, if I'm laid low by the infection coursing through my body?

She was looking for an argument, but he turned his back on her and headed through the morass of downed trees, picking the easiest, safest route he could find over the steep hills and deep gullies. He never looked back, trusting her to follow.

Except for warnings like "Watch that limb," or "See that crevice?" or "Be careful here!" they didn't speak for the next two hours. Brian did his best to control his limp and avoid stumbling, because he didn't want Tag to know how much his leg was bothering him. He drank often, knowing his excessive thirst was caused by fever, and because he felt sure they'd run into a stream before they ran out of water.

He was surprised at how much woodland the fire had demolished. They'd walked nine or ten miles over burned-out terrain, and he still couldn't see green forest.

"Brian?"

He didn't slow down, simply said, "What?"

"Stop and talk to me."

"We need to keep moving."

"Brian! Stop!"

He heaved an aggrieved sigh and turned around. "What is it?"

"Your limp has gotten worse."

"So?"

"You've been drinking a lot of water."

"So?"

"How's your—" She cut herself off. "I could use a break."

"Already? Are you tired?"

"Not really, but—"

"Then let's keep moving. We have another hour of daylight before we need to stop and make camp. With any luck, we'll be past the fire's devastation by then." He turned and started walking again. He didn't want her asking any more questions. He was worried that the fire had burned its way a lot farther across the backcountry than they could walk in another hour. He wanted green limbs he could use to make a cover over their heads and boughs for a bed. He wanted the hope of the odd wild blackberry or blueberry or strawberry they could pick and eat. He wanted rabbits and squirrels they could trap and a cool stream of water running through an even cooler forest.

The August sun was hot. His body was hot. He was walking through hell, with no end in sight.

"Brian, I'm hungry."

"Me, too."

"Can we eat the last Snickers?"

Brian realized it wouldn't be a bad idea to consume a few calories, since they had another hour of walking to do before dark. "Why not?"

He could use the break. Not that he would have admitted that to a living soul. He bit back a groan as he settled on a downed pine. It felt wonderful to give his leg a rest.

Tag reached for his PG bag, and he let it slide off his shoulder into her lap. She fished around inside until she came up with the Snickers.

"Should we eat the whole thing?" she asked. "Or just half of it?"

"Let's go whole hog. We need the energy."

He watched a smile flash on her face and disappear. "Thank goodness! It feels like my stomach is folded in half with nothing in the middle."

She opened the Snickers, which was gooey from the heat, and put the wrapper back in his PG bag—no littering in the forest—then broke it in half and handed him the larger portion. As she licked her fingers clean, he watched her with hungry eyes. But he made no attempt at playfulness. He didn't have the energy.

She shot him a grim smile as she knocked her half against his half and said, "Down the hatch."

He put the whole thing in his mouth at once, chewed it, and swallowed it. He watched her nibble off a tiny bite at one corner.

She caught him staring and said defensively, "I want to make it last."

He shook his head at her logic. "It's not going to fill you any fuller just because you eat it slower."

"My stomach doesn't know that. I'm tricking it into thinking this is the *whole bar.*"

Brian chuckled. He knew they ought to get moving, but he wasn't looking forward to putting weight on his injured leg.

"What are the chances of someone finding us now that we're out here walking around?" Tag asked.

"Better than they were. Not as good as I'd like."

"What does that mean?"

"It's a big forest. It would be easy to miss us."

"You don't think we'll be found?"

"Oh, they'll find us all right. I don't know about your family, but Aiden won't stop looking until he finds us— or our cold, dead bodies."

He saw Tag shudder and wished he hadn't been so blunt.

"Leah won't stop either," she said. "It's too bad they can't work together."

"What makes you think they haven't joined forces?"

She shot him a pained look. "After all the animosity? All the dirty tricks? Why would they?"

"Since we were lost together, they could agree to call a truce long enough to pool their search efforts."

"I suppose it's possible. I wouldn't count on it."

"Did all the drama between our families have anything to do with why you broke up with me in high school? Or was it all about you wanting to leave me before I left you?"

She looked startled that he'd brought up the subject of their brief stint as boyfriend and girlfriend.

The fever must be affecting my judgment. Do I really want to open this can of worms? Yes, I do.

If it was only her fear that he would abandon her that had kept them apart, he felt sure that could be overcome. Family pressure was a trickier proposition.

"Vick didn't trust you not to hurt me. She said she wasn't going to speak to me again until I broke up with you. She meant it."

"You couldn't tell me that at the time?"

"What difference would it have made? You obviously didn't care one way or the other. You never said a word to try and change my mind."

"Only because I didn't think it would do any good. You sent me a *note*. You didn't even tell me to my face."

"There was no way we could have kept dating once our families got involved," she argued.

"Within the past month, one of my brothers married one of your sisters. Despite our fathers. Despite opposition from me."

"You tried to stop Connor from marrying Eve?"

Brian snorted derisively. "I knew—from my own

experience—that getting together with a Grayhawk was an iffy proposition for a Flynn."

He watched Tag drop her gaze, acknowledging the guilty truth of what he'd said. "And I had my divorce as an example of what can go wrong when two people don't know each other well before they marry. But despite making a marriage of convenience, my brother and your sister seemed pretty damned happy the last time I saw them in church."

"That's because Eve had a crush on Connor in high school. She was already half in love with him."

He arched a rueful brow. "What makes you think I didn't love you?"

"You never said so."

"You weren't listening. Or you've conveniently forgotten what you don't want to recall. I distinctly remember saying the words."

"Flippantly. You said 'I love you' flippantly."

He frowned. "I don't think any man says those words without considering what they mean."

"Men say sweet things to get what they want from a woman."

"You mean sex? But we were already having sex. So why did you dismiss the possibility that I meant what I said?"

"Because I didn't for a minute believe you."

"Why not?"

She looked uncertain. "You couldn't have loved me."

"Why not?"

"What does saying 'I love you' even mean?" she countered. "How do those words change anything?"

"I wanted to share everything with you. I wanted to tell you my secrets and hear yours. I wanted to hold you close and take care of you and be together forever."

"Seventeen-year-old boys don't think like that."

He shot her a sardonic look. "They don't? How would you know that? You don't have brothers. From what you've told me, King wasn't around much. From whom—which brothers or uncles or cousins or other boyfriends—did you learn how boys think?"

She pursed her lips. "What kind of secrets would you have shared?"

"You're changing the subject."

"Not really. If you want me to believe you, tell me something you would have shared with me."

"All right. I was afraid when I first went out with you that you were dating me just so you could dump me at some embarrassing moment."

"I was."

He raised his eyebrows as though to say *Thought so!*

She hesitated, then asked, "If you believed that, why did you go out with me?"

"Have you looked at yourself? You were the most beautiful girl in school."

She wrinkled her nose.

"At least in my eyes. I remember you were always laughing. I wanted to be a part of whatever it was that kept you feeling so happy."

"Have you heard of laughing to hide the pain?"

"You weren't happy?"

"When I was with Vick, I always felt good, like I belonged. But most of the time, no, I wasn't happy."

"Why not?"

"Now you're asking for one of my secrets."

"I think I'm entitled."

She hesitated so long he thought she wasn't going to speak. At last she said, "My mom ran away. My dad was always gone. I grew up feeling like there must be something wrong with me, if my parents didn't love me enough to want to stick around."

"What about your twin? What about Leah and Eve? Are you going to tell me they didn't love you?"

"It's not the same thing. I wasn't very old when my mom took off, but she took something from me—something of me—when she left. Leah's done her best, but I think she feels the loss of our mother even more than I do. Maybe my father could have filled the hole inside me, if he'd hung around more. But he didn't."

"So you didn't believe I could love you?"

"I didn't believe *anyone* could love me."

He wanted to comfort her, but what did you say to someone who felt so unwanted? So invisible? Especially when you'd loved her yourself and that love had been so soundly rejected?

The silence stretched between them

"I'm glad you had Vick," he said at last. "The two of you were like this in high school." He twisted two fingers together.

She sighed. "For the past five years, Vick has been gone from the ranch most of the time, doing whatever it is she does to save endangered species."

"Like salamanders and butterflies?"

"Like grizzlies and wolves. She's got a place in Montana I haven't seen. I keep expecting her to invite me to stay with her, but she says she only uses the cabin as a base for travel. She's been giving Matt hell about taking the ranch away from us, but she's upset more for Leah's sake—and mine—than her own. She's only home for a few days at a time before she takes off again. We Skype, we talk on the phone, we text all the time. But it's not the same. Our lives have taken different paths—mine based here, hers in Montana."

"So she's rejected you as well."

She shot him a hurt, angry look. But she didn't contradict him. "People think I'm the outgoing twin, the happy one. But if I am, it's because Vick was always there beside me. I miss her."

"You should go visit her in Montana, whether she invites you or not."

"Maybe I will. If we get out of this alive." She glanced at him and said, "So you really loved me?"

"Yeah. I was mad for you. I got pressure from Aiden to break up, but I never would have done it. I would have kept dating you no matter what he said. You never gave me the chance."

He opened his mouth to tell her that he'd never really gotten over her, that he would always regret what might have been. What would be the point? Their moment had come and gone. Besides, he wasn't sure he could ever trust any woman again, let alone a Grayhawk. Especially one who'd already rejected him once because of her family, and who also had a terrible fear of abandonment.

What if I could keep her close long enough to convince her I'm not going anywhere?

As they walked through the desolate landscape, the lowering sun at their backs, Brian let himself imagine what it might be like to fall in love with Tag again, to be the one to fill the gaping hole her parents had left inside her, to hear her laugh and know that he was the one who'd put the radiant smile on her face.

The fantasy almost made him forget he was dying.

Chapter 17

TAYLOR SPENT THE next hour thinking about what Brian had admitted. He'd *loved* her. He'd wanted to keep dating her. He'd been willing to defy his family. She was the one who'd walked away. It was a novel idea, and she was having trouble accepting it.

His admission shouldn't have made any difference to her, coming as it had, so many years later. Except, if it wasn't important, why had he mentioned it? And why had she felt such a stirring inside when he'd told her how much he'd cared?

"Brian."

He ignored her and kept walking.

"Brian!"

"What is it now, Tag?"

She heard the irritation in his voice, which suggested his leg was hurting and his fever was worse. She bit her lip, unable to ask directly whether he still had feelings for her, or whether they'd died long ago. Their love-making in the cave had been the result of seeking comfort. It didn't have more meaning than that.

Maybe it was best to let sleeping dogs lie. Once they were safe, once they were back in the world where Grayhawks and Flynns were enemies, she could ask her question and get a more honest answer.

"Look!"

Brian stopped so abruptly Taylor ran into him, nearly knocking him down. She grabbed handfuls of his shirt at the waist to keep him upright, then let go and sidestepped so she could see where he was pointing.

"The forest," she said in a whispery voice. "The *evergreen* forest. Thank you, God."

"We're not out of the woods yet."

She laughed. "Actually, it looks like we're just heading into them."

Brian chuckled. "Let me try that again. We have a ways to go before we're home free."

Taylor put a hand up to shield her eyes and admired the yellow and orange and purple sunset. "Not a minute too soon. Once the sun gets below that mountain, it's going to be as black out here as it was in that cave. How long do you think it'll take us to reach the green stuff?"

"Another ten minutes ought to do it. What was it you wanted to say before?"

"Nothing important. It can wait."

"Let's hoof it, then. It'll be a lot easier to set up camp if we still have some light to work with."

Taylor marveled at Brian's fortitude as they trekked that final ten minutes. She hadn't realized how hot it had been in the charred landscape until they reached the cool, green forest. "Oh, this is heaven," she said as they moved into the trees.

"Find as many dead limbs as you can and stack them up near this tree." He pointed to a blue spruce. "We're going to need firewood to stay warm overnight."

"You really think it's going to get that cold?"

"Better safe than sorry."

It dawned on her that a fire would also keep predators— wolves and cougars and bears—away, and Brian likely hadn't wanted to remind her of the danger.

Brian dropped the parachute and his PG bag, then pulled out his knife and began trimming off limbs to use as a bed to keep them off the ground. Once he had a carpet on the ground under the spruce, he began making a contraption she realized was a snare for a small animal. He gave her a satisfied smile. "With any luck, we'll have meat for breakfast."

Taylor had grown up eating venison and buffalo, but she'd never tried squirrel or rabbit. Her mouth watered. Right now, at the end of the seventh day since she'd eaten a decent meal, either or both sounded pretty good.

"Should I look around for a stream?" she asked.

He glanced at the disappearing sun. "We can do that in the morning."

The sun was there, and then, suddenly, it wasn't. The darkness was astonishing.

Taylor grabbed for her headlamp and snapped the light on. "I've been camping in the wilderness, but I don't remember it ever being this dark."

"We should have started the fire sooner, I guess." He began breaking up some of the dry wood she'd retrieved.

She knelt beside him as he dug a fire pit in the dirt,

then put together flammable pine needles, small twigs, and larger branches for their fire.

"The last thing we want to do is start another forest fire," he said with a crooked grin.

"That would be one way to get the smoke jumpers in here to rescue us," she pointed out.

"Unless the fire got us first." He struck a match and lit the tinder. "I'm glad I brought a whole box of matches with me. I only had two left when I looked the evening I was planning to jump the fire, and I stopped to get another box. I'd hate to think of us trying to light a fire by rubbing two sticks together."

"You've done it before, though, haven't you?"

"Eagle Scout," he said. "Survival badge."

She smiled. "That's quite an accomplishment."

"Couldn't have done it without Aiden's help. Shit. Even if he's still looking, by now he probably thinks I'm dead. I wouldn't be surprised if he said 'good riddance' and gave up the search. He hates my guts."

"I thought you two were close. Why would he hate you?"

"It's nothing that concerns you."

"Oh, I see. Now that you think we're going to get out of here, you're clamming up. Spill, Mr. Flynn. What did you do to piss off your brother?"

"I don't think I can tell you."

"Why not?"

"It concerns your sister."

"Which one?"

"Leah."

"Now you *have* to tell me. What did you guys do?"

"I bet Aiden that he couldn't get Leah to fall in love with him."

"That was a safe bet," Taylor said as she settled cross-legged on the sleeping bag Brian had laid over the boughs, so she could be warmed by the fire.

"You'd have thought so." Brian settled a larger branch on the snapping fire and joined her.

"Are you telling me Aiden won the bet? I don't believe it."

"You'd better believe it."

"I never once saw Leah with Aiden, and she never mentioned a word about him. How on earth was he able to get her to fall in love with him?"

Brian shrugged. "You got me."

"All right, so now they're in love," Taylor said. "Why does Aiden hate your guts?"

"Because I told Leah about the bet."

Taylor felt her stomach twist. "Oh, no, Brian. How could you?"

"It was a shitty thing to do, and I regret it. I didn't think Aiden really cared for her. Leah hasn't let him near her since she found out."

"Poor, poor Leah!"

"Poor Aiden. You'd think your sister would give him a chance to explain."

"Explain what? That he manipulated her into loving him to win a bet? The more I think of what the two of you did, the more furious I am with both of you! How could you hurt Leah like that?"

"If it's any consolation, I think Aiden fell in love with her for real."

"Aiden can plead all he wants. Leah will never, ever trust him again."

"Well, hell. That makes her sound like a stubborn—"

"Don't go there, Brian. It isn't Leah's fault a man she loved turned out to be a liar. And you wonder why I didn't believe you ever loved me."

"So we're back to you and me?"

Taylor huffed out a breath. "There is no 'you and me.'" She opened her mouth to say, "And there never will be." But the words wouldn't come.

She liked Brian. She always had. If he'd loved her once, maybe he could love her again. She wasn't going to close the door on a future that included a relationship with him, even if it seemed far-fetched at the moment.

"We'd better get some shut-eye," Brian said.

Taylor's stomach growled. "I've had what amounts to an entire Snickers today, and I'm still hungry."

"Imagine that," he said sardonically. "Just think how great breakfast will taste on an empty stomach."

"Presuming you catch something with that flimsy trap you made."

"My snare is a superior example—"

"Shut up, Brian, and go to sleep."

He grabbed her by the waist and spooned her against him on the sleeping bag, close enough that she could feel he was burning up with fever. He pulled the parachute over them, for her sake, she realized, since the night air was surprisingly cool.

"Brian . . ."

"What?" he murmured.

What could she say? That she wanted to bathe his

body with cool water to see if she could get his fever down? They had to save their water to drink until they found a stream. That she should take a look at his wound to see if it was worse? It was surely worse. What good would looking do, if she had no way to treat him?

How long before the fever laid waste to his body? How much farther could he go? And what would she do if he collapsed before they found water—or somebody found them?

Chapter 18

TAYLOR SLEPT RESTLESSLY, aware of the strange night sounds in a way she never had been in the past. Brian moaned in his sleep, his body like a furnace beside her. She woke up shivering and realized the fire was nearly out—and that predatory eyes gleamed back at her in the flickering light.

"Shoo!" she said, leaping up and waving her arms.

Whatever it was scurried away in the night. She realized Brian hadn't moved when she'd risen from their bed. She fed the fire, then sank on her knees beside him and put her hand to his brow. She hissed out a breath and swore, using all the bad words Leah had tried so hard to ban from her vocabulary.

Taylor wondered if Brian would be able to get up in the morning. If he didn't, she would have to search out his trap and retrieve whatever was caught in it and gut it and skin it—

That was as far as she let her thoughts go before she reined them in. It was a job she'd done in the past, just to prove she could, but she'd been sick to her stomach afterward, where no one could see her. She'd do what had to be done. And since her stomach was empty, she supposed she'd end up retching nothing.

She tried lying back down but couldn't sleep. She wondered what she should do if Brian couldn't get up when the sun rose. She was afraid to leave him alone. He would be defenseless. But if she didn't leave him, they'd soon be out of drinking water. Water was also vitally necessary to bathe Brian's body and force down the fever.

And if he *could* walk? What then? Which way would take them where they needed to go?

Downhill. Downhill usually led to water. This area of the forest was flat, and the trees were too thick to see the mountains that she knew surrounded them. So which way was downhill?

Taylor tried to stay calm. Panicking wasn't going to help either of them. She needed to sleep, to rest her body, so she could do whatever needed to be done in the morning. She closed her eyes and heard Brian's ragged breathing. The scurrying sounds of small animals in the dark. The hoot of an owl. And the whisper of the pines in the gentle night breeze.

She tried to imagine what it would have been like to be a pioneer woman crossing this land for the first time. She smiled at the image of herself in homespun and farmer's boots. How strong—of body and heart—those first women must have been! How fearless! She wondered if she would've had the courage to get this far. At the moment, she needed all the nerve she could muster

just to face another day in the wilderness. Tamped-down
terror had her heart working overtime.

The next thing Taylor knew, freckles of sunlight were
dancing across her closed eyelids. She lay still, listening,
then slowly opened her eyes. She heard a magpie's rau-
cous wake-up call, and a gust of wind rustling the greener
than green pines. She could see bits of blue sky and a few
fluffy clouds. She might have been on a campout with her
sisters. Everything that had happened seemed like a horrible dream from which she was finally waking up. Taylor looked to her left, to share the enchanting moment
with Brian.

He was gone.

She leapt to her feet, certain he'd become delirious
with fever and wandered into the forest. "Brian! Where
are you?"

"Don't get your panties in a wad. I'm right here."

She whirled and saw him standing with a skinned rabbit hanging from one hand and a water bottle in the
other, a grin on his face.

She leapt at him and pounded his chest with her fists.
"Don't ever do that to me again!"

"Ow!" he said, stepping out of the way so he wouldn't
get pummeled. "That's a fine thanks for catching us
breakfast and finding us water."

"I woke up and you weren't here! Why did you leave
without saying something?"

"You looked like you needed the sleep. Besides, as I
recall, you're not too keen on butchering game."

She narrowed her eyes suspiciously. "How do you
know that?"

"We boys did a lot of spying on you girls back in the day."

She made a disgusted face. "I should've known."

"There's a shallow stream about a city block in that direction." He pointed toward the rising sun. "I took a quick dip with my bar of soap. You might like to do the same." He pointed to the soap, which he'd left out on a rock.

The thought of being able to wash her hair and scour her body sounded wonderful. "Is it safe for me to go there alone?"

"I didn't see any bear sign or cougar or wolf tracks. You'll be fine. Breakfast will be ready by the time you get back."

"A bath and breakfast both?" she quipped. "You *are* an Eagle Scout."

He laughed.

It wasn't until she was halfway to the stream that Taylor realized Brian had been acting so normally, she hadn't even asked how he was feeling. Last night she'd been sure he was dying of fever. This morning he was smiling like he didn't have a care in the world. What had happened? How had he bounced back so completely? Had he fought off the fever against all odds? Was his leg healing after all?

She started to turn around and ask, but the lure of enough water to bathe kept her moving forward. She found the shallow stream without any trouble and immediately shed her clothing and sat down. She knew enough not to drink the water before it had been boiled. Mountaineers who'd gone to Nepal, and returned to

Wyoming's Grand Tetons to hike and climb, had brought back foreign strains of giardia, a parasite living in the water that caused dysentery.

She was careful not to get the water in her mouth as she scooped up enough to splash on her face and into her hair. She lathered Brian's soap and washed everywhere, reveling in the feeling of being clean again. She hadn't realized how much she'd missed the luxury of bathing.

Taylor had her head bent low, rinsing her hair when she heard something move in the bushes behind her. She threw her head back to get her hair out of her eyes and rose from the water, ready to flee.

"Whoa there! It's just me."

She whirled, her heart hammering, swiping at the water and soap in her eyes and sputtering as water sluiced across her mouth. "Why did you sneak up on me like that?"

It never occurred to her to cover her body. Brian had already seen all there was to see when they were teenagers.

"Good lord." He said it softly, like a prayer.

It took her a moment to realize he was looking at her with awe. And with reverence.

"What's wrong? You've seen all this before."

"Never like this," he said. "The way you slung your hair back, you looked like some goddess rising from the sea. I don't know if I ever said it as a kid, but I'm saying it now. You're the most beautiful creature I've ever seen."

Taylor felt a sudden flush on her upper chest which

spread quickly, putting a blush on her cheeks. She wasn't sure what to say.

"I'm sorry I interrupted your bath," he said. "You were gone so long I was getting worried."

"How long have I been gone?"

"Almost an hour."

"I had no idea so much time had passed. I guess I was enjoying this too much." She plopped back down and splashed her fingers through the water, scaring away tiny fish. "This is heaven." She scooped up two handfuls of water and threw it onto her hair to continue rinsing out the soap.

"Want some help? I brought a bottle to fill with water to be boiled. I might as well use it to rinse your hair."

She wanted to refuse, but it was time-consuming to scoop water with her hands, and he could simply fill the bottle and pour it over her head. "All right. Thanks."

To her surprise, Brian sat on a flat stone and pulled off his shoes and socks, then stood and filled the bottle.

He stepped gingerly into the stream, the bottom of which was full of water-smoothed stones. Her skin felt warm where he laid a hand on her shoulder to steady himself as he kicked aside enough stones to make a comfortable spot to stand.

She leaned her body forward, so the soap would sluice off easily.

As Brian poured, he ran his hands gently through her hair. When the bottle was empty, he handed it to her and said, "Refill this."

While she did, he massaged her shoulders.

"That feels good," she murmured.

He took the filled bottle from her and poured, rinsing until she finally saw no more suds. She raised her head, pushed her hair back, and said, "Thanks. I'm good."

He squatted down so they were eye to eye. Taylor resisted the urge to cover her breasts. Instead, she met his gaze, stunned by the admiration she found there.

Brian pulled off his T-shirt, treating her to a view of a broad, muscular chest fanned with dark hair and a belly that looked concave. He used his shirt to dab the water from her eyelashes, from her cheeks, and from her lips. Then he leaned over and kissed her on the mouth.

She waited for him to touch. She wanted him to touch. When he didn't, she laid a hand on his chest, watching his muscles flex and his body quiver as she ran her fingertips through the thick mat of dark curls that covered his naked flesh. She looked up at him, an invitation in her eyes to do more than kiss. She watched the sudden flare of desire before he lowered his gaze to his hands, which were bunched into fists around his T-shirt.

Taylor felt the rejection all the way to her marrow.

They were out of the cave now. They were free. Brian might like her looks, but he didn't want anything more to do with *her*.

He rose abruptly, lifting her along with him.

Taylor swallowed her disappointment. She would be damned before she let Brian Flynn know he'd hurt her feelings.

He let go of her arms and said, "Thank you."

"Why are you thanking me? You did all the work."

"For allowing me the joy of seeing you like this."

Confused by the contradiction between the avid look

in Brian's eyes and the sweet words he was speaking—and the sting of his recent rejection—Taylor suddenly felt the need to cover herself. She turned her back on him, grabbed her chambray shirt, and pulled it on.

His hands settled on her shoulders as he turned her back around. "Let me."

Why was he suddenly being so tender? What did it mean? Did he want her? Or didn't he?

Brian kissed his way up her body as he buttoned the buttons that hadn't been lost when he'd stripped her in the cave. When he reached her throat, he kissed the space below her chin, then nuzzled her neck.

"I'm not completely dry. You're going to end up with giardia," she muttered.

He grinned. "It'll be worth it."

She took a step back, grabbed her bikini underwear—which she'd washed and hung on a nearby branch, and which was nearly dry—and pulled it on under her shirttails. Then she reached for her jeans and zipped herself into them. She grabbed her still-drying bra from another branch and stuffed it into her jeans pocket. She'd experienced her share of mistakes and misunderstandings. Her life was messed up enough. She didn't need Brian Flynn complicating it any more than it already was. If he wanted her at arm's length, that was where she'd stay.

"Why aren't you sick with fever?" she demanded.

"I have no idea."

"How's your leg?"

"Hurts like a sonofabitch."

"Then you're *not* well."

"Nope."

Maybe *that* was why, despite the desire she'd seen in his eyes, Brian had rejected her. Maybe he was in too much pain to be thinking about sex. Taylor felt awful, but not awful enough to relax her guard entirely. "Is your fever gone?"

"Yep."

"How did that happen?"

"I don't know, but I'm not going to hang around here waiting to find out. Let's eat breakfast, pack up our stuff, and get moving."

Taylor hadn't washed her socks because she wasn't sure they'd get dry. They were stiff with sweat and dirt. She sat on a rock and pulled them on anyway, then tugged her hiking boots on and laced them up. When she was done, she stood and gestured back in the direction of their camp. "After you."

He laughed, his eyes crinkling at the corners. "I'm glad you recognize who the leader is around here."

She linked her arm with his and said, "I'll follow anyone who'll get me back to civilization. Lead on, Mr. Flynn."

Chapter 19

BRIAN HEADED IN the same direction they'd been going when they'd stopped the night before. He was careful not to limp, even though his leg ached.

There was an easy explanation for why his fever had abated overnight, but he'd decided not to share it with Taylor. The truth was he'd woken in the middle of the night so hot that he'd gotten up to search for somewhere he could cool off. He might even have been a bit delirious, although he wasn't sure. He'd accidentally stumbled upon the stream, or rather, stumbled into the stream, where he'd spent the rest of the night.

His head had remained on the bank, while his body, including his wounded leg, had spent several hours being refreshed by cool flowing water. When he'd examined his leg this morning, it was still red, but the swelling was way down, and his fever seemed to be gone.

He had no doubt it would be back. Which was why he hadn't made love to Tag. When he'd seen her rise out of the water and watched it sluicing off her curves, he'd wanted her more than he'd wanted anything in a very long time. But he wasn't sure how long he had before his body betrayed him. How long he had before the lethal fever returned.

He hadn't been able to resist kissing her. Caressing her. Letting his eyes devour what he was afraid to take. He could see she was willing, which made it all the more difficult to refuse them both. She was clearly distressed by his behavior, and he'd wanted to explain. But he couldn't do that without revealing how dire his situation was. With any luck, they'd find help—or help would find them—before that became necessary.

In the end, he told himself that whatever energy he had left was better spent getting them back to civilization than indulging his need to touch her and taste her and put himself inside her. Once they were safe, he would have all the time in the world to make love to her.

If you get out of this mess, are you really going to pursue Tag? With all the shit Angus will rain on your head if you get involved with one of King's Brats? After what you did to fuck things up between Aiden and Leah, Aiden will go nuts.

Was he going to let his family dictate who he could and could not love? Both he and Tag had succumbed to family pressure when they were kids. They weren't kids anymore. He liked her. He wanted her. And he was damned well going to find out whether there was any hope that whatever spark had arced between them all those years ago could be fanned back into flame.

"Keep a lookout for Chaos Mountain," he said. "We weren't far from there when we left the plane."

"I can't see much past the trees," Tag replied.

The forest was so overgrown it was nearly impenetrable. The going was slow. But they had enough boiled water to last them for a couple of days, and they'd eaten a hearty breakfast that morning to give them the strength to keep moving. To his surprise, Tag had consumed the roasted hare with relish.

"You never told me how you liked the rabbit," he said.

"It could have used a little salt and maybe some sage or thyme, but overall, it was delicious. I think I could have eaten it raw, I was so hungry."

They were able to walk side by side for a short distance, and Brian took advantage of the opportunity to search Tag's face for signs of the brief starvation they'd endured in the cave. It was there in her gaunt cheeks. What he found more provocative was the worried look staring back at him from her blue eyes.

"Chin up," he said. "We're bound to find a logging trail or a Forest Service road or the spot where the jumpers dropped. It's only a matter of time before we get rescued or discover a way out on our own."

"Don't bullshit me. You forget I flew over this area. I know how isolated it is. We're miles from any road. We've got shade from the sun and food and water in this forest, but we're completely hidden from anyone searching for us from the sky." She paused, then added, "I don't know how you got rid of that fever, but without antibiotics, we both know it's coming back. Maybe we ought to find ourselves a spot in an open meadow to set up camp and lay out that parachute, so it can be seen from the air."

"What if no one happens to fly by and notice us?"

Tag made a disgruntled sound. "You're being pessimistic again."

"No. I'm calling it like I see it. Walking out of here is our best chance of surviving." He didn't mention the fact that if anything happened to him, her chances of lasting in the wilderness diminished. Two people had a far better chance of fending off predators and finding water and food than one. "Right now I feel fine," he said. "So long as I do, I don't intend to sit around in the sunshine and wait for help to arrive. So move your beautiful ass, Tag."

She shot him a narrow-eyed look and marched off ahead of him. "You're awfully bossy."

He remembered ordering her out of the plane with exactly those words. He wondered if they'd have been better off staying with the Otter. Certainly, it would have been easier for searchers to find them, especially if they'd remained near the plane. But he'd been fearful they would end up crash-landing in the middle of the fire, from which there would be no escape.

She stopped abruptly and said, "Do you hear that?"

He paused and listened. He heard aspen leaves fluttering in the wind. He heard chirping birds and buzzing flies.

And he heard a small plane.

"Move!" he ordered.

Tag looked at him helplessly until he gestured toward an open area to their right.

"Anywhere is better than here!" he snapped.

She began to run, the sleeping bag bouncing on her back. "It's too far!" she yelled breathlessly. "We'll never get there in time."

"The plane might be circling. Run!"

It was another one of those tiny meadows that appeared in the forest with no rhyme or reason. He slung the red-and-white parachute off his shoulder and shook it so the wind could catch it and spread it to its full size. Tag was waving her arms, her head back, her gaze aimed at the sky.

"We're down here! We're here!" she shouted.

He didn't point out that there was no way anyone in the air could hear her. Waving her arms couldn't hurt, but it probably wouldn't help much either. He was counting on the billowing parachute to announce their location. Assuming the plane flew over this meadow. And someone was looking down at the right moment and saw them.

He tried to find the plane in the sky but couldn't locate it. "Can you see where it is?"

She put a hand up to shade her eyes from the sun and searched the cloudless blue sky. "No. Can you?"

He shook his head but kept looking.

"Do you think it's searching for us?"

"I doubt it would be flying that low if it weren't."

"Why don't they see us?"

Because we're a dot on the landscape. Because they're at the wrong angle and the trees are blocking their view.

Because they're only in the air at all because someone is paying them to fly, and they've long since given up expecting to find us.

He thought all those things, but he didn't say them. He could hear the plane moving away.

"We need smoke," Tag said, her voice frantic.

"We couldn't get a fire built in time."

"We could try!"

"It would be a waste of time."

"They're leaving," she cried, shooting him a panicked look. "Do something, Brian!"

"I'm sorry, Tag. Maybe we'll get lucky next time."

"*Next time* you'll have us hidden in the forest again," she retorted.

They'd never seen the plane, only heard it. It hadn't seen them, or it would have done a flyover to let them know they'd been spotted. Brian offered what little encouragement he could. "Chances are they've found the Otter by now. They know which direction it was flying, and they did the math to figure out how far the plane glided before it hit the ground. If they found the plane, they know we got out alive."

"But they don't know whether we left the Otter after it crashed or by jumping," she protested.

"They likely searched the area near the plane first. Now we know they've finished their search there and have moved off to this area. There might even be people on the ground somewhere around here. They would have used the few roads that exist to drive in, so if we can find a road we're halfway home."

He saw her shoulders slump before she lifted her chin,

squared her shoulders and said, "All right, then. Let's get moving."

"That's my girl."

She arched a brow. "I'm not your girl or anyone else's. At least, not yet."

He laughed and said, "*That's* my girl."

Chapter 20

TAYLOR KEPT HER banter with Brian upbeat for the next four hours, as they made their way through the forest toward Chaos Mountain. He was limping—badly—and his face looked flushed, which told her his fever was back.

Maybe if she suggested a short rest, he would take one. "I'm ready for a break."

"Let's keep moving," he countered.

She considered his unwillingness to sit down as evidence that he knew how grim his situation was. She decided to bring up another subject that concerned her. "I've been smelling smoke."

"Me, too."

"Do you think it's the same fire? Or another one?"

"No way of knowing."

Taylor wondered if they were walking right back into danger. It wasn't beyond the realm of possibility that the forest fire they'd come here to fight wasn't yet out, eight days after they'd gone missing. "So there might be jumpers out here somewhere."

"If the fire's still out of control, they're out here."

"Aren't you worried that we might get ourselves into trouble again, if we keep walking without knowing where the fire is?"

"Have you seen the sky?"

She looked up. "What about it?"

"Those are rain clouds. They've been developing all morning."

She gave the sky a more lengthy examination through the tall pines. The clouds were merely gray overhead, but in the distance, they had darkened to an angry purple bruise. "How can you tell the storm is coming this way?"

"I've studied a bit. And I have lots of experience praying for rain."

She laughed. "I guess you would. I've seen how hard you smoke jumpers work on the ground. All that digging and cutting and whacking at flames. I don't know how you do it for hours—and days—on end. Or why you do it, for that matter. It's brutal work in awful conditions. I know the pay is good, but you don't need the money. What's the attraction?"

"I love the challenge of conquering the fire. It's the most primal sort of battle—man against the elements. I even appreciate the fear. That's part of what creates the excitement, knowing your life is on the line. The jump from an airplane into a small clearing surrounded by burning forest is literally a death-defying feat. The fire could turn and kill you in seconds. The cherry on top is the fact that you're doing something extraordinary, something not many people can physically or psychologically handle. It's addictive. That's why smoke jumpers come back year after year."

He plopped onto a knee-high stone shelf. "Okay. I admit it. I'm bushed."

That was quite a concession for a man who could fight a forest fire nonstop for three days without sleep. She slid to the ground beside him. "I'm glad you quit first. I didn't want to be a 'girl' and ask for special treatment."

He grinned. "God forbid."

She noticed he'd settled on a ledge instead of dropping to the ground. Was it because he thought he might not be able to get up again? Or that he might be tempted to stretch out and sleep? "I could use some water," she said.

He shifted his PG bag off his shoulder, pulled out one of the two water bottles, and handed it to her.

She drank, then handed the bottle back to him. Brian drank thirstily, then recapped the bottle, which she noticed was half empty, and stowed it again.

"How about something to eat?" she asked.

"I'm not hungry."

That wasn't good. He should be as starved as she felt. The fever must be curbing his appetite. She'd found a few blueberries—a very few—on a bush and stuffed them down, but her stomach had been gnawing at her to be fed for the past hour. "Would you mind if I have something?"

He handed the PG bag to her. "I'm not sure there's much left."

She rooted through the bag and realized there was

nothing left except a few packets of coffee. She'd forgotten that they'd eaten the last Snickers yesterday. No sense reminding him they were out of food, if he didn't already know. She handed the bag back to Brian and said, "I can wait if you can."

"Pretty soon there won't be enough of you left to squeeze," he teased.

Her lips twisted in a wry smile. "Look who's talking. If I'm not mistaken, you're an inch away from having your belly against your backbone."

He laughed. "You noticed?"

She focused her eyes on his belly and the memory of everything that had happened in the stream that morning came racing back. She lifted her gaze and saw her feelings of desire reflected back in his eyes.

He swallowed hard, then said, "Ready to go?"

"Not really."

"We can't stay here, Tag."

She knew he was right, but he looked flushed and feverish. She wondered where he was finding the will to go on . . . and what she would do when he could no longer keep moving.

"Shouldn't we have seen that mountain by now?" she asked.

"Yeah. But we could be off just a little and miss it."

"I've noticed you checking the compass. Which way have we been heading?"

"Southwest."

She didn't know why she'd bothered asking. They were in one of the most remote areas of the United States. No cell service, no roads, no nothing. It was beginning to dawn on her just how small their chances were of being found. She'd noticed Brian had followed the stream all morning, but she hadn't heard it for quite a while.

"How far are we from the stream?" she asked.

"It's off to the east a little."

"Why aren't we following it?"

"I didn't want to tell you, but it petered out."

"It just . . . stopped?"

"Headed underground, I guess."

"So, no bath tonight?" she said ruefully.

"Not unless we find a pond or a hot spring or another stream."

"I vote for a hot spring," she said, rising from the ground, conceding that it was necessary to keep walking.

"Just make sure before you jump into some pond that it isn't filled with sulfuric acid."

"Are you kidding? Yellowstone has springs that can dissolve bones?"

"The ones I know about are farther north, near Montana," he said. "But yeah, they're deadly. Any hot springs we find will more than likely roast human skin."

"Remind me to stick something in besides my finger to test the temperature," she muttered.

"Just be careful, and you'll be fine."

She wondered what other pitfalls lay in wait out here, things she knew nothing about. If anything happened to Brian, she'd be . . .

There was no longer an "if" attached to that statement. Brian was sick and getting sicker. She was going to need all her wits and wisdom to take care of both him and herself.

She heard a rumble of thunder and looked over her shoulder. "What do we do if we get lightning with this rainstorm?" she asked. "I mean, is it better or worse to be here in the forest?"

"It would be worse if we were out in the open. In that case, we would need to find a ravine where we could crouch and be the lowest thing on the horizon. Right now we need to look for a copse of trees smaller than the rest and hang out there. Not standing up, but not flat along the ground, either."

"Crouched, then."

He nodded.

She heard a thunderclap and felt the first raindrop hit her nose. It was followed quickly by several more. And then, by a deluge.

She shrieked and hurried to the closest tree to seek shelter under its limbs.

"Not there! Over here." He'd headed for a smaller group of trees, just as he'd instructed her to do not a minute ago.

She watched as he tried, and failed, to ease himself down on his haunches. He made a face and bit back an oath, then dropped onto his butt under one of the shorter trees. The flexibility that he'd had that morning, the ability to squat next to her, was gone, which meant his wound was inflamed again. Likely his leg had swollen too much for him to easily bend it.

"This is not how it's supposed to be done," he said. "But damn it, this is the best I can do."

She knelt beside him. "How about if I spread the chute in the limbs to give us a little protection from the rain?"

"Sure. If you want to bother with it. I doubt it's going to help much."

Taylor took the parachute from him and shook it out across several of the lower limbs and then crawled under it. She noticed that instead of standing to move under the chute, Brian simply used his arms to scoot closer to her, then leaned his back against the tree. She was sure there was some sort of rule against that, too, but he was obviously not in good enough shape anymore to keep himself upright without support.

"I love thunderstorms." She always had. But she'd rarely been out in the open like this when one occurred. A moment later, jagged lightning streaked across the sky and struck horrifyingly close to them. She could smell the stench of cordite and the hairs on her arms stood up as though electrified.

Taylor shuddered. "That was a bit too close for comfort."

She moved closer to Brian, and he slid a comforting arm around her shoulders.

"If we were doing this right," he said, "we should be keeping our distance from each other."

It took her a moment to realize what he meant. "So if lightning strikes one of us, it won't get both of us?"

His lips quirked. "You got it in one."

She heard thunder boom and pressed herself closer to him. "To hell with that."

Brian lifted her and settled her in his lap. "Might as well be hanged for a sheep as a lamb."

She laid her head against his shoulder and slid her arms around his neck. "I've never understood what that saying meant."

"If the punishment for a bad action (sitting too close together) and an even worse one (holding you in my lap) are the same (death by lightning strike), there's no reason not to do the worse one."

"Makes sense." She pulled his head down so she could reach his mouth and gently kissed him. She began tugging his shirt up with one hand while she slid the other into his hair.

They weren't going any farther today. Brian's fever was back. The only water they had was what he carried. It no longer mattered that she was a Grayhawk, and he was a Flynn. It no longer mattered that he'd used his pain as an excuse not to make love to her that morning. This was likely the beginning of the end for both of them, unless a miracle happened.

And she'd never had much faith in miracles.

"What are you doing, Tag?"

"Taking our lives in my hands by getting really, really close. After all," she said, smiling against his lips, "might as well be hanged for a sheep as a lamb."

Chapter 21

"WHAT IS THAT?" Leah said, pointing to a melted mess near a downed tree. "That looks like—"

"It's Brian's radio." Aiden shoved aside several burned limbs, then kicked at something metal. It was the half-crushed, blackened cargo box. "This burned up with a lot of stuff still inside."

She was surprised by how calm he sounded. Either they were very close to finding her sister and his brother, or they'd just found evidence that the two of them had perished. Either way, she'd expected more of . . . something . . . from Aiden.

Then she heard the excitement she'd been expecting.

"Look! Look here!"

She hurried over to see where he was pointing. "What am I supposed to see?"

"This tree trunk. See where the bark is missing on the other side? Someone's been hacking at it!"

Aiden leaned over the enormous trunk and peered into the wafer-thin opening.

"What do you see?"

"Nothing." He leaned his mouth closer and yelled, "Hello! Anybody in there?"

"Do you really think they're in there?" Leah said, trying to look in, but seeing the same "nothing" as Aiden. "Why aren't they answering?"

"Maybe they can't."

Taylor and Brian had been missing for eight days. They would die without water in three. Leah curled her hands into fists. *They're not dead. Please don't be dead.*

Aiden surveyed the clearing. "There's plenty of room here for a helicopter." He took out his satellite phone and ordered up a chain saw and more searchers, giving their coordinates.

"I don't understand why they're not saying anything," Leah said, pacing back and forth in front of the log.

"Maybe they were badly burned by the fire. Or maybe the smoke got them."

"Don't say things like that."

"I don't want you to get your hopes up, Leah. They've been missing a long time, especially if they've been stuck in that cave without water. I want you to prepare yourself—"

She put her hands to her ears. "Stop it! Just stop it! Don't say things like that."

She fought the comfort of his arms when he wrapped them around her. But his hold was inexorable, and a moment later she was sobbing against his chest, all the fear she'd been holding inside suddenly released in a torrent of tears. She put a hand to her mouth to stifle the agonized sounds, but the tears continued streaming from her eyes.

"Don't, Leah. You'll make yourself sick."

She choked back the next sob that threatened and took the handkerchief Aiden offered. His hands fell away as she stepped back to wipe her eyes and blow her nose. It took her a few moments to compose herself, and she was grateful he didn't offer platitudes. At last she said, "I can't believe they escaped the fire and ended up dying in some cave."

"Maybe I'm wrong," he said. "Maybe they got out before the tree came down."

She didn't ask the obvious questions. *Why is Brian's radio out here? Why didn't he take the supplies from the cargo box with him into the cave?* Instead she said, "I think my father's given up."

He rubbed the back of his neck. "Mine, too. Angus thinks we missed finding the bodies at the site where the plane went down."

"Finding Brian's equipment here proves they left the plane before it crashed. That chipped log suggests they found safety in this cave."

"Which might have become their tomb," Aiden added under his breath.

Leah couldn't contradict him. They'd both done more shouting into the mouth of the cave while waiting for the helicopter to arrive with reinforcements, to no avail.

"Leah . . ."

Leah had heard her name spoken more than once over the many days they'd spent searching together. She knew Aiden wanted to talk about their marriage. Or rather, the fiasco their marriage had become. She wasn't ready to do that. She hadn't made up her mind yet whether she wanted to stay in or get out, and she didn't want to be talked into some sort of reconciliation with clever words.

So far, she'd been able to keep Aiden from speaking merely by meeting his gaze with flattened lips and a narrow-eyed glance. This time, she saw a firming of his jaw and a lifting of his chin that suggested a warning glare wasn't going to do the job.

"I deserve a chance to explain myself," he said. "You owe me that."

She turned her back on him and walked away, desperate to put some space between them, even though there was nowhere she could really go to escape in this desolate landscape.

"Turn around, Leah," he said in a harsh voice. "Listen to me."

She whirled and stood with her arms crossed. "Nothing you say will ever make a difference."

"Then you might as well let me speak."

"Fine. Go ahead. Make your excuses."

She should have known he would close the distance between them, that he would end up right in front of her, close enough to touch. She wanted to lower her gaze and avoid looking at him. She wanted to take a step back, so she wouldn't feel the anger coming off of him in waves. She did neither.

"It's true I made a bet with Brian."

She felt her throat clog at his admission and her eyes burn with threatened tears. She would *not* cry. She'd already done too much of that. She lowered her gaze so he wouldn't see the tears that welled up despite her efforts to blink them back.

"I never thought . . . I didn't realize . . ." He made a disgusted sound. "Aw, hell, baby, I—"

Her head came up, along with a surge of anger that made her face flush with heat. "Don't you *dare* call me *baby*," she snarled. "I let you use a word like that to me because I was willing to be coddled—like a child—by a man I thought loved me. I'm a grown, thinking, rational human being, not a *baby*. So don't diminish me by calling me one."

She'd never in her life, before she'd dated Aiden, allowed herself to be pampered and called silly love names. It had felt too dangerous. If you were a *baby*, you were necessarily helpless. That was fine if the person calling you that was big and strong and you trusted him to protect you against any and all threats.

After discovering Aiden's deceit, his willing manipulation of her to win a bet with his brother, she felt stupid for believing one of "those awful Flynn boys" could fall in love with her. Aiden had said and done what was necessary to get her to fall in love with him. And she'd been so desperate for love that she'd willingly surrendered in his embrace.

Well, not again. Never again. No matter what he said.

"Well?" she said sarcastically. "What's your excuse for lying to me, Aiden? For allowing me to marry you under false pretenses? That's what I'll never understand. How could you allow a bet with your brother to go so far? I thought you loved me. I thought you cared about me. To find out—" Her throat was so thick and painful with emotion she couldn't speak.

"I'm sorry."

"Sorry?" she croaked. "Oh, God. You're *sorry*?" An apology meant it was all true. An apology meant he'd never loved her. An apology was the worst thing he could offer her.

"I—"

"No! Don't say another word. I can't bear to hear how sorry you are. It's too late. The time for explanations would have been *before* you made me your wife." No excuse for his betrayal was good enough to deserve her forgiveness now.

Leah believed she'd silenced him. She should have known better. A moment later he gripped her arms and pulled her close enough that she could feel his hot breath on her cheeks.

"I let it go so far because I fell in love with you. I let it go so far because I couldn't imagine my life without you. I let it go so far because I feared exactly what's happening now. I knew if you ever found out, you'd never forgive me, or believe me when I told you the truth."

He hesitated, then admitted, "I never intended to fall in love with you."

She winced and bit back a moan.

He shook her and said, "Look at me, damn it!"

When she did, his eyes were filled with anger . . . and hopelessness.

"Don't you get it?" he raged. "I didn't want to love you. I never intended to love you, but I do. More than I ever imagined it possible to love anyone."

Leah believed he hadn't wanted to fall in love with her. She was finding it impossible to believe that he had.

"How did this miraculous change in your feelings occur? When exactly? Why exactly?"

He seemed lost for words. She believed it was because he'd never actually fallen in love with her.

He yanked off his ball cap, shoved a hand through his hair, then pulled the hat back down low. "How the hell do I know when I started loving you? That first kiss? That awful wedding night, when *you* consoled *me* because the sex was so bad? Somewhere in between? The point is I love you, Leah. I didn't tell you about the bet, because I could see no good reason for forfeiting a lifetime of happiness over some ridiculous wager I'd made with my brother, which you had no way of ever discovering. I would have told you someday."

She snorted.

"But not before we'd been married so long, and you were so sure of my love, that it wouldn't matter."

He followed that proclamation with a searing kiss that curled her toes up in her boots. He might have kept on kissing her, except the helicopter appeared overhead, and a passionate kiss between Grayhawk and Flynn would have been difficult to explain. Instead, he let go of her and turned to wave a hand at the copter pilot and gesture toward a landing area he'd cleared while they'd been waiting.

Leah was left breathless. And speechless. She hadn't accepted Aiden's apology, but where excuses were concerned, he'd come up with a doozy.

I love you. More than I ever thought it possible to love anyone. A man didn't make a statement like that unless he meant it. Leah thought back to moments in their relationship when Aiden had started to speak and then stopped himself. Had those aborted efforts been attempts to tell her the truth? Had he really been so afraid that she wouldn't give him a chance to explain?

She heaved a sigh. He'd been right. That was exactly what she'd done. Refused to listen. Refused to hear the "truth." Even now, she was afraid to believe him. What if he was lying through his teeth?

Although, what would be the point of that? Why try so hard to make amends, if he didn't want to stay married? If he'd really been a scoundrel, why not simply let her get the annulment she'd been planning as soon as there was time?

That was another thing. She'd had plenty of time to end their marriage, if that was what she'd wanted. What had she been waiting for? Was it possible she didn't want an annulment? That she'd been waiting for an explanation from Aiden that wouldn't make her feel like the biggest fool alive for falling in love with him?

Did she still love him? More to the point, could she ever truly trust him again? Could she ever make herself vulnerable enough to be the one who was "cared for" in the relationship?

Leah had spent her whole life caring for others, which was why it had been such a novelty to be called "baby" and to willingly let Aiden "take care" of her. She'd done her best to reciprocate, cosseting Aiden in a way she'd never imagined a man might enjoy. She'd discovered that allowing someone else to see your faults and foibles could happen only when a person trusted the other enough to be vulnerable in his or her presence.

She'd revealed far more to Aiden of her insecurities than she'd ever told another living soul. Which was why his betrayal hurt so much.

What if he'd been telling the truth just now? What if he really did love her? Where did they go from here?

Nowhere until Brian and Taylor are found.

The sudden silence of the buzzing chain saw brought her back to the present. Leah realized that while she'd been caught up in her thoughts, Aiden had removed enough of the tree trunk to free the passage into the cave. The opening was surprisingly small. She could imagine Taylor making her way inside, but it didn't look large enough for Brian's broad shoulders.

A moment later, Aiden proved her wrong by donning a headlamp and wriggling into the hole himself. She stood there only a moment, before she threw herself down and crawled in after him.

She was grateful Aiden was there to catch her as she tumbled the last several feet headfirst into the cave. She pulled a flashlight from the pocket of a vest she wore and sprayed the light around the cave. Empty bean cans, aluminum foil, Kleenex, and other detritus littered the cave floor.

Leah picked up the empty tube of antibiotic ointment, and numerous bloody pieces of gauze. "One of them is injured."

She saw the furrows on Aiden's brow and knew he was wondering along with her which one was hurt, and how badly he or she was wounded.

Then she saw the shine on the cave wall. "They had water!"

"So they didn't die of thirst."

"Where are they now? They couldn't have gotten out the way we came in."

"Wait here while I check—"

Leah realized Aiden expected to find Taylor and Brian's bodies somewhere in the cave, perhaps dying of whatever injury had necessitated medical care—or already dead.

But there was no smell of decaying flesh.

"I'm going with you." She was glad he didn't argue. She followed him to the back of the cave, which their siblings had been using as a latrine, but there were no bodies, alive or dead. "Where are they?" she asked plaintively.

The use of the latrine proved they'd been in the cave for a week, at least. But there was no sign of what had happened to them. They'd simply disappeared into thin air.

"Look!" Aiden's headlamp shone on an opening high in the cave wall. "They must have gone out that way." He shot a grin at her and said, "Shall we?"

Leah realized that once Brian and Taylor were out of the cave, their chances of survival were greater. All she and Aiden would have to do was follow their tracks in the soft ashes and they'd surely find them.

Since the exit was so high, Aiden hefted her into it first. She held her flashlight out in front of her as she crawled, making first one sharp turn and then another, before coming out on the opposite side of an immense boulder that faced the meadow where the helicopter had landed.

Aiden appeared a moment later, shoving his way out into the sunshine. "I can't believe they found that exit. It looks like they had to do a lot of chopping to get rid of the roots around the opening. That suggests to me that at least one of them is able-bodied."

"And at least one of them is injured."

Aiden spoke to the helicopter on a walkie-talkie and arranged for them to do a survey from the air. He sent searchers out in several directions on foot, then turned to Leah and said, "Let's go."

It didn't take long, studying the tracks Taylor and Brian had left in the powdery soot, to figure out Brian was limping.

"At least he can walk," Aiden said. "They've got water, but they must be half starved. The sooner we find them, the better."

"Aiden, I . . ." Her heart was caught in her throat, keeping her from speaking. Which was a good thing, because she had no idea what she wanted to say.

As he frequently had in their brief relationship, Aiden came to the rescue. "Our problems can wait, Leah. Right now we need to focus on finding Taylor and Brian."

Chapter 22

THE RAINWATER DRIPPING onto his neck through the parachute overhead felt wonderful to Brian. He was tempted to stand up and let the rain pour over him to cool his fevered flesh. But a clap of thunder, and the smell of ozone as another bolt of lightning zinged through the air, reminded him how risky that would be. The storm was moving off, but he had no desire to abandon his position, wedged comfortably against a tree trunk.

Taylor had fallen asleep in his embrace. One of his arms had fallen asleep as well, but he didn't want to move, for fear of waking her. For the first time, he noticed the dark circles under her eyes. He wondered how little she'd slept when they were in the cave, and how little she was sleeping out here in the open, while his illness savaged him during the night.

He could feel the fever taking hold again. In a few minutes he'd need to wake her up and get moving. Every step counted, now that his strength was fading.

He was a man who'd always been very much in control of his life. As little as a year ago, he'd felt smug and cocksure, knowing he had the world by the tail, with both work and a woman he loved. That complacency had ended with his divorce. After that swift kick in the nuts, he'd concentrated on being a good firefighter and smoke jumper.

He'd never imagined Tag would come back into his life, that he might have another chance with her. But if they survived . . .

There was the rub. Things weren't looking too good for him, which was why he hadn't said anything to her about the future. Tag was in good shape, and she was smart. With a little luck, she might make it. Better not to say anything that would have her grieving once he was gone. She needed to concentrate on staying alive.

If she cares about you, and it seems she does, won't she grieve whether you speak or not? Tell her how you feel, Brian. While you still have time.

He heard Tag snuffle and felt her stretching in his arms. "Hey, sleepyhead. How do you feel?"

"Hmmph," she said.

He watched her open her eyes and saw in their troubled blue depths the sudden realization of where she was.

She sat up straight and looked around. "The storm's gone."

"It passed off a half hour ago."

"Why didn't you wake me?"

She started to rise, but he tightened his grip on her waist. "I'm not ready to go yet."

She pushed against his shoulders. "Half the day is

gone, Brian. We need to get moving and find a source of water."

"We have plenty of water."

"I want enough water to sponge you off and keep your fever down overnight."

That was plain speaking. There was no use arguing that he wasn't as sick as she believed he was.

"Come on, Brian. Let me up."

Reluctantly, he released her. She shoved her way onto her feet, then turned and gripped his hands to pull him upright.

It frightened him to realize he needed her help. Before he could reach for the parachute, she'd already pulled it off the branches where it had been hanging, shaken it to get rid of as much water as she could, and begun folding it up. Instead of handing it to him, she draped it over her own shoulder, along with the sleeping bag.

Brian had realized something else while he'd been watching Tag sleep. Their trail, which would have been simple to follow in the soft soot left by the fire, had likely been washed out by the heavy rain. Of course, none of that mattered unless someone had located the cave where they'd been hiding and started tracking them before the rain began.

Brian wanted to hope for the best, but he figured he'd better prepare Tag for the worst. Although, from the haunted look in her blue eyes, she'd already divined the worst for herself.

"I can't smell smoke anymore," she said as they started walking again.

"Let's hope the fire is out."

"Doesn't that mean all the smoke jumpers will be heading home?" she asked. "Won't that leave us out here all alone?"

"Our families are still searching. They're out here somewhere. All we have to do is hold on till they find us."

He tried to meet Tag's gaze, but she wouldn't look at him.

"Tag? Hey, brat!"

"What do you want, Brian?"

"I want you to look at me."

"I've seen all I need to see."

"Which is what?"

"You're flushed. You're sweaty. Your eyes are wells of pain. You're limping like a pirate with a stump for a leg. What is it you'd like me to notice?"

"Look at me!"

When she did, he grinned. Broadly.

"Oh, you crazy man," she said angrily. "How can you possibly be grinning at a time like this?"

"If a few days with you are all I have left, I intend to enjoy each and every one of them. That means being happy. That means thinking good thoughts. That means loving you while I can."

"What?"

"You heard me. Loving you. Might as well say it. I've got nothing to lose. Neither do you. Do you love me, Tag?"

"You're off your rocker. Sick with fever. You've lost it completely."

"Yeah, maybe. But do you love me?"

"That would be stupid, considering the fact that you've written yourself off. I mean, what would be the point of loving a guy who's only got a few days left to live."

"Aha! I see your clever plan. You get me to live in the hope that you'll say you love me, if I survive."

She shook her head, as though he were a pitiful excuse for a man. Maybe he was, but he didn't intend to waste whatever time he had left. Especially the time he had left when he wasn't out of his head with fever.

"Let's plan our life together after we get out of here," he suggested.

"You go home to the Lucky 7, and I go home to Kingdom Come. End of story."

"Except now that Matt's moved in, you aren't going to have a home at Kingdom Come for much longer. And life hasn't been too comfortable for me at the Lucky 7 since I messed things up between Aiden and Leah. I suppose that means we should get a place of our own. We need to know how many kids we're going to have, so we'll know how many bedrooms to get."

"We discussed this in high school," she said.

"We did? I don't remember any such conversation."

"I said I wanted two kids and you said you wanted four. We settled on three."

"Huh-uh. No way did I agree to that. If you have three, one gets left out. Two or four. That's my final offer."

"Did I mention you're crazy?"

"What does that have to do with anything. So three bedrooms."

"Three? I'm confused."

"You'll probably have two sets of twins, since they run in your family. One bedroom for the boys, one bedroom for the girls, and one bedroom for us."

She laughed, and he absorbed the happy sound as though it were a pail of cool water dumped over his head. "You with me?" he asked.

"Sure. Why not? The kids go to school in Jackson. No boarding schools."

"But college wherever they want."

She nodded, then said, "Barrel racing for the girls, calf roping for the boys."

"Agreed."

"No bareback bronc or bull riding!"

"I won't encourage it, but I won't discourage it, either."

She huffed out a breath of air. "I'm not raising sons to have their skulls crushed and their ribs gored by some nasty bull."

"They can wear helmets and flak jackets." When she made a face he said, "I don't want to tell my kids what they can and can't do. I'd rather advise them of the dangers and let them judge for themselves." He put up a hand to keep her from objecting and added, "When they're old enough to make those sorts of decisions for themselves, of course."

"I'm not going to stop flying."

"I never said you had to. I'm not going to stop firefighting and smoke jumping."

She shot him a look, and he knew what she was thinking.

If you're still able. If you aren't crippled. If you aren't dead.

He didn't say anything. There was nothing he could say. His leg hurt like a sonofabitch, and he was dizzy. He felt himself stagger and grabbed a pine branch to stay upright.

"Thank God," she whispered.

He was so disoriented, it took him a moment to realize that they'd stumbled onto another stream. This one was wider and deeper. He lurched a step or two farther and sank down in the shade of an aspen near the water. "Gotta take a little break."

He felt her hand on his forehead, calm and soothing, felt her brush the hair back from his face, as she helped him remove his PG bag and settle comfortably on his back. She was kneeling next to him, and he felt her cool cheek pressed against his, along with something warm and wet. A tear?

"Don't cry," he mumbled. "We're going to . . . make it. Just have to . . . hold on a . . . little . . ."

Chapter 23

THE NEXT FOUR days passed in a blur for Taylor. Every moment she wasn't setting traps or trying to catch fish, or cooking what she'd caught, she spent doing her best to cool Brian's fiery, fevered body.

On the first day, he had moments of lucidity.

"This is what I think you should do when I'm gone," he said.

"Don't you dare talk about your death as though it's going to happen," she snapped. "I don't want to hear it."

He tried again. "If anything happens to me—"

She cut him off before he got any further. "Don't bother speculating. I'm not listening."

"You have to listen."

"Blah. Blah. Blah," she said, putting her hands to her ears.

When he persisted, she got up and walked away, working on a parachute net she could use to catch one of the large trout in the stream. He was too sick to follow her. She came back bearing a smile and a fish. She was pleased and encouraged when he was able to eat some, after she broiled it over the fire.

The fever came back with a vengeance, and he was never coherent again for more than a few minutes at a time.

"Have you heard any planes?" he rasped.

She shook her head.

"Have you been shouting so they can hear you?"

She told him yes, even though the answer was no. What was the point of yelling when there was no one to hear?

The next time he woke up he asked, "Have you heard anyone yelling?"

She told him, "No, but I've been yelling like you told me to." She'd decided it couldn't hurt to yell for two or three minutes every half hour, just in case.

By the second day, Brian's wound looked awful. She wondered how he would feel if he survived but lost his leg. She wondered how she would feel if that happened. She tried not to think about it. Naturally, amputation was constantly on her mind. She tried to think how far up his leg a doctor would need to cut to get out all the infection. The longer they were lost, the more of his leg the imaginary doctor took off.

Brian wouldn't be able to fight fires anymore. Maybe he could do an administrative job with the Jackson Hole Fire Department.

He would hate that.

Smoke jumping would be out of the question.

He would hate that, too.

Sometimes she thought it might be better if Brian

died, because his life, if he survived, was going to be so different from anything he'd ever imagined. Then she would picture a world without Brian Flynn and knew it would be a darker, sadder place.

So she struggled to keep him alive.

She stripped off his shoes, socks, and jeans, so she'd have easy access to his leg. She saw the deepest claw mark was filled with pus. She wasn't sure what to do, and Brian was no help. He was out of his head with fever.

Taylor decided to lance the wound and drain the pus.

The thought of cutting into human flesh was nauseating. Cutting into *Brian's* flesh was horrifying, but she knew getting rid of as much of the putrefaction as she could was his best hope of survival.

So she did it. She cut open the wound and pressed out the awful gunk inside.

Brian cried. He howled and fought to be free.

She cried, too, but she didn't stop. She sat on his legs facing the wound to hold him down. It was a sign of how weak he was that he couldn't throw her off.

When she was done, she decided to do something she'd seen in movies that were set on the Western frontier. She didn't know if it would work, but she thought it couldn't hurt.

She heated Brian's Swiss army knife till it was red hot, then pressed it against the wound to cauterize the cut she'd made.

This time he screamed. She screamed too, frustrated by the awful need to hurt him so badly in order to help him.

When she thought the wound was sealed, she threw the knife aside, then turned to embrace Brian, pressing kisses to his hot face and holding him down on the sleeping bag to keep him from touching his leg or injuring himself further.

"Shh. Shh. It's all over now. You're okay. I won't hurt you anymore." She kissed away the salty tears that seeped from his closed eyes. She would willingly accept the condemnation she was sure to see, if he would only open them and recognize her.

On the third day, despite her efforts, he wasn't any better. She knew she had to do something to try and get his fever down. She loaded Brian onto the parachute and dragged him into the water, letting it cool his body and ease the swelling in his leg.

Although she was unable to get him to eat, she forced water down his throat. She took care of all his needs, even the most private, all the while watching his strong, masculine body waste away. She studied every shallow breath in and out of his chest, wondering when he would breathe his last.

Taylor woke up the morning of their fourth day at the stream, took one look at Brian, and knew he probably wouldn't survive until sundown. She splashed his body with cool water. She listened to him murmur and mumble in his delirium, and wondered who would take care of her when the end came.

Her stomach growled. She hadn't caught a fish or a squirrel or a rabbit in the past twenty-four hours. She felt weak and sick, although she was more sick at heart than anything else. She'd done everything she could to try and save Brian. She was out of tricks.

Brian was going to die.

It had been only twelve days since her Twin Otter flamed out, and they'd jumped into the wilderness. Twelve hungry days. Twelve terrifying days. Twelve wonderful days, because she'd finally found a man who loved her, a man she might have been able to love for the rest of her life, if only he managed to survive the infection in his leg.

It had been her habit to stoke a fire all night to keep the predators away and snatch a nap every morning. She was exhausted and having trouble keeping her eyes open. But she didn't want to be asleep when Brian passed away. She didn't want him to die all alone.

She sat beside him, lifted his head onto her thigh, and tried to force a little water into his mouth. It dribbled down the sides of his face.

"Damn it, Brian! Open your mouth and swallow. Do you hear me? I'm not going to die out here alone. We're going to be saved. So swallow!"

To her amazement, he did.

"See? You're not gone yet. Keep fighting. Just keep fighting. Don't give up. Please don't give up."

She sobbed. There was no one to hear her cry. No one to chastise her for being weak.

In a fierce voice she said, "I love you. Do you hear me? I admit it. I'm willing to take a chance with you. If we get out of here alive, I promise I'll give it a try. I'll love you more than anyone's ever loved you before, and I expect you to love me just as much. We'll have those twins—two sets of them—and raise them to care about their aunts and uncles and grandfathers on both sides. We'll put a stop to this feud as surely and completely as you've put a stop to all those fires."

She swiped at the tears blurring her eyes, unwilling to lose sight of his beloved face.

"Helloooo!" she screamed. "Is anybody out there! Can anyone hear me? Heeeelp! Somebody answer me! Just open your goddamn mouth and say something!"

"I can hear you!" a female voice called back. "Keep yelling!"

At the sound of another human voice, a voice that meant salvation, Taylor's throat had swollen completely closed, and though she opened her mouth, no sound came out. Tears of frustration spurted from her eyes. She swallowed hard, to get rid of the painful knot preventing speech, then took a deep breath and screamed at the top of her lungs, "We're here. We're right here!"

She reached out with two fingers to check the pulse at Brian's throat. She couldn't find it.

Chapter 24

"I TOLD YOU they were still alive," Leah cried. "That was Taylor's voice!"

"Brian!" Aiden shouted. "Brian, answer me!" What came back was the same female voice he and Leah had first heard, from somewhere west of them in the forest. Aiden fought back the rising fear that the reason Brian hadn't answered was because he *couldn't* answer. Maybe Brian had left Taylor behind and was off hunting somewhere.

In his heart of hearts, he didn't believe it. He'd seen Brian's limp in his footprints, seen him drag his right foot in the ashes rather than pick it up. Brian was badly hurt.

They'd followed Brian and Taylor's trail easily for about the first hour after they'd left the cave. Then the rainstorm had hit and washed it out. They'd headed in what they thought was a logical direction the two could have taken, but they didn't find their tracks again. They'd searched in one direction and then another. The past four days had been a nightmare of disappointments.

Aiden had begun to lose hope. It had been difficult to admit that Brian might be gone.

His father had exhorted him to give up the search and come home. "Either he'll walk out of the forest, or he won't," Angus had said. "You're not going to locate Brian in a wilderness that vast."

"Don't argue with me, Dad," he'd replied in a steely voice. "I'm not coming back until I find him."

King had apparently said pretty much the same thing to Leah. Her response had been considerably more blunt.

After she'd ended the satellite phone call to her father, Aiden had looked into Leah's desolate—and determined—hazel eyes and seen that she had no intention of giving up. He would cheerfully endure a little obstinacy in the woman he loved for the sake of spending his life with her. That is, assuming he could get her to forgo an annulment.

At least she'd been speaking to him, sharing stories about her sister. When they'd exhausted that topic, she'd asked him about Brian, to keep him talking. He'd realized that Leah needed their conversation to hold back the fear that threatened to overwhelm her.

He'd resisted the urge to offer the comfort of his arms. He could tell by the way Leah occasionally eyed him askance that he'd given her food for thought in his recent confession. It was equally clear, from the way she kept her distance, that she had no inclination—yet—of offering dispensation. It wasn't easy to give her the space to make up her mind, but he knew enough about Leah to understand that she measured all the pros and cons before coming to any decision. And she couldn't be rushed.

This morning, they'd finally stumbled onto Brian and Taylor's trail again, but it had been days old. Nevertheless, they'd shadowed their siblings' footsteps. Taylor's shouts confirmed that, at long last, they'd located their missing family.

"This way!" Leah cried, running off in the direction of Taylor's voice.

Aiden listened to Leah's frantic shouts and Taylor's hoarse replies until they could see Taylor sitting on the ground beneath an aspen, Brian lying beside her, his head in her lap.

Leah kept running until she was able to drop to her knees and wrap her arms around her sister.

Aiden stopped short, unable to breathe, his heart caught in his throat.

It was hard to believe that the gaunt woman Leah was hugging, her blond hair a mass of rat's nests, her face filthy, her clothes ragged and hanging off her body, was Taylor Grayhawk. He looked from Taylor to the equally emaciated man on the ground, his damp hair sticking up, brushed away from his brother's forehead, he imagined, by a soothing hand. Brian's bearded face was devoid of color and his chest lay still, with no air moving in or out, at least as far as Aiden could tell from where he stood.

He tried to take a step closer, but the shock of seeing Brian laid so low had rooted him in place. He met Taylor's despondent gaze and knew the awful truth without having to be told.

Taylor said it anyway. "He's dead."

Leah immediately pressed two fingers to Brian's carotid, then leaned over and held her cheek next to his nose. "No, Aiden. He's still alive!"

That bit of hope freed Aiden, and he threw himself across the last few feet, dropping to his knees at Brian's side. He took Brian's cold hand in his own and urged, "Hang in there, Brian. We're here. Help is on the way."

Then he smelled the gangrene that was killing his brother. He choked on the stench, then swallowed his gorge.

He might never forgive Leah for those few moments of hope he'd experienced when she'd told him Brian was alive, because now he would need to go through that awful moment of acceptance all over again. It was plain that Brian had traveled far more than halfway across death's doorstep.

"Brian needs a medivac," Leah said, one arm around Taylor and the other on Brian's shoulder. "Now!"

Aiden realized he'd been sitting doing nothing while Brian edged slowly, but surely, away from the world of the living. He grabbed his satellite phone and called for a helicopter, explaining what he needed.

"They can't get a basket in here," Leah pointed out. "The forest is too dense."

"I've got Primacord. I'll make a space big enough." He looked for the largest opening he could find in the trees, then set about wrapping Primacord around tree trunks, setting off explosions to neatly take down everything necessary to make a space sufficient for a medivac helicopter to lower a basket and get it back out.

He was grateful for the hard work. Even so, it took a lifetime—Brian's ebbing lifetime—for the helicopter to appear. Aiden had plenty of time to take another good look at Taylor. She was suffering from more than malnutrition. Her vivacious spirit seemed to have eked out of her, like air out of a balloon. He wondered how much longer she would have lasted, if she and Brian hadn't been found. He had no doubt that her tireless care of Brian was the reason his brother had lasted as long as he had.

He crossed to her and said, "Thank you."

She looked up at him with dull, despairing eyes in a skeletal face. "For what?"

"For keeping Brian alive."

He'd been surprised by her lack of tears in her emotional reunion with Leah, who'd been blubbering like a baby, but his words must have reminded her that Brian was hanging on to life by a thread, because her eyes suddenly filled with tears.

"I didn't know what to do," she whispered in a voice that sent chills down his spine. "There was nothing else I could do. I'm sorry. I'm so sorry."

Leah shot him a warning look and took her sister in her arms, holding her tight, as though to keep her from slipping away.

He heard the *flackita, flackita, flackita* that announced the helicopter had arrived.

"Help is here," Leah crooned to her sister. "Your work is done, Taylor. You can rest now."

Aiden watched Taylor's eyes slide closed and her chin drop to her chest.

"I'm so tired," she said.

Her body sagged and then went completely limp.

Leah met his gaze, her arms wrapped tightly around her unconscious sister, while silent tears streamed down her face.

Aiden couldn't look any longer at the desperate tableau. He stepped into the clearing he'd made and popped colored smoke to show their exact location.

He and Leah had done what they'd set out to do. They'd found Brian and Taylor. Now all they had to do was keep them both alive until they reached the hospital in Jackson.

Chapter 25

TAYLOR THOUGHT SHE was dreaming when she woke up and found herself in a hospital bed covered by pristine white sheets. She sat up slowly and ran her hands over the soft, worn cotton, to be sure she wasn't dreaming, worried that the hospital room would suddenly disappear, and she would find herself back in the forest. But the sheets stayed in place, the monitor to which she was attached kept on beeping, and the IV in her forearm, leading to a bag of clear liquid on a stand, was the real deal.

She sank weakly back onto the pillow, her eyes filling with tears of relief. "We made it," she whispered.

Then it dawned on her that Brian might *not* have made it. He'd been all but dead when Leah and Aiden had shown up. Taylor bolted upright and had to wait a moment for a wave of dizziness to pass. She looked for a phone, but there wasn't one in the room. She searched for some kind of call button for the nurse, but she couldn't find that either.

"Where the hell is everybody?" she said, surprised at

how hoarse she sounded and how sore her throat was. Then she remembered how she'd screamed for help, for someone to come and rescue them, when it seemed Brian was going to die and leave her alone.

She wondered how long she'd been in the hospital. The sun was coming up, but was it the next day? Or the day after that? How long had she been here? Brian could have died while she'd been sleeping! She needed to know what had happened to him.

Taylor frowned at the blue-patterned hospital gown she was wearing, then checked the back and discovered that it did, indeed, leave her ass hanging out. What had happened to her jeans and shirt? Not that she wanted to wear that outfit again in this lifetime, but she needed something better than an open-backed cotton gown if she was going to be running through the halls looking for Brian.

She snatched the flat white plastic contacts from her chest, and the machine stopped beeping. Then she removed the tape holding the IV needle in place and carefully slid the needle out. Once she was free, she pulled off the top sheet and wrapped it around herself like a toga. She didn't see slippers anywhere, so she left the room barefoot.

The fluorescent fixtures in the hall seemed brighter than the creeping sunlight in her room, and she hesitated in the doorway, waiting for her eyes to adjust.

A nurse was hurrying in her direction. "What are you doing out of bed? You can't just get up and walk around. What have you done with your IV?"

Instead of answering questions, Taylor said, "Where's Brian Flynn? I need to see him."

"I can't give you any information about another patient," the nurse said.

"Just tell me if he's alive."

"I can't comment on the condition of a patient."

Taylor had no patience with bullshit. "Either tell me where to go or get out of my way."

"I can't—"

Taylor brushed past the nurse and headed for the intensive care unit. That's where Brian would be if he was alive. She knew where the ICU was because King had stayed there briefly when he'd had a heart arrhythmia.

"I'm contacting your sister," the nurse called after her. "She's not going to be happy about this."

Taylor ignored her, hurrying down the hall toward the ICU, which was located in the middle of the one-story hospital near the emergency room. Leah would understand that she had to see Brian, and if she didn't, that was too damn bad.

The halls were strangely empty. Taylor realized she must have woken during a time when nurses were changing shifts, before breakfast was being served, or doctors were likely to be checking on patients. She ran past closed doors and slowed down at open doors to see if Brian might be in one of the beds.

She wondered where her sisters were. She would have expected to find not just Leah, but Vick and Eve conked out in chairs at her bedside. It was odd that not one of them had been in the room. Which suggested she'd been "out" more than twenty-four hours, enough time that they'd begun watching over her in shifts, and whoever was supposed to be there had gone to get coffee or to walk around outside.

She wondered if her father had visited and figured he'd probably been there for appearance's sake. She wondered what she would have said if she'd found King at her bedside. Something snotty, probably, about how he paid attention to her only when she was in trouble, and now that she was better he could take himself off to wherever he was spending his time these days.

She was nearing the ICU when she paused abruptly and stepped back into an empty room, where she couldn't be seen. She watched as Leah and Aiden leaned close, their eyes focused on each other as they spoke. For an instant, she thought they might kiss, but Leah stepped back abruptly and walked in the opposite direction.

She wondered if Leah had forgiven Aiden for making the bet with Brian. It was hard to imagine Leah falling in love with one of the Flynns. She wondered what would happen between her sister and Brian's brother, now that the necessity of working together was past.

Taylor stepped out from her hiding place and almost called out to Leah, but thought better of it. Taylor figured she had a better chance of getting past Aiden alone, than getting past both Aiden and her sister.

Aiden had thanked her for saving Brian's life. Aiden owed her a chance to see how Brian was faring, assuming Brian was in the room Aiden seemed to be guarding. Surely he was. Surely Brian had survived. But had he lost his leg?

Taylor waited for Aiden to go back inside, then hurried down the hall. She pushed the door open and stepped inside. And found herself facing every single one of "those awful Flynn boys."

"What are you doing in here?" Connor demanded.

Devon frowned. "How did you get loose? Last I heard, you were unconscious, attached to a heart monitor, and had a needle in your arm."

Taylor lifted her chin defiantly. She wasn't going to be kicked out. She wasn't going to go away. She wasn't going to be denied. "I came to see Brian."

"You should be in bed." Aiden's voice was kinder, but the message was the same.

You don't belong here.

She leaned around Aiden to peek at Brian. He looked awful. Thin, pale, and unshaven. A tent covered his right leg, making it impossible to tell whether it had been amputated. His hovering brothers looked to her like vultures hanging around a dying carcass.

"You should all get out of here and let him rest," she said as she stepped to the foot of Brian's bed.

"Who the hell—" Connor began.

"Back up and leave her alone," Aiden said.

Taylor felt her nose burning and tears sting her eyes as she gripped the foot rail. Brian had a tube down his throat and a needle in his arm and beeping sounds were coming from a nearby machine that looked like the one that had been attached to her.

He's alive. But is he going to stay that way?

Her stomach churned and emotion clogged her throat as she stared at the tent covering his leg. She shifted her gaze to Aiden and croaked, "Did they cut it off?"

He shook his head.

Devon took a step toward her and said, "You should leave."

Aiden whirled on him and snapped, "Shut the hell up! If not for her, we'd be burying Brian instead of standing vigil over him."

"She's the reason Brian's in this condition in the first place," Connor shot back. "She was flying too low."

"He's right, Aiden," Devon chimed in. "They're saying the plane went down because of pilot error. That makes this whole situation her fault."

Taylor felt like she'd been stabbed with a knife to the heart. *All her fault*. Were they right? Had she done this to Brian? She met Aiden's tortured gaze and asked, "Is he dying?"

"Who the hell knows? They've got him stuffed with antibiotics, but it's anybody's guess whether they're going to work."

"Why is that tent over his leg?"

"They cut out a big chunk of his calf, trying to save the leg. It might still have to come off, if they can't get the infection under control."

She crossed past Connor and Devon, daring them to try and stop her, so she could stand at the head of the bed. She brushed a lock of hair from Brian's forehead, then placed her palm against his cheek and felt the raging fever that might yet kill him. She bent down to whisper in his ear.

"Fight, Brian. Live. We aren't done yet. Not by a long shot."

Then she stood up and looked from one brother to the next.

"I owe your brother my life. He saved us both. I'll always be grateful to him for that." Everything suddenly caught up to her. Her whole body began to tremble, and she was afraid her knees were going to collapse.

"Are you all right?" Aiden asked.

Taylor looked at him, helpless either to move or to speak.

Aiden scooped her into his arms and said, "Open the door, Connor."

"Where are you going with her?"

"Back to her room, of course."

"Make sure she stays there," she heard someone mutter.

Her eyes sank closed, and her body relaxed like a rag doll in Aiden's arms. She was so exhausted. She wanted to go to sleep and have Brian be well again when she woke up. But that sort of magic only happened in fairy tales. She needed to find the strength to deal with what was really happening.

Brian's brothers probably thought they'd seen the last of her. Well, let them think what they wanted. She would be back. Tomorrow and the next day and the next, until Brian Flynn was fighting fires again.

She wanted a chance for a life together. The first step toward that goal was getting Brian back on his feet. With any luck, *both* feet. If that wasn't to be, they'd deal with it together.

"Those awful Flynn boys" could wish her to Hades, if they wanted. She wasn't going anywhere.

Chapter 26

"YOU NEED TO stop these visits to the hospital," Leah said, grabbing Taylor's arm to keep her from heading out the kitchen door.

"Brian needs me."

"You need to take care of yourself. You wake up in the middle of the night whimpering and wander the halls until dawn. You aren't eating."

"I have to go, Leah."

"Brian Flynn has been in a coma for the past ten days. He won't even know you're there."

"I'll know."

"I realize you've been through a lot together—"

Taylor gave her sister a look that shut her up. But only for a moment.

"Whatever feelings you might have had for each other were a result of the situation you were in," Leah persisted. "When Brian wakes up—if he wakes up—he's going to be concentrating on getting his life back together. He isn't going to be thinking about you."

Taylor's chin lifted, but she felt a spurt of fear that

her sister was right. "You weren't there, Leah. You don't know what it was like. You don't know anything."

"I know enough to warn you to protect your heart," she said in a voice so gentle it made Taylor's throat ache. "Whatever promises Brian made will be forgotten, I promise you. The Flynns, one and all, have grown up as cold and callous and uncaring as the bastard who raised them."

"You're wrong about Brian, Leah."

Leah's eyes looked both wounded and worried. "I know what I'm talking about."

"You weren't there," Taylor repeated.

"Have you spoken to Vick about this?"

"Of course."

"And?"

"She didn't change my mind." Taylor had gotten pretty much the same speech from her twin that she was getting from Leah, but she refused to be swayed. She'd allowed Vick to talk her into walking away from Brian when she was a teenager. She wasn't going to let it happen again.

"We spoke," Vick said, entering the kitchen still dressed in her cotton nightgown, yawning and ruffling her blond curls. "Argued half the night and into the wee hours this morning. I couldn't make her see reason, either."

"The Flynns can't all be as bad as you say," Taylor argued. "Look at Eve. She seems happy married to Connor."

"They haven't been together long enough for us to

know whether their marriage is going to survive," Leah said.

"Well, so far, it's working," Taylor replied, undeterred.

"What do the Flynns say when you show up at Brian's room?" Leah asked.

"Nothing." Aiden had made it clear to his brothers that she was welcome at Brian's bedside whenever she chose to come. So far, she hadn't run into Angus, but she was even willing to beard the lion, if necessary.

She spent her days sitting in a plastic chair beside Brian's bed, talking to him and holding his hand. His brothers showed up in shifts, but because they had ranch animals—and in Connor's case family—that had to be fed and cared for, they weren't able to stay for long. She left the room while they were visiting Brian and waited in the cafeteria.

"I have to be there, Leah," she said. "When he wakes up, I mean. Brian's going to need—"

"His family," Vick interrupted. "Not one of King's Brats. Wake up and smell the coffee, Taylor. The Flynns—father and sons—want nothing to do with us. If you're well enough to hang out at the hospital making a nuisance of yourself, you're well enough to go back to work—" Vick cut herself off and looked abashed.

Taylor huffed out a disgusted breath. "Dropping smoke jumpers? Flying over forest fires? I don't think the National Transportation Safety Board is going to let me do that until I've explained what I did to flame out both engines of my Twin Otter. I'll be lucky if they don't take away my pilot's license."

"You could . . ." Vick's voice trailed away.

Taylor couldn't work as a corporate pilot, either, until she'd been cleared by the NTSB. "Besides, I'm not ready to fly again. I need some time to cope with . . . everything."

Taylor wasn't sure she had the nerve to fly smoke jumpers again. She knew having both engines flame out had to be a one in a million incident, but she didn't think she'd ever again be so blithe about the dangers of dropping smoke jumpers on a hellish forest fire.

"Seems to me you've got enough to handle, without adding Brian's problems to your own," Leah said. "From what Aiden told me—"

"You've been talking to Aiden?" Taylor said. "What does he say? What's Brian's prognosis? The doctor won't tell me anything." She'd been unwilling to ask Brian's brothers for information they didn't freely offer.

They hadn't offered anything, which lent credence to Vick's suggestion that they'd just as soon she stayed away.

"Never mind what Aiden said," Vick interjected. "I want to know why you've been spending time with the enemy, Leah. I've never in my life heard you say a good thing about a Flynn, and suddenly you're best friends with Aiden?"

Taylor watched a rosy flush rise on Leah's face. Guilt? Embarrassment? Taylor knew far more than Leah realized about her relationship with Aiden. She hadn't used her knowledge against Leah in their argument, because it felt wrong, hurtful somehow, to expose Leah's secret.

She hadn't shared Leah's secret with Vick, either,

which was surprising, because she and Vick used to share everything, no matter how unimportant. And Leah's relationship with Aiden was far from unimportant. Something had been different between her and her twin over the past few years, pushing them apart, making it more difficult to share.

Taylor felt sure Vick was keeping a secret from her, something to do with that home she owned in Montana. She could have just shown up at what Vick had described as her "remote cabin in the woods," but she'd wanted Vick to invite her.

The invitation had never come.

Vick hadn't been as outgoing or seemed as happy as she once had. Taylor was afraid her twin was in some kind of trouble, but whenever she asked about anything to do with Montana, Vick shut her down. Taylor wanted to help, but Vick wasn't giving her the chance.

Taylor felt more worried and disappointed than resentful at being shut out. More than anything, she missed having her sister living in the next room, where they could share everything all the time.

Skyping wasn't always possible, and too many nuances were lost texting and talking on the phone. Maybe that wretched feeling of disconnectedness was why Taylor hadn't told Vick the story of Brian's bet with Aiden. Or maybe it was more in the nature of payback: *Let's see how she likes it when I start keeping secrets from her.*

Taylor was curious to hear Leah's answer to the question Vick had raised about their elder sister's relationship with Aiden. Had Leah forgiven him for the trick

he'd played on her? Was something more than information passing between the two of them? "What *is* going
on between you and Aiden?" she asked.

"We spent a lot of time together worrying about you
and Brian," Leah explained. "So Aiden's been keeping
me in the loop about his brother's situation."

"Why is it okay for you to talk to Aiden but not okay
for me to spend time with Brian?" Taylor asked.

Vick threw up her hands. "I give up. Why would either one of you want to spend time with either one of
them? You're both crazy as loons." She grabbed some
Cheerios from the cupboard, and set a bowl and spoon
on the breakfast bar, before striding to the refrigerator
for milk. She wet down the cereal, then stopped before
taking a bite to shoot her twin a perturbed look. "I still
don't get it. What's the point of spending time with an
unconscious man?"

"You've got plenty of sympathy for wolves and grizzlies. How about a little compassion for someone I care
about?"

Vick stopped with a spoonful of Cheerios halfway to
her mouth. She dropped it back in the bowl with a clatter and a splash of milk. "That's a low blow! You can't
expect me to care about *Flynns*."

"What happened to caring about *me*?" That was as
close as Taylor could come to saying that she missed the
tight bond between them that appeared to have frayed
over the past few years.

Vick shoved her bowl aside and hurried across the
room to fold Taylor in her arms. "I do care. I do! I just

don't understand this sudden need to forgive the Flynns all transgressions. You might as well be standing defenseless with a thousand-pound grizzly in your path. I'm frightened for you. I don't want your belly ripped out. All I see ahead is suffering, if you continue in the direction you're going."

Taylor stuck her nose against Vick's throat and blinked at the tears that threatened. How long had it been since they'd hugged like this? They said the words "I love you" all the time. But somewhere along the way, they'd stopped embracing when they met or when one of them went away.

Both sisters had held her close at the hospital. She'd cut their embraces short, because her feelings had been so near the surface, and she'd been afraid she would fall apart if she let down her guard. She hadn't realized how much she needed to be held, to be demonstrably loved. In Brian's absence, the constant fear she lived with, the knowledge of how unworthy, how undeserving of love she was, had crept back.

In truth, Taylor hadn't shared *everything* with her twin in the past. She'd never told Vick how empty she felt inside. Or just how unlovable she'd felt, until Brian Flynn had admitted to loving her. Vick had no way of knowing how Brian's love had filled that hole inside her, satisfying her need to feel valued in a way nothing and no one else ever had.

If she had known, Vick would've understood why Taylor sat by Brian's bedside praying that he would not only recover, but still feel the same way about her. Because Vick was ignorant of all the facts, Taylor had no one with whom to share the constant fear she felt that, when Brian was well, he would simply walk away.

Was it any wonder she didn't want to give up on that promise of love? She had a vested interest in seeing that Brian Flynn recovered. Until he was back on his feet, they couldn't move forward with their lives together.

It looked like Brian was going to keep his right leg, but a lot of the muscle had been cut away and wasn't coming back. Smoke jumping was out of the question, but depending on how well he rehabbed his right leg, he might be able to requalify as a firefighter with the Jackson Hole fire department.

Taylor didn't intend to let Brian fail, because her future happiness depended on his being a whole, healthy, happy person, ready to pursue a romantic relationship . . . with her.

"I'm leaving now," she said, pushing past Leah.

When Leah took a step forward to stand in her way, Vick said, "Let her go. If she's determined to jump into deep water without checking for unseen hazards, there's nothing either of us can do about it, except be there to fish her out."

Taylor saw that Leah's inclination was to physically restrain her from taking that dangerous—perhaps fatal—leap, but at last, she stepped aside and gestured toward the door.

"Go. Just be careful, Taylor. Be very careful."

Taylor didn't acknowledge Leah's warning. She couldn't afford to be careful. If she wanted to be safe, she'd keep her distance from Brian. She'd guard her heart and not take the chance of having it broken.

Being safe wasn't going to get her where she wanted to go. She had to be fearless. She had to take chances. She had to do whatever was necessary to get Brian Flynn back on his feet. Because she wasn't going to settle for less than happily ever after.

Chapter 27

BRIAN STRUGGLED TO open his eyes. It felt like he was swimming through Jell-O. He tried to swallow but something was in the way. He groped at his mouth and realized he had a tube down his throat.

"Easy. Breathe out."

He gagged, and then the tube was gone. He gasped a breath of air, then gasped again, as his eyes opened fully. He stared up at a doctor who didn't look much older than his youngest brother, and a nurse who looked like she might have been his grandmother. The doctor nodded to the nurse, who left the room.

"Don't try to talk," he said. "You're in the hospital in Jackson. You've been here for twelve days."

He'd been unconscious for twelve days? How close had he come to dying? Brian wondered.

"My leg," he rasped. Brian tried to sit up, but the doctor put a hand on his shoulder to keep him down. "Let go of me!" He got a look at the tent over his leg and panicked. "What did you do?"

"Your leg's still there, but I cut a pretty big chunk out

of your calf. It was touch and go for a while whether I'd have to take off the whole leg, but the infection is under control, and you're out of the woods, literally and figuratively." The doctor's eyes crinkled with humor.

Brian was in no mood for jokes. He met the young man's gaze, a question in his eyes that he couldn't voice aloud.

The doctor picked up his cue. "You'll likely walk again, but I can't say how well. It's going to take a lot of therapy, and a lot of hard work on your part."

"But I *will* walk, right?"

The doctor's eyes shifted away, and Brian felt his heart sink. "Will I walk again?" he demanded. "Or not?"

The doctor met his gaze and said, "You will."

Before Brian could interrupt again, he hurried to add, "There's very little muscle left on your right leg below the knee. Probably enough to keep you upright and allow you to walk. But in cases I've seen like this, you're going to need a cane to help support your weight."

Brian closed his eyes, shutting out the doctor's sympathetic face and the awful message he'd just been given. A man with a cane couldn't carry forty-five pounds of fire hose into a burning building. A man with a cane was never jumping out of a plane to fight a forest fire.

His life, as he'd known it, was over.

"Go away." His throat was swollen so tight he was afraid he was going to choke, and his heartbeat felt erratic enough to make breathing a struggle.

"I'll let your brothers know you're awake."

When the man didn't move, he croaked, "Get out!" Tears sprang to his eyes as he squeezed them shut, and he raised a hand—to which an IV was attached—in a futile attempt to soothe his sore throat. When he looked up, the doctor was gone.

Someone else had taken his place.

"Brian?"

Of course Tag was here. Any other time he might have been glad to see her. Not now. Not when he was most vulnerable. Not when he'd only had moments to absorb the disaster that had befallen him and crushed his world. "Go away, Tag," he rasped. "Get the hell out!" He turned his head to avoid looking at her. The pain in his heart was every bit as raw as the pain in his throat. He didn't want her here, couldn't have her here, pitying him.

"No."

Just the one word, denying him the peace he sought. He was fighting unmanly tears, fighting sobs that would completely undo him, and the damned woman wouldn't leave.

Suddenly, he felt her hand on his face, turning it back toward her, and then her lips were on his, offering comfort and seeking solace.

The kiss made his chest ache, because it spoke of what might have been. He couldn't make a commitment to her now. Not when he had no idea whether he would ever stand on his own two feet again. He put his hand on Tag's shoulder to push her away, but he was as weak as a kitten.

She held his face between her hands and said, "Look at me, Brian."

"Tag, don't do this," he said, fighting for control of his voice.

"You're awake. You're alive. We made it," she said in the softest voice he'd ever heard her use. "All we need to do now is get you well and back on your feet and back to work."

"*We* don't need to do anything," he said, forgetting about his throat and talking too loudly and paying the price with a pain like razors cutting into his flesh. "*You* need to haul your ass out of here."

"You mean my *beautiful* ass? The one you love to hold in your hands when we're making love," she teased, her eyes smiling down at him filled with . . . Oh, God . . . was that love?

"Not now, Tag," he said, closing his eyes, since she wouldn't allow him to look away. "It hurts my throat to argue."

"Good. Because there's nothing to fight about. I'm not going anywhere. I'm here to help."

He realized if he didn't nip this in the bud, she'd be here every day driving him crazy, making him feel worse than he already did. He opened his eyes and looked her right in the eye. "Listen to me, Tag, because I'm only going to say this once. Since it's painful to talk, I'm going to make this short and sweet. I don't want your help. I don't want you anywhere near me."

He kept his face as impassive as stone, while his stomach wrenched at the distraught look in her eyes. He gritted his teeth to keep from taking back what he'd said, but he didn't think he could bear to have her watching him struggle to walk again. He didn't want her hanging around while he stumbled and fell and sweated and swore. He'd rather do it by himself.

"What about us?" she said.

"Us?" He made the word an epithet. "Don't kid yourself. Nothing that happened out there was real." He put a hand to his ragged throat, then looked at her and realized the pain he'd caused—to her and himself—by speaking. He should just shut the hell up.

"Why are you pushing me away?"

"Do I need a reason?"

"You said—"

"Anything I said before I became a cripple should be taken with a grain of salt."

"Get over yourself, Brian! You've still got your leg. Lots of veterans—like the ones who come to Connor's ranch—have lost a lot more than a chunk of flesh and gone on to lead fulfilling lives doing some job that wasn't what they'd planned for themselves. Who do you think you are? What makes you so special?"

She was yelling at him, but he noticed she wasn't tearful. She was seriously pissed off.

He held up a hand to stop her tirade, but it wasn't necessary. The door to his room flew open and two of his brothers towered in the doorway. Aiden crossed the room in three strides and demanded of Taylor, "What's all this shouting about?"

Connor gripped the rail at the foot of Brian's bed and said, "Brian?"

Brian waved a hand and turned his face away without speaking.

"Your brother's being a horse's ass," Tag said.

"Brian?" Aiden said in the sort of gentle voice you

might use with a kid who'd just fallen off the horse he was learning to ride. "What's going on?"

Brian avoided looking at Tag as he said, "I want her gone."

"And I told him I'm staying," Tag shot back.

Connor focused his gaze on Tag and said pointedly, "We need to talk to Brian. Alone."

For a moment, he thought Tag would refuse to go. He watched her from the corner of his eye as she shot him a look fiery enough to burn down half of Yellowstone, then marched out of the room. She stopped at the door and said, "Don't think you can get rid of me this easily, Brian. I'll be back."

With all the destructive force of the Terminator, Brian thought with chagrin.

After the door slid closed, Connor said to Aiden, "I told you to keep her out of here. You should have listened to me."

"Are you okay?" Aiden asked.

Brian tried to shrug. It hurt. Everything hurt. His head was pounding. His leg ached. His face felt hot. Did he still have a fever? Was it something that might return? Could the infection come back and claim the rest of his leg? He shuddered at the thought of being out of his head again. He just wanted everyone to leave him alone. "Why are you here?" he whispered, saving his poor throat.

"We heard you were awake," Connor said. "We wanted to see for ourselves how you were doing. Devon would have been here, too, but he's got some horses that need—"

Brian cut him off. "I'm fine. Tell Devon I'm okay, and there's no need to come."

"Brian . . . About your leg . . ." Aiden said.

"The doctor told me what he did. And his prognosis. Is there something else you want?" He heard the annoyance in his voice but was helpless to control it. What did they want from him? An acknowledgment that he didn't mind what the doctor had done to him? That he was fine with being crippled because at least he was still alive?

Brian realized he'd probably needed the gut check Tag had given him. Every thought he'd had since he'd woken up had been filled with self-pity. He was lucky to have survived the infection. He could have lost his entire leg. Most of it was still attached. Why was he being such a crybaby?

What did his moaning and groaning say about his character? What did his despair say about him as a man? Was that why he'd wanted Tag gone? Because he didn't want her to see what a weak reed he was? Because he didn't want her to see that he wasn't man enough to meet the challenge life had dealt him without sobbing into his pillow?

Aiden touched him on the shoulder. "Brian? Are you all right?"

He realized his eyes had filled with tears and that one had run down his cheek. He swiped it away. "For Christ's sake, get out! Leave me alone!" He tried to turn on his side away from them and cried out when his cut-up leg brushed against the sheets.

He felt Aiden's hand on his shoulder, an offer of comfort that he desperately wanted but was afraid of accepting, for fear he'd break apart. He squeezed his eyes closed and bunched his hands into fists under the covers to keep his brothers from seeing how hard he was trembling. He would get through this misfortune on his own. He would do it to prove to himself that he could. He had as much courage as the next man. He'd demonstrated that every time he'd jumped a fire. He would do whatever it took, endure whatever pain there was, to walk again. And he would walk without a cane, or his name wasn't Brian Flynn.

Chapter 28

WHEN TAYLOR ARRIVED back at Kingdom Come from the hospital, she retreated to her room, closed the door, got into bed, and pulled the covers up over her head, making a dark, warm cocoon. Two hours later she emerged, like a bold and beautiful butterfly, with a plan.

It turned out that Brian needed to remain in the hospital for up to six weeks while his wound healed. After that, his doctor would schedule as much outpatient rehab as it took, measured in months, to get him back on his feet.

She planned to be there every step of the way.

Brian wasn't a quitter. He possessed loads of courage and perseverance. She felt sure those qualities would get him through this crisis. She just had to convince him to include her in the process.

All those hours of rehab would give them time to talk, time to catch up on everything they didn't know about each other, time to see whether the partnership they'd formed in the wilderness in order to survive could thrive in the real world.

She knew Brian loved his work, which worried her, because the loss of muscle in his leg was so devastating, it might be impossible for him to remain a firefighter. She had no idea what other interests he had that might suggest an alternative career. That was something else he'd need to decide.

Brian would want out of the hospital as soon as it was medically advisable to release him, and his family would support his decision. But she couldn't see him hanging out for long at the Lucky 7, which was an hour out of town, while he did his rehab every day at the center right next to the hospital in Jackson. Every time he got back home, his father and elder brother would be all over him like ants at a picnic.

Brian was going to want a place in town. His wife had gotten their house in the divorce a year past, and he hadn't yet bought himself another. Taylor figured if she played her cards right, she could offer him convenient housing—with her—while he learned to walk again.

She'd earned good money as a corporate pilot, mostly because King owned the plane she flew, and he'd allowed her to keep a portion of the rental for the use of it. She'd also earned a nice fee dropping smoke jumpers for whoever needed her, be it Forest Service, Bureau of Land Management, or some other entity.

Taylor had invested her money wisely, buying property in Jackson during the brief moments when the very expensive market was down. She was a landlord with six rental properties—and six mortgages. She'd chosen not to question the fact that her father owned the bank that had approved her six loan applications. As far as she was concerned, she was a qualified borrower. She had a steady income, good credit, and she'd never once been late paying her mortgages.

At the moment, Taylor was simply grateful that she would be able to offer Brian an alternative place to live. Her nicest rental, a single-story, four-bedroom, wood-and-stone house that backed up on a creek, in a neighborhood shaded by aspen and evergreens, was a summer week-to-week rental, and the latest tenants were leaving on Friday, which was the last day of August, and coincidentally, the end of the summer season in Jackson. Because she'd been aware she might find herself without a roof over her head if Matt kicked her out, she hadn't yet rented it out for the winter ski season.

She could take possession of the house in a matter of days, fix it up, paint it, store the current furnishings, and replace everything with things she liked and hoped Brian would like. When the time was right—that is, when he could no longer stand his hovering family—she would let Brian know that he was welcome to share the house with her.

Taylor's mind was racing a thousand miles a minute, but her heart was sinking lower and lower. It was all well and good to offer Brian a substitute place to stay during his rehabilitation. The trick was going to be getting him to accept it. He wasn't going to want to spend time with her while he was struggling to walk, any more than he wanted to be around his family.

She would need to come up with a way to pitch the idea so he wouldn't refuse. However, she was pretty sure that, if she timed it just right, whatever she said would be good enough, especially if he needed an escape from his loving, but overbearing, father and elder brother.

Taylor heaved a shuddering sigh at all the work she had ahead of her, work that needed to be completed on a short timeline. Failure was not an option. She had a vested interest in making sure that Brian was restored in body and spirit, because he was the man with whom she planned to spend the rest of her life.

Even if he wasn't on board with the idea at the moment.

It would have been far easier to take Brian at his word at the hospital, to fall back on her lifelong belief that she just wasn't the sort of person a man could love. But something had happened to her in the wilderness.

Brian had happened. He'd said he loved her, and she'd believed him. They'd planned their futures together. And when he'd been incapacitated, she'd found inner resources she hadn't known she had and fought for both Brian's life and her own. She'd kept them alive long enough to be rescued. And she'd done it because she wanted to spend her life sharing the love Brian had promised.

She wasn't about to give up now, just because Brian was feeling scared of what the future held. She was scared, too. There were no guarantees going forward that everything would turn out the way either of them hoped. But she wasn't going to let his fear keep her away.

Taylor wasn't stupid. Or naïve. Even though she'd grown up in a houseful of girls, or maybe because of it, she had some inkling of how fragile the male ego was. Men were like some of the most resilient sea creatures, soft and vulnerable on the inside, with a hard shell they hid behind whenever they felt threatened.

At the hospital, Brian had been doing and saying only what was necessary to protect himself, until he could come back stronger than ever. She'd gathered, from the way he was talking, that he wasn't sure he was ever going to be the man he once had been. His order to "go away" was simply the result of a vulnerable creature retreating into his protective shell.

Taylor could understand Brian's anger and grief over having to give up work he loved. She was perfectly willing to give him time to heal and adjust to his new reality.

But not too much time.

She wasn't going to wait until Brian was completely well and trust him to pick up their relationship where they'd left off in the wilderness. She was going to walk beside him every step along the way. Loving him. Letting him lean on her, letting him learn he could trust her not to walk away from him again.

"Taylor?"

Taylor started. "Leah. I didn't see you."

"You've been standing in the middle of the kitchen staring out the window for the past ten minutes. Is something wrong?"

"No. Nothing." Then she took a closer look at Leah and realized that her sister's stark hazel eyes were surrounded by deep, dark circles. "Are *you* all right?"

"I . . . I'll be fine."

"I've been back nearly two weeks, and you still look like death warmed over," Taylor said. "Something's keeping you up at night." She thought of the pain Leah must be suffering as a result of Aiden's bet with Brian. But unless Leah brought it up, she didn't want to mention it. "What is it, Leah? What's wrong?"

Leah opened her mouth to speak and shut it again. She found her way to a barstool and settled onto it, gesturing Taylor to the stool next to her. "King's in trouble."

Taylor snorted. That wasn't what she'd been expecting to hear. "*King's* in trouble? Why should you care what happens to him? He's treated you the worst of all of us. You're the one who planned to run Kingdom Come the rest of your life. You're the one being thrown out of house and home because he made a devil's bargain to get his 'Black Sheep' back in the fold.

"I suppose that's reason enough for those dark circles under your eyes," Taylor said. "But you've dealt with problems like this before and never looked this bad. What is it, Leah? What's keeping you awake at night?"

Is Aiden Flynn the one making you miserable? Would you like me to kick him in the balls? Would you like me to knock him down and—

"Angus has King by the throat, and this time it's a death grip."

So, not Aiden. Aiden's father.

Angus threatening King, or vice versa, was of more concern to Taylor than she was willing to admit to her sister. Anything that raised the stakes between her father and Brian's threatened the relationship she hoped to have with him. "What is it this time? Brian mentioned something about Angus interfering with King's efforts to renew the loan on some property in South America. Is that it?"

"King mortgaged everything he has to buy grassland in Argentina, and he doesn't have the money to pay off the note. He's going to lose everything, if Angus follows through on his threat to keep the banker from extending the loan."

"What is Daddy going to do?"

Leah's eyes flicked toward Taylor's when she used a name she'd rarely called their father since childhood. "King says he has a plan," Leah said, "but I can't imagine what it might be. I do the books. If there were any assets to be gleaned, I'd know about it."

"Is that why you haven't been yourself lately?"

"No. There's . . . something else."

Taylor's brow furrowed at the tremor in her sister's voice. Leah was the strong one, the anchor that kept them all from being adrift in a frightening and unfriendly world. Should she tell Leah she knew about the bet between Aiden and Brian? Or should she keep silent? "Can I help?"

Leah shook her head. "I have to make a decision about something. I may have a way to stop Angus in his tracks."

"What are you planning?"

Leah shook her head. "I can't tell you that. Not yet. If I do this . . . thing . . . it might backfire. I have no way of knowing. And the wrong decision could spell disaster for . . ."

"For whom, Leah?"

Leah's eyes looked bleak. "For me."

Taylor put her arms around her sister and realized Leah was trembling. This couldn't just be business. Aiden Flynn must be mixed up in this somewhere. "Leah," she said, putting her hands on her sister's arms and taking a step back so she could see into her eyes. "If there's anything I can do to help, you have to let me know."

Leah pressed her lips flat, as though to keep any request for help from coming out.

"Did you know I own six houses?" Taylor said.

A small smile curved Leah's lips. "King complained that you were on your way to becoming a real estate mogul when he okayed the loan for the most recent purchase."

Taylor pursed her lips. So much for getting those loans on her own merits. "I suppose he told them to loan me the money."

"He told them that if you didn't qualify, they shouldn't give you the loan."

"Oh." She thought about it and said, "Well, that was mean of him. What if I hadn't qualified?"

Leah laughed. "How could you not? From what I've seen, you've been pretty savvy with your investments."

"If I am, it's because I learned it from you."

"If I were better at managing the ranch—"

"You're great at managing the ranch. You can't help it if King got a wild hair up his ass and yanked the rug out from under you by offering it to Matt."

"Taylor," she admonished, speaking to her grown-up child with the authority of the mother she'd always been, "that's no way to speak about your father."

"I just want you to know that, if you get kicked out of here, you'll always have a place to stay. You can have your pick of—"

Leah hugged her tight and then let her go. "Thank you, Taylor. With any luck at all, that won't be necessary. I may have . . . other plans."

"Like what?" Taylor thought of Aiden Flynn and worked to keep the worry from her brow.

Leah smiled and said, "You'll know when I know."

Chapter 29

THE MORNING AFTER he woke up, when his fellow fire-fighters from the Jackson Hole fire station came by to visit, Brian could see in their eyes what they thought about his chances of getting back to work. Slim to none. Every time one of them shook his hand as he or she was leaving, Brian gritted his teeth and promised himself that he'd prove them all wrong.

Except he wasn't sure his leg was going to cooperate.

When the doctor changed his bandages later that morning, and he saw the extent of the damage for the first time, his heart sank to his toes. A six-inch stretch of his calf had been sheared of flesh to within an inch or so of the bone. He was still on an antibiotic IV drip, and would be for quite a while, to make sure the infection was gone for good. He was refusing painkillers because they made him groggy, and the resulting pain made him grouchy.

Brian hated being stuck in bed, but the doctor had warned him he would do more damage than good if he got out of it. Aiden had brought him the latest Jack

Reacher novel, but he didn't have the patience to read it. He felt like yelling. Hollering the roof down. He felt as surely imprisoned as if he'd never gotten out of that goddamned cave.

When Battalion Chief Fire Marshal Kathy Warren came by at noon, he sat up a little straighter and ignored the pounding in his maimed calf.

"You look better than I thought you would," she said, regarding him with a critical eye. "When are you coming back to work?"

Brian was so shocked by the chief's comment that he couldn't find his voice for a moment. "You're expecting me back?"

"Why not? You had the best scores I've ever seen on the Work Capacity Test. Presuming you can get that leg in shape and get an okay from your doctor, I don't see why you can't be one of my firefighters."

The chief laid a hand on his shoulder and said, "Keep your chin up, Brian. See you in a couple of months."

When she was gone, Brian remembered how hard he'd trained for his Work Capacity Test the previous year. He tried to imagine how, dressed in full Bunker gear, including air bottle, SCBA (self-contained breathing apparatus), pants, coat (three layers—thermal, waterproof, and rip-proof), boots, helmet, and gloves, he was going to perform the difficult series of firefighting skills required—and not just complete them, but do it within five minutes—on this bum leg.

Shit.

He understood from the doctor that there was no replacing the muscle he'd cut out. Where was he going to get the leg strength he needed?

He looked up, saw Aiden in the doorway, and said, "You look like your dog died. I'm the one with the crippled leg. What the hell is your problem?"

"You're my problem."

Brian's heartbeat ratcheted up. "Is there something the doctor didn't tell me? Is the infection worse? Does he want to cut off my leg?"

"Whoa there, Mr. Leaps-out-of-planes-into-burning-forests. Don't start jumping to conclusions."

"Then what is it?"

Aiden settled onto the foot of Brian's bed. "Would you believe a romance gone wrong?"

Brian hissed out a relieved breath. The infection wasn't back. And the doctor didn't want to cut off his leg. He suddenly realized what must be troubling Aiden. "Leah?"

"Who else?"

"I'm sorry, Aiden. What I did, telling her about the bet, was the pits. You can have my Harley as soon—" Brian yelped when Aiden jumped up quickly enough to jerk the sheets around his leg. "Ow! Watch it!"

Aiden didn't apologize, just glared at him. "I don't want your damned Harley. I want Leah back."

"So get her back!" Brian snapped. "And stay off my bed." He grimaced as he gently rearranged the sheet around his injured limb.

Aiden paced the room in agitation. "She says she can never trust me again. She's not giving me a second chance."

"Then move on."

He stopped and confronted Brian. "You just don't get it."

"Get what?"

"I love her. I want to spend my life with her."

Brian bit his tongue rather than say, "It'll never work." But he didn't think it would ever work. It wasn't just the animosity between their families. The obstacle keeping them apart was plain old logistics. Both Aiden and Leah ran their fathers' ranches, which meant they needed to live in two different places. Matt's appearance had complicated things for Leah, but Brian didn't think she'd give up Kingdom Come without one hell of a fight. And Aiden would never leave the Lucky 7. "If you're looking for suggestions," Brian said. "I don't have any."

Aiden groaned as he ruffled his hair, then smoothed it back down. "I just needed to vent with someone, and since you're the only other person who knows about this, you're it."

"Uh. That's not exactly true."

"Brian, if you've—" Aiden began.

Brian put up both hands to cut him off. "Hey! Tag and I thought we were going to die in that cave. I was feeling guilty about never being able to make things square with you, so I told her what I did."

His brother looked horrified. "She knows about me and Leah?"

"Not about you being married. But yeah, she knows about the bet. I didn't tell Tag not to say anything, but I don't think she will. I mean, she wouldn't want to hurt

Leah's feelings by telling her she knows what we did. Would she? Should I call her—"

"No! Hell, no. If you fuck this up any more than you already have, Brian, I swear I'll hack off both your legs myself."

"Don't worry. I won't be seeing Tag again."

Aiden frowned. "I thought you guys got kind of close. When Leah and I found the two of you, she was holding you in her arms like you were the love of her life. From what I saw, and what I heard later, she's the one who kept you alive."

Brian felt his face flush with embarrassment. "I have no idea what she did, because I was out of it. Nobody's said anything to me about her part in this before now."

"Well you should get down on your knees—when you can—and thank her."

Brian remembered how he'd kicked Tag out of his room. How he'd denied having any feelings for her. No wonder she'd been so mad.

He missed her. Missed her constant chatter. Missed holding her, touching her, being inside her. He had vivid memories of the two of them during the last days he'd been lucid. How he'd told Tag he loved her. How they'd planned their future together.

But he wasn't the same man who'd spoken those words of love. And he needed time and space to figure out whether he was going to have any sort of future to offer her.

Aiden had remained silent, and Brian realized the two of them made a great pair, both of them brooding over

Grayhawk women. He would have laughed, if the whole situation hadn't been so tragic.

"Sorry I couldn't be more help solving your problem with Leah," he said at last.

"Yeah. Me, too."

"What are you going to do?"

Aiden shrugged. "Wait. And hope. How about you?"

"Me?"

"Yeah, what about you and Tag?"

"There's nothing—"

"Don't try to bullshit me. She's in love with you. If I remember correctly, you spent a lot of time sulking in your room when she broke up with you in high school. You saved her life getting the two of you out of that plane and into the cave. She saved yours treating that wound in your leg. That sort of life-affirming experience tends to bond people."

"We're not stuck in a cave anymore. We have separate lives."

Aiden snorted. "If Tag's the woman you want, you should run after her as fast as you can."

"I can't *run* anywhere."

"You don't have to be standing on two feet to let her know you're interested. She showed up in this room the instant she got out of her hospital bed, and she sat there beside you day after day until you woke up. That says something."

"Shit."

"What's wrong now?"

"I threw her out. I told her not to come back."

"You'll kick yourself from here to Sunday," Aiden

said, "if you let her get away a second time. Maybe I won't end up with the love of my life, but there's no reason you have to screw up your love life as well. Don't just lie there." He gave Brian a slap on his back. "Do something about it."

He turned and marched out of the room, leaving Brian with a stinging shoulder and a great deal of food for thought.

Chapter 30

BRIAN WAS EXHAUSTED. And frustrated. Angry with both himself and his doctor. His recovery was progressing much slower than he'd expected. He'd been warned it would take six full weeks—from the end of August until mid-October—for him to heal enough to leave the hospital. But the slower his recovery, the less patience he had.

He missed Tag. Despite saying, with absolute certainty, "I'll be back," she hadn't come to the hospital again. Which left him wondering what had happened to keep her away. Aiden had urged him to call her, but he'd stubbornly refused, arguing, "I want to be off crutches first."

He hadn't seen or spoken to her since she'd left his room in a huff.

He'd been relieved at first that he didn't have to hide his suffering from her or pretend he was doing all right, when he felt discouraged and depressed at his lack of improvement. At the same time, it would have been nice to have her around to soothe his tattered soul as he struggled to get well.

He knew she was only a phone call away. But he never made the call.

Brian wasn't sure what had stopped him. Except, his leg looked like a mangled piece of meat, and he didn't want to subject Tag to the sight of it. He could hardly bear to look at it himself, and he didn't want her to hear him screaming—from the excruciating agony—when he tried to use the damned thing.

He left the hospital without telling her he was well enough to go home.

Aiden had insisted he stay at the ranch during rehab, even though it meant a drive back and forth to town, an hour each way every day.

"I need to know you're okay." The anxious look in Aiden's eyes had nearly undone him.

Brian was concerned when he learned that things hadn't improved between his brother and Leah. Aiden needed him to be nearby as much as he needed his brother to keep him on an even keel during his recuperation.

If that weren't enough reason to move home, his father had chimed in, "Who's going to cook for you if you stay in town? Who's going to do your laundry? Who's going to drive you back and forth to therapy? You're better off here."

Brian was certain he could have arranged everything if he'd been on his own, but it was easier to let his needs be taken care of for him.

At least, it was at the start. By the first week in November, he was like a bull with an unwanted rider on its back, bucking in all directions to get free.

Brian knew his family cared—and Aiden needed him as a sounding board for his romantic woes—which only worsened his guilt about wanting to get away. He still relied on crutches to walk. He hadn't even graduated to the cane he'd initially thought so abhorrent. He felt trapped.

So one day, while Aiden was out on the range, and Angus was locked behind the door of his office, he called an Uber and escaped to town.

During the long ride, Brian contemplated his situation. His slow recuperation was partly his own fault. He'd tried doing too much too soon and had set back his healing a couple of weeks. Not that healing had been going along without a hitch. He'd needed more antibiotics, and his leg throbbed even when he wasn't putting weight on it. And if he had to listen to Aiden say one more time, "Just be patient, Brian," he thought he might go bat-shit crazy.

Worst of all, his slow recovery meant he wasn't able to drive. He would have felt foolish buying a truck that had all the necessary equipment to operate the vehicle attached to the steering wheel, when he expected to be able to use his Chevy Silverado any day. But he'd been in rehab for five weeks—three weeks in the hospital and two weeks out—and "any day" hadn't arrived. He was at the mercy of his brother, his father, or one of the ranch hands, if he wanted to go anywhere or do anything. Which necessarily meant Angus and Aiden were able to keep track of where he was and what he was doing every second of every day.

Brian was tired of being dependent on other people, tired of asking for favors. Even his use of an Uber wasn't without its downside. One of his high school football buddies was driving and brought up the subject of all the girls the two of them had dated, including Taylor Grayhawk.

Tag was the last person he wanted to talk about, but his friend wouldn't let the subject go. Brian answered with "Yeah" and "Sure" and "Uh-huh" for the entire hour it took to get into town, and reconsidered the necessity of buying a truck intended for people without the use of their legs.

When he finally stepped inside the Million Dollar Cowboy Bar it was nearly dark, and the lights inside were inviting. He looked forward to having a drink without someone asking if it was a good idea for him to be consuming alcohol when he was taking medication.

Brian made his way to the bar on his crutches and realized when he got there how difficult it would be to seat himself on one of the saddles the bar used for stools. His lips flattened in disgust. He was going to have to think about such things for the rest of his life.

He was about to head for a table when he heard his name called.

"Brian?"

He recognized that sultry voice. He shifted his gaze and found Tag sitting on one of the saddles. His stomach did a quick somersault and landed sideways.

"Hi, Tag." He was so *glad* to see her.

She looked surprised to see him, but he wasn't sure how *glad* she was. He couldn't read her expression. Cautious? Anxious?

He didn't want her to take off, because he was pretty sure he wouldn't be able to move fast enough on crutches to catch up to her. He searched for something to say, but he was distracted by the sight of her.

She looked deliciously sexy. She'd let her blond hair grow even longer, and it looked bouncy and silky at the same time. She wore mascara that emphasized the long lashes above her blue eyes and lipstick that made him want to invade her mouth with his tongue. She wore a red cashmere sweater that fell off one smooth shoulder, a pair of jeans with a row of faux diamonds on the back pockets that emphasized her beautiful ass, and tooled leather cowboy boots.

"You look good," he said in a husky voice.

"Thanks."

After his stint in the hospital, he'd wondered if his libido was gone, along with a chunk of his leg. He got proof in the next thirty seconds that it was humming along on all cylinders, when a thick, hard ridge appeared behind the zipper of his jeans.

She searched his face and said, "You look good, too."

"Looks can be deceiving."

She glanced at the crutches he had propped under his arms. "Things not going as well as you hoped?"

"Not nearly as well as I'd hoped. I'm headed for one of those tables. Want to join me?"

He saw her hesitation and willed her to agree. At last she said, "All right."

She hadn't seemed enthusiastic, but at least she hadn't said no. He signaled the bartender, who brought him his regular drink, a twelve-year-old single-malt scotch. He pulled out a chair for her, then sat himself down to her right, laying the crutches on the floor. He eyed her drink, some kind of liquor mixed with what looked like Coke and a slice of lime, which she'd carried with her from the bar. "Can I buy you another one?"

She shook her head. "I'm driving."

"Lucky you, driving."

"You can't?"

"Not yet. To be honest, I'm not even close."

"Bummer."

She swallowed the last of her drink, and he had the feeling she was going to bolt. He wasn't sure what to do to keep her in her seat. He blurted, "I should have called."

"Yes, you should've." Her voice was decidedly cool.

"What have you been doing with yourself?"

"This and that."

She wasn't making this easy. But why should she? He was the one who'd kicked her out of his life. Apparently, she was in no hurry to step back in. Of course, now that she was running, he felt obliged to chase her. Even if he had to do it on crutches.

"I've been out of the hospital for two weeks," he said.

"I heard."

"I've been staying at home."

"How is that going?"

"What?" He was so distracted by the nipples that sud-

denly budded under her sweater that he'd lost his train
of thought.

"Recuperating at home," she said. "How's that
going?"

He pulled his gaze away from her chest and focused it
on her face. "Not as well as I'd like."

"It's too bad you don't live here in town," she said.
"At least then you could get around on your crutches,
you know, visit the guys at the firehouse, get to rehab
more easily."

She was right about that. Maybe he ought to stay at
a hotel tonight and spend time tomorrow looking for a
more convenient place to live.

"I moved to town last month," she said.

"Did Matt do something to piss you off?"

"No more than usual. I just decided to leave the ranch
on my own terms, rather than wait for him to shove me
out the door."

"Where are you living?"

"I've got a one-story place on Snow King Mountain."

He whistled. "Nice." Brian considered how great it
would be if he had a one-story place of his own in town.
No stairs, the convenience of being close to rehab and
the fire station, so he could drop in to bullshit with
the guys, or just go get himself some lunch or dinner in
one of the restaurants in town. No father asking when
he was going to get back to work. No brother asking
him how he was feeling.

And then he had a brilliant idea.

He took a drink and swallowed to give himself another moment to consider before he said, "How many bedrooms do you have?"

"Why do you ask?"

"How would you like to rent one to me?"

"I wouldn't."

"Come on, Tag. Have a heart. I'm a cripple. I—"

"You said you wanted me gone, Brian. Now you want to live in the same house? I don't think so."

"Aiden and Angus are killing me with kindness. If I don't get away from the Lucky 7 soon, I can't be held responsible for my actions. You don't want me ending up in prison for murder, do you?"

She laughed, and the bubbly sound woke up something inside him that had been dormant from the moment she'd walked out of his hospital room—and his life. He suddenly saw Tag stark naked in all her glory. He had no trouble imagining what it would be like to put himself inside her.

Then he remembered how ugly his right leg looked—a vein-streaked, hacked-up, scar-laden, red-and-purple mess. He'd have to hop his way to bed on one leg. He wasn't even sure whether he could support himself on his knees without causing some kind of cramping in his calf, which would be humiliating.

His arousal died a sobering death.

"How about it?" he said, his voice harsh with the realization that he had a long way to go before he could make love to her.

"It would never work, Brian. Our families would have a fit."

"Do you care? Aren't we past that? Didn't we already decide not to let them rule our lives?"

"That was before. This is after. Things have changed."

"What? Name one thing."

"You're not a whole man."

His face blanched. It felt as though she'd stabbed him in the heart.

She grabbed his arm to keep him from rising. "I didn't mean that the way it sounded. You still don't know how much use you'll have of your injured leg, whether it will allow you to resume your work as a firefighter—or not. You have a lot of decisions to make about your life.

"If you move in, it could complicate things even more. Sitting here, knowing how badly you treated me, I still want you. And I believe you want me." She shot him an expressive look from beneath lowered lashes that made it clear what she meant. His body reacted immediately, proving her right. "I don't see us denying ourselves what we want for long."

He would have jumped in, but she didn't give him a chance.

"I wish I could ignore the feelings I have when I'm with you. I can't. My point is I don't want to end up getting hurt—again—when you finally make up your mind what you're going to do with the rest of your life and decide you don't want me to be a part of it."

"Can I say something now?"

She nodded.

"All you're doing is renting me a room. I'll feed myself in town. I'll get myself to rehab. All I *want* is a place to stay that's far away from my loving family." He smiled to ease the bite of his words. He loved his family, he just needed some distance from them.

She smiled ruefully, and he held his breath, hoping that meant she was going to give in.

"You know this is a mistake, Brian."

"Please, Tag. I'm desperate."

He saw her uncertainty, her fear, and finally, her surrender. "All right," she said. "When do you want to move in?"

He felt a knot of tension ease in his shoulders. "Tonight."

She made a face. "Tonight? Isn't that a little sudden?"

"I told you, I'm at the end of my rope. I can buy whatever I need for now at the drugstore and get a bag of clothes from home some other time."

She looked skeptical. "Are you sure this is what you want to do?"

"Absolutely." He saw several thoughtful wrinkles appear in her forehead and asked, "Is there another problem?"

She looked sheepish. "I'm trying to remember whether I left dishes in the kitchen sink and magazines strewn all over the living room."

"Just so long as you have sheets for the bed—"

"Oh, I made up all the beds."

"*All* the beds? How many are there?"

"Four. One in each bedroom." She looked embarrassed as she admitted, "I was having so much fun, I got a little carried away decorating. I just . . ." She shrugged. "Did the whole place."

"I can't wait to see it."

"Finish up your drink, and I'll take you there."

Brian realized Tag might be right. He might be making a mistake moving in with her. She was clearly wary of renewing their romance. He would have to respect the limits she'd set and tell his libido to take a hike.

But he didn't see where he had a choice. It was move in with her or go certifiably crazy. One danger seemed a whole lot less frightening than the other.

Chapter 31

IN SEPTEMBER, WHEN Brian had thrown her out of his hospital room, Taylor had been shocked and hurt. In the days that followed, he hadn't called to apologize. He hadn't communicated at all. It was painful to admit that Leah might be right, but if Brian didn't want her, she sure as hell wasn't going to run after him—no matter what she'd told him when she'd made her defiant exit from his room.

Then she'd missed her period.

Taylor was as regular as clockwork, but she gave herself the benefit of the doubt. She'd been through a horrendous experience that could have thrown her body clock off.

She hadn't been suffering from any kind of trauma when she missed the second one in October.

Taylor had taken a drugstore pregnancy test, which turned out positive. So did the next three. She was definitely pregnant.

Her first response was elation: *I'm going to have a baby!* Her second response was a swollen throat and

tears stinging her eyes that were *not* the result of happiness: *The timing couldn't be worse.* And then, a combination of both: *This is Brian's baby, too. I have to tell
him. But when? And how?*

He'd kicked her out of his hospital room and told her
not to come back. Taylor didn't want Brian making
some kind of noble gesture, like marrying her to give the
baby his name. It didn't escape her notice that she pic-
tured him doing the old-fashioned "noble" thing, rather
than telling her, "It's your problem. Take care of it." The
point was she didn't need him to rescue her. Women all
over the world were bringing up children on their own.
She was certainly capable of raising a baby without Brian's help.

A good part of the reason why she hadn't told him
about the baby yet was the fact that she could never quite
imagine the smile—the shit-eating "I did that" grin—
she hoped would appear when she gave him the joyous
news. Instead, she envisioned a frown of concern laced
with shock and dismay. Brian had problems enough of
his own without her throwing a baby into the mix.

Because of her pregnancy, Taylor had completely
abandoned the idea of having Brian move in with her
when he got tired of his family. She needed to make plans
of her own—for a nursery, and for Lamaze and breast-
feeding classes, since she wanted to have natural childbirth and nurse the baby. She had to schedule a visit to
her ob-gyn to get a checkup and a prescription for pre-
natal vitamins. She was busy growing a baby inside her
belly, and frankly, didn't have the energy to cope with

another spoiled-rotten baby, who couldn't face the truth about his future.

That's a little harsh, don't you think?

No. I'm just telling it like I see it.

She had to face facts. She had to walk away from Brian Flynn and move on with her life.

The decision made, Taylor had visited her ob-gyn late this afternoon. Afterward, she'd headed to the Million Dollar Cowboy Bar to celebrate her good health, and the good health of her child. She'd asked the bartender for, "A rum and Coke, please. Hold the rum. And a slice of lime."

She was sitting at the bar, summoning up the courage to tell her family about the baby—a *Flynn* baby—when Brian Flynn walked in.

Taylor should have slid off that saddle seat and run like the devil was on her heels. She should never have said one single word to him. What on earth had possessed her to let Brian Flynn back into her life?

Hope. You're clinging to the hope that, once the cloud of pain and confusion about his future has cleared, Brian will be able to see you as the love of his life.

Taylor had known she was taking a terrible chance even speaking to him. The more time she spent with Brian, the more chance of becoming emotionally engaged. It had been heartbreaking when she made the completely logical decision to walk away from him after his rant at the hospital, to cut off her love like an amputated limb. She'd gone through several boxes of Kleenex and still left her pillow wet with tears. It would be devastating if she allowed herself to fall in love with Brian all over again, and he abandoned her for a second time.

And there was a ticking time bomb—

That's no way to describe your darling baby.

A *loudly ticking* time bomb growing in her belly. Brian was going to find out the truth. She ought to tell him sooner, rather than later, and give him a chance to back out of living in the same house with a woman who was carrying his baby, which he might or might not want to acknowledge.

Not now. Not yet. Give yourselves a little time.

For what? Brian's scarred flesh wasn't going to magically reconstitute itself. He was still on crutches. He'd winced with pain when he sat down in the bar, when he shifted in his chair, and when he got up again. He must always be on the edge of lashing out—at whoever was closest—when he suffered such constant torment.

At what point should she add to that burden by telling him she was pregnant with his baby?

Not now, for heaven's sake! Get hold of yourself. You'll know when the time is right. Just wait. Wait until you see which way the wind is blowing. And don't give up hope.

Brian threw his crutches into the back of her pickup, hopped—and huffed and puffed—his way to the door, then used his arms and his good leg to lift himself inside.

He heaved a sigh of relief that appeared as a cloud in front of his mouth before he closed the door. "Fall has fallen," he said. "I want to be off these crutches before I have to worry about navigating icy sidewalks."

Taylor started the engine and headed for the closest

overnight pharmacy, where Brian could buy the supplies he needed. "What does the physical therapist say?"

"The same thing Aiden is always saying."

"Which is?"

"Be patient."

"I take it that's not one of your better qualities."

"You noticed? I want to be back on both feet without the need for either crutches or a cane, and I want it now."

She shot him a teasing look and said, "You'll just have to be patient."

Brian's laughter was cut short when she hit a pothole that jarred his leg.

She watched him grit his teeth, but he didn't say anything, so she didn't either.

She bit the inside of her cheek to keep from suggesting that she be the one to shop at the drugstore. She simply parked in front of the brightly lit store and said, "Have fun!"

She saw him flinch when he exited the truck, gasp as he hopped to the back of the pickup for his crutches, and grit his teeth as he headed inside. He returned five minutes later with two plastic bags, which he threw onto the bench seat between them, before repeating the whole "throw the crutches in the back and hop to the seat" business.

Four tension-filled minutes later, without another word of conversation, they arrived at her house on the mountain.

"This is it," she said, as she hit the button for the door and pulled into the two-car garage.

Taylor couldn't help remembering how, earlier in the

day, she'd been moping around her lovely home, regretting the fact that Brian would never lounge on the leather couch or be sprawled beside her on the woolly buffalo hide in front of the stone fireplace.

Suddenly, he was here.

"Do you want me to get your crutches for you?" The words were out before she could stop them. She knew Brian didn't want her help, or anybody else's, which his next words confirmed.

"I can do it."

She stood at the kitchen door waiting for him, then stepped back to let him inside.

"Wow, Tag," he said, his gaze darting, taking in the sizeable main floor, which had an open concept. "This place is amazing."

"Thanks. It was trashed when I bought it, but I managed to put it back together a little bit at a time."

"I like the fact that it's perched on a mountain and tucked in among the trees, yet still walking distance to town. I'll bet it's beautiful here when the aspens turn gold."

"It was." That had happened during the last week of September and the first week of October, when she'd been pining for a moment with Brian just like this. Now the aspens were bare, but enough conifers were left— lodgepole pine and blue spruce—to make it feel like the house was nestled in the forest.

She watched Brian turn in a circle, using his crutches to prop him up. The great room, with its cathedral ceiling, included the living room, dining room, and kitchen.

"I love the wood in the floors and counters and the

stone in the walls and the fireplace," he said. "Best of all, you have a couch long enough for me to stretch out on."

She smiled, remembering how, when she'd first been planning to have Brian as a roommate, she'd argued with the furniture guy to get her a longer couch. "It was the biggest one I could find. You can have the couch, but the chair and ottoman are mine."

The seating area faced the wood-burning fireplace, which Taylor had been using often, now that the nights were cold. Snow already capped the Tetons, but the sun had melted what little precipitation they'd had in town.

She gestured toward the island that separated the kitchen and living room and said, "Help yourself to whatever you want from the fridge. Silverware is in the drawers, china and glasses are in the cupboards next to the sink."

"Thanks. Where's my room?"

Before Taylor had found out she was pregnant, when she was planning the best way to coax Brian into staying with her, she'd thought long and hard about where to put him. One bedroom was separated from the other three. She'd decided to give that one to him, since it had both a sitting room and an attached bath. She'd been living in the second largest bedroom, which had a Jack-and-Jill bathroom attached to another, equally large bedroom, which she planned to decorate for the baby.

Luckily, she hadn't yet begun that transformation.

Taylor walked ahead of Brian to his bedroom. Back when she'd been plotting and planning to get him here, she'd made the room as masculine as she could without giving away her game. The king-sized bed had a stripped-log headboard and footboard, and the dresser was pine. The curtains and bedspread were burnt sienna—what Brian would have called reddish brown—and the knobby-wool rug on the hardwood floor was the color of desert sand.

She'd decorated the bed with a stack of pillows in various sizes and complementary colors, just to make it look a bit more feminine, and to keep Brian from noticing that the room had been intended for use by a man. To be absolutely sure he didn't guess what she'd had in mind, she'd added a stuffed animal. The floppy-eared dog sat in front of the pillows.

Brian immediately reached down and picked it up. "Who's this?" he asked, grinning and wagging the black-and-white-spotted dog at her.

She reached for it and said, "Give him to me, Brian. That's Spot. Vick got him for me one Christmas."

"Do you have a watchdog guarding all your beds?"

She wrinkled her nose. "If it's any consolation, he doesn't bite."

Brian chuckled and pitched the stuffed animal to her. "I think he'll be happier in your room."

The two plastic bags full of stuff he'd bought at the drugstore were still hanging from one of his hands, where it was hooked over a crutch.

"Do you need any help putting those things away in the bathroom?" she asked.

"I can take care of it."

"Would you like a cup of coffee, or something stronger?" She hesitated and said, "Or something weaker? A cup of hot milk or cocoa?"

He shook his head. "No, but thank you. To be honest, I'm bushed. I've been working hard every day to get better, and I seem to need more sleep than I'm getting. If you don't mind, I'll just say good night."

"There's a TV behind the doors to that chest, and the bookcase in the corner has a few novels I've enjoyed." In fact, she'd chosen every book on the shelves with Brian in mind, and the TV had every sports package she could find. "The Broncos have a home game tomorrow, if you want to watch it with me in the living room," she added.

"That sounds like it might be fun. I have to admit I haven't paid much attention to football the past couple of months."

"The Broncos are undefeated so far this season. They have a new running back—"

He held up his hand. "I'll look forward to hearing all about it tomorrow. Good night, Tag."

It felt funny stepping out of the room and having Brian close the door in her face. Somehow, when she'd imagined him sleeping in that king-sized bed, she'd imagined herself lying right there beside him.

Brian might be tired, but Taylor was far too excited to sleep. He'd talked her into renting him a room. He was sleeping right down the hall.

Where did she go from here?

Taylor wondered if she ought to implement a few of the ideas she'd come up with when she'd first planned to lure Brian into her home. The most important thing she'd decided, which applied equally to their current circumstances, was to give him space to figure out what he wanted to do next. She wanted him to feel that the pressure was off, that he could recover at his own speed.

One of her more inventive ideas had involved dressing for *sex*-cess, that is, wearing outfits intended to spike Brian's desire and heighten his physical awareness of her. She debated the wisdom of doing that now. Did she want to incite Brian's passion? To what end?

Maybe he has feelings for you that have taken a backseat to getting well. Maybe, with a little encouragement, his desire—along with his deep feelings for you— will be rekindled.

Taylor got ready for bed, taking a quick shower and washing her hair, then put on a silky nightgown that left very little to the imagination. She lighted the wood fire she'd set earlier, then sat down in her chair in the living room, put her feet up on the ottoman, and continued reading her book, which she kept on a table beside the chair.

The room was silent, except for the crackling fire, when she heard the thump of Brian's crutches on the wood floor in the hall. Taylor sat up, but she didn't get up. The only light in the room came from the reading lamp over her chair and the blue and yellow flames in the fireplace. She waited for him to reach the living room and say something.

But he never did.

"Brian? Are you—" she cut herself off. *Do not ask if he's all right!* "Would you like to join me?" she called out instead, glancing over her shoulder toward the hall, where she found him in the shadows.

He was naked except for a pair of black briefs—the kind that hugged his sex. His chest looked even more powerful than it had the day they'd gotten trapped in the cave. His lower right leg was lost in darkness. She made a point of keeping her gaze focused on his face.

"I couldn't sleep after all," he said. "Do you mind?"

"Of course not." As a host, she should offer to get him whatever he wanted, but she was also determined to let him do things for himself. "Make yourself comfortable."

She focused her attention back on her book, but she couldn't make out a single word on the page.

"What are you reading?" he asked, once he was settled on the couch with his back against the arm farthest from her.

She glanced up and bit her cheek to keep from gasping at the sight of his calf, which wasn't more than three feet from the end of her nose. She worked hard not to shudder. "It's Stephen King. One of the scary ones." But not as scary as Brian's leg.

He chuckled. "Aren't they all scary?" He rearranged the pillow behind his back, then settled his wounded leg on a pillow at the other end of the couch. "My leg swells during the day, so I need to keep it elevated," he explained. "Pretty awful, huh?"

She saw the fear in his eyes that she would be revolted by the devastation wrought on his leg by the surgeon. She forced herself to look at his mutilated flesh, keeping her expression neutral. She was appalled at how much of the muscle was missing from his calf. There was not more than an inch or two of flesh covering the bone.

When she'd examined his calf thoroughly, she met his gaze and said, "I agree it's not a pretty sight." She bit back her next question: "How in the world do you walk on it?"

Taylor could see why anyone living with Brian would have a difficult time not asking "How are you?" or "How do you feel?" or "How's the rehab going?" She wanted to ask all those questions herself. But she stilled her tongue and let him do the talking.

"I thought I'd be further along by now," he said.

She kept her eyes focused on her book and said, "Uh-huh."

"The chief told me she'd take me back, if I can pass muster physically."

"That's good news," she said, reading the same sentence again.

"Hey! Look at me."

She looked up. "What?"

"Am I that boring?"

"I thought the whole reason you came here was because you were sick and tired of everyone asking about your injury. But that's pretty much all you've talked about since you sat down."

Taylor saw the shock on his face. She knew that getting back to normal must always be first and foremost in his thoughts. Part of what she hoped to accomplish by having Brian here was to get him focused on living a life that didn't necessarily depend on a leg that functioned normally.

Once that happened, she could tell him he was going to be a father.

He gave a self-deprecating laugh. "I guess I needed to hear that. I've been so absorbed by rehab that my life has shrunk down so it doesn't include much else."

"May I suggest Broncos football tomorrow afternoon?" she said with a playful smile.

"Sure. I'll make the popcorn."

"I just have 'girl' drinks in the fridge."

"Which are?"

"Diet Coke and a bottle of Chardonnay." The doctor had said she could have an occasional glass of wine, but she was waiting for one of her sisters to visit before opening the bottle.

"I'll have some Heineken delivered tomorrow along with my clothes," he said.

"Be sure to have whoever brings your stuff pick up some popcorn. I don't have any in the house."

He laughed. "You got it."

"Are you going to tell your family where you're staying?"

He thought about it for a moment. "I'll tell Aiden. He'll leave me alone and keep the rest of them from worrying. How about your family? What are they going to say when they find out we're roommates?"

"They won't like it, but it's my life." Taylor had long since realized she couldn't love Brian and keep fighting his family. Brian had more than once said he'd opted out of the feud between their fathers. Taylor wanted to try. She wasn't sure what Leah and Vick were going to say when they realized she was no longer going to wage war on the Flynns.

Taylor was lost in her thoughts when she heard Brian say, "By the way . . ."

She looked up. "By the way . . . what?"

He was grinning from ear to ear. "I like your taste in nightgowns."

Taylor glanced down and realized her nipples were clearly peaked beneath the ivory silk, and that the cloth was thin enough that Brian could see her areolas as clear as day. "Stop looking, Brian!" She dumped her book and jumped up, wrapping her arms around herself and lifting her breasts even higher, creating even more cleavage.

He bent over laughing. "That's like asking a wolf not to eat a piece of meat that's been thrown right into his mouth."

"You're a beast all right!" She grabbed for her book to cover her chest and stomped out of the room, his laughter following her all the way down the hall.

What Brian couldn't see was the delight on her face as she hurried into her bedroom and slammed the door. She hadn't purposely dressed for *sex*cess, but Brian had certainly noticed her as a woman. She was afraid to get her hopes up that she and Brian might have a future together, but they were sky-high nonetheless.

Taylor couldn't wait for the day when he was able to chase her down. And for what was sure to happen when she let him catch her.

Chapter 32

BRIAN WAS IN agony. He'd pushed too hard in rehab today, and his right leg was cramping. He was into his second week of living with Tag, and he just wanted to be off these damned crutches, so he didn't seem like such a cripple around her. The physical therapist kept saying he was well enough to walk with a cane, but he wasn't so sure. What if he tried and failed? Better not to attempt it until he was *absolutely sure* he would succeed. As for walking on his own two feet, that day seemed far in the future.

Or maybe impossible?

Tears of pain—and despair—squeezed from his eyes. He'd come home from rehab, plopped into Tag's chair in a T-shirt and thigh-length athletic shorts, and put his feet up on the ottoman, too tired even to get a shower. When he'd felt the first spasm, he'd done his best to point his toes toward his body to relax his calf muscle. The cramp had suddenly gone from a 4 to a 15. He'd bitten his lower lip until he tasted blood, to keep from shrieking.

"Brian?"

He uttered a tortured cry and gripped his right thigh so tightly with both hands he knew he was making bruises. But the muscles in his leg were strung as tight as barbed wire ready to snap, and he didn't know how else to counter the excruciating pain.

He heard several things land and roll on the wooden floor and then the sound of Tag running to the kitchen.

He arched his head back and clenched his jaw. He didn't want her to see him like this, but he didn't have the right to send her away. This was her home.

But he said it anyway. "Go away. Leave me be."

The next thing he knew, she was kneeling beside him, shifting a dish towel from hand to hand. "This might hurt."

When she slipped the towel around his calf and wrapped it tight, he realized why she'd been treating it like a hot potato. He hissed in a breath and yelped, "That's boiling hot!"

"It was the only thing I could think of to loosen your constricted muscles."

He realized she'd wet the towel from the dispenser at the sink that provided instant boiling water. "I'm going to end up with third degree burns on what flesh I have left," he muttered.

"Shut up and think of butterflies."

"What the hell do butterflies have to do with anything?"

She patted his hand where it gripped his thigh, then wrapped the towel more tightly around his leg. "Just think of something besides your leg and let this heat work."

Thirty seconds later he said, "It isn't working."

"The heat?"

"The physical therapy."

"Looks to me like you're doing too much too soon. Again."

"I want to walk with a cane. Is that asking so much?"

"It is if you end up torturing yourself with cramps."

"I'm afraid." He wanted to say more, but the words were caught in his throat. Did he dare tell her how scared he was that he'd never walk again without some sort of aid? That he didn't think his leg would ever be strong enough for him to go back to work as a firefighter? That he had no idea what he would do if he couldn't fight fires.

She met his gaze. "You're the bravest man I know, Brian. You can do this."

"I can't." He felt another spasm take hold and bit back a scream.

It took him a moment to realize she was gripping his injured calf—his ugly, deformed mess of an injured calf—in both hands as hard as she could. And it was easing the spasm.

"Oh, God, Tag. Hold on. Keep doing what you're doing. It's helping."

It took another thirty seconds—a lifetime—for the spasm to pass. He clenched his teeth and held his breath the whole time. It took him a moment to realize the pain was gone. He soughed out the breath of air he'd been holding and collapsed back against the chair.

He lowered his gaze to his hands, which were now knotted into helpless fists in his lap. "Thank you."

"I'm going to leave the towel wrapped around your calf."

She stood and headed toward the garage door.

"What did you drop?" he asked, glancing over his shoulder at her.

"The groceries." She gathered up a cucumber and a couple of apples that had rolled on the floor and set them on the kitchen counter.

"Come here, Tag."

She hurried toward him, and he knew she thought the cramps were back. When she reached him, he toppled her sideways into his lap.

"Brian! Your leg!"

"My leg is fine. But there are other body parts that need a little TLC." He nuzzled her neck and felt her stiffen in his arms, but only for a moment. Her body relaxed against his as her arms slid around his neck, and she laid her head on his shoulder.

"This is nice," he said.

"Yes, it is."

She gasped when he nibbled her earlobe and put a hand to his lips to stop him. "We have to be careful, Brian."

"Careful? I told you my leg is fine."

She sat up and looked him in the eye. "You said you loved me when we were lost in the forest. Then you kicked me out of your room at the hospital. Which Brian is holding me in his arms now?"

"Neither one of those idiots."

She laughed. "Were you an idiot for telling me you loved me? Or for kicking me out of your room?"

"I'm smart enough to know that when you have a beautiful woman in your arms the last thing you should do is talk."

He captured her mouth and tasted the honey inside. For a moment she was enthusiastically kissing him back. She suddenly withdrew and tucked her head under his chin, where he couldn't reach her mouth.

"There's something I need to tell you, Brian."

"I know. I know. What happened out there changed you. It changed me, too. I want to grab hold of everything good that comes my way and never let go." His arms tightened around her.

"Brian, I'm—"

He put two fingertips to her lips. "Shh. Don't say anything. Just sit here and let me hold you." He wasn't sure whether he was embracing her more to thank her or to comfort himself. Living with her was making him want a home of his own. Living with her was making him realize he'd never really gotten over her. That what he'd pronounced as love when he'd thought he was dying might turn out to be the real thing, now that death no longer loomed.

He understood why she was afraid of letting him get close. For the past two weeks, she'd been giving him conflicting signals, inviting him in, then backing off. She was ambivalent. Uncertain. Like tonight. Right there to help when he needed it but unwilling to accept the hug he'd wanted to give her as thanks.

"I think you need to give rehab more of a chance," she said.

"Even if it isn't working?"

"Do you want to walk with a cane? Or not?"

"I want to walk on my own two feet without help from anything or anyone."

He felt her hand on his cheek. "Then I think that's what you should do."

"But—"

She put two fingertips to his lips, then raised her head and kissed him lightly on the mouth. "That was for encouragement. So is this." She kissed him more deeply.

When they came up for air, she said, "Go back to rehab tomorrow and work hard, but know when it's time to rest, so you can be stronger the day after tomorrow."

"Will you be waiting here for me when I get back?"

"If boiling towels are your thing, I'm game."

He laughed. "I'll settle for a hug and a few lazy kisses."

She freed herself from his embrace and got to her feet. Her eyes looked troubled.

"What's wrong? I can tell there's something bothering you, Tag. Let me help."

"There's nothing you can do right now. It's something I have to deal with on my own."

"Are you sure?"

"I'm sure. You've got enough on your plate. I can handle this."

It dawned on him that he wanted to take care of her, to take her burdens on his shoulders. The problem was that he could barely take care of himself. She was wrong about taking the time to rest. He needed to work even harder to get well. If he had to suffer a few cramps now and then, it would be worth the pain to get back on his feet.

He didn't want to come wooing on crutches.

Chapter 33

KNEELING ON THE hard stone floor of her bathroom, her head perched over the toilet bowl, her stomach revolting against the piece of dry toast she'd dared to eat for breakfast, Taylor had time to contemplate what she'd done—or rather, had not done—last night.

The words "I'm pregnant" had been on the tip of her tongue. She couldn't believe she hadn't spoken them. She would never find a more propitious moment to break the news to Brian that he was going to become a father. But she'd chickened out.

The sharp knock on the door made her jerk fully upright, which unsettled her stomach, so she threw up again. Except she was vomiting with a completely empty stomach. Her eyes squeezed closed as she retched, then spit, then rinsed her mouth with water from the plastic cup sitting on the stone floor beside her and spit into the toilet, and finally, wiped her mouth with the hand towel in her lap.

She had the whole thing down to a handy system.

The door flew open and Brian was standing there, his brow furrowed, a look of worry in his eyes.

She stared at him with trepidation, certain he was going to figure out—jump to the conclusion—she had morning sickness. After all, as he'd pointed out himself, there had been no package of pills in her pocket, and they'd enjoyed plenty of sex in the wilderness.

He merely said, "I was headed to your room to ask you a question and heard you being sick. What's wrong?"

There it was staring her in the face. Another perfect opportunity to tell him about the whole pregnancy thing. She chickened out again.

"I think it must have been something I ate. You need to leave, or you'll be late for rehab."

Instead of making an about-face, he asked, "Have you taken anything for the nausea?"

As long as she kept her stomach full—which sometimes meant eating a peanut butter and jelly sandwich in midmorning, or having a bowl of soup an hour before having a late dinner with Brian—she was spared the indignity of actually throwing up. Not eating overnight was usually the problem. "I'll be fine. You need to leave." She wanted him gone before he was treated to the sight of her with her head over the toilet again. Except, it was already too late.

She lowered her head over the bowl and retched again.

"You poor thing." She heard his crutches clatter to the floor as he dropped to one knee beside her and held her hair out of the way.

When she finished, she grabbed for the cup of water

with her eyes still squeezed closed and ran into Brian's hand.

"Here. Is this what you want?" He pressed the cup into her hand.

She gratefully took it and rinsed and spit. Before she could set it down, he'd taken it from her and handed her the towel from her lap. If he wondered why, when she was sick without warning, she still had a cup of water to rinse her mouth and a towel to dry it, he didn't say anything.

She sank back and heaved a tremulous sigh.

"All done?" he asked.

She nodded, eyes closed. *Just leave. Please. I can handle this better if you'll just leave.*

"I want you to notice I dropped to one knee, without the aid of my crutches, and didn't fall flat on my face."

She opened her eyes. He was down on his left knee with his right leg bent at a ninety-degree angle. "Yeah. Yeah. But can you get back up?"

He laughed and shrugged. "If not, we can have a party here on the bathroom floor."

She couldn't believe he could make her laugh when she felt so awful. "Go away, Brian, and let me be sick."

"I thought you were all done."

It took her a moment to realize that her stomach, at long last, had settled down. "I am."

"Then let's get you into bed." He used the nearby bathroom counter to brace himself so he could get up and reached for one of his crutches to stabilize himself. "It's my turn to take care of you, young lady." He lowered the lid and flushed the toilet. Then he set the cup on the counter, threw the towel in the sink, and grasped her arm to pull her to her feet.

Once she was upright, she said, "I want to brush my teeth before I go back to bed."

He pulled her toothbrush out of the holder and opened the vanity drawer to find toothpaste, and handed both to her, then pulled the towel out of the sink. "Go for it."

Taylor was wearing a filmy nightgown, but she didn't think it was going to have much effect on Brian under the circumstances. Except, when she bent over the sink to spit out a mouthful of toothpaste, she was treated to a bird's-eye view of the bulge behind the placket of his Levi's.

Brian handed her the towel as she rose, and she met his heavy-lidded gaze as she wiped her mouth.

"You look surprised to see me in this condition," he said.

"You've got to admit, it's pretty nerdy to have the hots for a sick woman."

A grin spread across his face, showing off his perfect teeth. "What can I say? I'm the kind of guy who can fall for a woman in a cave full of bat guano and bear scat."

She laughed. She'd imagined a morning like this—without the morning sickness, of course—where the two of them would laugh together as they started their day. He'd been tender and kind and thoughtful. And funny. That was quite a combination in a man.

She opened her mouth to tell him he was going to be a father. And shut it again.

I'll tell him when he's off those crutches.

"Brian, you need to go to rehab."

"I'll call and change my appointment for later in the day. Let's get you into bed. I'll see if I can whip up some chicken soup to make you feel better."

"You don't know how to cook."

"Maybe not. But I'm pretty good with a delivery menu."

The only thing that would have made the morning more perfect was if Brian had been well enough to sweep her into his arms and carry her back to bed. She was happy enough to have him thump his way into her bedroom on his crutches and pull the covers up to tuck them under her chin. He finished by kissing her on the brow.

"Just in case you have a virus and not food poisoning."

She wanted to tell him she felt just fine, that she wouldn't mind if he joined her in bed. But she had to continue the charade until he knew the secret she was keeping from him.

"I'm okay now, Brian. Really. You should go to therapy."

He sat down beside her on the bed. "I don't know what I would have done last night if you hadn't shown up to help, Tag." He brushed a strand of hair behind her ear. "Let me return the favor."

"All right."

Tag had never had a man wait on her hand and foot for an entire day. Especially one with only one good leg. She fell asleep early in the afternoon, around the time Brian was headed to therapy. She'd been taking a nap every day when he was gone and wouldn't notice. When she woke up, he was sitting on the opposite side of the bed with his back against a pillow and his legs outstretched on the covers.

She yawned, then said, "I must have fallen asleep right in the middle of whatever you were saying before you left."

"You did."

"I'm so sorry!"

"You obviously needed the rest. Are you feeling better?"

Taylor sat up and waited for the nausea to rise. When it didn't, she smiled and said, "I'm good. Thanks for all the TLC, Brian. I think I feel well enough to get up and make us some dinner."

"So, not a virus?"

She shook her head. "I feel fine."

"Good. Then I can do this."

He put his hands on her waist and lifted her across the bed until she was seated facing him, her legs straddling his hips.

His hand caught her nape and drew her close for a gentle kiss.

"I've been wanting to do that all day."

"But refrained, so you wouldn't catch whatever I had?" she asked with an arched brow.

"I didn't because you looked pale and wan."

"And I don't now?"

He shook his head. "You look good enough to eat."

She laughed. "You're just hungry. You've been slurping up chicken soup with me instead of consuming the beef and potatoes you need to get strong."

"I'm plenty strong. In fact, watch this." He shifted her off his lap onto the bed, then dropped his legs off the side. She looked for his crutches but didn't see them. Instead, he reached for something on the floor.

It was a cane.

He shot her a look of triumph as he rose from the bed and stood using only a slender black cane. "Ta da!"

She scrambled off the bed and nearly knocked him over when she wrapped her arms around his waist to hug him.

"Whoa, there! I'm pretty new at this."

She stepped back but kept her hands on his chest. "How is this possible? Just yesterday you were still on crutches. What happened?"

He shot her a sheepish look. "The therapist's been telling me for a while that I should trust my leg to hold me. I was afraid to let go of my crutches for fear he was wrong. After last night, I was determined to give it a try."

He reached out to pull her into his embrace, using both arms.

"Your cane!"

She heard the gravel in his voice as he admitted, "I don't need it when I'm standing still. I only need it to walk."

"Brian, this is wonderful! I'm so happy for you."

Tell him now. Tell him!

But the words got stuck in her throat. It would change everything. And everything was so perfect right now.

"This is just the beginning, Tag. I'm going to walk without this cane. I'm going to get my job back at the fire station. You just wait and see."

She leaned her ear against his chest to hear his excited, galloping heartbeat. "Brian?"

"Hmm."

"Does this mean you can drive?"

"I guess it does."

She felt his body tense, as he realized the ramifications of being able to get around on his own.

"Are you kicking me out?"

She leaned back and looked into his eyes. "I thought you might want to get a place of your own, now that—"

"I don't. Is that all right?"

She wondered if her eyes looked as conflicted as she felt. What came out was "Sure."

He kissed her, his tongue inflaming her passion, his arms tight around her, pulling their bodies close.

She didn't want to push him away, but she knew where this was headed. She wasn't ready to make love to Brian. Not yet. Not when this terrible-wonderful-awful-amazing secret lay between them.

She tempered her refusal, because that's what it was, with a hand against his heart and a smile. "I'm hungry. Feed me?"

"A woman with an insatiable appetite. Who knew?" He gave her a quick, hard kiss. "One bedroom picnic coming right up."

He picked her up just long enough to toss her back into bed, and stuck his cane back on the ground in time to keep himself from toppling over. "Make yourself comfortable. I'll be right back with some food."

"Brian. I'm perfectly well. We should eat in the kitchen."

"Oh, I see," he said, pulling the covers back over her. "You don't want crumbs in your bed. Too bad. I've been hankering to go on a picnic for months. You're going to have to lie there and enjoy it."

"Brian—"

He kissed her to cut her off. "The longer you argue, the longer it's going to take to get your supper."

She opened her mouth, and he put a finger up to shush her. "Uh-uh."

"Fine. I want a hamburger and French fries."

"You've been sick all day."

"Yeah? Well, I'm fine now. A hamburger and French fries or nothing."

"A hamburger and French fries coming up. Don't go anywhere. I'll be right back."

She reached down for her purse, which she kept beside the bed and pulled out her car keys. "Brian?"

He turned back, and she threw the keys, which he caught.

"Make sure they're hot when they get here."

He grinned. "You trust me with your car?"

"I trusted you with my life. Why not my car?"

His face suddenly sobered.

Her attempt to be flippant had gone very wrong. Instead of making him laugh, it had reminded him of the near tragedy that had brought them to this point. "Be careful," she said in a soft voice. "I'd hate to have survived what we've survived and lose you in a car accident."

She only realized how possessive that sounded after the words were spoken. She tried to come up with something to say that would lighten the mood, but her heart was pounding and her face was flushed and all she could think of was the moment she'd held him in her arms believing he was dead.

"Just go, Brian," she said quietly. "I'll be here when you get back."

And if that wasn't an invitation for more than she intended, she didn't know what was.

Chapter 34

BRIAN'S DAYS IN rehab blended one into the next. His nights were another thing entirely. He spent them with Tag, who was turning out to be quite a puzzle. She was encouraging and supportive. She was fun and funny. And she was something else she'd never been in high school: a tease.

She was never mean or unkind to him. She just did . . . something . . . with her clothes or her hair or the look in her eyes that got him so hot and bothered he felt like some randy teenager again. He wasn't sure what her game was, but he was enjoying the hell out of playing it.

In the three weeks since he'd first walked with a cane, their evenings together had distracted him from a truth that was staring him in the face, one he didn't want to acknowledge. His leg had healed as much as it ever would. What muscle he had in his calf was all he would ever have. He might never be able to walk without additional support.

He'd long since let go of the possibility of returning to smoke jumping. What he found terrifying was the thought of never having the strength he needed to become a firefighter again.

Thanksgiving was coming up, and Aiden had invited him home for the holiday. He wanted to be with his family, but he wanted to be with Tag as well. He knew she planned to spend the holiday with her family, and he was pretty sure he wasn't going to be invited to sit at the supper table with King Grayhawk, so he might as well spend the day celebrating with his father and brothers.

Here they were again, divided by that stupid feud between their fathers.

"Hey!"

When he looked up from his seat in Tag's chair, she was waving her hands in his face.

"Taylor to Brian. Are you in there?"

When he focused his eyes on hers she said, "You're in my chair. Get out. I want to sit down."

He grabbed her by the waist and pulled her into his lap. "I say we share it."

She wriggled and giggled and said, "You're tickling me."

His hands had slid up her sides, but he moved them around to cup her breasts.

She froze in his arms. "Brian," she whispered. "We can't even share Thanksgiving together because of the battle going on between our families. You're still in rehab. You have no idea where you'll end up. Do you think this is a good idea?"

He didn't have a clue. He just knew he wanted her, and he couldn't wait any longer to have her.

"It's a great idea," he said, rolling her nipples in his fingers until they were hard buds.

She sucked in a breath. "I'm not sure—"

Something inside him snapped when he heard her wavering yet again. "Maybe what you aren't certain about is me. Is that it, Tag? Is that what this game is all about? Not sure you want to tie yourself to a gimp."

He propelled her upright as he rose and tried to get past her without the cane he'd been using, which was somewhere alongside the chair. She wrapped her arms around his waist from behind and pressed her cheek against his back. He didn't have the strength—the will, rather—to pull away.

She inched her way under his elbow and slid around his body to face him. He shivered when her fingers tunneled into the too-long hair at his nape. He stood with his hands at his sides, unwilling to play again until she'd told him the rules.

She met his gaze and said, "I've been waiting until you're completely well. It didn't seem fair to seduce you before you could break for the door, if you didn't want me."

"Not want you? Haven't you been paying attention? I'm lucky I have any jeans left without a busted zipper."

She laughed softly in his ear, sending a shudder of need running through him.

Brian enveloped her in his arms so swiftly and tightly that she gasped. He loosened his hold enough to get a hand between them, so he could shove her nightgown out of the way and palm her naked breast.

"If you don't want this, say so now," he said in a guttural voice.

"I want you, Brian. I've always wanted you. And I always will."

She could have no idea what a balm those words provided to his soul. His heart swelled with love for her—which startled the hell out of him. What was he doing? He still had a long road of recovery ahead of him. Months more of rehab before he could even think about a future for himself, let alone a future that included her.

But she had her hand inside his shorts and was doing something that made it impossible for him to think. Her thumb had found the tiny drop of liquid at the head of his shaft, sending sensations scattering and causing his body to harden beyond bearing. He would think later, after he'd slaked the unquenchable thirst he had to be inside her.

He picked her up without considering whether his injured leg could bear her weight and was astonished when it didn't buckle. He stayed close to the wall as he headed down the hall to his bedroom, just in case.

She missed seeing his amazement at his accomplishment because she was busy playing with his ears and kissing his neck and generally making his pulse race and his body catch fire.

When he reached his bedroom, he switched on the lamp and dropped her legs to the ground. He took her hand and drew her after him to the bed, pulling down the covers—the extra pillows had long since been banned from the room—and backing her up until her knees hit the edge and she sat down.

He laughed when she took his shorts down with her, leaving him wearing a T-shirt and nothing else. He pulled it off over his head and said, "Get rid of that nightgown, or I'll do it for you."

"Do it for me."

It must have been the timbre of her voice or the come-hither look in her eyes or the sight of the fragile cotton dipping in the shadow between her breasts. He didn't know what else could have compelled him to take the front of her nightgown in both hands and rip it down the middle.

She laughed with delight. "That's one way to get me naked," she said as she slid the remnants of fabric off her shoulders.

He wondered fleetingly if she always went to bed bare-assed. His temperature went up a few more degrees.

She lay back and held out her arms to him, and he realized he wanted to hold her, and be held by her, through the night. He shifted Tag so she was lying fully on the bed and covered her body with his own.

He'd forgotten completely about his injured leg, but it reminded him it was there when he rose to his knees. He ignored the stab of pain in his calf as he lifted her beautiful ass in his hands and thrust himself inside her, making them one.

She was wet and slick and welcoming.

She smiled up at him, and he felt an ache in his chest. He'd forgotten how good this felt. Not just the physical pleasure of joining his body with Tag's but the knowledge that she wanted him as much as he wanted her.

He slowed himself down, slowed everything down. He wanted to give her as much joy as she was giving him. So he took the time to kiss and to caress. To offer tender touches and whispered words. To arouse her until her body writhed beneath his, and she begged for release.

He arched his head back as he spilled his seed, and heard her cry out as her body spasmed along with his own. He lay atop her for a few moments, their lungs sucking air, before sliding to her side, separating their bodies. He slid his hand into her hair and tucked her head against his shoulder, sighing with contentment.

They lay wrapped in each other's embrace for a long time. Long enough for him to realize that he didn't want to let her go. He felt her belly pressing against his and slid a hand down between them to trace the shape of it. He realized she must have regained all the weight she'd lost while starving in the cave. "I love how soft and round you are. You feel . . . good."

She stiffened at his first words, then relaxed against him. She didn't say anything, just pressed her nose against his throat and kissed his sweat-salty flesh.

Brian felt sad and realized he was regretting the war between their fathers that had kept them apart all those years ago.

"Brian," she said. "I noticed you didn't have any trouble carrying me in here without extra support. How is that possible? I thought you couldn't walk without a cane."

"I haven't needed the cane for a little while now."

She lifted her head and looked down at him, a questioning furrow between her brows. "Then why have you been using it?"

"I guess because if I put it down, I'll have to concede that this is as good as it gets. That I'm no longer recuperating. That I'm healed."

She rested her chin on her hand, which lay on his chest. "What's the problem with that?"

"I don't think this leg is ever going to be strong enough for me to work as a firefighter."

"Have you taken the physical test you mentioned? Are you telling me you failed?"

"No to both questions."

"Ah," she said.

He waited for her to say more, but she didn't. On the other hand, the look in her eyes spoke volumes. "Don't stop there. Tell me what you really think."

"You haven't failed the test till you've *taken it* and failed."

"Why take it if I know I can't pass?"

"But you don't know that," she persisted. "You can't know how you'll do until you try. You might not finish, or you might not finish in time. If that happens, you won't be any worse off than you are now."

"Except I'll have tried and failed," he said, aware that his heart rate had accelerated and his face was flushed. "I've never failed at anything in my life, and I don't intend to start now."

"So you'd rather have everybody believe you still need a cane to walk?" she shot back. "You'd rather spend your life with a crutch—a cane—to keep you from having to find out the truth? Time for another gut check,

Brian," she said, flinging off the covers and sitting up. "Time to throw away your crutch, walk out of this house on your own two feet, and move on with your life."

"Are you telling me to leave?" he asked incredulously. "Now? In the middle of the night?"

She rose from the bed in naked splendor and headed for his bedroom door. When she got there, she eyed him over her shoulder and said, "You're a big boy. Figure it out for yourself."

Chapter 35

TAYLOR HAD AWOKEN to discover that Brian had packed up his stuff and taken off during the night.

Well, what did you expect? You tempted him out of his shell and then squashed him like a bug.

The house felt empty with Brian gone. She hadn't heard a word from him in six weeks. There was nothing she could do but wait and see what he did. Brian would either find the courage to take the test or he wouldn't. And he would find the courage to live with the results—whatever they were—or he wouldn't.

And he'll either come for you, or he won't.

Brian had trusted her enough to share his fears. She wished she'd told him she believed in him. She wished she'd told him she had faith he could do anything he set his mind to. She wished she'd told him she would love him whether he passed the test or not.

She wished she'd told him she was pregnant.

When Brian had made that remark about her rounded belly, she'd been afraid he'd guessed the truth. Luckily, he'd remained in the dark. Although, she didn't know how lucky that was, really. Because if he'd been the least bit suspicious, they could have discussed the baby before he'd walked out the door.

To make matters worse, she hadn't yet told her family she was pregnant. It didn't seem fair to tell them before she'd told Brian. She might have told Vick, if she'd been living at home, but her twin was back in Montana. Taylor didn't want to give her sister the news over the phone, or in a text or email.

Leah looked at her with a worried eye, but Taylor had been so exhaustingly exuberant during her elder sister's visits that she didn't leave room for Leah to ask, "Are you okay? Is something wrong? Why are you so flushed?"

She was planning to attend a Christmas dinner at Kingdom Come at noon. They usually opened presents after they ate. It would be a perfect opportunity to tell her family, all at once, that she was expecting Brian Flynn's child.

Then, somehow, some way, she had to tell Brian.

Maybe he'll call to wish you a Merry Christmas, and you can suggest a meeting. Maybe you should call him and tell him to come by, because you have a present for him.

Some present.

Taylor sighed and settled back in her chair and stretched her feet on the ottoman. The crackling fire was comforting, and she opened her book, yet another Stephen King novel. It was a good thing he was a prolific author, because she'd done a lot of reading lately to avoid thinking about how much she missed Brian.

The good news was that she'd been cleared of wrongdoing by the NTSB. The kind of flying she did was high risk, and surveying the landing area where she'd dropped jumpers was considered appropriate under the circumstances. The tornado of fire that had flamed out *both* engines had an infinitesimal probability of occurring in the future. She was certified to fly again.

Taylor was glad to have her license restored, but she wasn't sure she was ready to pilot a Twin Otter again anytime soon. She had her rental income—what was left after the mortgages and insurance were paid—to live on, so she didn't need to fly. Now that she was pregnant, and about to become a single mother, she didn't want to engage in the sorts of risks she incurred when she dropped smoke jumpers on the fringes of an out-of-control forest fire.

She'd begun "nesting," preparing her home for the baby's arrival. She'd bought a white baby sleeper that featured yellow ducklings, marveling at how tiny newborns were. She'd started looking at baby furniture online. And she'd cleared out the bedroom across from hers and painted it sunshine yellow.

If she was guilty of keeping the news that he was going to be a father from Brian, he was equally guilty of disappearing without a word. He could have called. He could have sent her a text. He could have shown up at her door, for that matter.

He'd kept his distance. So she'd kept hers.

She had trouble getting the zipper up on her jeans these days, but she could wear an untucked shirt and hide her baby bump. She still had time to speak to Brian before her pregnancy could no longer be hidden. And the baby wasn't going anywhere.

Taylor woke up in her chair an hour after she'd sat down. She supposed her body had needed the sleep, but she was going to be late for Christmas dinner. She jumped up and hurried to her bedroom to dress. She had to choose wisely, because she didn't want someone guessing she was pregnant. She wanted to make the announcement on her own terms.

She arrived at Kingdom Come at a quarter after twelve, surprised that no one was sitting at the dining room table. She'd figured they'd be waiting impatiently for her. Where was everyone?

"Hello? Anybody home?"

She was expecting Leah to answer her, but a male voice—not her father's or Matt's—called back, "We're in the great room."

Taylor hurried through the house to the great room, with its cathedral ceiling and spectacular view of the snowcapped Tetons, and stopped abruptly in the doorway. "I can't believe what I'm seeing," she muttered. The room was filled with an astounding number of people, both Grayhawks and Flynns.

Matt stood at the window looking out, his six-year-old son, Nathan, in his arms, pointing at something outside. Matt's daughter, Pippa, a blanket-wrapped baby in her arms, sat on the studded leather couch beside Devon Flynn. They'd eloped shortly after Brian and Taylor had been found alive. Pippa's child wasn't Devon's, but he'd fallen in love with her, and she with him, and they seemed delighted to be the parents of a beautiful baby girl.

A glowing Eve sat on the stone bench that ran along the front of the fireplace next to her husband, Connor Flynn. Connor's two children by his late wife, four-year-old Brooke and two-year-old Sawyer, sat cross-legged on the brindle cowhide in front of the fireplace playing with Legos.

They all seemed so happy. Taylor found herself fighting back envy. Somehow, two women in this family had made good marriages with Flynn men. Why couldn't she?

Because the Flynn man has to fall in love with you and ask you to marry him, that's why. Maybe Brian just doesn't love you enough. Maybe he never will.

Taylor suddenly felt queasy. She swallowed back the bile in her throat. If she threw up, Leah would figure things out in a flash. Which meant she absolutely, positively could not vomit.

She couldn't believe King hadn't objected to the presence of the two Flynn brothers since, in her lifetime, he'd never let a Flynn across the threshold. King sat glowering in "his" chair, an enormous studded leather monstrosity, holding court with a crystal glass in his hand that appeared to contain scotch.

Her twin perched on the arm of King's chair, holding a drink of her own.

Leah was walking toward her, hands outstretched, a smile on her face. "I'm so glad you're here." She winked and said, "For a while there, I was afraid we'd be outnumbered at the dinner table by Flynns."

"How is King taking all this . . . family?" Taylor asked.

"He's fine."

"How is he fine? He *hates* Flynns."

"I gave him an ultimatum," Leah said. "Behave himself—or else."

Taylor shuddered theatrically. "I've been the recipient of a few of those ultimatums. You're definitely not to be trifled with when armed with an 'or else.'"

They both laughed. Taylor let Leah lead her into the great room.

"You know everybody," Leah said, and then announced, "Taylor's here."

Taylor smiled and nodded to each family group in turn, pleasantly surprised by the cordial greetings she got from the two Flynn brothers. What else had she expected? Connor and Devon looked besotted with their respective spouses. Naturally, they'd been willing to grit their teeth and endure breaking bread in the home of their respective Grayhawk fathers-in-law—King and Matt—for the sake of the women they loved.

What was more amazing to Taylor was the fact that King seemed equally sanguine. Taylor gave Leah the credit for that miracle. Taylor would have liked to be a fly on the wall when her sister had arranged this Christmas dinner and laid down the law with King.

"Is anybody hungry?" Leah asked.

Brooke jumped to her feet, threw an arm in the air and yelled, "I am!"

Sawyer followed suit, jumping up and down as he shouted, "I am!"

"Then let's eat!" Leah said, looping her arm through Taylor's and heading back down the hall toward the dining room, letting everyone follow at their leisure.

"I wish you would've let me bring something," Taylor said.

"I had far too much fun planning a menu and decorating the table and cooking everything myself." Leah met Taylor's gaze and said, "The house has felt empty without you. How are you?"

Nothing happened in Jackson that everyone didn't know about. Leah had called when she heard Brian had moved out, but Taylor had explained, "He was only staying with me because it was too far to drive from the Lucky 7 for rehab. Once he was well, he left. There's no more to the story than that."

Leah hadn't been satisfied with that answer, but she hadn't pushed for more, for which Taylor was grateful.

Taylor had no experience with the family dinner that followed. Having kids at the table made for more confusion, but also a lot of laughter. The two brothers were able to speak to each other and their wives, even though King didn't deign to join the conversation.

Although her father presided at the head of the table, he didn't say more than ten words at dinner. It was clear to Taylor that Leah had put a leash on his tongue, because every time King opened his mouth to speak, Leah's chin lifted and her narrowed eyes turned in his direction.

Taylor sat beside her twin. Their conversation at dinner had been surprisingly stilted. She reached for her twin's hand under the table and asked, "Are you all right?"

To her amazement, Vick pulled her hand free. Taylor stared at her with shocked eyes and whispered, "Vick? What's wrong?"

Her twin looked miserable. They'd spoken as recently as two days ago, when Vick was packing to return home for Christmas, and her twin had seemed excited to be coming. Something dreadful must have happened since then. Why hadn't Vick called to share whatever calamity had occurred? Why was her sister being so reticent now?

Why haven't you told Vick you're pregnant?

Taylor was both stunned and shocked to realize that, sometime over the past year, the unbreakable bond that had held them together since birth had begun to unravel.

We never *keep secrets from each other. Or, at least, we never used to keep secrets.*

But she'd kept her pregnancy from Vick. And Vick was obviously keeping something—something terrible, she feared—from her.

Taylor was confused. And angry. Most of all, she was hurt. Everything had been different between them since Vick got that place in Montana. Why had she done it? What the hell was so special about some cabin in the woods?

It was only when Taylor got up to go to the bathroom before dessert that Vick said loud enough to stop all conversation at the table, "I'm glad to see you're not cozying up to Brian Flynn anymore. I don't think I could bear to have another Flynn at this table."

That was the last straw. Vick might not know about the pregnancy, but she knew Taylor loved Brian. How could she attack him at the dinner table in front of their father and his brothers?

She took a deep breath and said, "That's really a shame, because you've been sitting next to one the entire meal."

"What are you talking about?" Vick looked to her left, where Leah sat, and to her right, where Taylor stood. "What Flynn?"

"The one I'm carrying in my belly."

Chapter 36

BRIAN HAD LEFT Tag's home in the middle of the night and returned to the Lucky 7 with his tail between his legs, like the scared animal he was. Her accusations had hit far too close to home. Tag had made him take a hard look at his behavior, and he had to admit, she'd been right.

He needed to find the courage to take that test. And he needed to live with the results, whatever they were.

Brian had spent the past six weeks increasing his upper body strength to compensate for the weakness in his legs, and strengthening his left leg to compensate for the weakness in the right. He'd been eating a diet filled with protein and healthy carbohydrates and just the right amount of fat. He was as ready as he would ever be. He'd talked to the chief at the fire station and scheduled a Work Capacity Test for the first day the ground was dry after the New Year.

He missed Tag.

Night. Day. Every day. She was never out of his mind.

He'd promised himself he would see her again—and thank her—as soon as he'd taken his test.

Brian had finally begun to believe that what he'd thought was impossible, when he'd woken up in the hospital and seen his damaged leg, might be achieved. He'd set up a course in the barn for all the tests he had to pass, except climbing three flights of stairs. He had only two flights and ran up and down them twice. He'd conquered each challenge, one by one.

It hadn't been easy. He'd suffered cramps and pain in his injured leg. He'd had setbacks. He'd gotten discouraged. But he hadn't let anything deter him. He'd remembered the look on Tag's face the last time he'd seen her, gritted his teeth, and kept going.

The question was whether he could accomplish everything he needed to do within the required five minutes.

"Hey, Brian!" Aiden shouted up the stairs. "It's Christmas for Christ's sake. Give it a rest. Ten minutes till dinner is served."

Brian had set up free weights in his bedroom and worked with them every spare moment. He dropped the weights and headed to the shower. He was in and out in five minutes, and used the other five to dress in a starched, white oxford-cloth shirt, tooled leather belt, creased Levi's, and his Sunday best ostrich cowboy boots.

He took the stairs two at a time, stopping halfway down when he realized what he'd just done. A grin split his face. He'd trusted his leg not to buckle and hadn't thought twice about it. He was ready for that test.

He made it to the table as Aiden was setting a turkey

in front of his father to be carved. He took his place and realized both Connor and Devon were missing.

He looked at his watch. "It's twelve o'clock. Where is everybody?"

His father glared at him. "Where do you think?"

Brian had assumed, with good reason, that his two younger brothers would show up with their wives and Connor's kids. Christmas dinner, at precisely twelve o'clock, was a family tradition they'd observed all their lives. He turned to Aiden for an answer. "Well? Where are they?"

"Connor and Devon are celebrating the season with the Grayhawks."

Brian's jaw dropped. "Are you kidding?"

"Would I kid about a thing like that?" Aiden said. "They'll all be here for supper tonight. By 'all' I mean Devon will be here with Pippa and Connor will be here with Eve and the kids."

Brian turned to his father. "You're on board with this?"

His father scowled. "I don't have much choice, do I, if I want to see my sons and grandkids? Connor won't bring my grandkids if his wife isn't welcome, and Devon and Pippa won't show up if Connor isn't coming."

"Are we having leftovers tonight, or starting over with a brand-new turkey?" Brian asked.

His father grimaced and then guffawed.

Aiden turned to Brian and said, "I'm glad you've got your sense of humor back. My advice is eat all the turkey and mashed potatoes and stuffing you want, because we're having ham and sweet potatoes and green beans for supper." He lifted an amused brow and explained. "They're Brooke's favorite."

I could have invited Tag, Brian thought. *I still could.*

But what would she think, getting an invitation like that out of the blue? He hadn't called her in six weeks. She'd want some sort of explanation for why he was calling now.

I miss you. I love you. I need you.

He wasn't ready to say those things yet. He wanted to show her that he'd met the challenge she'd given him. He wanted to qualify as a firefighter first. And he wanted the chance to spend time with her before they had to face his father and brothers as a couple. Better to let well enough alone.

Brian smiled at his father and said, "Are you going to carve that bird or sit there looking at it?"

Angus carved the bird.

Brian ate till he was as stuffed as the turkey and retired to the great room with Aiden to watch football. Angus disappeared into his office.

"I'm proud of you," Aiden said during a break in play.

Brian groaned and rubbed his belly. "You should be. I think I ate half that bird."

"You know what I mean. I knew you had it in you to beat this thing. You couldn't have become a smoke jumper if you were the kind of man who quit when the going got tough."

"I might have quit," Brian admitted, "if Tag hadn't given me a swift kick in the butt."

"After what I saw when we found you in the wilderness, I have a lot of respect for her. Sounds like you do, too, if you made all this effort to get her approval."

"Tag made me take a good look at myself and decide what I really wanted."

"And that's being a firefighter?"

Brian nodded. "And Tag. I want Tag."

"Six months ago I would have said marrying a Grayhawk woman was a long shot. I don't know what to think anymore. I'd never have believed the old man would agree to have a couple of Grayhawks to the house for supper."

"Except, they're not Grayhawks anymore, are they? They're Flynn wives," Brian said. "Speaking of which, is your wife coming to supper?"

Aiden hissed in a breath. "Keep your voice down."

"There's no one here but us. What's happening between the two of you?"

"Nothing. Which is the problem."

"She hasn't forgiven you?"

"Not yet."

"Do you think she will?"

"I'm working on it."

"I'm really sorry, Aiden."

"It's water under the bridge."

"Are you going to see her today?"

Aiden shook his head. "Drop it, okay?"

Brian held up both hands. "It's dropped."

The football game wasn't over yet, and supper was still a long way off, when Brian heard a commotion in the kitchen. "Who do you suppose that is?"

"Hell if I know," Aiden replied.

A moment later, Connor and Devon entered the great room. Connor plopped onto the couch next to Brian. Devon settled himself on the floor next to Aiden's chair with his legs sprawled in front of him.

"Where are your wives?" Aiden asked.

"Pippa's upstairs in my old room taking a nap," Devon replied.

"Eve took the kids out to the barn to see that new batch of kittens," Connor said.

Brian hadn't taken his eyes off the screen, since the Broncos were playing, and they were still undefeated. But he had the odd feeling that he was being watched. He glanced sideways and saw Connor looking at him with something like awe. He shifted his gaze to Devon and saw confusion and disbelief. He shot a look at Aiden, whose gaze was still focused on the game.

He turned back to Devon and said, "Why are you staring at me like that?"

When Brian confronted Devon, Aiden turned and looked at his two youngest brothers with a question in his eyes.

"You don't know, do you?" Devon said.

"I don't think he does," Connor said, never taking his eyes off Brian.

"Know what?" Brian said. "Stop the bullshit, and tell me what's going on."

Devon and Connor exchanged glances.

"Do you know what this is all about?" Brian asked Aiden.

"Beats me. What's going on, guys? Spill."

"You want to tell him?" Devon asked.

"Maybe you better do it," Connor said.

"Tell me what?" Brian snapped. "Out with it! Now!"

"Taylor's pregnant," Devon blurted.

Brian opened his mouth to say, "That's impossible," and closed it again. When had it happened? In the cave? Surely he would have noticed the signs when he'd been living with her, if it had happened that long ago. She would have—

Brian thought back to the rounded belly that had been pressed against him the last night he'd spent with her.

Had she been pregnant then? Had that extra curve in her belly been a baby growing inside her? Or had she gotten pregnant, God forbid, the night he'd walked out on her?

He closed his eyes and groaned.

It dawned on him that his brothers might be mistaken. His eyes snapped open, and he focused his gaze on Connor. "How do you know Tag's pregnant?"

"Hell, Brian. She announced it at Christmas dinner, in front of God and everybody."

"How did she seem when she said it?" Brian asked. "Was she mad? Or sad? Or glad?"

"Hard to tell," Connor admitted. "She was late getting there, and she didn't say much during dinner. It happened when she was leaving. Her twin said something about being relieved that Taylor had broken up with you, because she couldn't have stood having one more Flynn at the table—"

"And Taylor said there'd been another Flynn at the

table the whole time. The one in her belly," Devon finished.

All the blood drained from Brian's face. He thought
he might faint.

I'm going to be a father.

Why hadn't Tag said something? Why had she told
her family before she'd told him? What did it mean?
And, Lord in heaven, what should he do now?

Chapter 37

TAYLOR HAD LEFT Kingdom Come within minutes of her revelation and without speaking to anyone. She'd planned to tell her family about her pregnancy, but not like that. She'd intended to sit down with her sisters and father and explain her plan to raise her child on her own. She couldn't believe she'd let her frustration with Vick goad her into revealing her pregnancy so abruptly to her family—and to Brian's brothers—while Brian remained in the dark.

Taylor knew about the two married Grayhawks' invitation to eat Christmas supper with Angus Flynn, which meant Connor and Devon were headed straight to the Lucky 7. Her pregnancy, with a Flynn baby, was a tidbit too juicy not to be shared with Brian.

When Taylor got home, she settled in her chair, stuck her feet on her ottoman, opened a Stephen King novel, and waited. She'd built the fire so high that flames were shooting up the chimney, but the heat did nothing to thaw the block of ice in her chest that lately had passed for her heart. Soon, she hoped, the awful coldness inside would be blanketed by the warmth of Brian's arms holding her close. She didn't think it would be long before she got a phone call. It was even more likely he would show up at her door.

Except, neither happened. There was no call. And no one knocked on her door.

Taylor found it hard to believe that Connor or Devon, or one of their wives, hadn't said something to Brian. He must know by now that she was pregnant with his child. He should have contacted her, if for no other reason than to discover how many months she was into her pregnancy. He could have no way of knowing whether she'd gotten pregnant when they were together in August, or whether their lovemaking in mid-November had resulted in a child.

The silence in her bedroom that evening, as she pulled the covers up over her shoulders, was deafening. She'd gone to bed at ten, unwilling to maintain the forlorn hope that Brian would appear on her doorstep. If he hadn't come or contacted her by now, hours and hours after he must have heard the news, he wasn't coming.

To say she was devastated by Brian's behavior was to underestimate her feelings. Taylor felt as though she'd been poleaxed. Her chest ached. Her stomach was tied up in knots. She felt alternately feverish and chilled to the bone. There was no reason, other than being on his deathbed, that could excuse Brian's failure to reach out to her.

She sat bolt upright in bed. Maybe he'd been so excited—so elated—by the news of her pregnancy that he'd been driving too fast on his way to her and had swerved off the icy roads and crashed and was even now in surgery to save his life.

Someone would have called you. Admit it, Tag. Brian didn't come, because he doesn't want this baby. He doesn't want you. You've been kidding yourself. You're the most unlovable person on the planet. How could you have ever believed that Brian Flynn had any intention of spending his life with you?

The sudden pounding on her front door shattered the ice in Taylor's frozen heart. Her feet got tangled in the sheets, and she swore in frustration as she struggled to get out of bed, threw on a robe, and turned on some lights on the way to the front door.

He came! He's here. He cares.

She opened the door and couldn't believe her eyes. "Vick! What are you doing here this time of the night?" She did her best to hide her severe disappointment. She didn't want to speak to anyone who wasn't Brian.

Her twin had obviously figured that out, because she shoved past Taylor and entered the house. She didn't stop, just kept going straight to the kitchen.

Taylor watched in disbelief as Vick filled the coffeemaker and set it to perking, then searched the cupboards until she found coffee cups.

"I don't usually drink coffee this late at night," Taylor felt compelled to point out. "Neither do you."

Vick set the coffee cups on the island that separated the two of them and said, "We need to talk."

"I need my sleep."

"I get it. You're pregnant. Your body needs rest. This is important."

"It can't wait till morning?" Her throat ached with unshed tears.

Please leave me alone. I want to curl up in a ball and pull the covers over my head and cry and cry and cry.

"No, it can't wait. I've put this off for too long as it is."

Taylor arched a brow and waited for her twin to speak.

Vick took a deep breath and said, "I'm sorry."

"You barged in here to say you're sorry?"

Vick came around the bar, grabbed Taylor by the arm, and hauled her into the living room, pressing her down on the couch with a hand on her shoulder and then sitting down next to her. "I've been keeping a secret from you."

Taylor frowned. "And this confession couldn't wait until tomorrow?"

Vick looked down at her hands, which were knotted so tightly in her lap that her knuckles were white. "I feel awful, because I know you couldn't have wanted to announce your pregnancy to the family that way. Or maybe at all."

"How do you know that?"

"Because when I was pregnant, I sat at the dinner table trying to get the courage to say something and never could."

Taylor's jaw dropped. "When were you pregnant? Why didn't you tell me? What happened to the baby?"

She saw the guilt and grief in Vick's eyes. "My son, Cody, is five. He lives in Montana with his father, Ryan Sullivan, to whom I'm not married."

Vick rose and began pacing in front of the fireplace. "I've been beside myself because Sullivan finally agreed to let me bring Cody to Wyoming for Christmas and then backed out of the deal. That's why I was so mean to you at dinner. I was upset and angry, and I had no one I could talk to because I've kept my son's existence a secret from the person I'm closest to in the whole world."

"Oh, my God, Vick. Who is this Sullivan guy? What right does he have to tell you what you can and can't do with your child?"

"Ryan Sullivan is a rancher in Montana. He has sole custody of our son. I only have visitation rights. Which is why I've been spending so much time away from Kingdom Come."

"Your cabin in the woods?"

"It borders Sullivan's ranch."

"Does Leah know any of this?"

"No one knows. Except you, now."

"Why on earth would you keep this a secret from all of us? From me?" Taylor's stomach churned. It was difficult—painful—to accept the fact that Vick had been leading a secret life in Montana.

Vick stopped and braced both palms against the mantel as she stared into the flames. "Getting pregnant was an accident. A one-night stand. I planned to have the child adopted by a loving family, but Sullivan refused to sign the papers to give up his parental rights. He said if I didn't want the baby, he'd take him. But he promised me that, once I handed over the child, that would be the last time I laid eyes on him."

"What did you say to that?"

Vick looked back at her with desolate eyes. "I agreed."

Taylor gasped. "Oh, Vick. How could you?"

Vick crossed her arms protectively over her chest and continued, "I was able to hide the later stages of my pregnancy from all of you by staying in Montana, supposedly to work. When Cody was born, Sullivan took him home from the hospital. He sued for sole custody of our son and won. My lawyer insisted that I have visitation rights, even though I told him I didn't want them."

Taylor was appalled. She'd thought she knew her sister. Vick was her other half. She couldn't imagine giving up her own flesh and blood. How had Vick done it? Why had she done it?

"Why, Vick? Help me understand this. What were you thinking?"

Vick turned to face her, and Taylor saw pure misery in her sister's blue eyes. "I was twenty-two years old. I didn't know Ryan Sullivan from Adam. He was just a good-looking cowboy I met in a bar. I wasn't ready to be a mother. I had grand plans for my life, plans to save endangered wildlife, plans that didn't include being tied down with a baby. You know what our lives have been like growing up—no mother and an absent father. I knew my child—my son—would be better off with two parents who wanted him—who would love and cherish him."

Tears welled in Vick's eyes and spilled over.

Taylor started toward her sister, but Vick held up a hand to stop her.

"Giving up Cody was the most impulsive, reckless, foolish, just-plain-dumb thing I've ever done. I will regret it to my dying day. I'm thankful for the lawyer who somehow knew I would have second thoughts and made it possible for me, when I came to my senses, to spend time with my son."

"At your cabin in the woods?"

Vick nodded. "The worst part is I've gotten to know Ryan Sullivan over the years. I like him." She shot Taylor a rueful look. "I love him."

"Oh, Vick, no." Taylor's heart went out to her sister. She knew how awful it felt to love, and not feel loved in return.

"Sullivan doesn't think much of tree-huggers. And he really doesn't like me—mostly for giving up my child. But also for trying to save the wolves and bears that kill his cattle. He was furious when I first exercised my visitation rights. He hates the fact that I have the legal right to see 'his' son. Sullivan has kept his promise, or as much of it as he legally can, by making sure I don't spend one more second with Cody than the court documents allow."

"But you said he was going to let you bring Cody here for Christmas. What happened to make him change his mind?"

"He asked me if I'd told my family about Cody, so he'd be welcome when he arrived. When I admitted I hadn't, he said I was still a spoiled-rotten brat who only thought of herself, and that he wasn't about to throw Cody into the sort of maelstrom that might occur when all of you found out he existed."

Taylor realized she agreed with Sullivan, at least about the storm of words that might have occurred when

Cody showed up unannounced, so she kept her mouth shut.

Vick sighed. "Of course, Sullivan was right. I wanted to take the easy way out, just show up with Cody and let the chips fall where they may." She swiped at another tear and smeared mascara on her cheek.

Taylor grabbed a Kleenex—she had boxes all over the house lately—and offered it to her sister. "Why are you telling me all this now?"

"Because I don't want you to make the same mistake I did. I don't want you to have any second thoughts about keeping your child and loving it and holding it as close as you can. And I want you to protect yourself legally, in case Brian decides to make a claim on the baby later."

"Brian would never—"

"There's no telling what a man might do when his child is at stake," Vick said in a deadly serious voice. "Brian's a Flynn. Angus might try to use custody of your child as a weapon against King. Have you thought of that?"

The legal consequences of having Brian's baby out of wedlock had never crossed Taylor's mind. "Surely Brian wouldn't—"

Vick interrupted her again. "Please, just protect yourself." She swiped at her eyes with the Kleenex, and then blew her nose. "And forgive me."

Taylor didn't offer forgiveness in words, she simply crossed the room and folded her sister in her arms. "I'm sorry you have to spend Christmas away from your son. But I'm so glad you came here to spend it with me." She rocked her twin in her arms, and felt Vick's arms tighten around her waist.

"We're a couple of sorry sights," Vick said, standing back and offering a wobbly grin.

"I don't see how Sullivan can resist you. You're beautiful and—"

"Not as beautiful as you. Or Eve. And Leah is so kind and good; everyone loves her." She shook her head. "Ryan Sullivan isn't the least bit interested in me."

Taylor couldn't believe what she was hearing. Here was Vick saying she wasn't the kind of woman a man would choose to love. "Ryan Sullivan would be lucky to have you," she said fiercely.

"I suppose I can always hope."

But she didn't look very hopeful.

"With any luck," Vick continued, "Brian will come to his senses and realize what he'll be giving up if he walks away from you and the baby. I'm happy for you. If you ever need anything—a godmother, a babysitter, anything at all—I'm here for you."

"Thanks, Vick. With any luck, that Montana rancher will figure out what a treasure you are."

"I'm working on it," Vick said.

Taylor voiced a question that had been niggling at her. "By the way, how did you know Brian didn't come here tonight?"

Vick dropped her gaze guiltily. "I don't suppose there's anyone who *doesn't* know. I mean, I heard from Eve that when Connor and Devon told Brian you were pregnant, he just sat there and watched the Broncos game to the very end."

Taylor felt a flush of humiliation rising up her throat and heating her cheeks. Talk about being forgettable. How could he! The rat. She would never forgive him. Never. He'd better not show up on her doorstep again. She was liable to do him great bodily injury if he did.

"Eve said she stayed as late as she could," Vick continued, "hoping to find out what Brian intended to do. After the game, he said good night to everybody and went upstairs to his room. He didn't come down again before they left."

"Thank you for coming, Vick," Taylor said through clenched teeth. She rose and took Vick by the elbow to get her started toward the door. She needed to get her sister out of here. In a moment, she was going to explode and start throwing things. She didn't need Vick telling Leah and Eve that she'd completely lost it.

"We didn't have our coffee."

"You know the coffee was just an excuse to get your foot through the door. I appreciate your coming, but I really do need to get my rest."

Vick impulsively hugged her again, and Taylor made herself hug her sister back, even though she was agitated beyond belief. She felt *violent*. She wanted to *hit* something. *Kick* something. *Pummel* something. And Brian wasn't around.

"I love you," Vick said as Taylor shoved her out the door.

Taylor smiled, but it felt like her face was in rictus. "Love you, too. Good night."

"Sleep tight. Don't let the bedbugs bite."

"I'll talk to you tomorrow." She closed the door as

quietly as she could and turned the deadbolt. "I can't afford to lose my temper," she said aloud. "I don't want to tear up my home, because I'll only have to clean it up again all by myself tomorrow."

In the end, she wasn't able to keep herself from throwing something. It ended up being one of the empty coffee cups on the bar. It landed against the stone fireplace with a satisfying *cccrraaaack!* and shattered into a million pieces.

"So there, Brian Flynn. That's what I'd do to you, if I could. You're dead to me. I will never speak to you again. Not if I live to be a hundred and two."

Her face felt even hotter than the tears streaming down her cheeks, and she was quivering with rage. She balled her hands into tight fists and squeezed them as hard as she could. She took a deep breath and let it out.

It didn't help. She was so . . . *angry.* How could he just *sit* there? Like she was *nothing.* Like their child was *nothing.*

She threw her head back and screamed, an ululating wail of grief that came from deep inside her. When the sound died, it felt as though she'd died along with it. She sank to the floor and curled into a ball and watched the unforgiving fire burning everything to ashes.

Chapter 38

"HOW WAS SHE?" Leah asked as Vick kicked off her snow boots in the mudroom and hung her coat on an antler rack by the kitchen door.

"About how you'd expect," Vick replied. "A hot mess."

Leah chewed a hangnail as she contemplated whether she should call Taylor. "This is all my fault."

"Brian's the one who left her high and dry. How is it your fault?"

"I'm the one who talked King into having the Flynns come to Christmas dinner."

"I'm the one who made the snarky remark about Brian that caused Taylor to spill the beans. If we're placing blame, that makes this all *my* fault."

Leah crossed to Vick and hugged her, rocking back and forth to comfort both herself and her sister. "I suppose we should put the shoe on the foot it really fits. King should have settled this grudge with Angus a long time ago."

Vick freed herself and asked, "How could he, if

Angus wasn't willing to let it go? I'm just grateful we Brats aren't still fighting with 'those awful Flynn boys.' It's a relief not to have to worry about getting marooned in the middle of nowhere with four flat tires or finding my Dodge Ram swathed in a thousand layers of plastic wrap."

Leah laughed and shook her head, recalling the "good old days" when the war between their fathers had resulted in skirmishes between their teenage kids. It was nothing short of amazing that every one of the Brats, except Vick, had ended up falling in love with a Flynn.

Including herself.

Unfortunately, the course of true love hadn't exactly run smoothly for any of them. It was downright rocky right now for Taylor, and Leah's own path had taken some surprising twists and turns.

Vick had been the only one to escape unscathed. But she'd been gone from the ranch a great deal over the past five years, working to maintain habitats for grizzlies and gray wolves.

Vick yawned and said, "I'm going to bed." She smirked and added, "Holidays with family are *soooo* exhausting."

Leah laughed in agreement. Even though it was nearly midnight, her day wasn't over yet. As Vick headed upstairs, Leah made her way to King's office. He'd been in there since their company had left. He hadn't come out for supper, and when she'd thumped the door and asked if he was hungry, he'd said, "Go away and leave me alone."

She opened the door without knocking to ask permission to enter. She had a feeling it wouldn't be given.

King jerked upright in the chair behind his desk when he heard the *snick* of the door closing. "Oh. It's you."

"Who were you expecting?"

"Most people know better than to knock when that door's closed."

"I didn't knock. I came right in," she said with a tentative smile. She had mixed feelings about her stepfather. He was a hard man to love, gruff and undemonstrative. He'd risked everything that should have been hers in a bid to regain a lost son, but she could hardly blame him for that. And she would always be grateful to him for giving her a home and a family.

King's face looked like a stone monument that was beginning to crumble at the edges. She was worried about him. His heart wasn't in the best shape. He'd also suffered a cancer scare recently. The disease hadn't been in remission for long, and she was afraid that all the stress he was under would bring it back. The silver wings that used to make him look so distinguished had disappeared into a head of hair that had gone completely white, or gray, or silver, depending on the light.

King made a disgruntled sound, but he didn't send her away.

"Have you figured out a way to stave off disaster?" she asked.

"No."

No explanation, no apology, no excuses. Just an admission that Angus had finally won.

She'd never seen King look so defeated. "You should go to bed."

"Sleep isn't going to solve my problem."

"No, but exhaustion isn't going to help, either." She walked around the desk and laid a hand on his shoulder. It was the first time she'd ever touched him in an effort to offer comfort. It felt strange. Awkward. She didn't know what to do next.

King put a hand up and patted hers. Then he stood, and her hand fell away. "We'll manage, girl. Something always comes along to save the day."

She took a step back to let him edge past her. "I've got a call to make. I'd like to do it in here, if that's all right."

He raised a curious brow but didn't question her. "Make yourself comfortable. Won't be much longer you'll have a chance to sit in that chair or make decisions about this ranch."

A moment later he was gone, closing the door behind him.

Leah had never been so aware of the fragility of her hold on the life she loved. She'd wanted family around her at Christmas, so she'd finagled and cajoled until she'd talked Eve into bringing her husband and children to dinner. Leah had mentioned to Matt what she was trying to arrange, and he'd done the heavy lifting to get Pippa and her husband to the table. She'd had no idea Taylor was pregnant. That revelation had been an unexpected result of her machinations.

In the end, King had been surrounded by his children and grandchildren—perhaps for the last time—at the hundred-and-fifty-year-old table in the dining room.

And she'd had the comfort and joy, however brief and
fleeting, of having her family together at Christmas, in
the home where they'd all grown up.

Leah didn't underestimate the looming disaster. The
deceptive friendliness evidenced at the dinner table between Grayhawks and Flynns might dissipate as quickly
as smoke in the Wyoming wind if Angus managed to
tighten the noose he'd slipped over King's head.

If King defaulted on the note he'd signed for the
250,000 acres of land in Argentina, and the bank fore-
closed on the assets he'd pledged as security for the loan,
she would lose the one thing that gave her life purpose—
the ranch. Taylor would lose the corporate plane that
provided much of her income. Vick would lose the home
base that gave her the freedom to roam the world saving
endangered species. And Eve would lose a family that
was likely to scatter to the four winds, once the ranch
was no longer the center of their lives.

It was hard to sympathize with Matt's situation, when
he was doing his best to steal Kingdom Come out from
under her, but if King lost everything, so did Matt. And
if Matt lost his bid for the ranch, Pippa might lose her
father, who could very well head back to Australia.

The solution then, to avoid all this calamity, was to
save King.

Leah had only one play to rescue her father, and she'd
decided to make it. It might not work, but she had to try.

She pulled her cellphone out of her jeans pocket and
dialed a number she'd deleted from her phone, but which
she knew by heart. It took several rings to be answered.

"Leah? Is that you? Is everything all right?" Aiden asked in a sleep-husky voice.

"I need to see you."

She heard the sheets rustle and something thump on the carpet before he said, "It's nearly midnight."

"I know. I need to see you. Can you meet me?"

"Where?"

"The usual place." When they'd been seeing each other clandestinely, they'd met near an isolated stock tank halfway between their two ranches.

"The road to the 'usual place' must have a foot of new snow and drifts a lot higher than that," he said. "It'll be damn near impossible to get there."

She wanted to meet on neutral ground. She wanted to meet somewhere freezing cold, where the air would cloud with each breath, so there'd be no chance of intimacy. She knew as well as he did that getting to that stock tank was going to be a pain in the ass. She was testing him. If Aiden didn't love her enough to get up in the middle of the night and meet her somewhere inconvenient, he didn't love her enough to do what she was going to ask him to do.

She waited to see what he would say.

After a ten-second silence he said, "Dress warm. I'll be there in half an hour."

Chapter 39

THE RINGING PHONE had woken Aiden from a sound sleep. He almost hadn't answered it. He'd looked at the time and groaned, then recognized Leah's number and answered. As he sat up, he juggled the phone and dropped it. The last time they'd spoken, she'd told him their marriage was over. She'd ordered him not to call her anymore and told him she wouldn't be contacting him. Her lawyer would send him the annulment papers. He'd spent the holiday in the depths of despair.

And yet, with Christmas not quite over, she'd extended an olive branch, offering to meet with him in the middle of the night. When he hung up the phone, Aiden had more questions than answers. Had she changed her mind? Was he going to get another chance to plead his case?

Something must have happened. He had no idea why Leah wanted to meet in the middle of nowhere on a frigid, moonless night, but nothing was going to keep him away, not even the occasional four-foot drifts he suspected were blocking the road.

To make sure he didn't get stuck in the snow, Aiden drove a pickup with a snowplow blade attached to the grille. If he ran into deep snow, he could plow himself a way through to Leah.

A smile flickered across his face when he arrived at the stock tank and saw that Leah had driven a pickup with a snowplow attached as well. She was sitting in the cab with the engine running to stay warm. The instant he arrived, she shut it off and stepped outside.

He left his lights on so he could see where he was going and trekked through two-foot-deep snow to reach her. "It would be warmer to have this conversation in your truck."

"This won't take long," she said. "Do you still want me for your wife?"

"Do you need to ask?" When she made a face he said, "Yes, of course. Always." He felt his throat knot with emotion. He didn't believe she'd ever stopped loving him. She'd simply stopped trusting him, because he'd lied to her—by omission. If she gave him a chance, he'd spend a lifetime proving he was the honorable man she'd thought he was when she first fell in love with him.

"You can have me," she said. "But there's something I want from you first."

His heart was suddenly thundering in his chest. "Name it."

"I want you to get Angus to call off his vendetta against my father. He can start with easing his choke hold on the banker who holds King's note on the South American land."

Aiden's heart beat even harder, this time with panic.

His father had spent half his life getting his foot on King's neck. He wasn't about to ease up on the pressure, not for anyone or anything.

"You're asking the impossible, Leah."

"If you want me in your life, you'll make it happen. That's all I came to say."

"Wait!"

He caught her by the arm as she turned away, and the deep snow caused her to stumble and nearly fall. He took a step and wrapped his arms around her and pulled her close.

She hid her face against his shearling coat, refusing to look at him.

"Leah," he pleaded. "Look at me. Please."

She lifted her face to his, and he saw the pain and fear in her eyes. His throat ached with unshed tears. He'd come here with such high hopes. Her request had dashed them.

"Ask me for something else," he said.

"There's nothing else I need."

"What about me, Leah? Don't you need me even a little bit? Would it be so terrible to let me help you carry some of the burdens you bear?"

"You can help me most by changing your father's mind."

"You really do want a Christmas miracle, don't you?" He felt helpless against the pleading look in her eyes. He sighed and said, "I'll try, Leah. That's all I can promise."

He felt her body lose its rigidity, as she sank against him. Two bulky coats separated them, but his memory was good enough to remember every sylphlike curve of the woman in his arms. Aiden slowly lowered his head, to give Leah a chance to turn away if she didn't want what was about to happen. He was a starving man, and she was a feast he'd been denied too long.

His gloved hands framed her face as he plundered her mouth, taking the sustenance he craved and giving back the nourishment she seemed to need every bit as much.

She pulled away far too soon, her plumed breaths rapid and uneven. "Aiden. Please. I can't . . . I don't . . ."

She pulled completely free and stared up at him with all the confusion she felt showing on her face. He reached out to caress her face, but she brushed his hand away.

"All right, Leah. I can wait." It might be a very long wait, if he couldn't change his father's mind. "Just don't forget how much I love you. Don't forget how much I need you. Don't forget how good we are together."

Her chin quivered as she said, "Merry Christmas, Aiden."

He swallowed over the knot in his throat and answered, "Merry Christmas, Leah."

He watched her struggle through the deep snow back to her truck. It started up with a roar, and she backed her way out and took off, her spinning wheels throwing up sheets of powdery snow. He got one last glimpse of her tear-streaked face in his headlights before she was gone.

He got back in his truck and headed home, slamming the steering wheel with frustration as he realized the task she'd set for him. "Why is she doing this?" he ranted. "She might as well have asked me to hand her the deed to the Lucky 7. I have about as much chance of tearing that out of my father's unshakable grip as I have of accomplishing the impossible task she set for me."

What plea could he make that would sway his father and convince him to forgo his revenge?

Tell him the truth. Tell him you want your wife back in your arms.

Unfortunately, even though his happiness depended on having Leah in his life, he didn't think that argument would hold much sway with his father. Angus would applaud the fact that he'd gotten one of King's Brats out of his son's life.

What else could he say? What else could he do? How in heaven's name was he going to thwart his father's revenge?

Chapter 40

AFTER HE'D GOTTEN the news that Tag was pregnant, Brian had watched the rest of the Broncos football game, but he had no idea whether they'd won or lost. He'd been in shock, and then completely distracted trying to figure out what he should do next. When the chatter and hubbub in the room indicated that the game was over, he'd said good night to everyone and gone upstairs, supposedly to bed. But he hadn't gone to sleep.

He'd tossed and turned, knowing he should call Tag but resisting the urge. After all, *she* hadn't told him she was having his baby. He'd heard the news from his brothers! As far as Tag knew, he had no idea she had his child growing in her belly. She'd been nowhere to be seen when the most momentous event of his life—learning he would become a father—had occurred.

Why hadn't she told him when she found out she was pregnant? Why had she kept it a secret? Why hadn't she called him as soon as she left her father's dinner table, having dropped that earth-shattering bombshell, to tell him the news herself.

You're not innocent in all this. Why haven't you spoken to Tag since you walked out of her house in the middle of the night? Why did you cut her out of your life? What is she supposed to think when you left and never came back?

He'd been planning to return. He'd just been waiting until he could prove her wrong. He'd wanted to pass that physical test with flying colors and show up on her doorstep knowing that he was a firefighter again.

He'd wanted her to be proud of him.

When he'd woken up this morning, Brian had made a phone call, but not to Tag. He knew he was being a stubborn ass, but she had just as much responsibility to call him as he did to call her. If that was the pot calling the kettle black, or a case of cutting off his nose to spite his face, then so be it.

The person he'd contacted was Chief Warren, and he'd asked her for a favor. Since there was no snow forecast, he wanted to take the Work Capacity Test today, a week early, instead of waiting until after the New Year.

Ever since the chief had agreed to clear the test site of the snow that had fallen overnight, and schedule his assessment this morning, a herd of wild mustangs had been stampeding in his stomach. Fear wasn't a strong enough word for the emotions churning through him. Terror was more like it.

What if he couldn't do it? What if his leg failed him after all?

Brian found Aiden with his head in his hands at the breakfast bar in the kitchen and said, "You don't look like you got any more sleep than I did last night. Something wrong?"

Aiden lifted his head and waved a dismissive hand. "Nothing you or I or anybody else can do anything about."

"You're the best I know at resolving difficult problems. What's your plan?"

"Don't have one. Yet."

"You'll figure it out," Brian said. "You always do." He was too nervous to eat, or to give any more attention to whatever was troubling Aiden, even though he knew he should do both. He poured coffee into a thermal cup he usually took with him in his pickup, took a sip, and hissed when he burned his tongue.

He was a moment from being out the door, when Aiden gave him a shrewd look and asked, "Where are you off to this morning, as if I didn't know."

Brian started. "How did you find out I arranged to take my test early?"

Aiden stopped his coffee cup halfway to his mouth. "You aren't on your way to see Tag?"

Brian shook his head.

"Then you spoke to her last night?"

Brian shook his head.

"You haven't talked to her yet?" Aiden said incredulously.

"No. I thought I'd wait—"

"Your lady tells you she's pregnant, and you blow her off?"

"*Tag* did not tell me she's pregnant," Brian retorted. "I had to hear it from Connor and Devon." Every time he thought about how he'd been ambushed, it made him mad all over again. "And I did *not* blow her off. I want to know whether I'm going to be able to keep working as a firefighter before I talk to her about what comes next."

"What comes next is that you're going to tell her how you feel about her and how glad you are that the two of you are going to have a baby. Do not pass GO, do not collect $200, just get your butt over there and do it!"

"She's going to have to wait until I take this test," Brian said stubbornly.

"Do you love her, Brian? Are you happy about the baby?"

Brian was surprised Aiden had asked so directly. He opened his mouth to say "Of course I love her!" and discovered his throat had swollen closed, preventing speech. He felt tears sting his nose and well in his eyes.

Aiden's hand squeezed his nape.

He glanced at his brother and saw that Aiden understood the power of the emotions he was feeling.

Of course I love her.

He'd always wanted kids, but having them was something he'd imagined happening "sometime in the future." The future had caught up to him. Tag was pregnant.

"Good luck," Aiden said. "I know you can do it. And go see Tag!"

Brian wished he was as certain he was going to pass as Aiden seemed to be. *Go see Tag.* He couldn't afford to think about anything right now except the upcoming test.

He'd worked hard. He was fit and ready. He should be able to complete the difficult tasks required in the time allotted. Knowing he'd trained for every situation was how he'd managed to fight all those fires in hazardous conditions without panicking. He had to ignore the rising fear that threatened to paralyze him and just *do the job*.

Because he'd changed the date and time of the test, Brian wasn't expecting to find anyone at the fire station except Chief Warren. He was moved almost to tears when he discovered that firefighters from every shift were there in full gear. They competed ferociously against one another to have the best score in the firehouse. They'd come to badger him, to hassle and plague him, as a means of goodwilled encouragement.

"How did you guys know—"

"The chief made a call, and that started the rest of us calling until we reached everybody," one firefighter said. "We all wanted to be here to cheer you on."

"We're going to make sure you bust your butt getting up those stairs and back down again," another said.

The crowd hooted and hollered and cheered, and Brian responded by slapping hands and bumping shoulders with firefighters on his way to the chief.

She stood at the foot of the stairs holding a stopwatch. Brian handed her the document from his physician confirming his physical fitness for duty. She glanced at it, stuck it in her back pocket, and said, "Gear up, firefighter."

Brian suited up in his jacket, pants, air bottle, SCBA, boots, helmet, and gloves. He'd worn his gear when he practiced, so it felt like a second skin.

"You have five minutes to complete all items on the Work Capacity Test. Are you ready, firefighter?"

"Ready," Brian said, taking an extra-deep breath and letting it out.

The chief clicked the stopwatch and yelled, "Go!"

Chapter 41

Aiden had done his best to hide his despair from Brian. He'd woken up suffering the sort of anguish he hadn't experienced since the day Leah had learned about the bet he'd made with Brian and walked out of his life. Actually, this was worse, because then he'd had a hope of winning her back someday. Now, he had the prize within his grasp—mere inches from his fingertips—and knew there was no way he could ever reach it.

His head was back in his hands, and his heart was lodged in the soles of his feet. He could think of no way to change his father's mind. He was sure his desire to marry a Grayhawk would not be the least encouragement for Angus to forgo his revenge. In fact, it might make him even more determined.

"Why are you sitting there with that hangdog look?"

Aiden raised his head at the sound of his father's voice and glowered at him from his seat at the breakfast bar. "You're the reason I look like this."

His father looked both startled and offended. "Me? What did I do?"

"It's what you're planning to do."

"I'm planning to have an English muffin with honey and butter and a cup of coffee. I fail to see how—"

Aiden rose like an avenging fury, his bar stool loudly scraping the floor, to confront his father. "You've got King Grayhawk in a vise from which he can't escape. Is it really necessary to crush him?"

Angus froze at the door to the refrigerator. "Are you suggesting I let him go?"

"Why not? What would you lose? How would it hurt you?"

Angus cocked his head and eyed his son. He closed the refrigerator without retrieving his English muffin.

Aiden had studied his father's business tactics all his life. Angus always searched for the hidden meaning in what his adversary said. What did the man want? What was his ultimate aim? For perhaps the first time, Aiden found himself on the dangerous end of his father's scrutiny.

"What's in it for you if I let him go free?" Angus asked.

Aiden balled his hands into fists below the bar so his father wouldn't see them trembling. "Not much. Just my future happiness."

Angus snorted. "Got to be a woman involved when you start talking 'happiness.' Since it's King you're trying to save, that makes it a Grayhawk woman. Which one?"

"Leah."

"Ah. King has a soft spot for that one. Never understood it, when there's not a drop of Grayhawk blood running through her veins."

He left Aiden standing with his heart in his throat—it had shot up there from the soles of his feet—and headed back to the refrigerator. Angus took out the package of muffins, removed the plastic catch and took one out, replaced the catch and threw the rest of the muffins back in the fridge before closing the door.

He took his muffin with him to the counter, grabbed a serrated knife from a block standing on the counter, cut the muffin in half, and dropped it in the toaster. He opened the cupboard above the toaster and took out a small plastic bear filled with honey. He took the lid off the butter dish sitting next to the toaster and found a knife in the silverware drawer with which to spread the butter once the muffin came up.

Aiden watched every step of the ritual his father followed every morning, waiting impatiently to hear whether his announcement had changed anything. Or nothing.

His father twirled the butter knife as he said, "I have to ask myself what *I* would get if I let King escape his just deserts."

Aiden recognized this ploy. He'd seen his father use it a hundred times. He gave the expected response. "What do you want?"

The muffin popped up, and his father left him in suspense while he buttered the muffin and drizzled honey into all the tiny holes that were distinctive to English muffins. When he set down the bear, he turned to Aiden and grinned. Broadly. Then he chuckled. And waggled his brows. And laughed with glee.

"I take it you've figured out something that will turn King's hair even whiter than it is."

"I have," Angus said. "In fact, this may be an even better—infinitely more satisfying—revenge than the one I had planned."

"I'm afraid to ask what you have in mind."

"I don't have to ruin King financially. I can take something else—something I suspect is infinitely more precious—from him."

"What is that?" Aiden asked.

"Leah."

"What does Leah have to do with your revenge?"

"You'll be bringing her here to live, correct?"

"That's my plan." He wasn't sure how easy it would be to get Leah to go along with it.

"Do the math. I get a daughter. He loses one."

"Is that it? That's your substitute for squashing King like a spider under your boot?" Aiden was unable to believe his father was giving up so much and gaining so little.

"There is one more thing."

Aiden held his breath, afraid to ask. This would be the kicker, the intolerable term to which he would have to agree to make the deal. "What is that?"

"I want a promise from you that when your first son is born, you'll name him Angus Ryan Flynn. After me." His father took a bite of his English muffin and made a satisfied sound in his throat.

Aiden eyed Angus askance. That was it? That was the intolerable term? "I'll have to talk to Leah before I can promise something like that."

"You do that."

Aiden didn't point out that they might have only girls.

No sense creating problems where they didn't exist. He was so excited, so *happy,* he wanted to grab Angus and dance around the room. He didn't because he was also suspicious of his father's capitulation. It had been far too easy to get him to back off.

"Dad . . ."

"What is it now?"

"Why are you doing this? Really?"

Angus threw the rest of his muffin on the counter and grabbed a dish towel to wipe the inevitable honey and butter off his hands. "Can't I love my eldest son?" he said gruffly. "Can't I want him to be happy?"

Aiden felt tears threaten and blinked them back.

"Besides." His father's grin reappeared. "I'm going to get a great deal of satisfaction from knowing King's favorite daughter is living in my home. Not to mention the fact that he'll have a grandson named Angus."

Aiden allowed himself to believe in the miracle. Leah was his. He might have to earn her love again, but once they were living together as husband and wife, anything was possible.

"Well? Is everything all right now?" Angus asked. "Are you happy?"

Aiden threw back his head and laughed. Then he grabbed his father and danced him in a circle. He let go of him suddenly, and Angus whirled away behind the breakfast bar.

"I have to go!" Aiden said. "I have someone to see."

His father calmly picked up his unfinished muffin and said, "You do that."

Aiden snatched his coat on the way out the door and ran to his pickup—the one with the plow. He had his cellphone out and had called Leah before he even cranked the engine.

"Angus agreed to forgo his vengeance, Leah! He's going to make whatever arrangements are necessary for King's loan to be renewed."

"How did you get him to do it?"

"I'll tell you all about it. Meet me at the stock tank."

"Now?"

"Right now. Oh, baby, I can hardly believe it myself. You're finally mine and—"

She interrupted to say, "I'll see you there," and hung up.

Aiden refused to let her lukewarm response dim his joy. Apparently, although she'd asked for the impossible, she hadn't expected him to succeed. He was going to hold her to their bargain. She would be coming to live at the Lucky 7, and they would start their life together as husband and wife within the next few days.

He would work out that little detail about naming their firstborn son Angus if and when the situation ever arose.

Chapter 42

LEAH HAD NEVER been so glad—or so troubled—at the same time. She'd been in the stable when she got Aiden's call, and she continued brushing down the horse she'd ridden that morning. Aiden could wait for her a few minutes if she was late getting to the stock tank.

Her life was about to change. King hadn't lost Kingdom Come, but she wouldn't be here to fight Matt over possession of it. She'd agreed to be a wife, which meant she would be living with her husband at the Lucky 7.

Presuming she didn't back out of their bargain.

She wanted to trust Aiden, but she didn't. She wanted to be with him, but she wanted them to live at Kingdom Come. That way, if he ever left her, she would still have the ranch.

Leah wished she believed in the fairy-tale version of happily ever after. That Aiden would never disappoint her again, that he would always be faithful, that he would never walk away from her.

She just didn't. She'd been disappointed and betrayed and abandoned by loved ones in the past. It wasn't that easy to shrug off a lifetime of negative experiences and believe that Aiden would turn out to be different.

She was scared. And wary. And wanted so badly to believe in him that she felt sick to her stomach.

The buckskin nickered, and she ran a comforting hand over its nose. "I know you're hungry. I'm done. I'll get you some oats and get out of your way."

She drove the truck with the snowplow attached. The wind had drifted last night's three inches of powder into eighteen across parts of the unplowed road.

Sure enough, Aiden was there before her. No wonder. He finally had what he wanted. She was the one being asked to step off a cliff and hope someone was there to catch her. She wanted to be married to Aiden and have his children. At the same time, she was terrified that he would walk away someday and leave her so devastated she would never recover.

Leah felt like a trapped animal. She'd heard a wolf would gnaw off its own foot to escape steel jaws. She felt equally desperate. What should she do? Which decision was the right one? Did she dare reach for happiness? Or was she just fooling herself?

Leah had no better idea of what she was going to say to Aiden now than she'd had when she answered his excited call early that morning.

Aiden didn't wait for her to come to him. He came running toward her, yanking her truck door open and pulling her out and into his arms. He swung her around, a smile as big as Wyoming on his face.

"Put me down!" she protested.

"I can't believe this is real." He stopped swinging her

long enough to kiss her with abandon. "Finally, you're mine."

She shoved at his shoulders, feeling panic at his possessive words and at her body's avid response to his kiss.

This feels real. This feels like love. But what if I'm wrong? What if it's just passion? What if he abandons me like my mother abandoned my father? She was happy at first, too.

Her fear overwhelmed her desire for a life with Aiden, and she kicked her booted feet until he released her. It seemed like she sank through the snow forever before she hit solid ground.

When he reached for her again she said, "Aiden, stop! We need to talk. Stop!"

She saw the sudden wariness in his eyes. And the love.

She held out her hands in supplication. "Please. Can we talk about this? I'll be happy to celebrate—"

"You will? Really?" he said sarcastically. "You asked me to perform a miracle, Leah, and I did it. Now you're acting like I should go away and leave you alone.

"We had a deal," he said in a hard voice. "And I'm, by God, holding you to it! You're my wife, and it's time—past time—you acknowledged that fact to your family and mine.

"I want us to live together. I want to wake up with you in the morning and make love to you in my own bed. I want to make babies with you. I want us to raise a family and—"

"Don't," she said. His voice had softened, and she wasn't unmoved by his entreaty. "Don't say any more." Tears glistened in her eyes and one spilled over.

In days gone by he would have offered comfort. But he stayed where he was, his hands stuffed in his pockets, probably to keep from reaching for her, while his jaw remained clenched.

"Tell me what I can do, Leah. Tell me what I can say to make things right between us. You can't be this unforgiving. You can't intend to hold one mistake against me forever."

"All right."

"All right, what? You'll tell everyone we're married? You'll move in with me? What?"

"Did you tell your father we're already married?"

His lips twisted cynically. "No."

"Why not?"

"I wasn't sure what he would do."

"Then we have time, Aiden. Let's take it. Let's tell everyone, and I mean everyone, we're dating."

"Dating?" He pulled his felt Stetson off his head and swatted it against his jeans. *"Dating?"*

"It's what people do to get to know each other better. It'll give me a chance to learn to trust you again."

He stuck his hat back on and yanked it low on his forehead. "We're already married," he shot back. "You've already said 'I do.'"

"That was before I knew you'd tricked me into liking you."

She saw him flinch when she used the word "liking" instead of "loving."

"How do I know what my feelings for you really are?" she said. "How do you know what you really feel for me? You had as much to drink as I did before we decided to get married in a wedding chapel in Vegas. You must admit, that's not the behavior of two rational adults."

"I wasn't drunk, and I wasn't out of my mind, Leah. I love you. My feelings haven't changed. What I want hasn't changed."

"If you love me, you'll give me a chance to be sure that marriage to you is what I want."

He looked sick, like he might throw up, at her suggestion that whatever love she might have felt for him no longer existed. He met her gaze and said, "I think you could learn everything you need to know about me more easily by living with me than by living apart from me."

"I don't agree." She took a deep breath and said, "There's something else."

He looked at her, his heart in his eyes, like a man waiting for the ax to fall and end his life.

"Matt doesn't own Kingdom Come yet. I don't intend that he ever should. Married or not, I intend to manage the ranch when he's gone."

"You know the Lucky 7 will be mine eventually," he said. "I need to live there."

"I know."

"How do you propose we resolve this little problem? Where do you suggest we raise our kids?" His lips twisted. "Assuming we're married, of course."

"When Kingdom Come is mine, and you have control of the Lucky 7, we'll merge the two ranches."

He looked stunned. "Our fathers—"

She interrupted in a steely voice, "Our fathers have messed up our lives plenty. I plan to consolidate my position and get my right to Kingdom Come in writing.

Once you've done the same thing at the Lucky 7, what's to keep us from doing whatever we want? There would be no question of you living at your ranch and me living at mine. We'd be living at *ours*."

Aiden whistled. "You think big, little lady. By the way, my father thinks I'm wooing you."

"You will be."

"He wants you to live at the Lucky 7 when we marry. That's his price for taking his foot off your father's neck."

"I will. When it's merged with Kingdom Come."

"He's going to want to see our courtship progress."

"You can bring me to dinner. I promise to bat my eyes at you."

He laughed. "I promise to be suitably impressed."

She grabbed the lapels of his sheepskin coat. "I need you to be honest with me from now on, Aiden. You need to prove yourself trustworthy."

"Just be aware that if you back off—if we end our relationship—my father will back off on his promise as well. Don't say I didn't warn you."

"I hear you. I understand. But I can't commit to a marriage I think will fail. Even to save my father."

"Fair enough. Just tell me what I have to do to make you trust me again."

She looked troubled. "I don't know, Aiden. I guess we'll just have to spend time together and see what happens."

They had plenty to do while they "dated." It could take months of planning to get legal possession of their respective ranches. Aiden would have to convince Angus to cede him the Lucky 7 sooner than his father might have wished. She would have to evict Matt and get King to transfer ownership of Kingdom Come to her. It wouldn't be easy, but the result would give them both what they wanted.

She held out her hand and said, "Do we have a deal?"

He pulled off her glove and his own, then took her cold hand in his warm one. "Remind me never to get on the wrong side of you, Miss Grayhawk. I mean, Mrs. Flynn. You have a positively devious mind. And yes, we have a deal. I suggest we seal it with a handshake." He shook her hand. "And a kiss."

Leah warned herself not to let her emotions get out of control. It was only a kiss. But when Aiden's lips touched hers, she felt as light as air. Her heart threatened to beat its way past her rib cage, and her insides did somersaults of joy.

Aiden broke the kiss before she was ready for it to end. He looked into her eyes and said, "You and I are more well-matched than you know, baby." He winked and said, "I don't give up on the things I want, either."

Chapter 43

WHEN CHIEF WARREN yelled "GO!" Brian's thundering heart was drowned out by the shouts of his friends. He had seven distinct tasks to complete. Some required dexterity, some required speed, some required strength, and some required all three.

He counted them out to himself as he began each task.

One. Hauling a 200-foot hose across a parking lot to a fire hydrant took a great deal of muscle. In a calf roping contest, once the cow had been roped and its legs tied with a pigging string, a cowboy threw his arms in the air to stop the clock. Brian did nothing so dramatic when he reached his goal, just yelled, "Got it!" and went on to the next task.

Two. He hefted 45 pounds of fire hose over his shoulder and headed up the stairs. He was more worried about his lung capacity than his leg, since he hadn't been able to practice going up three flights at one time. A few steps from the parapet at the top, the little bit of muscle remaining in his bad calf began to burn. He used his good leg to pull his body weight up the stairs and used the compromised one to keep him steady. He ignored the pain and pushed onward, moving even faster, until he reached the top, where he set down the hose.

The encouraging shouts of the firefighters and smoke jumpers rose up to him from below.

"Great work, Brian!"

"You did it!"

"Keep it up!"

Three. He had full confidence in his upper body strength and grabbed the rope which had a 45-pound, two-and-a-half-inch rolled hose attached, and pulled it to the top of the tower hand over hand in record time. He let it back down again, hand over hand, just as fast.

Four. He came down the stairs with the 45-pound hose the same way he'd gone up—putting most of his weight on his good leg and stabilizing with the injured one. As he covered the last few stairs, he felt a slight cramp. If his leg seized up completely, he wouldn't be able to finish the test. He did his best to ignore the twinge and kept going.

Five. Brian grabbed the 9-pound sledgehammer and pounded on the Keiser sled twenty-two times, using the strength in his arms and back to move it five feet. A door might be locked or blocked and need to be opened to rescue the folks inside, and he was the man to do it. The sled seemed to move like it was gliding on butter, and Brian realized he must be pumping a lot of adrenaline.

Six. He'd expected to have an equally easy time picking up a section of ladder and "setting" it against the side of a building at the correct angle so it wouldn't tip.

He hadn't counted on the buildup of lactic acid in his injured limb. His calf was definitely protesting now, and he knew that he didn't have much time before he would need to give it a rest or end up flat on his back in agony. He gritted his teeth and got the ladder up. Set it. And took it back down.

Seven. He could no longer hear the firefighters. He could only feel the pain throbbing in his scarred leg. He bent down to grab the strap on the double set of tires standing in for a 175-pound human—the firehouse's dummy was worn out—and began dragging it backward toward the orange cone fifty feet away. He got around the cone, but despite using mostly quads for the task, his compromised calf muscle was screaming for relief.

He looked up to see how far he was from the finish line and saw a glimpse of an unexpected face in the crowd. Tag must have caught him looking, because she ducked behind someone to avoid being seen. He could have sworn he heard her voice above all the others shouting, "Come on, Brian. You can do it!"

What is Tag doing here? How did she know about the test?

Brian realized he'd spent precious seconds speculating. He put his head down and forced himself to think of the unconscious victim of smoke inhalation he was rescuing from a burning building. A life was on the line. He was so consumed by the job he was doing that he didn't realize he'd crossed the finish line until he heard a tremendous roar from the assembled crowd.

He stood up and looked for Chief Warren, who'd

been keeping track of time. She grinned and put a thumb up.

I passed!

Brian could hardly believe it. The chief headed toward him, holding the stopwatch so he could see his time.

"Four minutes and fifty-eight seconds," she said. "Congratulations, Brian. And welcome back."

Brian was shocked at how close he'd come to failing. And so very glad that he'd passed. He felt the grin coming and let it spread across his face. Meanwhile, he surreptitiously manipulated his injured leg, circling it at the ankle and easing his toe upward to alleviate the cramp that had attacked with a vengeance.

His friends slapped him on the back and uttered words of congratulations, but he was busy looking for the one face he wanted to see again. He finally caught sight of Tag, glancing over her shoulder as she hurried away.

If she made the effort to come and cheer me on, why is she leaving without speaking to me?

He wanted to run after her, but running was out of the question at the moment. Besides, Brian realized he couldn't walk away without celebrating with the friends who'd come to support him.

It was several hours before he was free to go after Tag, and Brian headed immediately for her home on the mountain.

He found her outside shoveling snow from her sidewalk, which she never used, because she always entered the house from the garage. Was she shoveling snow because she'd known he might show up and didn't want him in the house?

She acted surprised to see him, as though she hadn't been standing in the crowd urging him on when he took his Work Capacity Test. He looked for signs of her pregnancy, but she was wearing a bulky coat that concealed her belly.

"Is this something a pregnant woman should be doing?" he asked.

She turned her back to him as she scooped a shovelful of snow and threw it into the yard. "I'm not speaking to you. In fact, I'll have to be a very old lady before I ever speak to you again."

He laughed. "You have a strange way of staying mum. I heard you, Tag. I know you were there."

She turned to face him, her eyes flashing. "That was different. Word was all over town that you were taking that test. I called Chief Warren, and she said I could come. I'd cheer for anyone who managed to come back from an injury as bad as yours."

"But it wasn't just anyone you cheered for," he said in a tender voice. "It was me."

She threw down the shovel, turned her back on him, and marched toward the front door.

He skip-hopped to catch up with her, amazed to realize that his bad leg was pain free and working fine. "I'm sorry."

She whirled and poked a finger in his chest. "You should be! Walking out without a word. Not calling, as though I no longer existed, just because I told you a few home truths."

"Truths I needed to hear."

"Exactly!"

She was beautiful when she was angry, and knowing she carried his child only made her more so.

"How could you not call me last night? You had to know I would be expecting to hear from you."

"I'm an idiot," he admitted. "A stupid idiot."

"If the shoe fits—"

"Who loves you," he added.

Her features crumpled, and tears pooled in her eyes. She scrubbed them away. "These stupid hormones make me cry all the time over *nothing*."

"I love you, Tag."

"You're just saying that because I'm pregnant with your child."

"I'm saying it because I mean it. I'm saying it because I want to marry you and raise our children together."

Her eyes opened wide with surprise. "How did you know it's twins?"

Brian's jaw dropped. *"Twins?"*

"Well, shoot. You didn't know." She turned and marched away again.

She reached the covered front porch before Brian caught up to her. He took her arm and swung her around so their bodies collided. He pulled her close and said, "Will you marry me, Tag?"

"Why should I marry a man who walks out and then stays gone without a word for six weeks? Why should I marry a man who doesn't call—even to say hello—when he finds out he got me pregnant?"

"Guilty. Of everything. There's no excuse for the way I've acted."

"Then why did you do it, Brian? That isn't how a man who's supposedly in love behaves."

"It isn't? What if he knew you were right, and that he'd been acting like a coward? What if he wanted to prove himself before he came back to you? What if he wanted to be worthy of your respect? And your love?"

She pressed her forehead against his chest. "Is that true?"

He put his forefinger under her chin to raise her face for his kiss. He touched her lips reverently with his own. "Every word of it. Please say yes, Tag."

"If you love me, I suppose I'll marry you."

"*If* I love you?" He picked her up and whirled her in a circle. "I love you so much I'll still be saying the words when I'm an old, old man." He set her down and looked into her eyes. "There's something you haven't said."

She looked up at him, her face flushed. "You don't have to ask, Brian. I know what you want to hear. I didn't withhold the words on purpose. I've just been waiting for the right moment to say them."

But she didn't say them.

"Is there some reason you're not speaking?"

"I have a confession to make."

He lifted a questioning brow.

"I've been a coward, too." She met his gaze earnestly and said, "I've been afraid to believe what my heart has been telling me. Afraid to believe you could really love me."

She put her fingertips to his lips to silence his protest,

then looked into his eyes and said, "I love you, Brian, more than—"

He cut her off with a kiss, sweeping her into his arms and holding her tight, wanting her to know that he would never let her go, that he was there for the long haul, and that he would still love her when he was old and gray and needed to walk with a cane.

He broke the kiss and began unbuttoning her coat so he could get his hands on her. "Just how pregnant are you?"

She laughed and put her hands over his, as he caressed her rounded belly. "Eighteen weeks."

"Four and a half months? I've already missed too much of these babies' lives," he said. "I don't intend to miss another day. What kind of a wedding do you want?"

"Nothing fancy," she said. "But I'd like my family to be there."

"I'd like mine to be there, too. First challenge of our lives together. Think we can make it happen?"

She grinned. "If we can survive a jump into an inferno, seven days trapped in a cave, and four more days in the wilderness—not to mention months of rehab for you—a little thing like a wedding between one of King's Brats and one of 'those awful Flynn boys' should be a piece of cake."

Brian laughed and hugged her close. "Can you make mine chocolate?"

Chapter 44

TAYLOR MARVELED AT the fact that both families had shown up in force at St. Michael's Catholic Church for her evening wedding to Brian. They'd decided to get married on Valentine's Day because, Brian joked, "That way I'll never forget our anniversary."

Taylor had been shocked to learn that Leah and Aiden were coming to the wedding as a couple, but it made getting the two families together a lot easier, because so many of them were paired off. She knew the next six weeks would be a tense time for Leah. According to Matt's contract with King, he would either take possession of the ranch on March 31—having remained at Kingdom Come for 365 consecutive days without leaving—or not.

Vick was Taylor's maid of honor and Aiden was Brian's best man. Brooke made an adorable flower girl, scattering rose petals with abandon, and tiny Sawyer, with a lot of laughs and a lot of help from Connor, acted as ring bearer.

The goodwill from both families at her small wedding, and the much larger reception at the church hall afterward, made it clear that the animosity that had defined the relationship between King's Brats and "those awful Flynn boys" was a thing of the past.

Unfortunately, the same could not be said of the animosity between their fathers. For some reason no one could fathom, Angus had not gone through with his threat to ruin King financially. Nevertheless, there was obviously no love lost between the two powerful men. They kept their distance both at the wedding and at the reception.

"Are you ready to go, honey?" Brian asked, already wearing his coat and holding hers over his arm. "Just about everybody is waiting outside in the cold to send us off."

Taylor swallowed the last of the hot apple cider she was drinking in lieu of champagne and set down the crystal flute. "I have one more thing to do."

She'd danced with her father. Now she crossed the room to Angus, who was putting on his coat to leave.

He turned to her and said, "You need to get moving, young lady, before folks outside freeze their—" He smiled sheepishly.

"I'm going," she said. "First, I wanted to thank you for what you did for my father."

He flushed and muttered, "Don't mention it."

"Why did you do it?"

"Doesn't matter now," he said, avoiding the question.

"Tag," Brian called. "Time to go!"

She rose on tiptoe and kissed her father-in-law's cheek.

He looked surprised. And pleased.

Then she hurried away to join Brian. She held out her arms so he could slip her coat on, then took his hand and let him lead her outside to be showered with rice and loving laughter.

Taylor couldn't remember a time when she'd been happier. Brian had adored her with his eyes since the ceremony began. She intended to let him adore her with his body for the rest of the night.

When they arrived at the door to her home—now their home—on the mountain, he said, "You've been awfully quiet since we left the church. Everything all right?"

"Everything is perfect." She laughed as he scooped her up in his arms. "What are you doing?"

"Carrying you across the threshold, of course."

"Will your leg—"

"If I can run up three flights of stairs with a ton of fire hose and knock down a heavy metal door with a sledgehammer and drag a hundred-and-seventy-five-pound unconscious person out of a building, I think I can carry my brand-new wife inside."

"Yes, dear."

They both laughed as she leaned down and opened the door, letting Brian kick it closed after they were inside. He gave her a quick kiss before setting her on her feet.

"Welcome home, Mrs. Flynn."

"I can't believe it! I've joined the other side. A year ago I was busy making Flynn lives miserable. Now I'm committed to making one of them *happy*."

He pulled her back into his arms. "Well, you're doing

a great job. Tonight I feel like the happiest man on the planet."

"That's a pretty big claim, Mr. Flynn. And you don't know the half of what I have in mind to keep a smile on my brand-new husband's face."

He grinned. "I'd love to find out."

"Oh!" Taylor's hands clutched her belly.

"What happened?"

"They kicked me!"

"Both of them? At the same time?" He unbuttoned her coat and slid it off, letting it drop to the floor. His coat met the same fate a moment later. "This I have to feel for myself."

He picked her up again and headed for the bedroom.

"Wait! I thought you wanted to feel the twins moving around."

"I can feel those tiny feet and elbows better when you're naked," he said with a leering grin.

Taylor laughed.

They undressed each other, their clothing thrown helter-skelter around the bedroom. His suit jacket. Her long, white, empire-waisted wedding dress. His shirt and tie. Her shoes and slip. His shoes and socks and trousers.

Taylor looked down at the extra-large support bra she was wearing—to hold already generous breasts that had grown with her pregnancy—along with a pair of white maternity underwear. She met Brian's gaze and said, "I wish I could be more attractive for you on our wedding night."

"You've never looked more beautiful," he said fiercely.

She didn't question him, because the look in his eyes told her he loved her and wanted her.

"I wish I weren't so tired." Taylor hadn't realized she'd said what she was thinking. She saw the dismay in Brian's eyes and quickly said, "I'm never *too* tired."

He pulled her close and rocked her in his arms. "We've got the rest of our lives to have sex."

"This is our wedding night," she protested. "I can't rob you—or myself—of that."

"We're going to have the most romantic night a couple ever had." Brian walked the two of them to the bed and pulled down the covers. "In you go."

Once Taylor was settled in bed, Brian joined her. He pulled her snugly into his arms, spooning her so his arms surrounded her just below her breasts, and pulled the covers up over both of them.

"There's nowhere else I'd rather be," Brian whispered in her ear. "I love you, Tag."

Taylor could feel Brian's arousal, hard and hot against her backside. It was their wedding night. How could she not make love with her new husband, whose obvious desire was pressed provocatively against her?

I'm so tired. Exhausted. I just can't . . .

She closed her eyes, just to rest them a moment.

Taylor wasn't sure what woke her. Maybe the ticking of the heater. Maybe the rustle of a pine against the windowpane. Maybe one of the babies had kicked her. It was pitch-black in the bedroom. Brian must have turned out the light after she'd fallen asleep. To her astonishment, she didn't feel scared. She realized Brian's arms surrounded her, making her feel safe—and loved.

She was feeling proud of herself, and happy, when it suddenly dawned on her that she'd fallen asleep on her wedding night! Without making love to her husband!

Taylor groaned.

"Sweetheart? Anything wrong? You okay?"

Now she'd woken Brian from a sound sleep. She fought back tears of frustration. "I'm fine. Go back to sleep."

Brian's arms tightened around her. In a husky, sleepy voice he asked, "Did you have a nice nap?"

"Nap? It's the middle of the night, Brian."

"Yes, it is. The middle of our *wedding* night."

Taylor drew in a sharp breath. Oh, what a good man she'd married. What a kind, considerate, wonderful man. She turned toward her husband and pressed one hand against his loving heart, and the other against his very aroused body. She leaned her lips close to his ear and whispered, "So it is."

Acknowledgments

I owe a great many people thanks for helping me craft this novel. First and foremost, I want to thank my editor, Shauna Summers, who always urges me to find the heart of the book and, once I get something down on paper, helps me make it better.

I'm eternally grateful for the support I receive from Gina Wachtel, and I'm indebted to Lynn Andreozzi for the amazing covers she designs for my books. I also want to thank the marketing and publicity folks at Dell for getting my books on the shelves and keeping them there.

My King's Brats series is set in Jackson Hole, Wyoming. With all the nearby national parks, and its views of the Grand Tetons, Jackson is one of the most beautiful places on earth. Lucky for me, I needed to do research in Jackson Hole to write this book, and therefore had a chance to interact with some of the nicest, friendliest people you'll ever meet.

Jackson Hole Battalion Chief Fire Marshal Kathy Clay not only provided me with the information I needed to write about firefighters in the town of Jackson, she also connected me with both male and female smoke jumpers, who filled me in on this dangerous but necessary work. In a gesture of true friendliness to an out-of-towner, Kathy loaned me her pepper spray, so I wouldn't get caught unawares by a grizzly while I hiked in Grand Teton National Park.

I'm eternally grateful to Leslie Gomez-Williams, with the U.S. Forest Service, and Noel (Chip) Gerdin, also with the U.S. Forest Service, both former smoke jumpers, for explaining the joys and dangers of jumping out of a plane to fight a raging forest fire. Both recommended *Jumping Fire,* by Murry A. Taylor, as the definitive book about smoke jumping. I found it both fascinating and enthralling.

Thanks also to Zachary Scott, a shop supervisor and technical administrator for the Twin Otter, for generously providing technical advice about the airplane.

Kudos to Nancy November Sloane, Rebel Marketing, for the amazing work she does on my newsletter and website.

I want to thank Kathleen Sullivan for being my beta reader and helping me to keep this book consistent with the previous books in the King's Brats series.

As always, hugs to my sister Joyce, for her willingness to be called at all hours as an expert resource for questions about spelling, grammar, and punctuation.

Dear Faithful Reader,

I'm already hard at work on the next book in the King's Brats series, *Sullivan's Promise,* which tells Victoria's story. Vick meets her match in Ryan Sullivan, a rancher who doesn't think much of her efforts to reclaim wilderness habitat for the very predators killing his cattle. *Sullivan's Promise* also features Matt Grayhawk and his one true love, Jennifer Hart, and concludes Aiden and Leah's romance. An excerpt from *Sullivan's Promise* is provided at the end of this book.

I've completed audio recordings (I did the reading!) for the first three books in my Bitter Creek series, *The Cowboy, The Texan,* and *The Loner.* They're now available from Audible. Enjoy!

Several of my backlist Western novels are now available with gorgeous new covers. Look for *Maverick Heart, Comanche Woman,* and *Sweetwater Seduction* wherever books are sold.

I appreciate hearing your comments and suggestions. You can reach me through my website, joanjohnston.com, at Facebook.com/joanjohnstonauthor, or on Twitter @joanjohnston. I look forward to hearing from you!

Happy reading,

Joan Johnston

Victoria and Ryan's story heats up in
the next installment of *New York Times* bestselling
author Joan Johnston's sizzling contemporary
Western romance series, where power, money,
and rivalries rule—and love is the best revenge.

Sullivan's Promise

A Bitter Creek Novel

Available from Dell

Continue reading for a special sneak peek

Prologue

"WHAT THE HELL are you doing here?" The image of a naked woman appeared in Ryan Sullivan's mind, her golden curls spilling across his pillow, her lithe body arched in ecstasy beneath him. He had to look again to see the same woman standing on his back porch fully clothed in belted Levi's, cowboy boots, and a starched white button-down shirt, open at the throat, the sleeves folded up to reveal slender forearms. Her striking blue eyes, which had been closed in that moment of extremis, looked wounded in the bright light of day. He realized she hadn't answered him, so he said, "I asked you a question."

Her chin lifted, and he saw a spark of the vibrant woman who'd attracted him when he'd first spotted her in the Million Dollar Cowboy Bar in Jackson Hole, Wyoming.

She looked him in the eye and said, "I made a mistake."

"Which mistake are we talking about here? The one

where you lied about being on the pill? Or the one where you wanted me to give up parental rights to my son?"

"I didn't lie. I was on the pill. I don't know why I got pregnant. And I only asked you to give up your parental rights because I wanted the child to be adopted by a loving family."

"Let me stop you right there. Cody isn't *the child* or *a child*. He's *my child,* since you gave up your right to have anything to do with him the day he was born."

She flinched, as well she should. He couldn't imagine any woman caring so little about her child that she would give him up to anyone—even his own father—and walk away without a second thought.

She met his gaze again, and he saw tears welling in her eyes. He hardened his heart. He didn't care what she wanted now. She'd had her chance to be a mother, and she'd thrown it away like trash. He wasn't going to let her back into Cody's life now. His son was a happy, healthy, six-month-old boy. He was doing fine without a mother. He had a doting father, a grandmother, an uncle, and a teenage aunt to give him all the love he needed.

"I know what I did was wrong," she said in a voice that sounded like a rusty gate. "You can't say anything to me—or about me—that I haven't said to myself a thousand times over the past six months. I made a mistake, Ryan. I never should have walked away. It was the dumbest, most idiotic, shameful thing I've ever done in my life. But I'm here now, and I want to see my son."

"He's *my* son," Sullivan shot back.

"I have visitation rights."

Sullivan remembered how surprised his lawyer had been when Victoria Grayhawk said she didn't want visitation rights, because she didn't plan to be a part of *the child's* life. It was her lawyer who'd insisted on writing in a clause allowing her to see their son "One weekend per month, from 5 P.M. on Friday to 5 P.M. on Sunday."

Sullivan remembered how she'd pursed her lips and shaken her head when her lawyer said, "You might change your mind." Sullivan had been tired of fighting and had agreed to her lawyer's terms, certain he would never see her again. They'd both signed the legal document, which was approved by a family court judge, making Ryan Andrew Sullivan the primary custodial parent and giving Victoria Alexandra Grayhawk visiting privileges one weekend a month.

For the past six months, he hadn't seen hide nor hair of her. Now, here she was at the back door of his Montana ranch house on a Friday afternoon demanding to see *his son*.

"You can't see Cody. You can't hold him. You can't have him for the weekend. Get the hell off my doorstep. Get the hell off my property. Go away and don't come back."

"He's *my* son, too! You can't deny me the right to be a mother to him."

The flash of fire in her eyes reminded him of the look she'd given him at the bar, when he'd asked if she'd come back to his room at the Wort Hotel. The one that had turned him hard as a rock. The one that had made it impossible to swallow. The one that had caused him to capture her nape and touch his mouth to hers. He felt a frisson of feeling skitter down his spine at the memory of that kiss.

He knotted his fists and forced the feeling down. "You're the one who walked away," he said in a voice made harsh by vivid memories he thought he'd put behind him. "You said you didn't want to be a mother. It's not something I'm ever likely to forget hearing."

"I told you, I made a mistake!"

"You sure as hell did!"

"I have legal rights," she protested.

"Good luck with that. Where were you planning to keep Cody for the weekend? You can't take him out of state without my permission, and I won't give it. Do you have a home here in Montana?"

"I've bought a cabin."

"Where?"

"On the edge of your property."

"Not the Wingate place," he said, horrified at the thought of having her so close.

"I think that was the old man's name."

Sullivan had been planning to buy that log cabin on the edge of Glacier National Park, and the five hundred acres that surrounded it, for himself. He'd just been waiting for old man Wingate to lower his price, since he didn't think there was anyone else willing to buy a place so deep in the woods. Now the mother of his child was going to be living right on the edge of his property, day in and day out.

"What happened to your grand plans to save grizzlies and wolves from extinction," he said with a sneer.

"I'm still working to save endangered species."

"I thought you had to travel to do your job. After all, that was the excuse you gave for not wanting to be a mother." That and the fact that she was only twenty-two when she'd gotten pregnant. He was nobody she knew, just a guy she'd met in a bar. It had been good sex, she told him (great sex as far as he was concerned, though he hadn't bothered to contradict her), but that had been the extent of it. The pregnancy was merely an unforeseen, entirely unexpected, consequence.

At twenty-five, he hadn't exactly been ready for parenthood, either, but he'd known he could never give his child up to someone else to raise.

"I still have to travel," she said defensively. "But I plan to be here at least one weekend a month to see my son."

"He's not yours. He's *mine*," Sullivan said. "And don't you forget it."

His gut clenched with fear for his son. He could probably put off the Grayhawk woman for a while, by bringing in social services to check out the living conditions in that old cabin in the woods. But eventually, she was going to get Cody one weekend a month. His son would be scared if he went off alone with some stranger. Which meant Sullivan was going to have to let that damned woman into his home to spend time with *his son,* before she took him away and kept him by herself.

Not to mention making sure she knew how and what to feed Cody, and how to change a diaper and what his bedtime ritual was and how he sometimes woke up at night and was scared of the dark—for no reason that Sullivan had ever been able to determine.

He studied the somber look on Victoria Alexandra

Grayhawk's face, so different from the bubbly smile and laughing eyes that had caught his attention at the bar. The air had shimmered with tension when he was still half a room away from her. It was as though she were tugging him toward her with an invisible rope, from which there was no escape. He felt the same attraction now and fought against it.

She wasn't the woman he'd imagined she was when he'd taken her to bed. That woman spoke of noble ideals and goals which, even though they ran counter to his personal feelings, had still resonated with him. She wanted to save wolves and grizzlies from extinction—the same wolves and grizzlies that killed his cattle every year. She hadn't changed her tune, even when she'd found out they were on opposite sides of the fence. She'd simply cozened him with kisses to convince him to take a look at her point of view.

He'd been willing to sacrifice every cow on his ranch to feed hungry bears and wolves by the time she got done with him. He was well and truly lost, ready—if she just said the word—to tie the knot and take her home with him to Montana.

Except, when he'd woken up the next morning, she'd been gone. And he'd never gotten her last name. She'd simply called herself "Lexie." He'd only been in town for a two-day cattlemen's meeting, and when he asked about a "Lexie" in the bar the next evening, no one knew a woman of her description by that name. Nor had there been anyone in the lobby when they'd entered the hotel who might have known her. It was only later he discovered her first name was Victoria, and that folks in Jackson called her Vick. It was one more transgression to add to the growing list.

"Lexie" had been more careful than he was, asking enough questions to find out his full name, and that he lived on a ranch in Montana. She'd come looking for him when she found out she was pregnant, and that whole sorry legal mess had started.

He wondered if he would be so mad at Lexie now, if he hadn't felt so foolish for wanting more time with her, when she'd apparently forgotten all about him once the sun hit the morning sky.

"Rye? Who's at the door?"

"No one, Mom." That's what Lexie was and always would be to him and his son.

He could hear his mother—who was nosy, but in a good way—crossing the mudroom to see for herself who'd come to visit.

The sudden intense look of longing on Lexie's face told him something was amiss. Then he heard the screen door screech behind him and turned to see his mother stepping onto the back porch with Cody in her arms.

Cody leaned over and thrust out both arms, but it wasn't Sullivan he was reaching for. As he'd turned to watch his mother's approach, Lexie had held out her arms to the child, her face lit with joy. He realized with a sudden pang that it was her smile he saw reflected on his son's face each morning when he greeted his child— the same bow on the upper lip, the same fullness of the lower one, and the wide, inviting mouth.

Her arms reached for the baby, who was grinning toothlessly back at her.

Sullivan saw what was going to happen and intercepted the child before his mother—this stranger—could touch him.

He felt disconcerted because his son was still straining to reach the woman, his tiny arms outstretched.

"Hello, Cody."

At the sound of Lexie's voice, low and husky, goosebumps rose all over Sullivan's body. That was the same mesmerizing voice that had coaxed *him* into her arms.

He tried to hand Cody back to his grandmother, to put him out of Lexie's reach, but his mom's arms were folded over her chest, and she had "that look" on her face that told him she knew exactly who was standing on their back porch. And that what Sullivan was doing—keeping a mother and her son apart—was wrong.

But he wasn't wrong. He knew it in his gut.

What if Lexie stepped into Cody's life and made his son love her, and then changed her mind again? He wanted to spare his son that pain. Better she never became a part of Cody's life in the first place.

Lexie had dropped her hands, and her smile had faded, but her eyes still implored him to let her hold the baby.

Cody settled his warm body against Sullivan's heart and stuck his thumb in his mouth, but his eyes were still focused on the woman standing in front of him.

"Go away, Miss Grayhawk," Sullivan said in a calm voice that wouldn't upset his son. "There's nothing for you here."

"Except my child, whom I love with every fiber of my being."

He was startled by the fierceness of the statement as much as by the words she'd spoken.

"You can't stop me from being a mother to my child, Rye. The courts are on my side. Make up your mind that this is going to happen."

His heart was beating frantically, pushing against his ribs like a terrified animal trying to escape, knowing there *is* no escape. "Fine." The single word was harsh, and startled both her and Cody, who lifted his head and looked up at him with a tiny furrow between his brows.

"Fine," he repeated in a more moderate voice.

"I can take him?" she said, a look as wary as his son's— the same look, reminding him that he saw her every day when he looked at his child—on her face.

"No."

"Then what—"

"Cody doesn't know you. And you don't know his routine. If you're going to do this, you might as well start from the beginning."

"May I hold him?" she asked.

Sullivan felt an ache in his chest. Why couldn't she have asked that at the hospital? But the time for regrets was past. She was here now, and he was going to have to make the best of a bad situation. He would do what had to be done for Cody's sake.

"He might not want to go to you," he said as she took a step toward him.

Cody put the lie to his words, as Lexie smiled again and held out her arms and cooed in a baby voice, "Hello, Cody. I'm your mother."

The little boy eagerly reached out to her and left the

safety of his father's arms for the far less certain ones of his mother.

She held *his son* awkwardly at first, shifting him until she had him sitting on her female hip, which God had apparently made for just that purpose. Her whole face was lit up so brightly it hurt to look at her. He saw before him the vivacious woman he'd met in a bar, who'd become his lover, and who was now the mother of his child.

He'd forgotten about his own mother. She pulled the screen door open wide with another loud screech and said, "Why don't you come inside?"

He stood helplessly by as Lexie Grayhawk, a woman he could never trust, a woman he both despised and desired, stepped into his kitchen . . . and into his life.